Praise for
Unfinished Desires

"[A] tender but clear-eyed exposé of the lost 'girl world' of a North Carolina school . . . Godwin's South has always been a place where charm and good manners can barely conceal the emotional drama pulsing beneath the surface. . . . Recalls the fraught family bonds of Godwin's best novels (notably *A Mother and Two Daughters*) . . . *Unfinished Desires* offers a door into the novelist's traditional Catholic education and roots as a writer." —*San Francisco Chronicle*

"Delicious . . . achieves its own sense of daring, freedom and grace . . . Appalling characters are rendered sympathetic as we learn their secrets; good characters are allowed a decency that's surprisingly bracing. . . . Convincing, funny, moving." —*The Washington Post*

"A spellbinding psychological ghost story, near operatic in intensity . . . sumptuous and spicy." —*NPR*

"Godwin's reserved yet powerful new novel, *Unfinished Desires*, is set in a Roman Catholic boarding school in the mountains of North Carolina. . . . Though it's a beautiful, well-intentioned institution, the school is anything but serene. . . . The novel switches back and forth between [the] official, sanctified version of events . . . and the richer, darker, uninhibited story of actual life among these manipulative, ambitious, gifted, fascinating adolescent girls. . . . Godwin's novel reminds us [that] no desire is ever finished." —*The New York Times Book Review*

ALSO BY GAIL GODWIN

NOVELS

Queen of the Underworld (2006)
Evenings at Five (2003)
Evensong (1999)
The Good Husband (1994)
Father Melancholy's Daughter (1991)
A Southern Family (1987)
The Finishing School (1984)
A Mother and Two Daughters (1982)
Violet Clay (1978)
The Odd Woman (1974)
Glass People (1972)
The Perfectionists (1970)

SHORT STORIES

Mr. Bedford and the Muses (1983)
Dream Children (1976)

NONFICTION

The Making of a Writer: Journals, 1961–1963 (2006)
Heart: A Natural History of the Heart-Filled Life (2001)

Unfinished
Desires

UNFINISHED DESIRES

A NOVEL

Gail Godwin

BALLANTINE BOOKS TRADE PAPERBACKS / NEW YORK

2010 Ballantine Books Trade Paperback Edition

Copyright © 2009 by Gail Godwin
Reading group guide copyright ©2010 by Random House, Inc.

Published in the United States by Ballantine Books, an imprint of
The Random House Publishing Group, a division of
Random House, Inc., New York.

BALLANTINE and colophon are registered trademarks of Random House, Inc.
RANDOM HOUSE READER'S CIRCLE & Design is a registered trademark of Random House, Inc.

Originally published in hardcover in the United States by Random House, an imprint of
The Random House Publishing Group, a division of Random House, Inc., in 2009.

LIBRARY OF CONGRESS CATALOGING-IN-PUBLICATION DATA
Godwin, Gail.
Unfinished desires: a novel / Gail Godwin.
p. cm.
ISBN 978-0-345-48321-8
1. Catholic schools—Fiction.   2. Women college graduates—Fiction.   3. Nuns—Fiction.
4. Teacher-student relationships—Fiction.   5. North Carolina—Fiction.
6. Nineteen fifties—Fiction.   I. Title.
PS3557.O315R43 2009
813'.54—dc22   2008049320

Printed in the United States of America

www.randomhousereaderscircle.com

2 4 6 8 9 7 5 3 1

Book design by Victoria Wong

To Father David Louis Bronson

If you go out walking in our dark wood
When the hawk's face is tucked beneath his wing
And mist has risen in the hollows
And the owl shrieks:
Do not shrink if on your path
You meet a solitary ghost.
Ask it, "What did you love most?
And what have you left undone?"

Prologue to Suzanne Ravenel's 1931
school play, *The Red Nun*

Prologue

A MEMOIR BEGUN

May 31, 2001
Feast of the Visitation
House of Olivia and Gudge Beeler
Mountain City, North Carolina

THE ROOM, THOUGH small, is light and airy. A highly polished writing table overlooks a square of lawn with flower borders. On the left side of the table, sharpened pencils have been placed slantwise across a brand-new yellow legal pad. Just behind the pad perches a small brass dinner bell. On the right side of the table is a silver serving tray. Laid out on its starched white cloth are a cut-glass water goblet, a silver pitcher beaded with frost, a tea napkin embroidered with a rose, a package of colored M&M's, and a designer box of Kleenex tissues.

In the center of the table a shiny ellipsoid tape recorder awaits its mistress.

Two women enter, arm in arm. The stylish one in crisp linen slacks is tactfully leading the old one, who is all but blind. She can still see shapes and colors, identify objects and—with a little assistance from them—the people she knows. Guided by her sense of smell and touch, and from long familiarity with the appropriate things and their happiest placements, she can still recognize a perfectly appointed room.

In her mid-eighties, she has a leonine thatch of crisp white hair, erect posture, and a noble profile. Her glittering blue eyes, set deep in their sockets, make her old girls feel she is seeing into them as keenly as ever, and perhaps she is, aided by other instincts developed and sharpened over her decades of girl-watching. She is dressed with the simple taste of one who prefers tailored over feminine, and the only indication that she is a nun is the Latin cross, pendant on its silver chain, resting on the modest bosom of her silk blouse.

Every spring since the school closed in 1990, a group of her girls have pooled their resources and flown her from the Order's retirement house in Boston down to Mountain City for a month's visit. They know how hard it was for her to leave Mountain City, which was home to her for sixty years, first as a seventh-grade boarder from Charleston, South Carolina, then as a boarding student in the academy, from which she took her postulant's vows in her senior year. From then on, except for semesters away at college after she was professed—and the one awful "leave of absence" (1952–53) enforced on her by her vow of obedience— her entire life as a teaching nun, the headmistress of the academy, and, finally, reverend mother was enacted within the blessed confines of Mount St. Gabriel's.

This year, she is staying with Olivia Stewart Beeler, class of 1974, possibly her most satisfying class in fifty years of teaching. The '74 girls were easy; they were spirited without being spiteful, resourceful without being destructive. Her year with them (as headmistress, she always taught the senior classes) had been a picnic after the stormy sixties and the detritus left in their wake. There had been other rewarding classes, of course, ranging from the bracingly challenging to the sweetly un- eventful, as well as the poignant and sad ones, such as '43 and '44, in which a total of six graduating seniors lost their fiancés in the European or Pacific theaters of war. And those once-in-a-while "star" classes, which kept her intellectually up to the mark, years in which a cluster of girls stood out and shone almost too brightly for the rest of the class's good, setting off undercurrents of resentment and grief in the less gifted. After that, the postwar daughters of the upwardly mobile, tak- ing for granted their security: even the pranks of those girls were fun- loving rather than mean.

AND THEN, IN the fall of 1951, the poisonous elements convened as the class of '55 entered their ninth-grade year and came under her charge. She still calls it the "toxic year" and is uncertain to this day how much of the damage can be laid at her feet.

A year better forgotten. Yet fifty years later she is still haunted by those girls.

But now her old girls have persisted and finally they have prevailed.

They have persuaded her that she must write a memoir of the school or, rather, *talk* it into this waiting machine shaped like a miniature spaceship. "Otherwise, Mother, it will all be lost. Mount St. Gabriel's was the school of schools. Please. Think about it over the winter. Remember all the assignments you gave us? Well, this is our assignment for you. It will be a fabulous story, Mother. Just start remembering and we'll do the rest. We have the scrapbooks, the yearbooks, and the press clippings; we've even lined up a publisher! But we can't do it without your memories."

That was last spring, and she had thought and prayed about it through the long Boston winter—and, if truth be told, had already composed substantial chunks of it in her head. Or, rather, allowed them to compose themselves. Now, this afternoon, in Olivia and Gudge's beautiful Mountain City home, she is about to begin.

"FIRST OF ALL, Mother, I want you to try this chair and see if it's comfortable for you at the table."

The nun traces her fingers lightly across the mahogany curves of the top of the chair. "It's one of your Chippendales."

"But this one has arms and a nice plain splat. I didn't want any *ornament* digging into your back."

"You are always so mindful of others, Olivia."

She settles into the chair. Her hands reach out and explore the shadowy and shiny items on the library table. "And you remembered I'm left-handed!"

"Well, of course, Mother. You made it fashionable for the other southpaws among us. And you always liked to doodle on a pad while you were thinking something out. Now I just want to show you how to operate this recorder. This model is also capable of voice-activated recording, but we needn't bother about that now. I told Gudge you like to be in charge and would prefer to have the old-fashioned option of starting and stopping on your own terms. But please remember, this is your *vacation.* Just do a little bit every day."

"And what do you call 'a little bit,' Olivia?"

"Well, a tape has sixty minutes on each side. When the tape cuts off, you might want to call it a day. But if you feel you really have to go on, just tinkle your bell and Sally or I will come and turn it over for you. Oh, and this little grille thing that runs along the front? That's the microphone. They told us that the sound quality of this model is so superior you won't even need to raise your voice. Just speak in your normal tone, like there's maybe one person across the table from you."

"That person had better be God," remarks the nun with her characteristic wryness, making Olivia laugh.

WHEN SHE IS alone, she centers herself in the sturdy Chippendale chair, resting her elbows lightly on its slender curving arms. She takes a deep breath, hears herself exhale. Her nostrils pick up lemon-scented furniture oil, the aftertraces of Olivia's Chanel No. 5, and the pineapple upside-down cake Sally is baking for her in the kitchen. Through the open windows, the lawn is a slab of chartreuse stamped with shadows, the flower border a blur of pastels with splotches of red and yellow.

Amazingly, she is experiencing the same uneasy flutter from her student days when the monitors at Mount St. Gabriel's were about to hand out the exam questions and she felt all her careful preparations draining through the holes of her mind.

She leans forward and clasps her hands on the table, then lays them flat, palms down, pleased with their shape and smoothness—they have held up well. Then she rotates the silver band on her left wedding finger. She has long since celebrated her Golden Jubilee—a gala affair at the basilica in Mountain City, covered by the newspapers, the bishop giving the homily "on service" and her old girls coming from as far away as Paris and Venezuela. Her seventy-fifth year as a nun, her Diamond Jubilee, is only eight years away. Will she make it? The age of ninety-three is only beginning to be ancient, these days. As long as she can keep her wits.

She prepares to say a prayer before starting, then decides that the spoken prayer should inaugurate the tape and presses the Record button. There's a discreet click, followed by a barely audible sibilance—a far cry from the rattletrap machine she practiced on all last winter in Boston.

"Let the words of my mouth and the meditation of my heart be acceptable in Thy sight, O Lord, my strength, and my Redeemer."

She stops, rewinds, and plays herself back. After all those years in the western North Carolina mountains, she has kept the lowland Charleston drawl of her childhood. People have told her it's charming, "aristocratic," but there's something undeniably frivolous about it, too, especially when reciting a prayer. Did Teresa of Ávila sound frivolous when praying aloud in her aristocratic Spanish?

She knows she can rewind again and record something else over it. But she decides to leave the prayer and continue. In the published memoir, you won't hear the Charleston drawl.

Lord, what if I am not up to this task? The girls so much want this little history. And who is better equipped than I to do it? I was at Mount St. Gabriel's the longest of anybody, first as student then teacher. I am the only living person who actually knew our foundress, Mother Elizabeth Wallingford, during her last days in the infirmary. For better or for worse, I am the walking deposit box of what's left. In every way, I am the most qualified person alive to preserve the memory of Mount St. Gabriel's, if it is meant to be preserved. And, besides: I *want* to do it.

Well, Suzanne, as usual you have answered your own question.

But I need to know if you're with me in this undertaking, Lord. Is it Your will, or am I just being driven by ambition?

For the most part, your ambition has served us well. It has produced many good results, but it has chipped away some of your soul.

(*"WHEN YOU SAY you hear 'His' side of the dialogue," her retreat master, Father Krafft, had queried her, "does the voice seem to be speaking to you from the outside? Would you say it is a corporeal audition? That is, do you hear it in the same way you are hearing my voice?"*

She was on her month-long retreat before taking final vows.

"No, Father, it's not outside me, but it's a perfectly articulate voice and it's not my voice."

"What do you mean it's not your voice?"

"Well, first of all, the pitch is lower. It's a man's voice. And He doesn't have my accent. And it's wise. He comes up with things I wouldn't have thought of."

"Can you be more specific, Sister?"

"He has answers to things I couldn't begin to solve for myself. He points out places in me I didn't know existed. It's not always pleasant, either, Father. He can chastise or diminish. At other times He's droll, almost teasing. His sense of humor is more the masculine sort.")

. . .

I'M NOT SURE I'm following you, Lord, when You say my ambition has produced good results, yet chipped away my soul. If only I could see a *plan* of this little history I am going to dictate!

Just go tape by tape, Suzanne. Your ambition and your habits of discipline will serve you well. As for the undictated part that is going to restore your soul, remember your Ignatian exercises. Visualize the story of the year that haunts you. Go scene by scene. Inhabit each participant with all your faculties.

This afternoon I am beginning the school history of Mount St. Gabriel's in Mountain City, North Carolina. This is a great undertaking, but I will do the best I can. There are scrapbooks covering the years from the school's opening in 1910 to its closing in 1990, and we have yearbooks for all the years except for the first three years of the Great Depression, when the school couldn't afford them. No girl was sent home because her family could no longer pay board or tuition. We ate a lot of oatmeal and beans in those years, but every girl was fed.

I came to Mount St. Gabriel's as a seventh-grade boarder in 1929 and was kept on at the school when my father lost everything. That was just nineteen years from the school's beginning. And I was to remain until its closing. So I was part of very much that happened in that unique place, and with the help of Our Gracious Lord I hope to make this account as interesting as the story of Mount St. Gabriel's.

> —from the preface to *Mount St. Gabriel's*
> *Remembered: A Historical Memoir,* by Mother Suzanne
> Ravenel, Order of St. Scholastica, 2006; published by
> Mountain City Printing Company

PART ONE

CHAPTER 1

Tour of the Grounds

Third Saturday in August 1951
Mount St. Gabriel's
Mountain City, North Carolina

"WHEN YOU'VE DONE as much girl-watching as I have, Mother Malloy, you can see even as they're coming up through the lower grades how each class reveals itself as an *organism* in its own right. You're not too tired for a bit of a ramble, I hope."

"Not at all, Mother Ravenel. I've only been sitting on trains for two days."

"Good, in that case"—the headmistress, as quick of step as she was in speech, veered suddenly off the gravel walk and, snatching up her ankle-length skirts, plunged down a woodland path—"we'll take a turn around the new athletic field and then go up to the grotto and sit with the Red Nun awhile and have a little prayer to Our Lady in front of our Della Robbia."

"Who is the Red Nun?"

Without slowing her pace, the headmistress turned back to reward the new young teacher with an appreciative smile.

"You know, I often still catch *myself* thinking of her as a 'who.' After all these years! The shortest way to put it is, she's our mascot. If you can rightly call a six-foot-high ton of red marble a mascot. She's been unfinished since the middle of the First World War. It's quite a story, and you know what? I'm going to save it until we're at the grotto. There are so many things I want to point out to you first. Now, where was I?"

"You were saying about—organisms?"

"Oh, yes. A class is never just a collection of individual girls, though it is certainly *that*, too, when you're considering one girl at a time. But a class as a whole develops a group consciousness. It's an organic unit, with its own special properties. While we're having our walk, I will tell you a little about your ninth-grade girls, the upcoming freshman class. They are a challenging group, those girls. They will require control."

"As a—an organism, you mean? Or—some ones in particular?"

"Both, Mother Malloy."

In the presence of the headmistress, Mother Malloy, who was by habit cool and exact in speech, found herself stumbling and blurting. From my responses so far, she thought, this voluble, assured woman must be wondering how I am going to take charge of *any* class, not to mention a "challenging" one that requires "control." Mother Malloy was vexed by the clumsiness that had come over her even as she had been descending the steps of the train, taking caution with her long skirts, thanking the conductor who steadied her by the elbow, when a nun wearing aviator's sunglasses shot forward to claim her. Mother Ravenel was a vigorously handsome woman of medium height, with a high-colored face and fine white teeth. Snappy phrases, bathed in southern drawl, assailed the young nun from Boston. Her hand was clapped firmly between Mother Ravenel's immaculately gloved ones and she was mortified that she had not remembered to put on her own gloves.

There was worse to come. Mother Ravenel introduced her uniformed Negro driver and a lighter-skinned young man: "This is Jovan—we call him our Angel of Transportation—and this is his grandson Mark, who will be going off to college next year."

Mother Malloy extended her hand first to gray-haired Jovan, who took it after the merest hesitation. Though sensing she had done something outside of protocol, she had no choice but to repeat the gesture to young Mark, who, after a quick glance at his grandfather, shook her hand and bolted away to see to her trunk. While the two men loaded it into the back of the wood-paneled station wagon bearing the Mount St. Gabriel's crest (the archangel with upturned palms floating protectively above mountain ranges), Mother Ravenel tipped her veiled head close to the new nun's and gently confided, "We do things a little differently down here, Mother, but you'll get used to our ways. I think you'll find there's a great regard between the races and just as much love—if not actually *more*."

I have never seen a nun wearing sunglasses, Mother Malloy thought at the train station, trying to contain her mortification and offer it up.

"Of course, girls in their early teens are always difficult," Mother Ravenel was saying now. She zigzagged off the woodland path and into a clearing. "Do you have sisters, Mother?"

I have never known a nun to dart about so, thought Mother Malloy, struggling to keep up with her guide. They taught us to glide and keep custody of the limbs in the Boston novitiate. Perhaps religious formation is another thing they "do differently" in the South. The accent is melodious, but somehow it doesn't lend itself to gravity.

"Except for my sisters in the Order, none, Mother."

"Ah, same as myself. I grew up with two older brothers. I was the baby sister. You had brothers, perhaps?"

"No, no brothers, either."

"An only child. That has its advantages. For instance, I could never go off by myself and read and daydream, as I imagine you could. My beastly brothers were always dragging me up into their tree houses or out on their boats. We lived on the East Battery, in Charleston."

"You were saying about these girls—the rising ninth grade?" Kate Malloy had been raised in a Catholic foster home in West Newton, near Boston, but saw no point in tempting Mother Ravenel into further asides. "Their challenging aspects?"

"Yes, well, my point was, *all* girls are challenging at that age. They're sensitive and acute and they have a cruel streak—a *different* cruelty from boys, has been my experience—and a shocking amount of energy. Their bodies are ready for childbirth, but their cognitive development isn't complete yet. You have only to recall your own feelings at fourteen. You felt you were capable of making your own life decisions. You felt that most adults, besides being over the hill, had compromised themselves and were to be pitied rather than listened to. Am I right?"

No, but you're my superior. "I was lucky to have several adults I truly admired. What I do recall feeling is wishing I could spend more time with them."

"Ah, mentors, you mean. But a mentor is not in the same category as your average compromised adult, wouldn't you agree? And since you have brought up the subject of mentors, Mother, that's exactly what I'm praying these girls will find in you. Their specialty is intimidation. In sixth grade they demoralized a popular lay teacher. I'll supply the gory details later, but right now, I want you to take in Mount St. Gabriel's picturesque view. It's at its most sublime from here. That's why we chose this site for the new athletic field, even though the excavation and tree-topping costs completely wrecked our budget."

Mother Malloy took in the vista from this place into which her vow of obedience had so abruptly landed her. In three weeks she was to have begun her second year of graduate work at Boston College. But a week ago Reverend Mother had summoned her. "I know it's a great disappointment, my dear, but Mother Ravenel down at Mount St. Gabriel's is in a bind. The junior college lost their shorthand-and-typing mistress, a young novice who has asked to be released from her vows, and Mother Sharp, who normally takes the ninth grade, is the only one qualified to teach secretarial courses. Offer it up to Our Lord, and we'll see if we can arrange for you to come back to Boston for summer courses."

The spot on which Mother Malloy and Mother Ravenel stood commanded a panorama of mountain ranges stacked one behind the other, their hues fading from deep smoky purple into the milk blue of the horizon. Below them was Mountain City, its downtown buildings and curving river twinkling with late-afternoon sun. A solitary hawk dipped and soared, riding the air streams above them. Mother Malloy was in the midst of composing a suitable line of praise for the school's picturesque view when Mother Ravenel, off on another tack, rendered the effort unnecessary.

"And *next* year we will be taking on the boys."

"The boys?"

"Newman Hall for grades one through eight, and Maturin Hall for the high school. Though there's still some lobbying going on about calling the upper grades 'forms,' like the prep schools and the English public schools. If you look over through those pines, you can see the slate roof of what will be Newman, when the renovations are finished."

Mother Malloy followed the tanned pointing finger. She took in the gabled roof; she also took in the headmistress's youthful, well-kept hands. The older nun's silver ring flashed in the sunlight.

"What will be Newman and Maturin were lovely adjoining estates. Within a single year they were left to us by two cousins: grateful mothers of satisfied alumnae. I told the bishop, I said, 'We must be doing something right at Mount St. Gabriel's.' His nose was a little out of joint because the properties were deeded to *us,* the Order of St. Scholastica, and not to the diocese. Isn't this a grand athletic field? When the boys come, we'll put in goalposts for football. Howard, our handyman, is so proud of the turf and of his new tractor mower that we have to restrain him from mowing twice a week. Only yesterday I told him, 'Howard, this is not a golf course,' but I can see and smell perfectly well that it has been mowed again since. What sports did you play, Mother Malloy?"

"I can't say I played anything well, but I liked swimming in the ocean. And badminton as a teenager."

"I still crave a set of tennis, even with the restraints of the habit. Do you play tennis?"

"I'm afraid not."

"I could coach you. What a treat, to have someone to play with besides Miss Farber, our gym teacher, who never has time for more than a game. You're still young enough to learn properly, and we'd be equally handicapped with our long skirts and veils."

"What sports do the girls in the academy play?"

"Everyone gets basketball, tennis, volleyball, and modern dance. We also offer gymnastics, ballroom, ballet and tap, and horseback riding, but for those, additional fees are required. There's a movement afoot by the parents, abetted by Miss Farber, to open up the indoor pool—Mount St. Gabriel's was a famous mountain resort in the Victorian era—and have swimming for the upper grades. Reverend Mother, who likes to make people happy, seems to be leaning that way. Being of a more practical nature, I have to consider the wet hair, the monthly period excuses, and the girls' uncharitable appraisals of one another's figures. Your rising ninth grade has made the critique of others into a high form of torture."

"Is there a ringleader?"

"That's a good *first* question. It was my first question, back when they were sixth graders and their, shall we say, effects began taking their toll on others."

"What happened in sixth grade?"

At Mother Ravenel's brisk pace they had already walked half the length of the athletic field, and Mother Malloy found herself slightly out of breath.

"We lost a devoted lay teacher who'd been with us for twenty-two years. Mrs. Prince taught arithmetic from grades six through eight and home economics in the academy and junior college. She was much loved, especially by the older girls."

"Lost her—how?"

"After three months with the sixth grade that will be your ninth grade, she resigned. She told Reverend Mother she felt she was getting thin-skinned and could no longer keep discipline. She also said that 'little girls seemed to be changing into something different.' We begged her to stay on, at least for home economics with the older girls, but she said she had begun to shake and feel sick at her stomach as soon as she drove through our entrance gates every morning, so we had to honor her wishes. She's since become a substitute teacher in the public school system."

"What did they do, the sixth grade?"

"Well, for a start, Mrs. Prince liked to bring homemade fudge to school. After the girls had done their lessons well, she'd pass it around and read to them from *Uncle Remus*. Until one day when she was passing it around to the sixth graders and girl after girl turned her down. Very politely, of course; they had all manner of excuses. 'Thank you so much, Mrs. Prince, but I've just found out I'm allergic to chocolate' . . . 'Thank you, Mrs. Prince, but I'm on a diet' . . . 'Thank you, but I'm not hungry, Mrs. Prince.' One girl even said she was fasting!"

"The entire class turned down the fudge?"

"Oh, there were some holdouts. But they got fewer each time. Finally she stopped bringing fudge to school for any of the classes."

"And the readings that accompanied the fudge? Did they continue?"

"Ah, that was their next target. Do you know the Uncle Remus stories? No? Up there in Yankeeland, I guess not. Joel Chandler Harris was an Atlanta newspaperman who wrote humorous adaptations of the folktales of Negro slaves. Dealing chiefly with animals like Brer Rabbit, who has a cunning instinct for survival and is always outwitting his enemies. Uncle Remus was the old slave who narrated the stories, and Mrs. Prince had the dialect down pat. When she did the different animals' voices you were in stitches. 'Oh, *please,* Brer Fox, *don't* throw me into that briar patch!' "

"You heard her read?"

"Why, yes, many a time. I laughed myself out of my chair the first time. I'd just come to Mount St. Gabriel's as a boarder. She was our seventh-grade math teacher."

"You were a student here?"

"Indeed I was. I was in the class of '34. In my time, the state didn't have an eighth grade. You went from seventh grade into the academy. Oh, I should also tell you, three of your ninth graders have mothers from our class of '34, and two of the girls share an aunt. At first it was going to be just *two* mothers and an aunt, but now Chloe Starnes, whose mother died tragically this past spring, will be joining us as a boarder. What she will add to the mix, who can predict? Her mother, Agnes, was a well-thought-of girl—I admired Agnes Vick, though we were not close. Young Chloe seems a more interior sort—though, of course, she's in deep mourning right now. Her uncle, Henry Vick, Agnes's brother, is a prominent architect in town—right now he's designing the new public library—and he's a staunch supporter of the school. But add to *that*—well, you see, Chloe's uncle Henry was married to the aunt I mentioned—a dreadful thing; Antonia Tilden was killed in a traffic accident on their honeymoon in Rome. Henry has never remarried. Antonia was my best friend at Mount St. Gabriel's. And, you see, by her marriage to Henry, she is also *Chloe's* aunt, or late aunt, as well as Tildy Stratton's. Cornelia, Tildy's mother, and Antonia were identical twins."

Mother Malloy's mind was now a vertiginous whirl of aunts, uncles, mothers, identical twins, friendships, tragedies, and accidents, all of which she must match to individual girls she hadn't even met. Also she was feeling light-headed from the walk.

"What did the girls do—about the Uncle Remus readings?"

"Well, first they stopped laughing. And then they stopped smiling. As a group. They just faced front and stared straight ahead. They stopped looking at Mrs. Prince when she read to them. And then they stopped looking at her when she taught them math."

"It's hard to imagine little girls being so organized in their cruelty. Surely there must be a leader, or a few main girls."

"Of course there's always a core of leadership. And every class has its main girls. I could rattle off some names, though you'll quickly be able to pick them out for yourself. I'd rather you rely on your own instincts, Mother Malloy. Provide us with the fresh view of someone coming in from the outside. I'm such a dyed-in-the-wool Mount St. Gabriel's girl—I entered the Order as a postulant during my senior year. There may be something here I'm not seeing because it's been staring me in the face the whole time. After all, I was in the same class with some of the mothers and aunts. And as I said, one of them, poor Tony, was my dearest friend."

"I hope I—"

"And here are the steps leading up to our grotto. It's lovely and cool up there, an ideal spot for meditation and just turning things over to the Blessed Mother. You'll be meeting all of your girls on registration day, but now it's time for you to see our beautiful Della Robbia and meet our Red Nun."

✠

SHE HAS THE face of an alabaster saint, the headmistress was thinking, sprinting ahead up the winding stone steps to the grotto. The vigorous swish of her habit set the giant ferns on either side bowing and swaying, like obeisant minions.

Yet she seems unaware of her beauty. And she's less *commanding* than I was given to expect. But the looks alone will carry her—they'll have nothing to criticize *there*—until they locate her weak spots.

Is she panting? In her early twenties and already short of breath after our little climb? I'm her senior by more than a decade and feel as fit as I did as a girl when I foot-raced my brothers on the beach. Probably our academy up in Boston doesn't put enough of a premium on exercise. And of course there's their colder weather, and they're located right in town.

I will coach her in tennis. It will loosen her up a little. Put some color in her cheeks; she's way too pale. There's something almost Quakerish about her. Not easy to draw out. In conversation she reminds me of a hound dog, intent on retrieving a single bird at a time.

"Oh—!"

Now she's gone and turned her ankle or something! "What is it, Mother?"

"A baby rabbit." The young nun was crouched on the path, raptly squinting through a thicket of old rhododendrons. The fringed sash of her habit trailed in the undergrowth.

"Oh, if it's rabbits you want, we've got them by the dozens, the procreative little creatures. Mother Finney, our cellaress, finally had to get Howard to build her a chain-link fence around the vegetable garden."

"I've never seen a brown one before."

"I can tell you're going to enjoy your forest walks. Mount St. Gabriel's has thirty acres of woodlands and riding paths just teeming with wildlife. You name it, we've got it: wild turkeys, great horned owls, hawks, bobcats, foxes in both red and gray, and of course raccoons and skunks and possums and an oversupply of rabbits, chipmunks, and squirrels. Not so many black bears anymore, though in late spring almost every year, a girl will come flying in to report that she *thinks* she spotted one."

"What is a bobcat?"

"Basically just a smaller-sized wildcat that sounds exactly like a house cat when it vocalizes. They're tan with black spots. Jovan, who met you at the station, found an abandoned bob-kitten and took it home to raise it. But it gnawed its way out of its box and was so spiteful and snappish to his children he brought it back to the woods."

Talk about "vocalizing"—I am worn out with my own. People with no small talk are exhausting; you're obliged to carry the whole load yourself. Well, maybe she's just taking it all in, showing respect. I am her immediate superior, after all. Reverend Mother in Boston said she was a first-rate graduate assistant at Boston College. Students work hard to impress her, and she puts up with no foolishness. How odd that Reverend Mother had said nothing about the striking good looks. "I think you'll find her effective" was all she volunteered. Well, Lord, You always provide more than I know to ask for. These supercritical girls will be subdued by their teacher's beauty—at least until they have time to ferret out her vulnerabilities, of which I suspect there are some.

"Not much farther, now, Mother Malloy. The grotto is just up around the next turn."

I sound like I sound when I'm showing parents of prospective students around the grounds. I don't have to sell *her* on the school—she already belongs to us!

⁜

MOTHER MALLOY CONTINUED to call on her filtering powers to stanch the overflow of information and the competing new sights and sensations. First the rambling eighty-bedroom Victorian edifice, the former hotel, complete with its tower and gables and porches, in which she was to live. Her third-story bedroom, in which Mother Ravenel had allowed her a half-hour respite (she lay down as soon as she was alone, putting off unpacking until later), looked down upon a sunny inner courtyard where one black woman peeled vegetables and another hung laundry. And now the rustling presences of this primeval woodland setting, and the discovery of her own breathlessness, new to her at age twenty-four, as she climbed up and up. Her skin was damp beneath her habit, and perspiration trickled down the back of her neck. As the train had pulled into the station, a banner on the depot had announced "Welcome to the Land of the Sky. You are now ONE MILE above sea level!"

The headmistress seemed never to have need to pause for breath, nipping round the edges of Howard's too-often-mowed athletic field and dashing up the steep woodland steps, discoursing on everything from extracurricular fees to the unfortunate Mrs. Prince and the coil of all these histories leading to the unpredictable chemical mix of the rising ninth grade.

Help me, PLEASE, to listen and hear without making premature judgments. Later You will help me discern between the significant and the interesting. Or the merely diverting.

In the meantime, please help me not to be overwhelmed.

CHAPTER 2

Uncle

IN THE DAPPLED shade of the grotto, Henry Vick was slouched upon the cool marble ledge—or lap, as the girls called it—of the Red Nun, taking reflective draws on his pipe and preparing for his encounter with the headmistress as soon as their paths should intersect. She would not be pleased with his news. Suzanne Ravenel had never taken it well when her plans were revised or thwarted.

He had not found her in her trophy-and-memorabilia-filled office overlooking the western ranges. But he had met old Mother Finney returning from the garden, bent double with her basketful of summer vegetables. The Irish nun had come over with the English foundress to open the school in 1910. Mother Ravenel was taking the new teacher from Boston on a tour of the school's grounds, Mother Finney told him, adding, "And, you know, she likes to save the grotto for last." Henry carried Mother Finney's basket to the kitchen, where she rewarded him with an oatmeal cookie, soft and hot from the oven.

"These are the best," he said. "Did you learn to cook as a girl in Ireland?"

"I wasn't allowed near our kitchen in Ireland. Too busy mucking out the stalls. Jovan's wife, Betty, taught me everything I know about cooking, in this very kitchen."

Henry looked around at the clean, shiny surfaces of Mount St. Gabriel's kitchen. "It's good to be here. I miss—I've missed you all."

"Ah, but we will be seeing more of you, Henry, now that your niece Chloe is to be with us. I am desolate over Agnes. Your sister was dear to my heart. I know we aren't supposed to have favorites, but even Our Lord had His favorites."

"And you were dear to Agnes. Do you remember the Halloween when she dressed up as Fiona Finney, the Irish horse trainer?"

"Remember? I should say so! I dressed her myself. It was my own riding boots she wore. And to die so young."

"Agnes turned thirty-five this past January."

A worn-out thirty-five, the last time Henry had seen his sister. The future plighted with her great love, Merriweather Starnes, had been scuttled when his fighter plane went down on Okinawa less than two months before the end of the war. Chloe had been eight at the time. Agnes's second marriage, to Rex Wright, a member of Merry's squadron, had turned out to be, Agnes had confided to Henry at their last meeting, "my mortal mistake."

This disclosure took place in a booth in a diner in Barlow, two hours down the hairpin curves from Mountain City, Agnes having telephoned Henry the night before. "I want to send Chloe home with you for the Easter holidays," she'd told him. "Perhaps for longer. I'll say more when I see you. Don't come to the house. I don't want him to know she's leaving till she's gone. There's a little diner in the middle of town."

Agnes was one who took great care with words—"mortal" as in human, or as in fatal? He wished he'd asked. Then later, when it was too late to ask, he wondered if his sister could have meant "mortal" as in mortal sin: grave matter, full knowledge, full consent.

"There are some things in my life now, Henry, that are better left undescribed. Chloe will come here to the diner straight from school. Her suitcase is packed and in my car. By the way, I haven't told her that it may be longer than the Easter break. It may not be. I'll just have to see."

Henry had been glad of the solitary drive down the mountain to Barlow: two hours in which to get used to the prospect of a young teenage girl he hardly knew sharing his home for an unspecified duration. However, by the time he reached the town where Rex Wright had his crop-dusting service, he found himself anticipating certain changes his niece might bring to his bachelor life. They would go out to dinner, to the basilica during Holy Week. He would have the moral satisfaction of being an uncle and godfather called to account for his baptismal promises.

And having got that far on the drive, he was able in all sincerity to say to Agnes in the diner, "Why don't you come along, too? You and Chloe can make your home with me as long as you want. It is your house as much as mine."

"Please don't tempt me, Henry. I have to stay here and see what can be salvaged of this marriage."

"What can be salvaged of a thing you've just admitted was a mortal mistake?"

"Nothing more or less than just my honor, dear." She had laughed her self-mocking laugh and narrowed her eyes at him and for a moment was his baby sister again. "For better or worse, Henry, I'm still ferociously attached to my honor. Rex hasn't had it easy since the war. Bombing the enemy was a lot more exciting than bombing bugs. And I did marry him before God. I said the same vows to him that I said to Merry."

WOMEN'S VOICES FLOATED up through the trees. Ravenel's familiar hustling cadences raced ahead of the lower-pitched, monosyllabic responses of the other.

Henry rose to his feet just as the ruddy-complexioned headmistress, wearing her customary sunglasses, entered the grotto, followed by a pale young nun.

"Why, Henry, what a nice surprise. Were you having an audience with our Della Robbia or our Red Nun?"

Even now, when Henry saw his sister's classmate and his bride's best friend in her habit, he could imagine Suzanne impulsively snatching off her veil and demanding of her audience, "There, now! Didn't I play that part well?"

"Actually, I was hoping to have an audience with you, Mother Ravenel."

"Well, here I am. And this is Mother Malloy, fresh off the train from Boston. I've been giving her the grand tour. Mother, this is Henry Vick, the uncle I was telling you about, Chloe's guardian. Mother Malloy will be taking charge of Chloe's class, Henry."

"How do you do, Mother Malloy."

"How do you do, Mr. Vick. I'm looking forward to knowing your niece." Her voice was low and precise. Only the "*fah*-ward" proclaimed her Boston roots. But behind those few words about Chloe, which in themselves stopped at the perfunctory, he wanted to believe he heard empathy and a warmth of heart. She was lovely despite her pallor.

"I am still getting to know her myself," he said. "And the more I know her, the better I like her. She is deep and she is hurting. She lost her mother at Easter—it was all very sudden, unexpected. This has been a period of adjustment for both of us."

"You have been a godsend to that child, Henry," Mother Ravenel assured him, "and now you are doing exactly right in letting us help you. We will do our best to give her round-the-clock motherhood and guidance, won't we, Mother Malloy?"

"The thing is," said Henry, realizing that the presence of the other nun might ease his task. "I have decided—that is, *we* have decided, Chloe and I—that we prefer to go on as we are. Chloe will be coming to Mount St. Gabriel's as a day student and living with me. We agreed on this only this morning, but I wanted to inform you as soon as possible."

He could see Suzanne admirably suppressing her annoyance.

"Well, Henry, this *is* news. But if it's what you all have decided, I appreciate you letting me know so promptly. Of course, you understand I can't refund Chloe's boarding fee. There are no exceptions, even for an old friend. Besides"—here she managed a laugh—"your money's probably already been spent."

"If it hasn't been," was his gallant comeback, "spend it on something wonderful."

"And what would you consider wonderful, Henry?"

"Oh, a memorial ciborium for Chloe's mother, encrusted with garnets. That was Agnes's birthstone."

"Well, I don't know if the fee will cover *garnets*, Henry."

"It will if I make up the difference. Have Haywood Silversmiths do it. Her dates on the rim."

"What about 'Class of '34'?"

"That, too, of course," Henry magnanimously conceded.

☩

DURING THIS MELLIFLUOUS sparring between the headmistress and the uncle, Mother Malloy took what she hoped were unobserved ragged breaths. Or, rather, she was trying to find her breath. These two persons were well matched. There was history between them. Though Mother Ravenel had clearly been caught off guard by Mr. Vick's announcement, she had remained in control. What, though, had she meant by "you *all*"? Didn't that imply that more than two people were involved in the decision to keep Chloe at home? Or was this a regional quirk of speech? Mr. Vick had an astringent manner, yet was courtly in combat. He reminded her of her professor of Renaissance history at Boston College, Father Galliard: dry, exacting, but always cordial.

But then, to her dismay, her light-headedness increased. Blue and purple spots showered inside her eyes. She caught herself tilting forward and would have fallen had she not reached out to grab the hulk of russet marble from which Mr. Vick had risen to greet them.

The next thing she knew, she herself was semireclining on its benchlike ledge, their concerned faces floating above her.

"—entirely my fault," Mother Ravenel was saying. "I've been dragging her up our hills like she was a mountain goat. Speak to us, Mother Malloy."

Henry Vick was offering to bring a glass of water from the kitchen. "Or I have a flask of cognac in my car."

"No, please. It was—whatever it was has passed."

"When did you last eat something?" he asked.

"Mother Finney had iced tea and a chicken salad sandwich waiting for her when she arrived," the headmistress answered for her.

"Really, I'm better now. It's very cool—" She was aware that her cheek lay against the red marble and hastened to pull herself upright. "Is this a sculpture I'm seated on?"

"Why, you've gone straight for the protection of our Red Nun," Mother Ravenel said. "Now you're truly one of us. Henry, I'm going to presume on you to tell Mother Malloy the story of our guardian spirit. I have been bending her ear until I am weary of the sound of my voice. Meanwhile, Mother Malloy, you take it easy. I'll be back in a flash with some ice water."

Off she dashed, fringed sash flying.

"Are you subject to fainting spells, Mother Malloy?" Fiddling with his pipe, Henry Vick stood a little apart: a lanky man in his mid- to late thirties; soft voice, furrowed brow, graying brown hair receding at the temples; rumpled seersucker suit. His kind, abstracted manner put her at her ease.

"I've never fainted before. If that was what it was."

"My sister, Agnes, was a champion fainter. Always at the dentist's and sometimes just before an exam. Anytime she was tense or uncertain, you could see the blood leave her face. Then she had to put her head between her knees or she was out cold. The first time she fainted was right after her first communion. She was walking back to her seat with her hands clasped properly in front of her and then suddenly she hit the floor with a thud."

"It was the fasting, of course," Mother Malloy said. "Now children are allowed to drink a glass of juice before."

"The monsignor told her afterward that it was a sign of grace; it meant she was taking the sacrament seriously. But she was furious with herself. 'Everyone saw my panties,' she told us when we got home."

They both laughed. In his telling, she felt the personality of his lost sister. In his laughter, she saw that Henry Vick gained relief in bringing her back through anecdotes like this.

"Do you have sisters or brothers, Mother Malloy?"

"I was in a foster home, but there were certain of the children that I felt sisterly toward."

"I see. Would it make you queasy if I relit my pipe?"

"No, I like the smell of a pipe. If I were a man, I would probably smoke one. Please do tell me about the Red Nun."

"It's an unfinished memorial to a young woman who was a student here in the early years of the school. Malaria carried her off the summer before she was to enter the novitiate. Her people were rich Charlestonians; they ordered the marble from Italy and commissioned a famous funerary sculptor. But from the start, things took on a life of their own. White marble was ordered; red was delivered. Then came 1914, war broke out in Europe, and there was no more Italian marble to be had. The sculptor said he was delighted to work with the red—it was Veronese red, more than a hundred million years old. He said he could make something distinctive, really fine. The plan was to have a life-scale young nun in all her particulars, even down to her rosary, seated in front of that Della Robbia Annunciation across from you."

Both transferred their attention to the glazed terra-cotta bas-relief of the Virgin looking up, startled, from the open book on her lap to the kneeling Gabriel. The white dove hovered in the blue-enameled air between them. A Grecian vase crammed with lilies was placed equidistantly between Virgin and angel.

"The young woman—her name was Caroline DuPree—had prayed rosaries here in the grotto, asking Our Lady to persuade her parents to let her be a nun. But the sculptor died while the piece was in its half-finished form. There was talk of the family finding another sculptor, but nothing ever came of it. I've always been glad in a way. There is a certain power in her rough form."

"Like Michelangelo's Captives."

"You've seen them?"

"Only in my college textbook on Renaissance history. But I felt what you said about them: the power of the unfinished. How I would love to go to Italy!"

Too late she realized her blunder: this man's bride had been killed on their Roman honeymoon.

But he was applying the lit match to the bowl of his pipe with the same tranquil focus—the awful memory seemingly unstirred.

When the tobacco caught flame, he continued to speak in his equable tone.

"Mount St. Gabriel girls have made her their guardian spirit. That unfinished marble lap you're resting on, Mother Malloy, has been snuggled into and worn down by generations of girls begging her to intercede with the Madonna and heal their sorrows or grant their desires. Suz—Mother Ravenel wrote a play about her for the freshman class in 1931. It was called *The Red Nun.* My parents and I were in the audience. My sister, Agnes, and Antonia, the girl I was later to marry, had prominent roles. Mother Ravenel—she was Suzanne in those days—directed the play and divided her acting talents between several roles, including the voice of God. Since that time, the actual history of the memorial to Caroline DuPree has become entwined with Mother Ravenel's play, which is revived from time to time. Each class in the academy does a play every year, but the *Red Nun* revivals are for the freshmen only because Mother Ravenel was a freshman when she wrote it. It's the tradition. And you know how traditions and legends tend to grow tentacles. And the girls are permitted to add their own material. Within reason, of course. That's another tradition."

"Let's hope the next production will be soon," said Mother Malloy, feeling her strength flowing back. "You have made me very eager to see it, Mr. Vick."

Early Beginnings

Over the years the girls have never tired of hearing the story of how our Order was formed. And I never tire of retelling it, because it is such a wonderful example of how intricately God works His purposes in our lives. We must go back in time to the small village of Cowley, just outside of Oxford, England. The year was 1889 and a remarkable Anglican preacher and monk, Father Basil Maturin, recently returned from a very successful ten-year mission in Philadelphia, was leading a retreat at Cowley. One of the retreatants was Elizabeth Wallingford, the future foundress of our Order. Like Father Maturin, Elizabeth was still a member of the Church of England at that time. Her family, the Wallingfords, was a very, very old Oxfordshire family; they and their property holdings are listed in the Domesday Book.

Now, Elizabeth's brothers had been educated at Oxford, but in those days women were not admitted to universities. We know from the brief account of her life she has left us that she keenly felt her lack of education. At the time of the Cowley retreat, she had reached the age of twenty-eight, which back then would more than qualify you for spinsterhood. After she had turned down several acceptable proposals of marriage, her father, who doted on her, offered to set her up as head of a school for young ladies in a dower house on the Wallingford estate, but she refused him. How can I teach others, she asked, when I myself have been denied the subjects that were daily fare for my brothers? She said the world did not need any more "schools" to teach girls how to stay home and do needlework and play the piano and manage the servants. She was very much ahead of her time but was powerless to do anything about it.

Or so she thought until she went to Cowley and heard Father Maturin preach. "Don't be content simply to speculate what you *might* be capable of," he challenged his retreatants. She felt he was speaking directly to her. "You don't know what is in you till you try. There was much about the Magdalene that she had never used, perhaps never dreamed that she possessed, until she met Our Lord and He set her on the path of true self-development."

Ironically, Elizabeth had heard about "the spellbinding Father Maturin" from a former suitor who was now a vicar in the Church of England. He had accompanied her on the retreat, perhaps thinking he might induce her to reconsider his proposal of marriage. But for Elizabeth Wallingford, God had more far-reaching plans in store. "Discontent," Father Maturin said, enunciating the word with a strange vigor and looking straight at Elizabeth, "may be God's catapult, His way of saying: 'Go and try yourself *now*.' "

—from *Mount St. Gabriel's Remembered: A Historical Memoir,* by Mother Suzanne Ravenel

CHAPTER 3

Drawing the Dead

Third Saturday in August 1951
Henry Vick's house
Mountain City, North Carolina

"IT'S AS THOUGH *you were back in my girlhood, watching over me like a guardian angel . . ."*

The girlhood room of Chloe's mother, from the days when she was still Agnes Vick, looked down over a gently rolling back lawn surrounded by mature boxwoods. The window seat, nestled beneath the slant of the roof, was at present awash in the fiery brilliance of the late-summer afternoon.

In drawing his plans for this room in 1927, Agnes's architect father, Malcolm Vick, had included a sketch of his daughter fitted into this space, her long legs doubled to form a prop for her book. Already, by age ten, Agnes had reached the height of five feet six and, though it would throw the house design slightly out of proportion, her father had added a second window to increase the length of the seat and provide for her teenage extensions. It was his hope that Agnes would grace this new house for at least nine or ten years before a husband carried her off to another.

Chloe had never seen those plans for the Vick house at the corner of Montgomery Avenue and Riverside Drive, but from her mother's descriptions she had conjured up her own vision of Malcolm Vick's sketch of his daughter in the proposed window seat.

And when Chloe herself began drawing in earnest, in the months after her father died, she felt compelled to reproduce that long-legged girl in the window seat again and again. "How do you *do* this, darling?"

her mother would ask. "I know draftsmanship runs in our family, but this is something more. It's as though you are watching over my girl-hood like a guardian angel." And then her mother had wept, saying, "If I didn't have you, I might think my whole marriage with Merry was a dream." And Chloe had said, "Yes, and we can remember him to-gether."

The drawings got more interesting as Chloe's skills improved. She experimented with angles: the girl Agnes as seen from above, from across the room, from outside the window.

If my mother could observe this window seat from wherever she is now, with me in it, how could I send her the message that I am all right and that I know that we will go on taking care of each other? After all, we spent one night together in this very room, before Rex showed up early in his new plane and cut short our weekend visit with Uncle Henry.

Chloe could not swallow the notion, put forward too often in recent weeks by people wishing to console her, that Agnes was up in heaven with her adored first husband and her mother and father and all the company of saints as well as Jesus and the Blessed Mother and God Himself. This seemed too simplistic an elevation: the newly dead get-ting lifted up on their death day ("Going up, folks!") to eternal life. Where they would then do what? Roam around like they were at a big party, recognizing old friends (and surely some enemies, too)?

Whereas Chloe could accommodate the existence of purgatory—in which her mother had firmly believed. It was an extension of life's im-perfections, Agnes had said. You stopped in purgatory because you weren't yet prepared for perfection. Rushing off to heaven before you were ready would make you feel soiled and uncomfortable in the pres-ence of perfection.

"Would you come straight home from a sweaty day at school and drag your best dress off the hanger and rush off to a fabulous dance without showering and fixing your hair first?" That was Agnes during one of their "Catechism in Secret" sessions at the downtown diner after Rex Wright had forbidden his wife and stepdaughter to discuss religion "in his house." ("You two have made your damned Catholicism into a snooty secret society.")

It was easy to imagine Agnes in purgatory, and Chloe liked dwelling there with her, just as she had spent much of this phantasmal summer sketching her mother in favorite remembered poses: Agnes as seen from behind, hair in a kerchief, stooping to collect the eggs in the henhouse; Agnes in the diner, leaning forward on her elbows to say something, her face, stretched and framed by her hands, looking suddenly younger.

If purgatory was like an extension of what most people meant by "daily life," a place where you found yourself stuck in the middle of a routine you had neither wanted nor expected, but where there was still a chance that something you did or learned today would move you closer to the exit of this disappointing place, then she could follow Agnes through her daily purgatorial assignments.

In purgatory, there would be things Agnes had to do, things that corresponded to her duties in their house in Barlow. But instead of laundry and chickens and meals and a husband to pacify and a daughter to educate and protect, there would be—

Chloe faltered. It was like going uphill in your mind; gears needed to shift, but what would the gears in a car translate to if you were talking about human beings?

In purgatory, the people wouldn't be there, or the house or the chickens, but Agnes's soul would be going through the motions until she got it right, until she understood what she had done and what she had left undone.

There would be no mirrors in purgatory. Agnes wouldn't need to see her image in a mirror; she would be intent on carrying, with the same care that she transported between her palms a new-laid egg for Chloe's breakfast, her own immortal soul.

It felt okay to Chloe to compare her mother's soul to an egg. With both, the hard part was to carry them intact to their assigned destinations. Which would be—in life—feeding a daughter. And—in purgatory—in purgatory—

Here Chloe's metaphor-making powers stalled just as she heard her uncle's car purr smoothly into the garage.

⊹

"WELL, THE DEED is done," Henry Vick said, sipping his scotch as Chloe sipped her Coke, he lounging in a wicker chair and she upright in the back porch swing. The shadows had lengthened on the rear lawn, the shiny boxwood hedge had become a deep purple wall, but there was still gold left in the sky. In the kitchen, Rosa, the family cook, reputed to be in her nineties, was frying up chicken to go with the potato salad she and Chloe had made earlier. ("Good child! You know to pull the strings off the celery." "My mother taught me." "And guess who taught your mother?")

"How did she take it?"

"Admirably. Mother Ravenel is always at her best when there's an audience. There was another nun with her. Your ninth-grade teacher, as a matter of fact. Mother Malloy had just arrived on the train from Boston."

"What's she like?"

"She's an impressive person; beautiful, in a nunlike way. I found her both informed and easy to talk to."

He left out Mother Malloy's fainting spell. These days he was very conscious of monitoring Chloe's grieving; he didn't want to overload her with too many reminders, though he didn't wish to prevaricate, either. Accepting in advance that he would make some wrong calls, he kept up a constant effort to strike a delicate balance between what she needed to know now and what could wait till later.

The fainting was something her mother had done, and it was assumed to have caused her death on Easter eve. Her husband came home from giving Saturday flying lessons at the airfield and found her body slumped on the floor of their bedroom. There were cranial bruises from the impact against the radiator. That much Chloe had been told.

Even Rex Wright hadn't known that his wife had been carrying a six-week-old fetus, until the coroner informed him. "She hadn't even told me she was expecting my child!" he wailed to Henry on the phone. "She was always keeping secrets, her and Chloe both. They shut me out every chance they got. For all I know, she told Chloe about the baby, but not me."

Henry doubted this and told Rex so. It would go against his sister's ferocious attachment to her honor. But he wasn't about to ask Chloe. Henry scrupulously avoided any quizzing of the girl about her last days with her mother. When and if she was ready to tell him anything, he would be there to listen.

"I wonder what it will be like," Chloe said, leaning forward suddenly in the porch swing.

"The school?"

"The whole thing. The ninth grade. Mother Malloy. The girls in my class. I hope I won't be too far behind."

"Why should you be? You've always done well in school."

"But they weren't schools like Mount St. Gabriel's. Mother said sometimes the nuns would put a girl who'd transferred from another school back a grade."

"That's not going to happen to you."

"No," Chloe calmly agreed, surprising him. "All through eighth grade, Mother's been teaching me the extras. I know my catechism and we were doing European history and starting Latin. I'd meet her at the diner after school and we'd have Cokes and cheese crackers in the back booth and she'd tutor me out of her old Mount St. Gabriel's notebooks."

"Well, then. You'll certainly be on equal footing with the other girls. Maybe ahead."

This was the first he'd heard about the tutorials at the diner. Had Agnes been preparing to send Chloe off to school months before she summoned him?

"No, not ahead. Though I've been going on with my schoolbooks and her notebooks this summer, since I didn't get to finish the last month at the junior high. But there's so much *else* I won't know."

With the tips of her toes Chloe set the old porch swing going until it sang on its chains. She could not know how much she resembled Agnes at fourteen. The same proud posture, Agnes's identical jutting chin and beaky nose, the same inward gaze even though she could be looking straight at you. The prehensile way the long feet controlled the motion of the swing. Though she was more serious than Agnes. There was not that flash and crackle of wit always lurking beneath the surface.

"What sort of 'elses' won't you know?"

The fine skin between Chloe's brows crinkled. She licked her lips and shot out her chin. This was her concentration mode. Like a young animal about to leap, she was gathering herself to explore a further outlook. Henry was suddenly pierced to the depths by his young charge. Had he taken on too much? Would it have been wiser to go ahead as planned and let her board at Mount St. Gabriel's, where, as Mother Ravenel said, she would have a host of mothers? But Chloe had told him last night that she would be sorry to leave the house her mother had been a girl in. She felt, Chloe said, the presence of her mother watching over her. "And, you know, Uncle Henry, I watch over her, as well."

And he, being one of those grown men who still prayed nightly, had fallen asleep praying about it.

"Well, the other girls, they've been together since first grade. To them I'll be a new girl in the ninth grade—an outsider."

"I hardly see how you can be an outsider when there are so many connections. Mother Ravenel was your aunt Antonia's best friend. And Antonia's niece Tildy Stratton will be your classmate. Antonia and her twin sister, Cornelia, and your mother were all in the class of '34. I'd say you're as . . . as *entrenched* as anyone can be."

She paused in her swinging to consider this, then set the swing going again, but in slower motion.

"No," she said thoughtfully, "there's all the stuff these girls have done that I wasn't there for. And besides that . . . besides that . . . Mother was never in the oblates of the Red Nun. Aunt Tony and her twin sister, Corny Tilden, and Suzanne Ravenel *were.*"

The otiose oblates, Agnes had scornfully christened them behind their back after she had turned down Suzanne's invitation to join. *Of all the silly, pointless societies, Suzanne's little group takes the cake.* He hadn't thought of the oblates in years, not even earlier this afternoon when he had been filling Mother Malloy in on the lore surrounding the hulk of red marble.

"I doubt if your classmates will know anything about that little society."

"Well, if Mother, who wasn't one, told me about them, why shouldn't Tildy Stratton, whose mother and aunt *were,* have told her friends about the oblates?"

"Because it isn't the kind of thing a grown woman would be proud to tell her daughter. It would be as though I had joined some secret high school society where we gathered in the dark and swore solemn oaths beyond our boyish understanding."

"Did—Aunt Antonia tell you what the oaths were?"

"We didn't have a whole lot of time together, as you know," he said, avoiding the issue for now. What good would it do Chloe, when she had to be friends with these girls and respect Mother Ravenel as head-mistress, to know that his wife had lain next to him in bed on that brief honeymoon and reminisced about Suzy Ravenel's high-flown promises they had all solemnly recited, holding hands in front of the Red Nun. ("Oh, dear, we were so earnest, pledging to be true to selves that we hadn't even met yet. But Suzy convinced us—she adored having secrets with just a few select people.")

"Maybe that's why Mother wouldn't join—because of the oaths," Chloe said. "Suzanne—Mother Ravenel—was really put out with her over it. They had to ask this other girl to make up the required number. You had to have five before you could start a club."

Registration Days at Mount St. Gabriel's

Every fall at Mount St. Gabriel's we had two full days of registration. Day one was for the preparatory grades, first through seventh—until, in 1943, the state added an eighth grade. The second day was for the high school grades, which we called the academy.

By the late 1940s, after the anti-Catholic prejudice had died down in Mountain City and people realized what a fine school "the nuns from England" had created in their midst, enrollment in the prep was up to 200 and there were 78 girls in the academy, 15 to 20 girls in each class. We also had a junior college and secretarial school for day students, with an enrollment of about 50 girls.

In fact, so many prominent local families desired their daughters to have a Mount St. Gabriel's education that the bishop of our diocese jokingly complained that the Order of St. Scholastica was running a school for Protestant and Jewish girls with a few Catholics thrown in!

Now, back in the 1880s and 1890s, our school had been a very famous mountain resort, Clingman's Sky Top Inn. People came to Clingman's from all over the country for its pure mountain air—one mile above sea level—and its matchless panoramic views. You could face west and see the ranges of the Great Smokies backed up all the way to Tennessee, and you could spin right around the other way and have a commanding view of Mountain City and Long Man River, one of the few north-flowing rivers in the United States, with Beaucatcher Mountain in the background.

Our building was an imposing three-storied wooden structure in the Victorian style. It had a fabulous gothic air about it. Even after it was razed to the ground in 1963, many an old girl reported that she regularly roamed its corridors and porches in her dreams. It had eighty bedrooms, two dining rooms, a ballroom, an indoor swimming pool, and many parlors. It also had its own water tower, which could be seen from all over Mountain City. The tower was a local landmark. When our foundress, Mother Elizabeth Wallingford, purchased the site in 1909, the tower no longer contained water and she asked a Mountain City architect, Malcolm Vick, to design a room up there where nuns and girls could go and meditate and have the wonderful "God's-eye view," as she called it. As she herself had grown up in a large country house in Oxford-shire with tower rooms, Mother Wallingford was able to help Mr. Vick with the design.

You approached Mount St. Gabriel's by a long entrance drive lined with Norway spruces that got more majestic as the years went by. The first thing a visitor would notice when the building loomed into sight was the handsome porch that wrapped around three sides of the building. In the summertime the nuns would enjoy the gracious coolness of the porch from their rocking chairs, and on warm days during the school year the academy girls would have their study period on the porches. This was considered a treat. We had boards made that went across the arms of the chairs so the girls could write their lessons in the fresh air. However, the girls had to turn their chairs to face inward because the views would be too distracting. But at the end of the study period they turned the chairs around again and we had a final prayer while "lifting our eyes up to the hills."

On registration days, parents would park their automobiles around the edge of the circular driveway and come up the stairs to the formal front entrance with their daughters.

Inside was a grand, spacious lobby that we called the "main parlor." It was presided over by our Infant of Prague, who wore vestments, handmade by the nuns, to match the church seasons. And all around this big lobby were small private parlors. For two full days, starting with the prep and finishing with the academy, the teachers in charge of each of the classes would sit in the small parlors and each nun would interview every girl entering her class and that girl's accompanying parent. These parlor interviews were scheduled alphabetically and, though they lasted only fifteen minutes apiece, much was accomplished.

—from chapter 2 ("The School Year") of
Mount St. Gabriel's Remembered: A Historical Memoir, by Mother Suzanne Ravenel

CHAPTER 4

Switching Friends

Academy registration day 1951
Mount St. Gabriel's

THE AUTOMOBILES BEARING girls scheduled for the late-afternoon registration interviews swept punctually through the entrance pillars of Mount St. Gabriel's and decelerated to a ceremonious crawl up the shady tree-lined drive. The Norway spruces had reached their full maturity and the downward-dipping branches from either side formed a gloomy canopy above the cars. The approach had been open and sunny when eighteen-year-old Henry Vick, serving in the role of parent, had driven his fourteen-year-old sister, Agnes, to register for her freshman year in September 1930. Their father was out of town, drumming up much-needed commissions after the Crash the year before, and their mother was on one of her discreet drying-out vacations at a West Virginia sanatorium.

"Well, there it is," Henry said to his niece, Chloe, as the picturesque old firetrap came into view.

"Yes, and there *they* are," said the girl. "All lined up like satisfied crows waiting to welcome us. Just like Mother described."

There they were, indeed, the nuns in their row of rocking chairs, taking in the fine late-summer weather from the porch, some of them past their teaching years and a few, like Mother Finney, old enough to have been part of the original faculty. Henry felt the friendly scrutiny of these hooded figures—"satisfied crows" was so typically *Agnes*—as they identified the arriving automobiles and commented among themselves on the persons inside them. He knew what they would be saying about himself and Chloe—and the remembered Agnes.

And likewise—having happened to glance in his rearview mirror—he could imagine what they would be saying about the two girls in the yellow Oldsmobile convertible following him.

"That's Tildy Stratton just behind us. Her older sister, Madeline, is driving them."

Henry could see from the sudden stiffening of Chloe's shoulders that she was restraining herself from looking back.

"Is Madeline in the upper academy?"

"No, not anymore. Madeline's a junior at Mountain City High."

"Ah, she wasn't invited back to Mount St. Gabriel's."

"How did you know that?"

"Because Mother told me about those letters that go out at the end of the year. 'Your daughter is—or is not—invited back.' "

You and your mother must have talked a lot about Mount St. Gabriel's, Henry almost said, but then stopped himself from venturing further.

But Chloe answered as naturally as though he'd spoken his thought aloud. Henry was growing increasingly aware of this mind-reading propensity of his niece's.

"Mother told me lots about the school because we liked going there together in our imaginations. It was a place she'd been happy and safe in, she said. And nobody could follow us there."

✠

"THAT MUST BE her up ahead," said the insolently beautiful sixteen-year-old girl at the wheel of the yellow convertible.

"Her, *who?*" Tildy Stratton was in a foul mood, having been dragged by Madeline out of the country club pool even though it would be closing at the end of this week. Creighton Rivers, the scrumptious lifeguard who had taught her the swan dive and called her "Tantalizing Tildy," would be leaving town for Emory University. And all for the stupid purpose of putting on a dress with sleeves too tight under the arms (no cap sleeves allowed by Raving Ravenel!) and shoes and *socks*—Mount St. Gabriel girls did not go bare-legged—to throw away the remainder of a beautiful day sitting on a straight chair in a stuffy little parlor, being grilled—and accordingly prejudged—by the teacher you were going to be stuck with for the whole next year.

"Chloe Starnes. Up front, in Henry's Jag. At last you two will meet."

Tildy perked up. All summer she had been rehearsing her first encounter with Chloe Starnes: what she would say to Chloe, and to what desired effect. "He's certainly keeping that little orphan niece wrapped in black tissue paper," Mama had said. Finally, back in June, Mama had phoned Henry and invited him and Chloe for tea or supper, but Henry had said she wasn't quite up to it yet; would Cornelia ask them again in a month or so?

"Of *course,* Henry, I'll phone you again 'in a month or so.'" Mama had repeated his exact words back to him in her "social" voice. But after hanging up she had made a sour face. "It will be a cold day in hell before I invite that pompous stick again. Even if he is still officially my brother-in-law."

More than anything, Tildy was anxious to set eyes on Maud, whose letters and postcards from Florida had grown dippier and more enraging over the summer—the first extended period they had been apart since they became best friends back in third grade. Maud's mother and grandmother operated the Pine Cone Lodge, which Mama said was just a fancy name for a run-down boardinghouse for traveling salesmen and older tourists on budgets. Maud's grandmother, a Sluder, was a descendant of old settlers, and that claim allowed some leeway for Maud's mother to be a divorced woman and for Maud to look gypsyish, even, some guessed, Jewish.

Every summer before this one, Tildy's father had arranged a special pool membership so Maud could go to the club with Tildy as often as she wanted. Tildy had taught Maud to dive and, under the tutelage of her older sister, Madeline, the girls had begun their apprenticeship in flirting with older boys.

And then suddenly last spring, Maud's long-lost father, Mr. Norton, whom many of the girls had suspected of not even existing, invited his daughter to spend the summer in Palm Beach with him and his present wife, Anabel.

"It'll completely wreck our plans!" Tildy had screamed. "We were going to learn to water-ski. Madeline's already arranged for Creighton's motorboat on his day off."

"Oh, Tiddly, I really am sorry. But Granny and Mother say I ought to give it a chance. If they like me, they might offer to help with college. Apparently Anabel's loaded."

"Don't be silly, Maud. With your grades, you can get a scholarship to any college in the universe. You don't need them. Can't you postpone it? He's postponed *you* long enough."

That's when Maud had suddenly turned on her. "You don't understand. He's my father. I want to know him. And—and, I mean, maybe he had his own reasons for *postponing* me, which, by the way, is an extremely cruel way to put it, Tildy."

It was like having cold water thrown in her face. First the abrupt abandonment of the funny, cherished nickname "Tiddly," invented by Maud, who was the only one Tildy allowed to call her that. And then being accused of cruelty. *Cruelty!* By her best friend since third grade.

But there was worse to come, something Tildy could hardly bear to acknowledge as it rolled inexorably toward her like a dangerous wave. All these years Tildy had rested secure in the certainty that she was the most important person in Maud's life. She had reveled in her role as patron and benefactor. In many ways Tildy had created the Maud who faced her now, a bold new hostility flaming in her cheeks.

Extremely cruel!

In third grade, before Tildy had taken pity on her and embarked on her Magnanimous Experiment, Maud Norton had been nothing: an uncertain newcomer, voice scarcely above a whisper, trailing shady rumors behind her. Her mother divorced (or so she claimed). Returned to town from somewhere in New Jersey to help the grandmother run the Pine Cone Lodge. Down on her luck? Ashamed? *Abandoned?* She said she was keeping her married name so it would "be the same as my daughter's." Maud's mother had a stuck-up air about her, Lily Roberts who now called herself Lily Norton. She was always like that, Mama said, even back in high school, though she hadn't gone to Mount St. Gabriel's. Grandfather Roberts was violently anti-Catholic; he bragged that he had jumped off the back of a Mountain City streetcar when two nuns from Mount St. Gabriel's boarded it. But now Grandfather Roberts was dead and the grandmother wanted Maud to have the advantages of a Mount St. Gabriel's education, even if it did cost a hundred and fifty a year for a day student.

But who was "Mr. Norton"? And, as first the months and then the years went by, why did he never show up to visit his daughter?

"Do you think Maud even has a father?" Tildy had asked her mother after she and Maud had become best friends.

"Everybody has a father, Tildy," said Cornelia Stratton. "Whether he's in the picture or not. What has Maud said?"

"She doesn't remember him very well. He sold college jewelry and traveled a lot. But I was thinking, if her father *is* out of the picture and, say, her mother died, our family could legally adopt her, couldn't we?"

"What would be the point of that, Tildy?"

"Well, I just thought—"

"Don't you two see enough of each other as it is? And besides," Tildy's mother drily added, "Lily Norton hardly looks as if she's wasting away. She's frequently seen dining and dancing with the town's most eligible bachelors at the Casa Loma Club. If anything, someone else might be adopting Maud before too long."

However, third, fourth, fifth, sixth, seventh, and eighth grade passed, and nobody adopted Maud. Lily Norton continued to be seen dancing and dining at the Casa Loma with the town's current crop of eligible bachelors; the former ones had married and begun raising families. "At this rate," Tildy's mother remarked, "Lily Norton will be dating the sons of her old dates before long."

Cornelia Stratton was known for her caustic tongue. The last thing you wanted was to inspire one of her "dry ice" comments, as her daughter Madeline called them. No one was spared, including Cornelia's husband, Bernard, whom she had renamed Smoky Bear when they became engaged, because he took parties of men bear hunting, living cheerfully and guiltlessly on his inherited lumber income. Even Cornelia's adored twin sister was fair game, both the living and the dead Antonia. "That's just like Tony, so eager to get into a damn *church* on her *honeymoon* that she runs in front of a van," Cornelia had raged in her grief after the telephone call had come from Rome. Over the years, her daughters had suffered dry-ice burns so often that they had turned them into humorous scars, each bearing its story. At some point Madeline and Tildy had tacitly decided to regard their dry-ice scars as signs of Cornelia's close attention to them, proofs of motherly love.

But what had been happening this summer to Maud in Palm Beach with Mr. Norton and the wife, Anabel, who was loaded? Tildy was dying to see Maud in the flesh and make her own conclusions. Norton was far enough down the alphabet for Maud's interview to be scheduled, like those for Stratton and Starnes, for late afternoon. But first

Tildy intended to punish her best friend. Maud's scatty letters and post-cards, when they trickled through the mail slot, had been so disappointing they had verged on insult. Whole dimensions had been left out. And Maud had a jillion dimensions. Tildy had been the one to spot these promises and depths in Maud and coax them into the light for others to admire. But in these stingy summer missives, for which Tildy had first waited avidly, then reproachfully, and at last angrily—Jesus, it was like Maud was under a spell or had undergone a lobotomy; even her classic, slanting penmanship everybody admired had become debased with circles now floating above the *i*'s and squatting beneath the far-too-many exclamation points. And, for some reason, she put the names of all her new acquaintances, including her stepmother, in quotes.

Yes, first I will have to punish Maud a little, hit her with a dose of the "shunning treatment" we mastered together and taught the rest of the class to such advantage in sixth grade. She needs to be reminded of all I have done for her and how much more we can do as a combined force. She needs to understand how boring ninth grade would be without me beside her.

"So, little one," said Madeline, "you want me to pull in behind Henry in the driveway, or should I tootle on down to the parking lot to give you more time?"

"More time for *what*?"

"My, we are cranky this afternoon. But I forgive you; I used to loathe the registration interview. All I meant was, if I park behind Henry, you can meet Chloe right away and get the introductions over with. Or maybe you want to prepare your tactical approach."

"Oh, Christ, it's not that important. Park behind the Jag."

"Watch all those Christs and Jesuses, honey. Summer's over—you're back on the Ravenel firing range. I was only trying to be helpful. I re-member what it was like when a new girl came. A mutual appraisal has to take place, like dogs sniffing one another."

"Well, I certainly am not planning to *sniff* her. Isn't she my sort of cousin by marriage—if our aunt Tony was married to her uncle?"

"Oh, by southern standards, everybody's a sort of cousin. I'd say you can either be one or not, depending on how you all get on."

In her spaghetti-strap sundress, Madeline looked irresistible when angling the wheel, showing off the swanlike arch of her neck and her tanned bare shoulders. Tildy could have greatly benefited from an inch or so of Madeline's neck without her big sister being any poorer for the loss.

Ahead of them, Henry Vick, spruce in a panama hat and cotton cord suit, was unfolding his lanky self from his automobile. On the passenger side, the dome of the girl's head had not moved. Henry sauntered around the rear of the Jaguar, raising his hands in mock alarm as Madeline's convertible leapt forward and stopped inches from his legs. He opened the door for his niece, who took her time in emerging.

"Hop on out, Tildy, and make the first move," said Madeline. "I'll just get my sweater out of the trunk to conceal my brazen arms so the Ravenel won't take it out on you—but she'll just have to swallow my bare ankles. Of course, she'll be teed off when she sees *I* brought you instead of Mama."

("Tell her I've got stuff to do in the darkroom," Mama had instructed Madeline. Cornelia Stratton had a successful studio in town, specializing in social occasions and group photographs. "Today I'm just not up to Suzanne's registration fervors.")

Tildy put herself into noblesse oblige mode and stepped out onto the driveway to meet Chloe. Introductions were easier if you pretended you were acting a part in a play. She walked up to the girl blinking at her in the bright sunlight, stuck out her hand, and said, "Hi, I'm Tildy Stratton. I believe we're in the same class."

Now, why had she spoiled it with that stupid *believe*? Chloe would think she was an idiot.

But the girl's face relaxed and her hand came out and met Tildy's. She was pale as the moon. She must have spent the whole summer indoors, "wrapped in black tissue paper." Her cool hand nestling in Tildy's grasp, Chloe said, not very audibly, "Hi, I've been looking forward to meeting you."

So much for that. Then uncle and big sister took up their parts and the four of them swept as a social unit toward the main entrance, from which two women were just emerging.

"Oh, great galloping *Jesus*!" Tildy sputtered. The two women were Lily Norton and her daughter, Maud. Maud looked about twenty. She had shot up in height and grown boobs. She was dressed like a model in a sheath skirt and matching jacket with a nipped-in waist and peplum. Her brown hair was cut short in a stylish pixie, and her earlobes were pierced with little gold studs. Worse, Tildy could see that Maud had already seen her, but was pretending—from some ominous, yet-to-be-revealed motive—that she hadn't.

"At this rate, little one, you'll be over at Mountain City High with me before the leaves turn," said Madeline to her sister. "Expelled for profanity. Oh, good grief, it's Maud." To Henry Vick, Madeline explained, "That glamour girl mincing toward us is Tildy's best friend."

"Oh, yes, Lily Norton and her daughter," Henry said.

Tildy could have killed Madeline for blabbing that Maud was her best friend when Maud hadn't even deigned to acknowledge her yet. Chloe was probably thinking, This Tildy must be one big dope.

But Tildy was not about to be made a fool of by the person she had rescued in third grade and practically created from scratch. Maud might have all kinds of subtle dimensions, brought out by Tildy, but Tildy's inborn ruling powers were very much intact. Once more she slid into noblesse oblige mode and, taking Chloe gently by the elbow, advanced on the mincing Maud and her mother, Lily Norton, looking rather glamorous herself—for a middle-aged woman.

"Maud. Long time no see," Tildy said brightly. "How was your summer? I hope it wasn't too *hot* down there in Florida."

"Oh goodness, no!" Maud, startled, was already on the defensive. "My father has central air-conditioning, and their house is right on—"

"And how are you, Mrs. Norton?" Tildy pressed on, drowning out Maud's plaintive "—the beach."

"Oh, I can't complain, Tildy," said Lily Norton in the affected Yankee accent she had brought back from New Jersey. "Too busy, as always. The lodge was filled to capacity all summer. Mother and I were even forced to turn some old clients away. Well, Henry Vick, how's life treating *you* these days?" This was said familiarly, as though to recall former intimacies. As a widower, Henry had dated Maud's mother for a while, then withdrew. ("She threw herself at him" was Cornelia Stratton's take on it. "She succeeded in scaring him off local women completely and, I sometimes think, women in general.")

"Hello, Lily. Hello there, Maud," said Henry with a little bow to each. "Actually, Lily, I'd have to say I'm about the same as you. Too busy, but I can't complain. You know Madeline, of course, and this is my—"

"Oh, Madeline and I are old buddies," Lily pertly acknowledged, though she had totally forgotten to include Madeline in her greeting. That was the trouble, thought Tildy, with underbred people: they never could keep track of all the amenities you had to get through first.

"And this is my niece Chloe Starnes, who has come to live with me. She's going into the ninth grade, too."

"Oh, yes," said Lily Norton, looking Chloe meaningfully up and down. She seemed on the verge of saying something particular to Chloe when Tildy sprang her coup.

"Chloe is the nearest thing I have to a cousin," she told Maud. "Uncle Henry, you know, was married to my aunt Antonia, and I've always wished I had a cousin. I think ninth grade is going to be a really interesting year, don't you?"

"Oh, *that's* for sure," said Maud, with a fakey new laugh. She offered Chloe a blasé handshake. So far she had not even looked at Tildy. "Just wait till you all go inside that parlor and meet *her*."

"Her, *who*?" Tildy irritably demanded.

"Our teacher. Mother Malloy, from Boston. She's a knockout. We won't be wanting to get rid of *her* anytime soon. Well, we have to run—Mother and I have some shopping to do. By the way, Tiddle-dy, I *loved* all your letters. I'm sorry I didn't write back more, but Daddy and Anabel kept me on the go from morning till night."

Tiddle-dy! The added syllable seemed like a mockery. Maud would be punished for that, too.

"Maud's father and his new wife just fell in love with her," said Lily Norton. "My daughter was a complete success in Palm Beach."

"That's not very hard to imagine," Henry gallantly replied as mother and daughter set themselves in motion to mince off to their next expedition. "Though I know you must be happy to have her home again."

CHAPTER 5

Mother Malloy's Ninth Grade, 1951

The morning interviews

SEVEN GIRLS — SURNAMES A through L—from nine-thirty until the noon Angelus bell, followed by chapel and lunch. Day students accompanied by mothers, except for one father, Dr. Galvin, whose wife was in the hospital, about to give birth to their sixth child. Galvin, a general practitioner, also doctored the nuns. He brought his two high-school-age daughters, Josie for ninth grade and Sally for twelfth. He had been to Mount St. Gabriel's the day before, he told Mother Malloy, to register his two younger daughters in the prep. There was, so far, one Galvin boy-child, who would be ready for first grade at Newman Hall when it opened next year. Josie Galvin, a small brunette with sly eyes, seemed sure of herself and of her father's regard. Was Josie, perhaps, one of the ringleaders in Mother Malloy's new ninth grade?

The two ninth-grade Cuban boarders presented themselves as a pair for their interview, as the new girl had so little English; Marta Andreu and Gilda Gomez had come down on yesterday's train from New York, where their fathers were diplomats. Outgoing Gilda, whose heavily accented English rolled off her tongue in impulsive dashes and tumbles, was returning for her third year. She had been at Mount St. Gabriel's since seventh grade. Her oversized blouses, she explained, laughing, to Mother Malloy, were always tight by Thanksgiving break, and her father said it was a waste of money to buy two sizes of everything. "At Sain' Gabriel, Mother, my clothes they begin beeg and then they grow small. Jus' the opposite of me!"

Marta looked, and was, more mature than her classmates. She had been held back in school in Havana, Mother Ravenel had told Mother Malloy, and during her year of shame at having to repeat a grade had formed an unsuitable attachment. Subsequently she had been sent off to Spain to spend a year with a great-aunt. "I am making an exception," said Mother Ravenel, "by letting her room with Gilda Gomez, who is a good, cheerful girl and knows our ways. I am allowing them to speak Spanish when they are alone, though that's generally against our rules. Marta is from a prominent Cuban family, and she has a baby sister who will be coming to us in a few years."

Four of the new day girls were graduates of St. Jerome's, the parochial grammar school across the river. They would be bused the fifteen miles back and forth daily for the privilege of receiving a higher Catholic education. Even though one of them had a surname beginning with Y, Mother Ravenel had seen fit to bend the rule so they could arrive as a morning group, minus one mother, who worked as a court recorder. These girls and their mothers hung together, wary and faintly scornful of Mount St. Gabriel's interview day with the parents. "Lora Jean could have come here just fine by herself, Mother Malloy. She's the one who's going to be at Mount St. Gabriel's, not me."

Lora Jean Cramer. Kay Lee Jones. Mikell Lunsford. Dot Yount. Tonight, before Compline, go through the roll and match images to names. Lora Jean, no-nonsense and stocky, a junior edition of her mother. Kay Lee, green-eyed and fey, with a strawberry-shaped birthmark on her neck—Mrs. Jones was the absent court stenographer. Mikell, tall, straw-haired, and tomboyish: must take after her father, since Mrs. Lunsford was dark, tiny, and demure. Dot, sneezing apologetically into a wet handkerchief, was allergic to goldenrod, Mrs. Yount explained. Also, as though ticking off her daughter's further accomplishments, to eggs, tuna fish, nuts, and chalk dust.

Thus the four transfer girls from St. Jerome's across the river. But try to fix them in your mind as individuals.

A last-minute cancellation: Lidia Caballos, from Venezuela, had eloped with her cousin. "Her father is taking steps to have it annulled," Mother Ravenel told Mother Malloy. "He's furious about the nonrefundable boarder's deposit. He didn't see why, if the annulment goes through, Lidia can't come to Mount St. Gabriel's next semester. I told him I was very sorry, but it would be setting the wrong tone with the other girls."

Mrs. Frew had driven all the way from Knoxville to enter her stately daughter, Elaine, as a boarder in the academy as Mrs. Frew herself, the former Francine Barfoot, had entered as a freshman boarder in the fall of 1930. "I was in Mother Ravenel's class, back when she was our talented Suzanne and our class president. She chose me to compose and play the flute music for our freshman play, *The Red Nun,* which she wrote herself. My time at Mount St. Gabriel's was so happy, Mother Malloy. Unfortunately, Daddy passed away and I had to drop out my junior year. It broke my heart. But here is my Elaine, to finish what I started."

Elaine Frew, an advanced musician, was to have piano lessons twice a week from a retired concert artist in town who handpicked his few students and charged a fortune.

"Except for her flute, Francine Barfoot was rather undistinguished, but she tried hard at whatever she did and you could trust her to be loyal. Not enough is said about those girls who are content to lend bulk to the class pudding rather than always having to be the cherry on top": that was Mother Ravenel's thumbnail sketch of "the third mother" in the class of '34.

Noon—the hour of Sext—the Angelus

Five minutes before noon, Mother Finney turned off the gas oven, leaving the trays of macaroni and cheese inside to keep warm. She washed her hands under the tap, dried them on a fresh towel with the priestly care that precedes sacred duties, and set off, with her slight limp from a girlhood horse fall, down the trophy-lined hall to ring the Angelus.

The knotted end of the thick bell rope ended in a stairwell and was cordoned off by a circular wrought-iron gate, which Mother Finney now unlocked with a key from her deep pocket. The temptation of an accessible rope connected to the thundering peal of a bell that could be heard for miles around had proved too much for several generations of little girls—and even some older ones. In 1939 a senior had announced her engagement via the bell and narrowly escaped being expelled. The last unauthorized bell ringer, before the gate went up in 1944, was a fifth-grade boarder, overexcited by the Friday night movie, *Arsenic and Old Lace.* She had yanked and swung on the forbidden rope to the horror and delight of her fellow boarders and, while its wild peals were still echoing from the tower, had raced up the stairs screeching Cary Grant's infamous lines: "Insanity runs in my family. It practically *gallops!*"

Mother Finney often thought of that little girl when ringing the Angelus bell. The child hadn't stayed at Mount St. Gabriel's for long, though she hadn't been expelled. There were always those comers and goers, the ones dropped off by out-of-town parents, then just as suddenly whisked away. Mother Finney kept a special place in her heart for the bolder, high-spirited girls. She hoped God would grant that little bell ringer enough suitable outlets for her energies and would help her to distinguish between exuberant mischief and what Mother Wallingford, who had supremely embodied it, had called "holy daring."

Three rings and a pause; three rings and a pause; three rings and a pause. Hark, drop your tools, and remember you are inside the Eternal Presence. Followed by the nine consecutive peals heralding the hour of no shadows, the end of morning's work: resonating through the building and billowing out into the valley below. If the wind was blowing the right way, jail prisoners on the tenth floor of the downtown courthouse could count the rings of the Mount St. Gabriel's bell.

Mother Finney's frail, curved body belied her still powerful arms. She rang the bell cleanly, with no irresolute half measures. As a young woman she had broken recalcitrant yearlings on her family's horse farm in Galway. Now she was in her eighty-ninth year, having outlived Elizabeth Wallingford, her fellow adventurer and beloved foundress, by two long decades.

The afternoon interviews

Eight girls, from one-thirty to five, M through Y, followed by Vespers and dinner.

Mrs. Saul Meyer, a stylish woman with a piquant mix of guttural German and Carolina drawl, introduced herself as "Judy Meyer." "Rebecca has been at Mount St. Gabriel's since first grade, Mother Malloy. We emigrated here in forty-one. She loves this school, and so do we. Her father and I are observant Jews, and we're raising Becky in our traditions. But, you know, in Vienna, both Saul and I attended Catholic *gymnasia.* The nun who taught me penmanship had us copy out the cat-echism, so I know it almost as well as I do the Torah!"

Rebecca Meyer: small for her age, with poised, old-world child's manners. A thick flame-red braid descending to her waist. Spoke with a Carolina drawl, but said very little.

Ashley Nettle, new day girl, and her mother, Virginia Nettle, who spoke in haughty, theatrical phrases. Jumpy, nervous Ashley, flyaway hair the color of tinsel, swallowed her words; she jiggled her legs under the table and her eyes darted about the parlor, as though looking for a way out. "Ashley's father is the new assistant headmaster at Pisgah Prep—the private school for boys. Ashley will be riding in with the Dutch contingent from Enka Village. It's so convenient, as we're right on their route."

Later, Mother Malloy asked Mother Ravenel if Mrs. Nettle was British. "No, she just gives herself airs," replied the headmistress. "That Ashley will certainly need some work. I wish she were boarding with us, but at least she'll be riding with the Dutch girls from the Enka rayon plant. They'll be a good influence. They're relaxed and friendly and speak better English than she does."

Maud Norton, a tall, handsome, physically developed girl, and her mother, Lily Norton. "We're old-timers in Mountain City, Mother. My mother was a Sluder, one of the pioneer families here. Mother and I run the Pine Cone Lodge. What is your accent? Boston! I thought so! I worked for a while up in Cape May, New Jersey, that's where I met my husband, Mr. Norton. When I came back to Mountain City, everyone swore I had a 'northern' accent, but I don't think so, do you? Mr. Nor-ton and I are no longer married, but it was a very amicable parting. Maud spent this summer in Palm Beach with her father and his present wife. They both fell head over heels in love with her."

Maud, who had been staring almost rudely at her new teacher, blushed from the neck up and rolled her eyes.

"Was it a good summer for you in Florida, Maud?" the nun asked.

"Everything was wonderful, Mother, but I'm glad to be back in school."

"Maud loves her schoolwork," Lily Norton chimed in, "and of course she missed her best friend, Tildy Stratton, didn't you, hon? Those two have been hand in glove since third grade. They—"

"Tildy and I corresponded regularly," said Maud coolly, cutting her mother off.

Mother Malloy had not realized how depleting the long day of continuous interviews had been until she looked up and saw Henry Vick escorting a slight girl with a pronounced chin and a dark fringe of bangs. Their entrance made the parlor, which had grown smaller and more oppressive in the afternoon heat, suddenly feel airier. Mother Malloy felt lighter of spirit and surer of her ground. Here was the kind man she had first encountered smoking his pipe on the marble ledge of the unfinished sculpture of the Red Nun. On whose cool ledge she had rested after her breathlessness, or whatever it was, while he stood close by and conversed with her in his easy way, saying much without seeming to. And this would be Chloe, another orphan like herself. Though Chloe had known her parents. And Kate Malloy had not been blessed with an uncle like Mr. Vick.

"It's good to see you again, Mother Malloy. This is my niece, Chloe Starnes."

"How do you do, Chloe. I hope you'll soon feel at home with us at Mount St. Gabriel's."

"I expect I will, Mother. My mother, Agnes Vick, went here from first grade through high school. She told me all about how things are at Mount St. Gabriel's."

"In that case, you can be a great help to me." Mother Malloy felt herself smiling without trying to. "I've been here less than a week and have almost everything to learn about how things are."

It was rare for someone Chloe's age to look you in the eye without defenses and let herself be looked back at. Perhaps you had to have suffered a great loss first.

Mary Tilden ("Tildy") Stratton was accompanied by her older sister, Madeline, a beauty with the gift of gab. "Our mama sends her apologies, Mother Malloy, but she's backed up on her darkroom work down at the studio—she had a bunch of weddings in August. So I'm being mother to Tildy today. I'm an old Mount St. Gabriel's girl myself, until I got uninvited back at the end of my freshman year. Though things have turned out well enough for me at Mountain City High."

"Do you go by your full name, Mary Tilden, or do you prefer Tildy?" Mother Malloy asked the younger girl. She was not a beauty like her sister, though appealing in a sweet, stalwart way. Her face was so sunburned you had to look closely for the expressions. But they were there.

"I almost *think*—" the girl began haughtily. Then she seemed about to cry, but switched to anger. "I *might* change my name to—"

"Don't make any sudden decisions," her sister advised. To Mother Malloy, she said, "She's just had the strangest little *contretemps* in the driveway with her best friend, Maud—"

"You shut *up*!"

"*Sorry*, little one. I'm always overstepping, aren't I? I guess I'm not used to being motherly. I was once in ninth grade myself, Mother Malloy, and interview day at Mount St. Gabriel's makes everyone cross. Listen, Tildy, run ahead and stop Henry Vick before he drives away with Chloe and ask if they'd like to come by our house for cocktails or tea or anything at all."

Thus Tildy's dignity was salvaged before any tears fell, and Madeline stayed behind for a word with Mother Malloy. "I guess you don't think much of me, Mother, but I love my baby sister, and, oh, this place is such a hotbed of bitchery. Generations of bitchery and intrigue! I can say it now, I can say anything I want. I can even say you are beautiful and I hope you enjoy being a nun. I had a beautiful aunt, my mother's twin sister, who also had a vocation, but something went wrong and then later she married Henry Vick and was killed on their honeymoon. They were in Rome and she was knocked down by a van. I want Tildy to keep her intrepid little soul—I have half a mind to coach her in how to get expelled so I can keep better watch over her over at Mountain City High, only you can't go there till tenth grade."

"On the contrary, Madeline, I think I like you very much," said Mother Malloy. "I hope you'll come and see me again. In the meantime, I promise to do my best to watch over your sister's intrepid soul."

The last were the two Dutch girls: Hansje Van Kleek and Beatrix Wynkoop, from Enka Village, the rayon plant. The largest in the world, Mother Ravenel had informed her. ("When the Dutch set out to do something, they do it right.") The mothers of the two girls, looking hardly older than their offspring, paid their cheerful respects to the new teacher and then went off to visit Mother Finney. "We could smell her oatmeal cookies all the way from the parking lot!"

Both Hansje and Beatrix spoke excellent, unaccented English, from which word-swallowing Ashley Nettle would surely profit as they rode to and from the school together. Mother Malloy made every effort to distinguish Hansje from Beatrix, both tall blond girls with perfect manners, both returning for their third year at Mount St. Gabriel's. She noted, like a possibly significant punctuation mark, the down-turned left corner of Hansje's mouth, as though she had a reservation about life even as she smiled, and Beatrix's seemingly unconscious gesture of twirling a lock of hair around her finger as she attended to you expectantly, as if you were on the verge of saying something wonderful.

Before Compline tonight, I will sit at the little desk in my room, open my roll book, and go down this list of girls. And I will say each name aloud, followed by a short prayer: "Help me to see what I need to see about this young human soul."

Mother Malloy's Ninth Grade, 1951

Marta Andreu

Lidia Caballos (last-minute cancellation)

Lora Jean Cramer

Elaine Barfoot Frew (mother, Francine Barfoot, '34)

Josephine (Josie) Teresa Galvin

Gilda Gomez

Kay Lee Jones

Mikell Maria Lunsford

Rebecca Meyer

Ashley Nettle

Maud Norton

Chloe Vick Starnes (mother, Agnes Vick, '34; aunt by marriage, Antonia Tilden, '34)

Mary Tilden (Tildy) Stratton (mother, Cornelia Tilden, '34; aunt, Antonia Tilden, '34)

Hansje Van Kleek

Beatrix Wynkoop

Dorothy Yount

CHAPTER 6

The Afterrunner

Sunday, June 24, 2001
Feast of St. John the Baptist
House of Olivia and Gudge Beeler
Mountain City, North Carolina

THIS IS HER last night in what Olivia Stewart Beeler, class of 1974, refers to as "your very own VIP guest suite, Mother Ravenel."

Tomorrow morning Gudge and Olivia will drive her to the airport to check her luggage—Olivia has lent her a second suitcase to carry the tape recorder plus other gifts from the girls—and impress on airline personnel that this legally blind old lady must be conveyed like a precious heirloom to her destination. Unfortunately, there are no direct flights to Boston, so a wheelchair will be waiting at her gate at Dulles to speed her to her connection. It has all been arranged and she is grateful.

At Logan Airport in Boston, she will be met by Sister Bridget, who will promptly disabuse her of any notions of heirloom status picked up in Mountain City. Sister Bridget, sixty-five, is the "young" superior of all that is left of the Order of St. Scholastica, though there's not much left for her to be superior to. She is the only one in the house who still has a driver's license, and will make sure to squeeze in as many errands as possible between the baggage carousel at Logan ("Two suitcases, Sister Suzanne? How can that be when you left with only one?") and the Order's retirement house in Milton. Sister Bridget calls all the nuns "Sister," followed by their given name, even though the old ones have been accustomed to "Mother," followed by their surname, for most of their professed lives.

Fortunately, all the young in power are not as mirthless and bullying as Sister Bridget. At Mass at the basilica this morning, Father Thad, the new monsignor, had preached a lively sermon on John the Baptist.

"It's not easy to be a forerunner," Father Thad had said. "But when something larger than life is about to appear in our midst, *someone* has to go first . . . you know, like those cars with flashing headlights that precede a truck bearing an oversize load. People have to be prepared. The forerunner has to announce—has, even, to *forewarn:* 'Pay attention! Something larger than you're used to is riding into town.' "

After Mass, Father Thad, a towering blur clothed in red vestments for the martyr's feast, greeted his congregation as they filed out through the narthex. When her turn came, he swooped down and gathered her in his arms. His garments smelled of incense; his warm neck exuded a spicy aftershave.

"Ah, Mother Ravenel, I don't like this at all! In a month's Sundays I've gone and lost my heart to you, and now you're leaving us tomorrow. What do you expect me to do?"

"I expect you to be right here when I come back next year," she volleyed back in her headmistress tone. "And, Father, your sermon has helped me to see what I may be, in a larger sense. I am just the opposite of a forerunner. I am what comes afterward—an 'afterrunner,' if there is such a word."

"Well," he replied, delighted, "there is now."

"Yes, Father, you've helped me to see that I am to be an *afterrunner.* My old girls have talked me into writing a history of Mount St. Gabriel's. I've been speaking it into the tape recorder, which I'll be taking back to Boston with me tomorrow. Please pray that I live to complete my assignment to the glory of God and that I do justice to my material."

"You may be sure I will, and I expect to get a personally inscribed copy. Have a safe journey, Mother. May He carry you in the palm of His hand."

It is nice to be among people who are aware that you were once in power. It is a blessing, at eighty-five, to lie on these soft sheets in "your very own VIP guest suite," surrounded by comforts, cherished and picnicked and partied and toasted by those who were actually present during your strongest hours. Yesterday's final picnic lunch, at the mountaintop aerie of Beatrix De Groot Bradford, née Wynkoop, class of 1955:

"Oh, Mother, what a sad time that was, the end of our ninth-grade year. I always felt bad that it was our class that sent you away on sick leave."

Beatrix, at sixty-four, is a comfortable woman who has a Christmas tree farm on top of the mountain and performs countless services for her church and community. She has been twice widowed, lost a son in a boating accident, and survived cancer, yet she still maintains her cheerful, expectant outlook and her old schoolgirl habit of playing with her hair.

"There were extenuating circumstances, dear. My mother was dying in Charleston and my brother asked me to come and nurse her and Reverend Mother gave the permission. She thought it would be a restorative thing for me to get away. And at the same time, I would be helping out my family. But after all those regrettable things happened, you must remember, Beatrix, the composition of the class changed. By the time I had you all for your senior year, there were more of you, for one thing, a graduating class of twenty-one—"

"—and some were no longer there."

"Some were no longer there," Mother Ravenel echoed meaningfully, tipping up her face to feel the midday sun on her bare neck. Although she does miss being called "Mother" up in Boston under Sister Bridget's leveling jurisdiction, she doesn't miss the old stifling habit one bit.

"You prevailed, Mother."

"*We* prevailed, Beatrix. God was beside us through all of it."

Through her sunglasses the light was the golden platinum of high noon and Beatrix, facing her in an Adirondack chair, was a bright, beloved blur. "Well, Mother, it's been eleven years and my doctor says I'm still cancer-free. And I still have this mountaintop with three thousand little spruces growing diligently into Christmas money, and I still have God, and I still have you. Of course, I can't pop out to see you at the convent whenever I feel the urge, but I know you're there at the other end of the telephone and you're still on the same earth. And now, the girls have given me the privilege of transcribing your tapes as you send them."

In the noonday light, Mother Ravenel could make out Beatrix absently raking her hand back and forth over her new head of hair, which sprang out from the blur of her face like a sizzling halo of steel wool.

"It will be like having you in the room with me all year long,

Mother, telling me stories about my favorite place and the stories behind the stories," Beatrix said. "Are you going to tell the sad parts, as well? I remember Mother Malloy so clearly."

"I still dream of her. Mother Malloy was with us such a short time, but all these years later she's remained a faithful visitor to my night life. Do you have that, Beatrix? People who reappear regularly in your dreams and bring you messages and themselves often go on growing and changing in the dreams?"

"Oh, Mother, yes. And even if they never knew one another when they were on this earth, they can mingle and exchange information in the most amazing ways."

"What do you hear about Chloe Starnes, Beatrix? Olivia told me she changed her name to Vick so the firm could stay Vick & Vick."

"Well, they say that after business hours Chloe has always kept pretty much to herself. She's on the alumnae mailing list, of course, but she never answers the questionnaires. If I happen to run into her in the Fresh Market, she's always cordial, but she keeps pushing her cart. She attends the Episcopal church now, and designed them a beautiful labyrinth. That's become one of her specialties. Sacred spaces."

"I was invited to her wedding, back in the sixties, the one that never took place. I've always wondered why."

"So have many of us. There are speculations that she was in love with someone else, but I try to stay clear of those. She sent all her presents back and, as far as I know, never dated again."

"Well, I'm sorry she didn't finish at Mount St. Gabriel's, but I wish her well. Apparently, she was a great comfort to old Mother Finney, the year I was away. I wish them all well. Even those we lost track of. You must pray for me, Beatrix. I so much want to do a good job on this little memoir of the school."

"I always pray for you, Mother, and how could you do anything but the best?"

Thank you, Lord, for this noonday brilliance on Beatrix's mountaintop. It's like going to heaven and finding my girls in charge. I mean, under You, of course.

CHAPTER 7

The Swag

Saturday, September 15, 1951
Tildy Stratton's fourteenth birthday
Smoky Stratton's hunting cabin

"I WANT TO have a *different* kind of party this year," Tildy announced to her parents at the end of her first week of ninth grade.

"Oh-oh," groaned Tildy's father with a comic wince of his burly shoulders. "How much is it going to cost me this time?"

"Very little, Daddy. Less than ever. I plan to invite only one person."

"Little Maudie, I suppose."

"Maud and I are *very* past tense, Daddy. And she is not at all 'little' anymore."

"Maudie has shot up like a weed and grown a substantial bosom over the summer, according to Madeline," Tildy's mother informed her husband. "So who will be your distinguished guest, Tildy?"

"What I'd like for my birthday this year is to have Chloe Starnes out to spend the weekend at the Swag. We could cook over a fire and make our own food, and I promise we'd wear life jackets if we even *thought about* walking close to the lake."

"You don't mean go alone—just you and Chloe?"

"Of course not." Tildy had planned her approach. "What I thought was, Flavia and John would go with us, just like they do for Daddy's hunting and fishing guests. Only we wouldn't ask Flavia to cook or clean for us; she'd just be there to chaperone. And John would drive us and fish his heart out."

"But what would you girls do for a whole weekend?" Mama asked.

"The lake's way too cold for swimming by then, and the Swag, you know, doesn't offer much in the way of entertainment."

"We can entertain ourselves. Chloe is a very interesting person to be with, and she finds me interesting."

"Well, I don't know," said Mama. "Give Daddy and me time to talk it over."

"The one thing I don't want is you girls trying to build any fires," said Daddy. "John would have to build the fires and extinguish them. That is, if your mother and I decide you can go."

"And Henry Vick would have to give his okay for Chloe," said Tildy's mother. "But your father and I *haven't* decided yet, so don't go rhapsodizing prematurely."

Tildy knew she had won.

✠

CHLOE, SITTING NEXT to Tildy in the roomy backseat of the Packard gliding quietly through the countryside, executed a few just-so strokes on her drawing pad and a figure sprang to life.

"Oh my God, it's her!" cried Tildy. "How do you *do* this, Chloe?"

"I don't know, exactly. First, I need for that person to appear, and then I try to see them, and if I get it right they sort of come out through the tip of my pencil."

"But it's her to the life. The way she stands when she's writing on the blackboard. Oh, I love it. Can I have it?"

"Not until your birthday."

"But it *is* my birthday."

"It is not totally *yet* your birthday. You were born at five this afternoon and it's only ten in the morning."

Though the two presences in the front seat occasionally spoke in murmurs to each other, they bore themselves with monolithic remoteness: John, the conveyer and fire builder, and his wife, Flavia, the protectress and overseer of foodstuffs. It was a new thing to Chloe, black people living on the premises with their white families. Rosa took the bus from Uncle Henry's home to Colored Town every evening, despite her advanced age. Chloe's own mother and Rex Wright had never employed "help," as Rex made no secret of his distrust of Negroes.

John and Flavia lived in an apartment over the Strattons' garage. John ran the family's errands in the black Packard and drove Mr. Stratton wherever he wanted to go; he transported Tildy to and from Mount St. Gabriel's. Tildy's mother and big sister dashed about in their own cars, while Flavia stayed home and made soups and Creole dishes and Tildy's school lunches and seemed to hold the Stratton household completely under her dominance. She was neither friendly nor talkative, but you could feel her sort of enveloping you in her idea of how the day should properly go. As long as you fit into her choreography of things, you felt taken care of, even brooded over, within her aloof protectorship.

"Oh, Chloe, you've got the sleeve, the elbow, the veil always floating out a little when she moves, and the way she tucks her chin in when she's writing. God, on her, even those old-lady shoes look good. I wonder what she was like at our age. She told your uncle she was an orphan."

"No, she said she had been in a foster home."

"But that could go either way, couldn't it? I mean, she could have been an orphan or she could have been abandoned by her parents. She didn't say which?"

"She only said that much because Uncle Henry asked if she had any sisters or brothers." Chloe herself had pumped Uncle Henry about his conversation with Mother Malloy in the grotto. Like every other girl in ninth grade, she was under the spell of their teacher from Boston.

"Maybe they had to give her up," Tildy said ominously.

"Who?"

"Her parents. I mean, what if . . ." Tildy lowered her voice. "Maybe her father was a priest or something and their love had to remain secret, so the woman was forced to go away and have the baby and give it up for adoption to a foster home. Maybe the mother was a nun."

"If someone is adopted," Chloe quietly pointed out, "they don't go to a foster home. They go home with their new parents." Whenever Tildy's flights of imagination dispensed too cavalierly with the way things worked, Chloe felt obliged to return her new friend to the plausible. It had been three weeks now—they were going into their fourth week of friendship—and Chloe still glowed at the memory of Tildy stepping forth in the school driveway, like a young prince claiming her for the dance, and presenting her to Maud Norton as "the nearest thing I have to a cousin."

For reasons Chloe was still piecing together from Tildy's brusque remarks and her own intuition, the partnership of Tildy and Maud had been ruptured during their separation this past summer. Now the former best friends regarded each other slantwise and warily; they conversed, when necessary, in guarded commonplaces, as though trying to outdo each other in nonchalance. Though once, when Maud had addressed her old friend as "Tiddle-dy," Tildy had blazed out, "Don't *ever* call me that again."

"Oh, okay, fine," Maud had replied, with a cool smile. "If I call you anything, I'll call you for dinner."

"I really do think they scooped out part of her brain down there in Palm Beach," Tildy had told Chloe. "Her letters got shallower and shallower, even her handwriting got silly, with little circles and things, and now she's come back with all these trite sayings to fill in for real talk. This new ninny is nothing like the person I was friends with all those years. I want you to understand that. It's almost like the real Maud had *died* or something."

Then poor Tildy had flushed beet red, and Chloe knew she was thinking, How could I have said such a dumb thing, when Chloe's mother really *has* died?

"I do understand it," Chloe said. "It's bound to make you feel sad."

"Not so much sad as disgusted," corrected Tildy.

Maud Norton—the "new" Maud—appraised Tildy's new best friend with an affronted sort of curiosity that recalled to Chloe Rex Wright's begrudging, puzzled glances at his stepdaughter during the four years they had shared Agnes. Like Rex, Maud also looked at Chloe as though she had taken away something rightfully belonging to her. Like Rex, Maud seemed to be trying to figure out the source of Chloe's power without sacrificing her pride.

Once again, Chloe felt herself in the middle of a spoiled relationship. Not just passively in the middle, taking up space, but filling in the space between antagonists and receiving the arrows from both sides. For, of course, the connection between Tildy and Maud was still there, as strong as before, maybe stronger, but now the forces had turned negative. Just as when Agnes and Rex became disenchanted with each other, Chloe felt the arrows from either side.

Because of their frequent moves while her daddy was in the war, Chloe had never had time to make a best friend. Her best friend had been her mother, Agnes. They had played together, read together, slept together, while waiting for the war to be over so they could be a family again. Then when Daddy's plane was shot down in the last weeks of the war, Chloe had to be the "older and wiser" friend for a while. Making Agnes eat, reading to Agnes aloud, dragging her out for walks, coming up with little treats and surprises, making Agnes want to get up in the morning. And then Rex Wright had come courting and Agnes convinced Chloe they would be a family again. After the marriage, Chloe settled into one place—Rex's hometown, Barlow—and went to the same school for four years. A quiet, composed girl who listened as much as she talked, she attracted friends, both girls and boys, but not a particular best friend. Her one best friend was still her mother, whom she frequently called Agnes.

Rex's family was respected in the town and Rex himself had come home a war hero. So far, so good. Then, after a while, Chloe stopped bringing her friends home; she never knew when there would be raised voices, or weeping behind a closed door, or the thud of someone falling. Before Rex, Chloe hadn't known that men struck women. When Agnes was married to Daddy and they had an argument, Daddy almost always gave in first and then Mother would tease him that he'd let her win. Mother often said Merry had been the perfect name for Chloe's father.

Somewhere just before Rex's hitting started, there was a much anticipated weekend bus trip with her mother to the mountains to visit Uncle Henry. Mother and daughter had shared Agnes's girlhood room under the eaves. They were to have visited Mount St. Gabriel's the next day—Agnes wanted to introduce Chloe to her beloved Mother Finney—but it was not to be: Rex surprised everybody by showing up a day early in his new Beechcraft and insisted on flying them back with him immediately. Agnes cried. Rex blew up.

"Nothing I ever do for you is enough!" he had screamed after take-off, banking the plane so steeply Chloe thought she was going to up-chuck. "What I ought to do is smash us all three into the side of your beloved *mountains* and be done with it!"

And then, that final year, Agnes and she had become closer friends than ever. The private lessons at the diner began. The Latin, the catechism, the stories told hurriedly, one after the other, as though there was a deadline looming, about Mount St. Gabriel's, where Agnes had been so happy. Mother and daughter keeping back more and more of themselves from the increasingly furious Rex.

Evening, Tildy's birthday
The Swag

Tildy and Chloe, faces bathed in red light from the campfire, stood turning their sticks, watching their marshmallows blacken and blister to perfection. A sickle moon had risen on the eastern horizon and stars popped out like little lights going on in the sky.

Tildy withdrew her stick from the flames; Chloe followed suit.

"These are exactly right," pronounced Tildy. "And this is *exactly* the birthday I wanted."

"Now you are officially fourteen," said Chloe, pleased by Tildy's words.

"And *you've* been officially fourteen since back in June," said Tildy.

A clumsy silence followed in which Chloe was sure Tildy was thinking how sad Chloe's last birthday must have been, coming so soon after Agnes's death. Chloe rescued the moment by restoring Agnes to the living. "You know, my mother was out here at the Swag once. It was in the fall of their senior year, at your mother and father's engagement party. Agnes was about to get engaged herself but she didn't know it. She already knew she was in love, but my father hadn't asked her yet. He told her later he was afraid she might turn him down."

"God!" cried Tildy. "So there they were, suffering in silence because they were afraid of not being loved back! All that wasted time! Can you imagine being in love, Chloe?"

"I expect I will be sometime, but right now I guess I wonder more about other people—what it was like for them. My uncle Henry, for instance, with your aunt Antonia."

"That was kind of strange," said Tildy.

"How do you mean?"

"Well, Aunt Tony had a vocation. From early on, she was very serious about becoming a nun. And my grandparents approved. It wasn't like that poor girl who never got to be the Red Nun, that girl who died while her parents were still hoping to talk her out of it. My grandparents were *proud* of Aunt Tony's decision. They had her dowry money put in a special account and everything. The way it was supposed to be, Mama said, was that Antonia and her best friend, Suzanne Ravenel, were going to enter as postulants together at the end of their senior year. But Suzanne jumped the gun without telling anybody and entered at spring break, with Reverend Mother's permission. It just stunned Antonia, it broke her heart."

"My mother told me something about that," said Chloe. "But she said it was because Antonia was having doubts, and Suzanne wanted to spare her friend the embarrassment of backing down."

"That's what Mama calls 'the Ravenel alibi.' Aunt Tony never had doubts till after Suzanne went behind her back. Then she just sort of caved in. She got through her studies with decent grades, she kept going to Mass, but she was like a robot, Mama said. At the end of their senior year Antonia was voted Queen of the School—that had always been expected; everybody knew Aunt Antonia was the most admired girl in the school."

"And Antonia turned down being queen," Chloe said, taking up the story. "She said she didn't deserve it and asked Mother Delaney, the headmistress, to have another election. But Mother Delaney decided against it, and the tradition was discontinued."

"Aunt Antonia was the last person to be voted queen of Mount St. Gabriel's and she wasn't ever even crowned." With her marshmallow stick, Tildy poked at the dying fire. Then she sank to her knees and blew on it vigorously. "Does your uncle Henry ever say anything about Aunt Antonia after she was his wife?"

"Oh, he mentions her at least once every day."

"What kind of 'mentions'? Does he ever talk about how they fell in love?"

"No, it's more like 'Antonia once said . . .' or 'Antonia always felt . . .' or just 'We weren't together very long.' "

"Maybe you could ask him. You could just casually say when he's having his cocktail, 'Uncle Henry, how did you two decide to get married?' "

"I could maybe do that," said Chloe. "But didn't your mother tell you any stories about them as a couple?"

"Just that they started dating after Antonia was running the photography studio—when Mama was pregnant with my sister."

"But doesn't your mama remember how they fell in love?" asked Chloe. "I mean, she and Antonia were twins. They must have whispered together in the dark."

"I can see them whispering in the dark about Aunt Antonia's wanting to be a nun, because that's when they were girls. Mama was already a mother when Aunt Antonia married your uncle Henry. They weren't sisters whispering in the dark anymore."

"I wonder why Mother Ravenel—back when she was Suzanne— why did she go ahead like that and enter without telling her best friend? I mean, when they had planned to enter together?"

"Best friends have been known to do hurtful things to each other," said Tildy with a less enthusiastic poke at the dying fire, making Chloe feel sad in advance at the possibility that she and Tildy might one day hurt each other and cover their hurts with guarded commonplaces.

It was getting chilly out here in the darkness, and Flavia could be seen brooding out at them from the cabin's lit kitchen window.

✠

A summer morning, very early, 2001
St. Scholastica Retirement House
Milton, Massachusetts

Lord, when are You going to deliver me from this mortifying dream? Each time I have it, I wake embarrassed to address You and I would probably be more so if You chose to reply. So just let me talk. Maybe I will run out of things to say and then it will stop. Not that I don't love to elicit Your voice, but this is distressing. St. Augustine was distressed in his chaste thirties and forties when his body continued to betray him in sleep. But, Lord, I am going on eighty-six.

It's always the same place, the Swag. Or, rather, what has come to be my dream construction of the Swag. Antonia and I are walking away from the campfire, away from the others. We can hardly wait until we are far enough away to clasp hands. And then we start running and we lift off together and mount the night sky. The culmination is always the embrace, but before the embrace comes the foretaste of union—when we know we are going to be inseparable and, through each other, utterly changed forever. If I had come across such sentiments in a novel

one of my girls was reading I would have confiscated the book with a re-
vulsive snort. But, you see, in the dream this is my peak moment of ful-
fillment: *it is going to happen, nothing can stop us now.* With the embrace
comes the knowledge of sin, the one we will repeat as often as we can.
Then comes the bad part: waking inside this old body still throbbing
guiltily with satisfaction, my mouth and cheeks swollen and gritty
from the prolonged contact—all in a mere dream!

And yet, Lord, I only kissed her that once, at Cornelia's engagement
party out at the Swag. And she returned my kiss. We both lost ourselves in what we had discovered. But after that night, I could feel Antonia withdrawing from me.

Early Beginnings, Continued

As I've already said, Elizabeth Wallingford was twenty-eight when she went to
the Cowley retreat, preached by the charismatic Anglican monk Basil Maturin,
and afterward confided to Father Maturin in a private conference that she
knew she wanted to dedicate her life to God but didn't know how to go about
it. Father Maturin sent her to visit his sister, an Anglican nun in Oxfordshire,
who advised Elizabeth to go home and pray about it and ask God for His suggestions. "Don't be afraid to ask for specifics," this wise nun said. "God loves
specifics."

Now, at this time there was a young horse trainer from Ireland staying with
the family. The Wallingfords were avid horse people and the Finneys from Galway were avid horse people and the squire's interest had been piqued when
his friend Brendan Finney had boasted that his youngest daughter could break
any recalcitrant yearling on the Finney horse farm. "Let her come and visit us,"
said the squire. "I'm sure we can find some recalcitrant horses for your daughter to break, and my daughter would enjoy the company of another horse-
woman."

This young woman who came to stay with the Wallingfords was Fiona
Finney.

In 1889, she was twenty-three, five years younger than Elizabeth. Both
were excellent horsewomen, both had great independence and vitality, and
both were seeking strenuous ways to serve God. It wasn't long before the two
friends were riding their horses over to Littlemore, a village just outside of Oxford, to visit a Catholic priest Fiona had been consulting about a possible
vocation.

Now, Littlemore, you remember, was where John Henry Newman had experienced the crisis of conscience that led him to leave the Church of England and become a Catholic. His conversion in 1845 changed the religious complexion of the nation. In the forty-four years to follow, the Catholic Church became the church educated middle-class people in England were attracted to. No longer was Catholicism just for Irish immigrants and stubborn old Catholic aristocrats who had survived Henry VIII's dissolution.

Growing up in western Ireland, Fiona had always felt so at home inside her Catholicism that she had never really examined it. Being Catholic was the same to her as being a Galway Finney. Unlike Elizabeth, Fiona was not an intellectual or a scholar, but now she mustered all her powers of mind to examine her religion in order to convert Elizabeth. Because by now it was clear to both of them that they had vocations. And they felt certain that they could accomplish more staying together and supporting each other than going off to be nuns in different religions.

Elizabeth went back to Cowley to see Father Maturin a number of times and talk with him about her growing interest in the Catholic Church. The more she came to know about the Catholic faith, through worshipping with Fiona and through her own reading—she devoured Newman's *Apologia* and afterward wrote her own spritely commentary on the book of Acts—the clearer it seemed to Elizabeth that the straightest, purest line was that which stretched between the church Peter and Paul had worked so tirelessly to establish and the present-day Catholic Church.

It would be wonderful to have listened in on Elizabeth Wallingford's talks with Father Maturin, because, as we know, he himself converted to Catholicism in 1897. By that time Mother Wallingford and Mother Finney had taken their final vows and established their Order under the aegis of the Benedictines and were running their first academy for girls in Boston. You can't help wonder to what degree Elizabeth Wallingford's avid questionings led her famous mentor to follow her example!

—from *Mount St. Gabriel's Remembered: A Historical Memoir,* by Mother Suzanne Ravenel

CHAPTER 8

The Pungent Ache of the Soul

Monday evening, October 15, 1951
Pine Cone Lodge
Mountain City, North Carolina

MAUD NORTON HAD always loved reading, but *David Copperfield* was introducing her to the idea that someone else's story, if told a certain way, could make you ache as though it were your own.

From the lodge's screened porch three floors below, her mother's coquettish murmurs alternated with Mr. Foley's oily baritone replies. Maud was glad their words were inaudible. The rhythms themselves were bad enough. It was still warm enough for them to sit out on the porch if they wore wraps. The mingled aromas of Lily Norton's cigarette and Mr. Foley's cigar floated up into the open window of Maud's "ivory tower," as Lily preciously called it. The tower room was too hot in summer and too cold in winter, and you had to go down steep circular stairs to get to the bathroom, but Maud treasured its remoteness from the rest of Pine Cone's compromised life. Despite the room's coming winter chill, she looked forward to the hard frost, when the porch furniture down there would be covered with plastic and turned to the wall and her mother and Mr. Foley would be forced to carry on their furtive courtship indoors or downtown at the movies.

Art Foley, who sold fancy foods ("choice comestibles," his brochure said) for a wholesale company based in Atlanta, was a star boarder at the Pine Cone from the second Tuesday to the third Monday in every month. He had the prize corner bedroom with its own bath. He brought them gift baskets full of questionable treats: mustard with ale in it, goose liver with blackish mushrooms called "truffles," English "biscuits" that were actually just dry tasteless crackers, and mottled cheeses that looked and smelled as though they should have been thrown out a long time ago.

Down below, in the darkened living room, Grandmother Roberts sat in her late husband's armchair, her swollen legs elevated on the ottoman, listening to her radio programs and keeping watch on the hallway leading to the kitchen. Certain guests had a tendency to pilfer from the Pine Cone's refrigerator.

By tomorrow the class was supposed to have read to the end of chapter 11 and updated their life chart on David. "When you finish the book," Mother Malloy had told them, "you will see the progress of a life on your chart." Maud had skipped ahead to find out if David would definitely go to live with Mr. Micawber so she could enter his new address on her chart. Assured of that, she could go back to the chapter's beginnings, where they were just being introduced, and savor the certainty that things were going to get a little better for David, who had been sent away by Mr. Murdstone to wash bottles in a slummy warehouse.

Not that Maud's mother had married a villain like Mr. Murdstone and herself died soon after. Lily was very much alive, sometimes embarrassingly so. And now everyone at school, thanks to Lily's shameless broadcasting, knew that Maud had a respectable father in Palm Beach, and that both he and his wealthy wife, Anabel, had been "captivated" by Maud this past summer, with hints of more benefits to come. Yes, Maud possessed a father every bit as "real" as Tildy's. Tildy's father had more gruff masculine charm, but the way the two men spent their days was remarkably similar. Smoky Bear Stratton, with nothing very urgent to do, oiled his guns in the den and rode around town in the front seat with his chauffeur. Cyril Norton, with nothing very urgent to do, drove himself around town in his wife's second-best Cadillac and was growing fat from snacking in the kitchen while chatting up the cook.

Far from being sent off to wash bottles in a slum and be mocked by inferiors, Maud was in a top school, with a beautiful teacher everyone worshipped, and once again she had been elected class president—the first time without the help of Tildy's officious campaigning. The other girls looked up to her, to Maud Norton, and not to that former monster-duo known as "TildyandMaud."

Yet why did her heart exult as she reread and savored the passage where David confided to the reader that no words could express the secret agony of his soul as he washed bottles with his low-life companions and felt his hopes of growing up to be a learned and distinguished man crushed in his bosom?

To be "utterly without hope"! What secret agony in her soul corresponded to this? What feelings of shame? What fears that all her learning would pass away from her, little by little? What had happened in her past, or could happen now, to make her plight match his? When everything in her life was going so well, when every school day brought her six hours of proximity with the superior Malloy, what chords were being struck here by this English boy in another century in poverty and despair? And yet they *were* being struck, over and over, with a pungent ache.

After the class finished reading and discussing the novel, Mother Malloy expected a five-page paper from each girl. "Please, do not go to the library and look up what others have said about *David Copperfield*. I will have read any critical works you are likely to find there. I am interested in *your* experience of the novel. Not 'What does this mean?' or 'What have others said about it?' or 'What would impress my teacher?' but 'What does this move in my soul?'"

Could you write a paper called "The Pungent Ache of the Soul in *David Copperfield*"? Malloy encouraged you to think for yourself but came down hard on anything that smacked of the impertinent or the slangy.

Do I or don't I miss Tildy?

Standing alone was a little scary—so exposed—but at least you were just yourself, not tethered to somebody whose name always came first in the mouths of others: TildyandMaud. Standing alone was like starting your own club and waiting to see who wanted to join it, rather than having to be grateful for your measly visitor's pass to someone else's country club so you could swim beside your friend and be patronized by her.

Not that it didn't rankle when Tildy found a replacement so quickly, a brand-new person to boss around—the mousy little orphan "cousin" who would now partake in Tildy's schemes and owe Tildy gratitude.

Was I ever that mousy? Was I ever that grateful that she had chosen me to collaborate with her in what she called "making things turn out the way *we* want"?

I probably was. Until this past summer in Palm Beach when Anabel Norton raised her plucked eyebrows at me on Worth Avenue and asked, "But what exactly do you *see* in her, darling?"

That whole thing with Mrs. Prince back in sixth grade. We weren't learning anything. Mrs. Prince, who smelled of old-lady talcum powder, had taught Tildy's *mother's* sixth-grade class arithmetic and read the Uncle Remus stories and brought the fudge to *them*. "Poor Mrs. Prince—her trouble was she wanted to be liked too much," Tildy's mother had declared. "That's always the undoing of anyone." Tildy's mother could be devastating when she narrowed in on some person's shortcomings. She could pronounce death sentences with a corrosive turn of phrase.

"Let's try something, Maud," Tildy had proposed after Mrs. Stratton had pronounced Mrs. Prince's death sentence. "Let's see how far we can go by *asserting our will over Mrs. Prince* and setting an example for the others."

It had worked. Within two months, Mrs. Prince was gone. They got a new teacher, hatchet-faced Mother Odom, who taught the upper girls in the academy and said it was never too early to start on algebra. Tildy was giddy with their success. Maud felt a little shaky at first; she felt like a witch: if they could accomplish this, what else might they do?

"I think you should be class president next year" had been Tildy's next proposal. "If we start planning now, you'll be a shoo-in for seventh grade. You're the smartest person in the class and people respect you."

They respect *us,* Maud had thought; they respect the strange animal called TildyandMaud. Though Tildy's grades were mediocre and her reading problems a secret shame, she seemed to take it for granted that Maud's superior abilities were hers to share and would cover them both in glory. And as long as they were harnessed together like a pair of horses, their carriage skimmed swiftly forward, ahead of everyone else's, borne by Maud's abilities and Tildy's fantasies and Tildy's implacable self-regard.

In the seventh grade Maud was elected class president. In the eighth grade, likewise.

But now, for the first time without the benefit of Tildy's electioneering, Maud found herself class president of the ninth grade, having beat out the other contender, Kay Lee Jones, nine to six by secret ballot. If Kay Lee, the prettiest and sauciest of the transfers, despite the strawberry birthmark on her neck, had voted for herself (and why not? Maud had voted for *her*self), that would put all four of the St. Jerome's transfers—Kay Lee, Lora Jean Cramer, Mikell Lunsford, and Dorothy Yount—in the Kay Lee corner.

Given the rupture between Tildy and Maud, Tildy and her new best friend, Chloe, could easily be expected to have voted for Kay Lee. Except Maud could perfectly well hear Tildy telling Chloe, "Though Maud and I are no longer best friends, Maud is a *known quantity.* She takes being president seriously. It's a job, like with her grades. Whereas Kay Lee Jones and her bunch aren't truly Mount St. Gabriel's girls yet. I mean, they're hardly individuals; they're more like a *clump* of something from across the river."

Maud was appalled at Tildy's flagrant snobbery. It could so easily have been turned on herself, if Tildy had not chosen her for her best friend.

No, it must be two other new girls who'd voted for Kay Lee Jones. Not Marta Andreu, the new Cuban girl, because she would vote however Gilda Gomez did, and Gilda had always liked Maud. Perhaps stuck-up Elaine Frew, then, who lived for her piano practice and couldn't care less who was class president.

And probably the other Kay Lee vote came from Ashley Nettle. Those first days of school Maud had seen Kay Lee playing up to nervous Ashley.

Now, however, Ashley had joined the constituency made up of Josie Galvin, the doctor's daughter, and the Dutch girls, Hansje Van Kleek and Beatrix Wynkoop—and sometimes Rebecca Meyer, when she wasn't involved in her synagogue activities. Rebecca Meyer had never liked Tildy much, though she was too aloof to come right out and say so.

How was Tildy coping on her own with these *David Copperfield* assignments? Though Tildy, like her mother and sister, commanded an impressive speaking vocabulary, she was strangely defeated by the sight of words lying flat on a page. Last year, in eighth grade, she had threatened to have a nervous breakdown over *Silas Marner.* Maud had to drag her through that book, one-fourth the size of *David Copperfield,* kicking and screaming all the way.

("Oh, God, God, God, it makes me want to *puke,* Maud. This story isn't written in English, it's in murky old-fashioned hieroglyphics that make me dizzy! Who cares about spinning wheels, and what the be-jesus are 'nutty hedgerows'?"

"It's what they've assigned us, Tiddly. We've got to get through it. Don't get sucked into the spinning wheels and nutty hedgerows. Let's just go along, a chapter at a time, and get what they want us to get from it.")

Was Chloe Starnes performing that function for Tildy now? Was Chloe as amazed and grateful as I was when Tildy came up to me in third grade and said, "You want to sit together at lunch?"

And all those years I went on being amazed and grateful that she had chosen me. Until Anabel Norton asked me, when we were shopping on Worth Avenue, "Do you have a picture of this special friend you're always talking about?" And I pulled the snapshot of Tildy out of my wallet—lovably arrogant Tildy, hands on hips, narrowing her eyes at me like a cat at its owner ("You belong to me")—and proudly handed it over to Anabel.

The plucked line of Anabel's brows shot up a full inch and then she laughed. "*This* is the superior being called Tildy? Why, Maud, she looks like—Orphan Annie without a neck. She is such a little girl compared to you. You're already a stunning young woman. What exactly do you *see* in her, darling?"

Oh, Tildy, how I hurt for you when Anabel said that. It's like Granny is always saying to Mother: "Don't let them pull the wool over your eyes again." But what do you call it when somebody pulls the wool *away* from your eyes?

After Anabel said it, even though she tends to judge everyone by their looks and clothes, I couldn't make the wool go back. I felt sick about it, but it had changed something. For the first time I wondered, What would it be like to be just Maud without the "Tildyand" in front? I had to find out. But how, without hurting you? Maybe if I acted shallow and stupid you would get disgusted and think you were dropping me. And you, the one who was always saying, "Oh, Maud, you're so deep, you have a jillion facets"—poor Tildy, you didn't even see through me!

"You want to sit together at lunch?" you said that miraculous day in third grade. And I said, "Sure, why not?" Trying to hide my amazement. We'd both brought our lunches from home, but when we got to the cafeteria you went to the counter and bought each of us a bag of potato chips. You handed me my bag and then put yours on the bench and sat down on it. *Crunch.*

"I like to do that," you said in your uppity way. "It makes more of them. Why don't you try it?"

So I did. *Crunch.* It became a thing we did, and soon the other girls were copying us.

Oh, Tiddly. You could be so funny!

✠

LILY NORTON, SHOULDERS draped in an afghan, leaned back against Art Foley's sweatered arm lying casually along the back of the glider. It was quite dark now. No nosy gossip passing on the sidewalk, even someone with twenty-twenty night vision, could see anything more than two figures sitting respectably upright on the porch of the Pine Cone Lodge.

"Yes, Maud and I are very close," Lily said. "We are more like sisters than mother and daughter. Of course, I had her so young. I was practically a child bride. Mr. Norton used to call me that: his child bride. Maud tells me absolutely everything. We have no secrets from each other."

"Do you tell her absolutely everything, too?" Art Foley's voice was laced with lazy insinuation. As the syllables rolled out, his hand on the back of the glider stroked the nape of Lily Norton's neck.

"Well, not *quite* everything," said Lily with a skittish laugh. "I am her mother, after all. There are things that a young girl being carefully brought up isn't supposed to be thinking about yet. Maud is so much less sophisticated than I was at her age. Much of it's due to her school, Mount St. Gabriel's, and those nuns—though I'm glad Mother and I have been able to scrape together the tuition. And last year she won a four-year scholarship to the academy. She's getting a superior education, and meeting the right kind of girls. As I told you, I went to the public high school because my father hated Catholics and he thought nuns were an abomination."

"The time he jumped off the bus when the nuns got on," remembered Art Foley, now actively kneading Lily's neck and shoulders.

"Oh, that feels so good. Don't stop."

"Who says I'm planning to?"

"It's just that—oh, sometimes, I get so tired. It's not easy being a woman on your own with a daughter to raise properly in a small town where everyone is watching you and waiting for you to make a mistake. I'm so glad that Mr. Norton and his wife, Anabel, have taken such a shine to Maud. Anabel is a very wealthy woman, and Maud likes her. Of course, Anabel's a good bit *older* than Mr. Norton, but I daresay the arrangement suits him. He was never one to *strive.* Mr. Norton had his attractive points but being a good provider was not one of them."

Art Foley chuckled.

"What?" asked Lily.

"I was just wondering if Mr. Norton had a first name? Or did you call him 'Mr. Norton' the whole time you were married?"

"It was—Cyril," said Lily, rather stiffly. She hadn't used the first name of Maud's father for so long it sounded strange.

"You called him Cyril, then? 'Will you take the garbage out, Cyril?' 'Oh, Cyril, that feels so good.' 'Oh, *Cyyy-ril*!' "

"You are very naughty, Mr. Foley."

"Yes, I expect I am. But you were talking about your lovely daughter and meeting the right girls at school and so on. How about sharing some of that afghan with me? There's plenty of it to go around if we just drape it over our knees, like so. It's getting kind of nippy but I'm not ready to go in yet, are you?"

"Oh, no. Mother's in the midst of her programs. She likes to turn off the light and *live* in them, you know."

"Go on about Maud's friends." Under cover of the rearranged afghan, his other hand got to work on the inside of her thigh.

"Maud has this whole new set of friends. Mmm, this *is* comfy. But are you sure you have enough room under there, Art?"

"More room than I need, Lily."

"You see, when she started to Mount St. Gabriel's in third grade— that's after Mr. Norton—*Cyril*—and I had parted ways and I came back to Mountain City to help Mother run the lodge. It wasn't my idea of an exciting life, but I had a hostage to fortune to think about now. Well, in third grade Tildy Stratton made a beeline for Maud, and after that they became inseparable."

"Yes, I've met Tildy. Saucy little number. Parents are society people, you said."

"His great-grandfather founded Stratton Lumber. But other people run it now. He mostly just takes rich people hunting out at his cabin and rides around in the front seat of his automobile with the black chauffeur."

"I guess Stratton Lumber has cut down enough virgin forests by now to let him do that," said Art Foley with his lazy insinuating good humor.

"I have nothing against the Strattons," said Lily. "*She*—Tildy's mother—has a mean tongue, but Cornelia does go out to work every day. She has this very successful photography studio in town. She does all the important weddings and clubs."

"I shouldn't wonder," crooned Art Foley, taking a few more liberties under the afghan.

CHAPTER 9

Nuns' Dormitory

Monday evening, October 15, 1951
Feast of St. Teresa of Ávila
Mount St. Gabriel's

Ignatian Examen of Conscience

1. First, ask for God's light. Then try to review the day from God's viewpoint.
2. Pray for the grace to see clearly the guidance God is giving you in your daily history.
3. When reviewing the day, ask to be shown concrete instances of the presence of God and of the activity and influence of evil. These can be detected by paying attention to strong feelings you experienced during situations and encounters.
4. When did you and God act together? When did you yield to the influence of evil? Ask pardon for your failings and ask for the strength to overcome them.
5. Plan how you can do better on the morrow. Then entrust yourself to God's grace. Conclude with an "Our Father."

Mother Malloy unpinned her veil, folded it according to custom, and laid it in its drawer, the two straight pins arranged on top of the black square of georgette crepe in the form of a cross.

In the portfolio on the desk were her handwritten preparations for tomorrow's classes: portions of Cicero's *Second Philippic,* that masterpiece of invective against Mark Antony, with its many shadings and tones of attack, though nothing too brutal or salacious in their Latin textbook with its imprimatur; in medieval history, they were doing guilds and festivals and the visual arts. What riches she could have checked out for them from Boston libraries!

For English class, she had brought up-to-date her own chart of David's life. "Goes to live with Micawber family at Windsor Terrace, City Road."

With reminders to herself in the margins:

1. Mr. Micawber based on Dickens's father's experience of debtors' prison.
2. The author's use of recognizable speech tags ("I never will desert Mr. Micawber") to identify characters.
3. "Flat" vs. "round" characters: advantages and disadvantages of each.

Removing the starched coif, Mother Malloy rotated her neck, enjoying the freed expanse of side vision and the coolness of a bare head. All those years of wondering what kind of unsightly remnants must lurk beneath nuns' coifs—and then her surprise, after profession, to find out that the majority of her sisters *opted* to retain squashed clumps of hair under their veils. In the Order of St. Scholastica, the choice was left to the individual. Old Mother Finney, who had remained clear-sighted and steady-handed into her eighties, fulfilled a wide range of convent roles, from sacristan to school archivist, cellaress, and barber. "Finney's Clip 'n' Shave Parlor," as she called it, opened for business once a month in the nuns' sunroom on the third floor. You sat on a kitchen stool facing the mountains and the western sky, a ragged sheet pinned around your shoulders, and requested either the scissors or the electric razor. Mother Finney herself was a shaver, she told Mother Malloy. "They do come back wilder and thicker—it's as though each hair rejoices in its freedom to start over. All the same, like you, Mother Malloy, I prefer a tidy scalp."

First, ask for God's light. Then try to review the day from God's viewpoint.

In her flannel nightgown, Mother Malloy dropped to her knees on the prie-dieu beneath the wooden crucifix. After asking for God's light, she launched into his empyrean, circling like a hawk in the dawn air above Mount St. Gabriel's. This precept of taking a God's-eye view came naturally to her. As a child, Kate Malloy had gone on frequent night journeys after lights-out in the foster home. This satisfying form of recreation was to be had simply by closing your eyes and envisioning whatever scene you chose—whether floating above and looking down on your own body curled in its narrow bed, or observing the foster home as a bird in West Newton might see it from the rooftop, or spotting the lights of Boston Harbor as they might appear to a night traveler aboard an incoming ship. These journeys were perfected during a long convalescence in her ninth year, when a strep throat followed by severe bronchitis kept her out of school for weeks; they continued unabated throughout her teens. It was not until she became a postulant, overscrupulous about everything in her mental life, that she confessed them to her spiritual director, who, luckily, was a man grounded in the physical realities, a priest who taught high school physics and chemistry.

"What do *you* think of these little excursions, Sister? Do you feel you are performing a mystical feat when you go floating around? Or that maybe God has graced you with these visions as a token of His special regard?"

"They don't feel at all mystical, Father. It's more of a visual shift in perspective. And the scenes don't appear out of nowhere. First I have to want to go there—and I have to have seen the places, or to have seen pictures of them. It's just that I can look at them from other angles."

He brought her a test booklet from the high school. She looked at diagrams and chose the picture closest to how the object would appear when assembled from the diagram. She gauged distances in her mind or transposed angles, then chose from the pictures how the field of view would be altered. She made a perfect score on the test.

"I thought so, Sister. Yours isn't a case of spiritual presumption; God has simply given you a high degree of spatial apperception. You would have made a damn good pilot."

Go back to this morning. Be in God's point of view as He rides the dawn, then banks and swoops and penetrates the chapel roof as an invisible, all-seeing presence.

The community is at morning prayer. Today is the feast of St. Teresa of Ávila. Mother Ravenel reads the lectionary with her fast-paced southern brio, weaving in her own asides, as though she is a confidante of the sixteenth-century nun and perhaps believes she is a likely candidate for a modern Teresa.

". . . and as you all know, she was a first-rate organizer, a vigorous and practical woman who had become so close to God that she talked right back to Him. *If this is the way You treat Your friends, no wonder You have so few!* Yes, that's just what she told him when her carriage over-turned in the mud while she was on the road to found another convent."

A ripple of nun laughter from the pews. A few had not heard the story; the rest laughed to register their good-natured acceptance of Mother Ravenel, the vigorous and voluble organizer among them, engaged in an act of being typically herself.

("The hardest part of convent life is the day-to-day coexistence with your sisters in Christ," Mother Malloy's novice mistress in Boston had warned her. "Some personalities will rub you the wrong way from the start; others will cause you to lie in the dark at night, grinding your teeth. Some will bore you, some will earn your esteem, others you will cheerfully dismiss. But they are all vital pieces in God's human kaleido-scope. That's the thing you have to remember when you kneel next to them in chapel or watch them chewing their food across the table. But it will be especially trying for you, Sister, because you are fastidious and have the same high expectations of others as you do for yourself.")

Mother Malloy had not been much discomfited by any friction with her sisters since she had been at Mount St. Gabriel's. She was simply too tired at the end of each day to lie in the dark and grind her teeth over anyone. She often dozed off while doing her examen and saying her evening prayers. Up here in the mountains, one mile above sea level, the oxygen was scarcer. The southern food, fried meats and grits and starches and cobblers, cooked and served by the black kitchen staff, sat on her chest for hours after a meal. No wonder Gilda Gomez grew into her outsized blouses by Thanksgiving.

Except for the nuns' noon chapel break, Mother Malloy was generally with her ninth-grade girls from eight forty-five in the morning until the end of last period, at two fifty-five in the afternoon. The exception was their after-lunch math class with Mother Odom on Mondays, Wednesdays, and Fridays, during which time Mother Malloy liked to walk the grounds—not the strenuous "mountain goat" hike of her first day with Mother Ravenel, but just strolling and breathing deeply and recollecting herself in the presence of God. Even when other faculty members were teaching the combined academy grades in the big study hall, Mother Malloy was expected to hover somewhere in the background, monitoring her fifteen girls.

The combined classes included Miss Bianca Mendoza's popular Spanish conversation classes and Professor Staunton's Friday afternoon lectures on current events (not so popular: Chloe Starnes doodled quite accomplished sketches in the margins of her current events notebook; Marta Andreu, whose comprehension of English remained minimal, gazed longingly out the window; the piano prodigy Elaine Frew drummed scales on her desktop).

There were also Mother Ravenel's sprightly biweekly addresses to the entire academy, which went under the rubric "Moral Guidance for Modern Girls," which Mother Malloy had overheard Tildy Stratton refer to as "Moral Guidance for Modern Goats." (She was sure Tildy had meant her to overhear.)

She respected Mother Ravenel, was a little in awe of her, and yearned for a mere fraction of the headmistress's stamina. Mother Malloy could not remember a time, even as a child, when she could command such reserves of energy.

WHEN REVIEWING THE day, ask to be shown concrete instances of the presence of God and of the activity and influence of evil. These can be detected by paying attention to strong feelings you experienced during situations and encounters.

On this Monday, the feast of Teresa of Ávila, Mother Malloy had experienced two definite instances of God's love made manifest in human exchanges. She also had felt, in her classroom, stirrings of rivalry that might attract a devil alert to opportunity. She had difficulty with the concept of pure evil, but she could comprehend Aquinas's definition ("a tear in the fabric of the good") and had worked out for herself that temptation is anything that encourages us to be less than we are or that tries to separate us from God.

She remembered Tildy Stratton's older sister, Madeline, on registration day saying, "I want Tildy to keep her intrepid little soul," and her own promise to keep watch over it. She had wanted to see the interesting sister again, and on this very Monday, during her free hour after lunch, her wish had been granted.

For lunch she had taken a minuscule helping of the frankfurter-and-bean casserole, passed up the berry cobbler, and hurried out to take advantage of the crisp October air while Mother Odom did algebra with the ninth grade. She headed straight for the grotto, not by the strenuous route Mother Ravenel had chosen on her first day, but along a gentler path that branched off from the circular driveway in front of the school.

Once seated on the cool marble lap of the Red Nun, facing the Della Robbia Annunciation, Mother Malloy took deep breaths (she had walked fast in order to make the most of her hour) and tried to get a head start on her nightly examen by examining the day so far. The "keeping track" part of the religious life was difficult when there was a full teaching load as well. Was young Mother Galyon, the new principal of the lower grades, who had been granted uninterrupted years to finish her graduate work, able to keep track of her soul along with all her class preparations?

Where, Mother Malloy asked herself in the grotto, nestled against the unfinished memorial to a dead girl, *have I, so far today, discerned God's presence? And where the influence and activity of evil? Or spotted a tear in the fabric of the good?*

She was aware of God's presence most mornings when she took the ninth-grade roll. She felt herself inside the nimbus of Christ as Good Shepherd, alphabetically naming her sheep, checking on the well-being of each. Every routine "Present, Mother" came back to her in a particular accent and emotional tone. During this brief antiphonal exchange with her flock, Mother Malloy acknowledged each girl's essence—Lora Jean Cramer's stolid complacency, Mikell Lunsford's tomboyish inattention. She also looked for signs of a girl's current state: edgy or despondent this morning? Keyed up over something? Teary or sullen?

They were at such a molting age. Not yet divested of childish wrappings, their womanly selves poked out in spurts. Mother Malloy noted the almost daily changes. Tildy Stratton's face had new cheekbones—she was going to be striking, if not pretty—but her grades were close to failing. (Mother Malloy had sent a note to Mrs. Stratton last week but had not yet heard back.) Flat-chested, word-swallowing Ashley Nettle had sprouted breasts, and under the influence of her Dutch friends Beatrix and Hansje, with whom she rode to and from school, was now speaking (almost) coherent English sentences. Dorothy Yount, holding herself like a diva since Mother Lacy had discovered her voice and become her coach, seemed to have mislaid her allergies altogether.

("Remember, girls: you are a work in progress!" This was Mother Ravenel's signature sign-off at the end of every "Moral Guidance for Modern Girls" lecture.)

Circling back, inside God's point of view, to her classroom this morning, Mother Malloy recalled those stirrings of girl rancor in the classroom that might well flag the interest of a passing devil. It was hardly more than a distant rumble of thunder, but Mother Malloy had witnessed the face-off. It was just before roll call and Maud Norton and Becky Meyer, class president and vice president respectively, were busy updating the bulletin board, putting up new notices of meetings (choir practice, Sodality of Mary, the decorating committee for the Christmas tea with the Pisgah Prep boys). Then in came Tildy Stratton, with quiet little Chloe close behind. Tildy, grumpily on the lookout for something to find fault with, immediately spotted it.

"Wonders never cease," she sarcastically murmured to Chloe. "Our humdrum old bulletin board is getting a makeover."

Becky Meyer, with her characteristic standoffishness from all classroom intrigues, continued on with her thumbtacking. Maud, however, spun slowly around, a strange smile lighting her face, and addressed herself to Tildy's friend alone.

"Oh good, Chloe, you can help us. Will you please think of something *artistic* so it won't look like everybody else's bulletin board?"

Chloe blinked. Tildy looked momentarily stunned, then narrowed her eyes. Pushing Chloe forward with the tips of her fingers, she said, "*You* go give it a bit of *pizzazz*," as though the idea had originated with her. "Good *morning*, Mother Malloy."

"Good morning, Tildy."

"Good morning, Mother Malloy," echoed Chloe.

"Good morning, Chloe. Now, everyone, please be seated for roll call. And let's all of us think of ways we can make our bulletin board uniquely ours."

Careful to eschew the pet words of either faction. No mention of artistic or "humdrum" or "pizzazz." If you were too humble and submissive in your conduct to young people, St. Augustine warned, your authority would be undermined.

The problem of discerning mischief from good, thought Mother Malloy (closing her eyes against the flickering sunlight and leaning back against the Red Nun) was that, very often, the two grew together. Our Lord knew this: His parable of the wheat and the tares. If you ripped out the menacing weed prematurely, you risked killing the tiny seedlings of goodness struggling for life around its root.

CHAPTER 10

Madeline

Early Monday afternoon, October 15, 1951
Feast of St. Teresa of Ávila
Mount St. Gabriel's grotto

WANTING TO STAY off Mother Ravenel's radar, Madeline Stratton
parked her yellow convertible down the road, behind the junior college.
Head lowered modestly, she made her way up the drive toward the old
building where her baby sister was having algebra class. This morning
she had dressed for stealth and invisibility rather than toward her usual
standard of glamour.

Today Mountain City High students had a half day off. They were
always having half days off at Mountain City High, to make room for
the really important things in life, like football rallies and electing the
homecoming queen and her court. "I really think we ought to change
our name to Mountain City *Low* School," Madeline remarked recently
to her mother, the occasion being another of the half days off, when she
had sought relief from aimlessness by helping at her mother's downtown studio.

"Oh, Maddy, you do miss Mount St. Gabriel's." Mother and daughter were in the darkroom together. Below them in the developer tray
the faces and bodies of this year's first-form boys at stylish Pisgah Prep
floated up at them piecemeal, like ghosts emerging through a fog.

"Not the creaky old place itself. I miss the feeling of being kept on
my toes."

"And there's nothing to keep you on your toes at—*Mountain City
Low.*" Her mother's droll tone indicated approval of Madeline's witti-
cism.

"Not really, no. I'm liked by the girls one would prefer to be liked by. And the boys, well, I can more or less pick and choose. Though it's sort of like choosing to go out with one Hershey's Kiss instead of another. I guess I miss hating certain people. Hating definitely keeps you on your toes."

"I take my share of the blame for your having to leave. You wouldn't have sassed Mother Ravenel at that vocation day thing if you hadn't had so many years of my running her down at home."

"I didn't sass her, Mama. I just said what was true—"

"The one thing in the world you ought not to have said."

"Well, it was true, wasn't it? I just said I didn't want to jump the gun on my vocation, the way some people had."

"You know, Maddy, I often fantasize where we'd all be today if our parents had sent Antonia and me to the public schools after seventh grade. Back then we didn't have an eighth grade. Lots of other Catholic girls transferred to public high. They wanted to go; they'd had it with restrictions. Mount St. Gabriel's would have laid our religious groundwork perfectly well by then, and without Suzanne clinging like a leech Tony might have stuck with her vocation. Oh, drat and damnation, just look at that!"

"What?"

"That wretched boy on the end of the front row."

"What about him?"

"Well, look. He has his eyes shut."

"But you always take backup shots for each group."

"Yes, but the light was perfect in that one. In the others there was too much sun and all the boys looked bleached out." Then Cornelia giggled wickedly and bumped her hip against her daughter's. "Like identical bleached-out Hershey's Kisses."

TO SPARE HERSELF parading past Ravenel watch points, Madeline detoured down an overgrown path that led in a roundabout way to the grotto. Inside her shoulder bag was Mother Malloy's letter, in exquisite nun cursive, received last Friday at the Stratton home.

Thursday, October 11, 1951

Dear Mrs. Stratton,
    This is a follow-up to Tildy's first six weeks' report card,

which she took home yesterday. Would there be a convenient time for us to get together? I have a free period on Mondays, Wednesdays, and Fridays during the girls' algebra class, from one until two. Weather permitting, I walk about the grounds or sit in the grotto. Otherwise I can be found in my office. I am also in my office following three o'clock chapel, if that is better for your schedule.

Tildy has a vivacious spirit and many leadership qualities, though she must guard against haughtiness and impertinence. She enjoys working out math problems, and she is an enthusiastic participant in the Spanish conversation classes. Her vocabulary and range of expression in speaking are truly exceptional for a girl her age. However, they far exceed her written work. As you can see from the six weeks' report, her grades in History (75), Composition (70), and English (70) are on the borderline of failing. What I am hoping is that we can put our heads together and come up with a plan for Tildy's improvement. I look forward to meeting you, Mrs. Stratton.

Yours sincerely,
Mother Kate Malloy, O.S.S.

PS. Please give my warm regards to your daughter Madeline and tell her that I hope she will come and see me sometime.

"Well, she must think I'm a very neglectful mother" had been Cornelia Stratton's outburst of self-reproach as she passed the letter to Madeline. "I didn't accompany Tildy to the sacred rite of registration day, and last Wednesday, when Tildy handed me her report card, I didn't go rushing out to the school, demanding why my daughter was failing in three subjects. Yes, this Mother Malloy must think I'm a very poor excuse for a parent."

"She writes 'on the borderline,' " said Madeline, scanning the letter. "Seventy isn't failing."

"It's just one little point *away* from it, Madeline."

"Well, but she got a 92 in Algebra and 75 in History. That's only five points below a C. And Tildy's always hovered around a C in English. You know how she hates to read."

"You always loved reading."

"But I was a slug at math. Still am. Though at Mountain City High, which is a year behind Mount St. Gabriel's, I'm a dazzling B plus in Algebra. "

"But, look—" Cornelia snatched back the letter. "Right here she says Tildy's vocabulary and range of expression are 'truly exceptional for a girl her age.' Tildy is the most articulate child I know, Maddy. She surpasses you at her age. She's never at a loss for words."

"I think it has something to do with the print on the page, Mama. When I'd read to her when she was little, she'd say trying to follow all those up and down flat marks made her want to throw up, and she'd rather listen to the story with her eyes shut."

"But she *has* been reading all these years, whether she hates it or not—I don't see why now, all of a sudden, she should backslide. Do you?"

"Well, it could be because Maud's not around anymore. They studied together so much."

"You're not trying to tell me Tildy kept her eyes closed all those years while Maud read aloud to her."

"No, but maybe talking it through with Maud made it less oppressive."

"And now Tildy's teacher expects me just to drop all my professional commitments and head out to the *grotto* so we can 'put our heads together.' And I should, I should! But, damn it all, this week of all weeks, I've got the Jaycees lunch and the Toastmasters' dinner and the opening of the new Jewish Community Center, not to mention I'm way behind on the Pisgah Prep job because I have to go back and reshoot the first form because of that little boy with his eyes closed."

Madeline saw that her mother was warming up for one of her "Nobody understands a professional woman's life" arias.

"Why not let me go on Monday, Mama? We're getting another half day off for float decoration."

"But you have your *social* obligations at school, too, Madeline."

"I've just been elected to the homecoming court, Mama. That should fulfill my quota of social obligations for the semester."

"But I hate to always be imposing myself on your young life—"

"Oh, my young life. Mother Malloy said in her PS she wants me to come and see her. I can be your emissary, like the Pope's—'Her Excellency says she can meet with you in the near future, but at the moment her schedule—' "

"Well, maybe if you *could* just drop by the school on Monday and explain to her about my dratted schedule and ask if we can set up a meeting the following week—oh, Madeline, you are such a support. You're probably sick of hearing this, but you remind me so much of Antonia. So coolheaded and so giving of herself. The complete opposite of me. How I wish you could have known her better."

"I'll never be sick of hearing it, Mama, and I do think I remember Aunt Tony playing games with me in her room."

"She adored you. She felt you were partly hers, you know, because we went through it together."

When eighteen-year-old Cornelia Tilden had married Smoky Stratton after graduating from Mount St. Gabriel's in 1934, her parents had turned over their Mountain City house to the new couple and moved out to the farm left to them by Great-grandmother Tilden. Antonia, at loose ends since her sudden decision not to take vows, went with them and threw herself into getting them acclimated to their new life. But no sooner did she get the three of them settled into the farmhouse than Cornelia sent an SOS and begged her twin to move back into her old upstairs room and help her endure the intimidating ordeal of pregnancy.

"We spent so many hours, Tony and I, curled up on her bed together, with you, Maddy, right there in my stomach between us, getting bigger by the day. When I felt really awful, she was the only person I could stand to have near me. Poor old Smoky had to sleep all by himself."

Her late aunt Tony's room was now Madeline's room, had been so ever since Antonia had married Henry Vick in 1938, when Madeline was three, and gone off on their unlucky Italian honeymoon. Madeline wished she could remember more about Aunt Tony playing games with her in that room. There were vestigial recollections of sweet afternoon light and the stately swish of cars passing outside beneath the leafy old elms, and stifled breaths behind a curtain, or someone flinging open the lid of the window seat and pulling the warm hidden child squealing from its depths. But who was the child? Little Madeline enfolded by Aunt Tony, or warm little Tildy, wriggling and squealing in the arms of the not much older Madeline? She could never be sure.

TO MADELINE, ENTERING the grotto was like stepping into a moody illustration in an old book others had read, or thought they had read, and then told you about maybe once too often. Today, however, she was struck by the juxtaposition of the alabaster-pale nun resting against the rough, ruddy memorial to the dead girl who had not achieved nunhood. Straight-down October sunshine pierced the turning leaves, bathing the hulking figure in a mottled, moving light. At first Madeline presumed Mother Malloy was deep in prayer, then saw that she was asleep, wedged upright in the marble embrace of the Red Nun. She stood transfixed, not wanting to startle.

Then the breeze parted a patch of shade and sunlight shone direct into Mother Malloy's face. She woke, blinking up at Madeline.

"I'm sorry, Mother—"

"Whatever for? I've hoped you would come, Madeline."

"Mama got your letter about Tildy and wants to meet with you early next week, if that's okay. Her schedule is just crazy this time of year—all these lunches and things opening in town. She runs the business all by herself, you see. And since they were giving us a half day off today at Mountain City High, I said I'd stop by—"

This was coming out all wrong. As if Mama's schedule were more important than Tildy, and like I'm doing everyone a favor, when it was my idea in the first place.

But Mother Malloy smiled as if Madeline had given back something equal to her own frank-hearted welcome.

"And here you are. Come, let's sit over there." Mother Malloy rose from the red marble shelf, a perfect "lap" for two young girls to snuggle in, side by side, but too small for two adults. As the nun gracefully shook out her long skirts and readjusted her sash, it struck Madeline that this woman was not much older than herself.

Would I want to enclose myself in all that *fabric* for the rest of my life, she wondered, taking a seat beside Mother Malloy on the wooden bench facing the Della Robbia. It would depend, I suppose, on how many boring or unfriendly elements it would keep out. There would be a certain release of having chosen your so-called destiny, so you could get on with whatever came next.

"Tell me about your school, Madeline. Do you like it there?"

To her disgust, Madeline heard herself regurgitating the "Mountain City Low School" quip that had amused her mother in the darkroom.

Though Mother Malloy did not laugh, she continued to regard Madeline with fond attention. "The work isn't challenging enough?" she suggested.

"It's not just the work—it's the whole life of *school*. I feel I've been held back to repeat what I already know how to do. It's like you've learned to swim really well, and now you're ready to cross a huge body of water and see what's on the other side, and then someone tells you, No, no, dear, you have to stay in this pool and tread water until—until I don't know what. Whatever comes next. I wish I could get to it!"

Clumsy! But at least she was flailing toward something, not coasting on her earlier bon mots.

"May I ask what you did to get yourself banished from Mount St. Gabriel's?"

"I said something really rude to Mother Ravenel. It was on vocation day—every year we celebrate the birthday of our foundress, Mother Elizabeth Wallingford; there's a program put on by the whole school. It's the day girls in the academy are invited to ask God if they might have a vocation. And if they do, they march up to the stage and declare themselves, and then right after the program they meet with Mother Ravenel in her office."

"What you said must have been very seriously rude."

"It just sprang out, like a toad that had been crouched inside my mouth for years. It was something only someone in our family was entitled to say to her, but it was also the one thing that should have been left unsaid by anyone under her control. It hurt her, as it should have, and made her absolutely furious."

Mother Malloy was listening in profile now, head lowered, pale hands folded upon her lap.

"I said it out of nervousness, to protect myself. We were in her office by then. She had summoned me after the program. No girl that year had marched up to the stage to declare a budding vocation, and she was put out and, I suppose, ready to blame it on me. She was giving me a real dressing-down, saying it was time we got to the bottom of my puerile behavior.

"What I had done was, well, what I did every vocation day since I was ten: gotten my usual fit of giggles and had to excuse myself from the auditorium. There always came a point during the program when I lost control. I never knew what was going to set it off, but something always did. This time it was a girl reciting a poem she had written for the occasion, a bunch of cloying little couplets with predictable rhymes. The poem was supposed to be about the night before our foundress is to take her first vows, and she goes out in the moonlight on her family's Oxfordshire estate—she's in her nightgown—to say good-bye to her—oh, dear, here I go—to say farewell to her—oh, ha, ha!— 'pulchritudinous hair'—!" Madeline shot up from the bench and paced back and forth until she got her convulsions under control.

She was just about to conclude repentantly, "See? That's how I disgraced myself every vocation day," when she saw that Mother Malloy, hands still folded upon her lap, was also shaking with laughter.

"Oh, please, Mother, you have to say what *you* find funny."

"I will, I promise. But do go on. I am enjoying the way you tell it."

"Well, first of all, our foundress was twenty-nine when she took vows; she was a certifiable old maid who had been saving herself up for God. She and her friend Fiona Finney had been working on this scheme together, and Elizabeth had just converted to Catholicism—she'd gone through instruction and all of *that*. The last thing in the world she would have been thinking about was her hair. Who knows or cares if she even had pulchritudinous hair?"

Laughter brought agreeable color to Mother Malloy's face. "Go on."

"Well, as I say, I lost control and Mother Ravenel shot me a withering look and I slunk out of the auditorium. Of course, by then these outbursts of mine had achieved their own notoriety—my exits had become part of the yearly show. What made it different this time was that no girls had marched up to declare vocations to keep Mother Ravenel busy afterward. So there I was, in her office, and she pulled out this little black spiral notebook from a drawer and found the page she wanted and said: 'Now, Madeline, you have been finding vocation day sidesplitting since you were a child in fifth grade. You see, I have kept a record. And now you are a freshman in the academy, a young woman. Why are you still behaving like a ten-year-old?' "

Madeline, a good actress, spoke the headmistress's lines in a fast-paced drawl very like Mother Ravenel's.

"Then she closed the book, but kept a finger in it to mark her place.

She looked up at me from under her eyebrows the way she does when she's about to skewer you, and she said, 'You know, Madeline, the psychologists tell us that helpless laughter often masks fear. If this is true in your case, don't you think it's time we get to the root of why the vocation day program makes you fearful?'

"And I was also wondering what else about me was on those pages. She was always saying to us that she was going to write down this or that about us in her 'little black book,' but I always thought she meant it as a figure of speech. That the book actually existed was pretty scary.

"She went on probing me. Did I have any idea what this root cause might be? I said that something just came over me and I couldn't control it.

"She asked what that 'something' might be, and I said I really didn't know, and that's when she asked would I like to hear her idea about it.

"What could I say but 'Yes, Mother,' and that's when she skewered me. 'I think it is God calling you, Madeline, and you're scared, as any sensible young woman should be.'

"Then the Rav—Mother Ravenel started quoting from 'The Hound of Heaven,' that whole first stanza all the academy girls have to memorize for Moral Guidance—about fleeing Him down the labyrinthine ways and in the mist of tears. By the time she got to hiding from Him 'under running laughter,' I knew exactly where she was going.

"But the toad was already perched on my tongue, ready to spring. I let her finish the stanza—'All things betray thee, who betrayest Me'— and give me that self-congratulatory, victorious look, and then I said, 'Whatever it is that might be calling me through my laughter, Mother, I hope I will have the restraint not to jump the gun on my vocation and ruin someone else's life.' "

Madeline paused for effect. "I guess I'd better stop here and explain that my aunt Antonia was the one whose life got ruined. She and Mother Ravenel, who was then her best friend, Suzanne, had pledged to take their first vows together at the end of their senior year. My Tilden grandparents were planning this huge party for both of them— Suzanne's family had disowned her, you see, and wouldn't even come up with the dowry; the Order ended up paying for her—and then Suzanne jumps the gun and enters at spring break, without telling anyone. It broke Aunt Tony's heart. Aunt Tony was my mother's twin."

"Yes, I knew that. But then your aunt married Mr. Vick—"

"That was later. That was a whole other story. Though my mother sometimes says it was the same story played out to its ill-fated end."

"But there must have been more to it than that," said Mother Malloy. "Your having to leave Mount St. Gabriel's."

"Oh, it ended up being a mutual agreement between the Ravenel and me," said Madeline, not bothering this time to censure the family's pet sobriquet for the headmistress. "I was given a chance to apologize, and did so right there on the spot. I admitted I had been rude and disrespectful. I also knew I had hurt her and that I didn't regret it, but I did *not* admit that. Then she said we both needed to pray about what had taken place between us, and I was to come back a week later for another talk. Meanwhile, she said, we should keep this 'just between ourselves.' She likes to isolate people that way—keep all the secrets just between them and herself. But of course I went right home and told Mother and Daddy, and they both agreed I had gone too far to ever get back in her good graces. Daddy, who can't stand for anyone to find fault with his daughters, was all for my transferring to Mountain City High the very next day; he was even working out how he could buy me a car, though I was all of fourteen and couldn't have driven it. But Mama said it would look bad on my record if I didn't finish out my freshman year at Mount St. Gabriel's. She advised me to eat humble pie and let Mother Ravenel *think* she had awakened something in my heart, but say that I 'needed time to grow into it.' So I went back the following week and was modest and repentant and agreed with Mother Ravenel that I had lashed out at her because maybe I *was* afraid of the Big Somebody Who might be following me. The upshot was that before we parted we were hugging and she had made a huge concession—for her. I was allowed to finish out the year with my best efforts and she would just leave the part blank where a girl is invited, or not invited, back the following year and sign her name below. She said, 'I am going to take a chance on you. You know, St. Ignatius of Loyola said, Give me a child until he is seven and after that he is ours. Well, we will have had you for nine years, Madeline, and I believe wherever you go you will always be a lady and you will always belong to God.' "

"That is quite a story, Madeline," said Mother Malloy, after a thoughtful interim. "You'll understand why it wouldn't be appropriate for me to make any comment beyond that."

"Oh, sure, of course," agreed the girl, resuming her place on the bench beside the nun. "But you did promise to tell why you laughed."

"You said it yourself. It's such romantic nonsense. The night before her vows, Elizabeth Wallingford was surely caught up with all the challenges of founding her order. And she and Fiona Finney were already making plans to go to America. And here we are, as a result of their dreams." She pulled a watch from a deep pocket. "And I'm due back for my next class. Thank you, dear Madeline, you have revived me. Please tell your mother I'm eager to meet with her as soon as she can find time. And I want you to know I haven't forgotten what I promised you that first day: I'm doing my best to watch over Tildy's intrepid soul."

"I'll walk part of the way back with you, Mother." But not far enough to pass a Ravenel-manned window. "Now I'm feeling guilty that I talked the whole time about myself."

"But I asked you. Needless to say, what you've told me won't go any further."

"Oh, everybody knows all about it, Mother. It's just one more story bubbling away in the school stewpot. More stuff gets added every year and everyone tosses in their favorite spices and keeps stirring away. It's pretty thick, by now. And our family's various *contretemps* figure prominently in the mixture, of course, though I'd say by this time Mother Ravenel's contributions dominate the brew."

"You and Tildy have such a command of language."

"Wait till you meet Mama. She adds a tang all her own, a bit like Tabasco sauce served over dry ice. Uh-oh!"

Mother Ravenel, traveling at her usual velocity, had wheeled suddenly into view on the path. "Why, Madeline, how nice to see you!" she drawled, her aviator sunglasses concealing whatever else she might be feeling.

Once more, Madeline regurgitated her spiel about the half days at "Mountain City Low School," which seemed to go down well with Mother Ravenel.

"And so you just came by for a little meditation in our grotto," prompted the headmistress.

"Well, no, Mother. Actually, Mama asked me to drop by and tell Mother Malloy that she'll meet with her next week to discuss Tildy's grades."

"Oh, is there some problem with Tildy I wasn't informed of? Maybe you could stop by my office after chapel, Mother Malloy, and fill me in."

"Certainly, Mother," replied the younger nun, looking discomfited by the implied reprimand from her superior.

Now look what I've gone and done, thought Madeline, thoroughly peeved with herself. Why couldn't I just have told a little white lie about needing a spot of meditation in the good old grotto? The Ravenel always does that. Makes you say more than you meant to, and then somebody always gets skewered.

CHAPTER 11

Sister Bridget's Chore List

Around noon, July 31, 2001
Feast of St. Ignatius of Loyola
Grounds of the St. Scholastica Retirement House
   (formerly the Sanderson estate)
Milton, Massachusetts

I AM BROUGHT particularly low today, Lord. I have no money of my own and my eyes are failing and I have no means of escape. Though I can follow the sunlight on the white gravel of this driveway back and forth between the house and the gates, and though I can still walk without a cane if I choose my steps with care, someone persecutes me with relish. You know who I'm talking about. She is younger and stronger and grinds down my soul. Her heart is a stony place. If she were one of my old girls, I would summon her to my office and have a very serious talk with her about the advantages of *imitating* compassion until she learns to feel it. And if she didn't show improvement by the end of the year, out she'd go. But, and I am trying to appreciate the irony of this, Lord, I am one of *her* old girls now, and I can't go anywhere. What am I going to do?

This sun is hot, Suzanne. Let's go into the summerhouse. Be careful of the rickety steps.

I'll sit here, where I can't be watched from the house. She watches everything. Lord, please do something.

What would you have me do?

I won't ask You to smite her; we're not back in Old Testament times. I wouldn't even ask You to afflict her with some illness, because

I do feel compassion. Sister Bridget is one of Your sparrows and You know her exact feather count, just as You know mine.

What do you need in order to complete your soul's tasks?

The girls will be heartbroken if I don't get to finish *Mount St. Gabriel's Remembered.* I've made such a good start.

Why shouldn't you finish it?

You know why. But You want me to put it into words so I will see it for myself. My best time for dictating is the twilight hour before Compline. As You know, we have our ridiculously early supper so the cook can load the dishwasher and go home, and then I take a turn up and down the driveway and assemble my thoughts. By the time I go back to my room and press the Record button, the words pour out in fully formed sentences. But that's because they've had all day to organize themselves. That is my method; that is how I have always worked best.

You've always saved the evenings for your reflective composing, yes.

And then she posts the midsummer-to-Advent chore list on the refrigerator. Midsummer to Advent. In Your sight, a thousand years are the same as one evening, according to the Psalmist. But, given the life expectancy of an eighty-five-year-old human, midsummer to Advent is equivalent to roughly a decade in the life of a young adult. And, under the vow of obedience, I must now squander this precious portion of what is left of my creative span by telephoning all the hospitals and assisted-living facilities in the Boston area for their Catholic deaths that day. I dictate the names to Mother Galyon—excuse me, "Sister *Frances*"—who still has her eyesight. She sits across from me in the stifling little telephone parlor and writes them out for Compline prayers that night. The next day, Sister Bridget, who is both superior and provincial of our deplorably shrunken Order, sits down in her air-conditioned office and pens personal notes to the next of kin: *Just wanted you to know that our community of St. Scholastica prayed for your loved one, N, on the day of his/her death.* It makes for good PR, she says, and of course the next of kin join our mailing list for end-of-year solicitations.

As You know, Lord, I went to Sister Bridget and asked whether Sister Frances couldn't do the phoning as well as the writing part. "Sister Frances has offered it," I said. "She's right there in the room anyway; she can hear *and* see. It doesn't need the two of us." And You heard what my superior said: "Your voice has class, Sister Suzanne. People remember it." I always warned my girls away from that word. It's the quickest way in the world, I used to tell them, to let people know you don't have any. I just wish I'd stopped myself from adding that Sister Frances knew how important this project was to me, and that I am always most fluent in the evening, after having had the day to organize my material. Because that gave Sister Bridget the perfect opportunity to say I had become obsessed with this "vanity project" backed by wealthy alumnae and with "glorifying my own creativity" at the expense of the community.

She's all of sixty-five, and she disciplines sisters twenty years her senior as though she were their novice mistress. Always on the lookout for faults. Like when Sister Odelie—I must say it's hard for me to think of our math-whiz Mother Odom as "Odelie"—was preparing our meals on the cook's Thursdays off and Sister Bridget made her stop in the middle of whisking a hollandaise because she was "puffed up with pride." I hope I was never guilty of misusing my power like that—back when I had some. Lord, I have been in Your service for sixty-seven years. But my heart is in this school memoir, which she calls a "vanity project." The question is, How can I honor my vow of obedience and follow my heart?

You always wake early, Suzanne.

Always have. Before the light, before the birds.

What then?

Well, first, as You know, I feel my way down the hall to the community bathroom. A full bladder can certainly dull the ardor of an elderly person's morning prayers. Then, since my knees have gone stiff, I get back in bed and You and I have our first exchange of the day. My mind is rested and receptive and I think I hear You best then.

You're hearing me now.

Yes, Lord.

We're going to change your routine. Tomorrow morning, as soon as you come back from the community bathroom, go straight to your desk. Press Record on your machine and speak to whatever floats up about the school. Don't stop to arrange topics or prettify sentences.

Even before I pray?

Look on it as a form of prayer. Your first offering, uncluttered, unedited.

But this "floating" method may pose a problem, Lord. What worries me is, How do I keep the thoughts meant for my soul's repair . . . from infiltrating the published memoir?

You can't.

But the whole project will be changed.

If you are changed already by this project, why shouldn't your narrative have room for change, too? No more analysis for now, Suzanne. Tomorrow morning, after the community bathroom, sit down at your desk, press Record, and simply speak to your girls from the urgency of your heart. Let's see where that takes you.

Holy Daring: A Predawn Digression

My dear girls, this morning I want us to consider together what our foundress meant by "holy daring."

That Mother Wallingford (1863–1930) was a remarkable woman is evident from what she accomplished in her lifetime and the legacy she has left to all of us who had the good fortune to pass through the portals of Mount St. Gabriel's.

Elizabeth Wallingford embraced a life of "holy daring." She coined the phrase in her 1890 commentary on the book of Acts,[1] written during her twenty-ninth year when she was drawing near to her conversion, going to Mass daily at John Henry Newman's church in Littlemore with her good friend Fiona Finney, and seeking guidance about a vocation from Father Basil Maturin at Cowley, Oxfordshire. It was Father Maturin, just returned from a ten-year preaching tour in the United States, who enchanted Elizabeth with stories of American opportunities for the religious. And, as I've said to you before, I think it is very likely that his talks at Cowley with Elizabeth were what ultimately tipped him toward the Catholic faith he was to embrace in his fiftieth year, in 1897.

Another of our foundress's alluring phrases, one she came to use more and more frequently during the course of her work in America, according to Mother Finney,[2] was "a woman's freedom in God." I'm sure you remember that one! I sprinkled it liberally, like seeds that would fall where they might, into our biweekly "Moral Guidance for Modern Girls" sessions, though I never went into much detail: it would have been precipitate of me, and now I will tell you why.

1. This lively and passionate commentary, "Charged by the Holy Ghost," is preserved in the appendix of Mother Fiona Finney's invaluable chapbook, *Adventures with Our Foundress* (Mountain City Printing Company, 1933).

2. *Ibid.,* passim.

The concept of "a woman's freedom," to a group of teenage girls in those pre–"women's lib" times, was a very incendiary notion all by itself. It would have invited reckless misuse. And "a woman's freedom in God" would have been—well, how can I best put it? If "a woman's freedom" evokes a stack of firewood laced with nice dry kindling in the home fireplace, then "a woman's freedom in God" would be like my handing over a box of matches, back when you were under my care, and saying, "Girls, this box of matches has been blessed by the Pope: help yourselves and strike as you will!"

When you came to me in the academy, most of you were fourteen going on eighteen. Over the years, some of you would seek me out after the "Moral Guidance" sessions and say, "Please, Mother, I want to hear more about this holy daring and freedom in God our foundress was always talking about."

And to those of you I thought were ready, I doled it out with discretion. If there are any of you who felt I "jumped the gun," I ask your pardon, wherever you are.

Well, digressions must not go on too long; otherwise they might usurp the flow. But perhaps in a future digression further along in this school memoir, I will elaborate, as much for myself as for you, on these connected topics of holy daring and a woman's freedom in God.

—from *Mount St. Gabriel's Remembered: A Historical Memoir,* by Mother Suzanne Ravenel

CHAPTER 12

Girls' Voices Upstairs

A Sunday evening in late October 1951
The Vick house
Mountain City, North Carolina

HENRY VICK WAS not the sort of person whom one would casually ask, "Are you happy?" But if someone *had* asked, he would have said he was happy at his drawing board, at home or at the office. He loved watching buildings go up; perhaps the excavations thrilled him even more. He looked forward to his first sip of scotch in the evenings, enjoyed playing through the Bach preludes and Chopin ballades he had worked up over the years, and was at his happiest in conversations that kindled some degree of enlightenment in both parties. He loved the Mass and felt himself replenished by God's mystery each time he received the sacrament.

Chloe's coming to live with him had brought added items to the list: the many ways the girl reminded him of his sister, Agnes: the neat turn of the long, narrow foot as she set the porch swing in motion; the same profile, the stubborn chin and beaky family nose sweetened by the pursed lips and delicate stem of neck. Perhaps more dear to him were the moments when Chloe was like no one but herself.

At the forefront of Agnes's personality had been the flash and stab of her wit, the apt conceit ("Rex hasn't had it easy since the war. Bombing the enemy was a lot more exciting than bombing bugs") and the mordant self-directed put-down ("Everyone saw my panties").

At first Henry had wondered if his niece lacked a sense of humor. Then he realized that what Chloe found funny came from her quiet perusal of what went on around her, until out would come a response worth waiting for. ("Don't you think Mother Ravenel would have made a neat leading lady, Uncle Henry? I mean, if she hadn't already found her perfect role.")

The two of them could work in the same room, Henry drafting plans for the new library and Chloe curled up in her favorite armchair doing lessons or making sketches of her uncle on his high stool at the drafting board or playing the piano. She was so easy to be with that he missed her ahead of time when he toted up the few years left of her girlhood in his house. He hoped her future husband would treasure her rare form of tact. Her quiet, steady gift for keeping you company without invading your solitude was probably, Henry thought, why she could produce such uncanny likenesses of people going about their business.

Recently, Chloe's new friend had entered the picture. On the nights when Tildy stayed over, the girls kept to themselves in Chloe's room, which Henry had stopped thinking of as "Agnes's room" even before he and Smoky Stratton had rearranged its furniture to accommodate a sofa bed for Tildy, carried up on the capable shoulders of Smoky's versatile retainer and chauffeur, John.

The two girls were upstairs now (they had left the door open, which honored him), and he could hear Tildy's regular barrage of prompts and pronouncements interspersed with Chloe's murmurs as she concentrated on their very important project, for which he had loaned his (and his late father's) drafting table, dismantling it from the corner where it had stood since this house was built and carrying it upstairs piece by piece, along with the high swivel stool, to reassemble it in Chloe's room.

So this is love, Henry thought, smiling at his own discomfort: the prominent architect scrunched into his niece's abandoned armchair, his drafting pad backed by Rosa's breadboard balanced awkwardly on his crossed thighs, hoping to smuggle a few clean lines of his proposed new municipal library back through the trustees' clutter of antiquated add-ons and impractical revisions.

So that Chloe, upstairs with her best friend, Henry's niece by marriage, could have access to the best drafting surface on which to compose her ambitious group portrait of their classmates for the ninth-grade bulletin board.

✠

"YOU KNOW WHAT I can't wait for," said Tildy, balancing on one leg beside Chloe's drafting stool, "is when you walk into class with it rolled up under your arm. And you go up to her desk on the platform in your usual modest way and hand it up to her and say, 'Mother Malloy, here is something I created for our bulletin board. That is, if, in your judgment, it's good enough.' Then you'll say, 'Remember how, the other day, our class president asked me to come up with something artistic and then *you* said, Mother, that we should all think of ways we could make our bulletin board uniquely our own . . .' "

"You don't think I should say her name?"

"You have already *said* her name, and just 'Mother' is respectful enough for the second time round. Even Raving Ravenel would say so."

"No, I meant . . . Maud's name."

"I think it carries more weight if you say 'our class president.' *Her* saying it would be like just any old person in the class had asked you. Oh, for Christ's sake, say whatever you like. *I* don't care."

"Now don't go getting huffy with me, Mary Tilden, or you'll wobble my concentration."

"Oh, heaven forfend, Miss Chloe, that your artistic concentration be *wobbled* by this huffy peon. I don't give a piddle what you say, I really don't. I'm not even mad at her anymore. She serves her purpose in the firmament. I merely thought that 'class president' is the kind of protocol that cool Boston Malloy laps up."

"Uncle Henry is right. You are never at a loss for words, Tildy. Though I'm not sure I'd want to hear you exercising your vocabulary on me behind my back."

"I wouldn't want you to, either. If you heard me describe you behind your back, your precious modesty would be a thing of the past."

"Well . . ." Chloe disguised her pleasure by frowning over her choice of brown shades from the handsome box of pencils her uncle had given her. She plucked out the raw umber and, for contrast, etched in some shadows behind the flaxen-haired Dutch girls.

"Why are you doing the girls in the back row first?"

"Because they're at the top. I always work down. It keeps you from smearing."

"When I used to color, I always did my favorite parts first and filled in the rest after."

"That was with crayons. Besides, how do you know Hansje Van Kleek and Beatrix Wynkoop aren't my favorite parts?" Teasing, Chloe had learned, went a long way toward deterring Tildy from rampant bossiness.

"Ha, ha. But seriously, just between us, Chloe, why is it that some girls are just always *background*?"

"How do you mean, background?" Hansje and Beatrix had the same blunt haircuts. They both wore gray double-breasted topcoats with velvet collars. But Beatrix had her expectant smile, whereas things in Hansje's expression didn't match. It was as though two people were having a fight on Hansje's face.

"I mean background for the others."

"What others?"

"The ones who matter."

"And who might they be?" Tildy's snobbery was sometimes just breathtaking.

"Now, don't go all arch with me, Miss Chloe. You know as well as I do that some girls just stand out—you think of them first—and the rest make a sort of fill-in. Of course, it's not the kind of thing I would say in public."

"You're not in public, so why not name names?" Chloe moved on across the back row of her sketch: next came sultry Marta Andreu with her cast-down velvety lashes and her ultrafeminine way of hugging herself against the North American cold. Chloe's mouth watered at the prospect of doing justice to Marta's purple shawl with green fringe worn over the vicuña coat her father had sent from New York.

"Well, take our mothers' class for a start, the class of '34. There were twelve girls in that class; you can count them in the yearbook. But how many can you name from memory? Okay: your mother, Agnes Vick. And my mother and aunt, Cornelia and Tony Tilden. And Ringleader Ravenel, the former Suzanne. After that the mind just blanks."

"Tildy, your argument has about a million holes in it. We're naming them first because they're ours. I mean, there was Elaine Frew's mother, Francine Barfoot. She was one of the oblates, and if the oblates weren't the inner circle I don't know what was. My own mother wasn't even an oblate."

"But the oblates *wanted* Agnes. Old Francine was just a fill-in. She played the flute and did what everyone told her because she was so thrilled to be included."

Chloe slammed down her pencil. She had put too many purple highlights in Marta's hair, detracting from the purple shawl before she even started on it. She felt suddenly hostile toward her friend and was glad Tildy would be leaving soon. Under the strict new regime following Mother Ravenel's recent ultimatum about grades, Tildy was allowed to spend only one night away from home, and that night had been last night. In a half hour or so, the Stratton Packard would roll into the driveway and Tildy, with a martyr's sigh, would stuff her hairbrush and last-minute incidentals into her smart patent leather bandbox and clump peevishly downstairs into John's silent custody.

And when, at that moment, a motor's thrum was heard in the driveway, making Tildy cry out, "Oh, no! This isn't fair!" Chloe felt vindicated.

Tildy went flying across the room and flung up a window sash. "John, you are *way* too early," she screeched into the darkness.

"It's me, little one," Madeline Stratton's blithe voice trilled back. "But I'm going to visit with Uncle Henry first, so you girls still have some time."

☩

HENRY VICK, OF course, heard the indoor-outdoor calling between the sisters and stifled his disappointment that it was not the Strattons' chauffeur. It had been dark for hours and he had been anticipating a neat, cordial transition. ("Ah, John, come in. Tildy, John is waiting downstairs. You're very welcome, honey, always good to have you. Come back soon, hear?") And then maybe he'd play a little Bach and, as his father used to put it, climb the wooden hill for an early Sunday night bedtime. He was meeting with the library board again tomorrow and not looking forward to standing his ground against their pigheaded insistence on a superfluous portico with columns.

But instead here was Madeline, whom he genuinely liked. She

brought her own aura into the room, not at all turbulent, like Tildy's. She was debonair and conversant, but seemed to keep the emotional side of herself in reserve. Unusual for a girl of sixteen, though tonight, wearing her hair skinned back by a bandanna, she could have passed for a woman of twenty-five. She looked, in fact, ready to have an early night herself.

"What a nice surprise," he said. "Come to keep an old man company."

"That was my intention, but—oh dear," she said, spotting the drafting pad facedown on the arm of the chair, "I've interrupted your work. And, I didn't mean"—she colored slightly—"that I think you're old."

"I know. I'm the one who said it. What can I get you, Madeline?"

"Thank you, nothing. I bolted down practically a whole pitcher of ice water before I left home. Oh, Henry, I am so pleased with myself tonight."

"Sit down and tell me all about it."

Madeline did look triumphant, in her dungarees and an enormous old cable-knit pullover that Henry figured must be from her father's closet.

"Please excuse my slovenly getup," she said, seating herself at the corner of the sofa with the straight-backed aplomb of a full-skirted deb, "but I've been switching rooms with Tildy. It's a surprise for her. Flavia and I have been slaving nonstop, emptying drawers and dragging furniture, ever since I saw you all at Mass this morning. Tildy has no idea—I only thought of it myself during Monsignor's sermon. Then Flavia reminded me it was getting close to Tildy's curfew and there was nobody but me to come get her. John's out at the Swag with Daddy, putting in some improvements before hunting season starts, and Mama's working late at the studio. I'm hoping this will give Tildy a new start. She's always coveted my room."

"Now your room is—which?"

"On the upstairs front. Aunt Tony's old room. It gets the afternoon sun and will be more cheery for studying. Mother Ravenel skewered the poor child last week, as only the Ravenel can skewer. Tildy has six weeks to bump up her grades and improve her attitude, or else."

"Or else, what?"

"Or else Mother Ravenel writes 'On probation' on the back of

Tildy's next report card. And it will go on Tildy's 'permanent record,' which the Ravenel always makes sound like eternal damnation."

"That does sound ominous."

Henry recalled several chaste trips upstairs to Antonia's room for the purpose of carrying down boxes to be stored in his father's house while they enjoyed their Roman wedding trip. Both of them had been virgins, she by choice, he by default. Antonia was twenty-one, working full-time in the sisters' fledgling photography studio. He was the twenty-five-year-old junior partner of Vick & Vick, feeling himself agreeably stretched by sudden new responsibilities, drawing and re-drawing to scale his father's frenzied sketches for the ambitious indoor shopping arcade (touted by the press as "the first of its kind in the South" but left in limbo at Malcolm Vick's death, the site later requisi-tioned by the Defense Department when Roosevelt entered the war) and rushing around town collecting paperwork and signatures so his fi-ancée's passport could be issued with her married name. Neither had traveled abroad. A few locals who considered themselves politically au courant opined that honeymooning in Mussolini's Italy could be iffy. But Henry wanted to see the architecture and Antonia wanted to visit the churches. And Henry's father had arranged for the couple to have an audience with the Pope.

"Tildy's always loved my room—she'd bring in her storybooks and curl up beside me on the bed and we'd read. Or, rather, I would read to her. Flavia and I left my bed for her; it was too heavy for the two of us to move anyway. What I'm hoping is all those good memories of read-ing in it will make it more congenial for studying. She's really got to turn things around. There are no shades of gray in the Ravenel's color chart."

"But what about you? Will you feel congenial in your new room? Which room is it, by the way?"

"It's the back room on the same side of the house. It used to be Granny Tilden's sewing room, because it gets north light. It's never been cozy, but since they've made the new tunnel cut through the ravine, it faces a sea of red mud and monster machines. A very uncozy view for a young girl going through so many changes herself."

"But you can dispense with coziness?"

"Oh, Henry, there's so much I'm ready to dispense with! I just wish I'd thought of the room switch a lot sooner. Thank God the monsignor is an uninspiring preacher, or poor little Tildy would still be sleeping there tonight."

Henry strained to hear the girls' voices upstairs. His wish for Madeline to take Tildy and go home so he could have his early night had been completely preempted by astonishment: how could this vivid young woman speak so passionately about letting things go?

"At sixteen, I would think, a person like yourself would want to . . . consume life—stuff as much of it as you could into your pocket."

"Is that what you wanted at sixteen, Henry? To stuff as much life as you could into your pocket?" She squinted up at him as though spying at the remnants of his sixteen-year-old soul through a narrow opening.

"I said a person like yourself. I was more—well—" He grabbed for the nearest comparison: "Uninspiring, like Monsignor's preaching. I did my duties, I put in my preparations, but the result was never brilliant. Not even close to it."

"Why, that's just criminal modesty, Henry Vick. Who did the newspaper building and who's designed the new library? You are one of the most distinguished men in this town."

He let this pass. Poor girl: in this town, it might possibly be true. "At sixteen, the thing I was probably best at was being a good brother to Agnes. Though she was always the quicker one, she *was* four years younger, and I guess I took it on myself to make sure she felt protected and appreciated."

"Why don't I have any memories of your sister? I can see your father striding to his office with his rolled umbrella and, I'm sorry to say, always frowning, and I remember your mother once in a floaty gown at the club. I couldn't have been more than five—she stooped down and kissed me and called me 'Adelaide.' Mama told me I said afterward, 'That lady's perfume smells like Lavoris,' though I don't remember saying it."

"Well, you were right on target." Henry laughed ruefully. "Poor Mother. The reason you wouldn't have seen Agnes around town when you were little was that she went away with Merry while he finished engineering school and then he joined the Air Corps and they moved from pillar to post."

"And there was Chloe growing up in all those strange places. Speaking of wanting one's little sister to feel protected and appreciated, I'm glad about Tildy's friendship with Chloe. It seems so healthy—more

like a fair exchange." Madeline's countenance clouded with an unspoken afterthought.

"A fair exchange?"

"Their qualities complement each other's. Each contributes something. Tildy's last friendship didn't really bring out the best in either
girl."

"You mean Maud Norton. She has certainly become a handsome
girl, though a bit flighty." He did not add *like her mother.*

"Everyone assumed Tildy was the stronger personality, certainly our
family did, but now I'm not so sure. I think there was something in the
combination of those two that created a sort of unholy alliance. When
Maud entered third grade and the other girls were speculating about
her, it gratified Tildy to take the new girl under her wing and play pa-
troness. Once Tildy even proposed to Mother and Daddy that they *adopt*
Maud. Mama said that someone else would most likely be adopting
Maud any day now, because Lily was not exactly suffering for boy-
friends. And then as time went on, Mama said Lily would soon be dating the sons of her former dates. Gracious, Henry, how rude of me! You
went out with Lily, didn't you?"

"For a little while, yes. But she was way too lively and ambitious to
put up with a morose widower like me for very long. What about this
unholy alliance you say the girls created?"

"As a team they influenced the others, made the class do whatever
they had decided on. But it was a joint thing. I don't think Tildy could
have done it all by herself, even with her wild imagination, and Maud
certainly couldn't have by *herself:* she was a social nonentity until Tildy
chose her. But the two of them made a powerful little engine—who was
the engine and who was the fuel I'm not sure even matters. You need
them both to drive anywhere."

"So where did they drive?"

"Well, their first drive was, pardon the pun, driving off a lay teacher
who had been there forever. Mrs. Prince."

"Oh, Agnes had Mrs. Prince."

"Yes, Mama's class had her, I had her. She was a well-meaning fix-
ture. Mama always said that Mrs. Prince wanted too much to be liked
and that could be the undoing of anyone."

"Uh-oh. Watch out for wanting to be liked too much." Henry could
just hear Cornelia Stratton's pitiless tone as she framed her pronounce-

ment, and he couldn't help wondering to what degree she had inspired the driving out of Mrs. Prince.

"Why, Henry, you don't strike me as giving two hoots about being liked."

"I like to be respected, which is a version of the same thing. But what about yourself, Madeline? How much do you care about being liked?"

Madeline drew her father's baggy sweater up around her neck. "I'd first need to ask, Liked by whom? Even if you are, in your usual way, Henry, deflecting the spotlight from yourself."

"By all means, do ask it."

Am I so starved for adult company that I am enjoying this dialogue with a sixteen-year-old girl, he wondered, or is it that we have found our way to topics I don't ordinarily touch on during the course of a business day?

"Well, unlike Tildy, I never needed to have just one special 'best friend' I could tell everything to. Probably Mama has filled that role for me. We're still girls together, giggling in the darkroom about how interchangeable most boys are. Mama had me when she was nineteen, which is only three years older than I am now, and she's often told me she didn't really feel like a mother until she had Tildy, who was more of a childlike child. Mama says I was born an old soul, like her sister. Like Antonia, she says, I am wiser and larger-hearted than the average adult. I'm not sure that's so, but I am sure that Mama likes me as much as Mama likes anyone. Of course, Daddy would walk barefoot over broken glass for me or Tildy, but we're talking about liking here."

I'm sick of being told I'm an old soul, Antonia said to Henry during the very short span of time they were privileged to lie together as a sanctified couple and say whatever they pleased in the dark. *I want to be a brand-new soul starting out on life's adventure.* And he had said something not quite inspiring enough, like *Well, I hope you'll let me go with you.* To which she had responded with an impatient laugh, sounding in the darkness exactly like her caustic twin: *You already are with me, Henry, in case you hadn't noticed.*

"I've said something tactless, Henry. I see it in your face."

"No. I was recalling something Antonia said."

He saw how valiantly the girl strained to suppress her curiosity.

"While we were in Rome, Antonia told me she wanted to be a

brand-new soul starting out on life's adventure. I just wish she could have been granted the opportunity."

"Oh, *why* did she have to cross that street without looking?"

"Well, we were crossing together and I guess she assumed I was looking out for us both. She turned to say something. But she must have been a little ahead of me, because there was a roar and a thump and only one of us was on the ground. It was a small gray van, taking the corner too sharply. It went right on without slowing down and disappeared in traffic. Maybe the driver was unaware anything had been hit. Then people were shouting in Italian, and two very efficient *carabinieri* materialized instantly. The ambulance came remarkably soon after. This was Il Duce's faultlessly run city. But she was already gone."

"It must have been just— I can't imagine what I would have done in your place."

"I didn't do much of anything. Everything was organized for us. Our embassy and even the Vatican stepped in. Antonia and I had been received by Pope Pius XI the day before. All I had to do was sit in a room and speak into the receiver to my father and to the Tildens. Someone else even did the work of placing the calls. And then I was back in my old bedroom with Antonia's unpacked boxes in the corner. And not long after that, Father died, and after that came the war."

The girls chattered on upstairs.

"Oh, Uncle Henry, I didn't mean to dredge up all that old sorrow."

"Actually," Henry said, "it's nice to have remembered something so particular about her. To hear her say something she really did say. And you dredged that up for me, Madeline, for which I thank you."

"Oh my God, that is priceless!" Tildy shrieked.

Madeline stood up, all business, and marched to the foot of the stairs. "Okay, little one," she called up in her strong, trilling voice, "time for us to get going."

Did Henry only imagine he heard a note of relief at being ejected by duty from an embarrassing conversation?

CHAPTER 13

All Souls

Friday, November 2, 1951
All Souls' Day
Mount St. Gabriel's

FATHER LOHAN, HIS back to the people, knelt at the altar for the
noon Requiem Mass of All Souls' Day. *"Munda cor meum ac labia mea, om-*
nipotens Deus, qui labia Isaiae Prophetae calculo mundasti ignito . . ."

Maud, the non-Catholic, also on her knees, read the English trans-
lation on the right side of the missal. *Cleanse my heart and my lips, O*
Almighty God, Who didst cleanse the lips of the Prophet Isaias with a burning
coal . . .

She liked following along in the missal. This one, new to the pew
racks this school year, was arranged better, had larger type, and was
more lavish with illustrations. That must please Tildy, she thought. Before the coming of Chloe, Maud had knelt next to Tildy. Not because
they had been best friends but because everything at Mount St.
Gabriel's was alphabetical, and in their class, Norton had been followed
by Stratton. Even if Chloe hadn't been Tildy's new best friend, she
would still be placed now between Maud and Tildy, because Starnes
came between Norton and Stratton.

Maud could see Tildy, on the other side of Chloe, kneeling with her
gaze fastened on her open missal. Tildy did not turn the pages. In the
old days, Tildy would watch until Maud beside her turned her page, or
flipped back and forth between the front part of the book and the feast
of the day, and then Tildy would follow suit. Tildy could read the numbers at the tops of the pages fine, but letters played mean tricks on her.

In order to read, or do what passed for reading when Maud was not around to expedite things, Tildy had to go letter by letter, like making her way, she said, through a bunch of nasty, belligerent sheep, *dragging* the ones who had strayed into their proper places. It took her twice as long to do assignments and gave her headaches, but she had learned to do it. Now Chloe could be seen turning the page, but Tildy kept her gaze stubbornly riveted on the previous one. Had she stopped trying to keep up appearances? Or had she not chosen to share her weakness with her new friend?

Suddenly Maud felt close to tears.

"If we haven't heard something by Thanksgiving, it's not a good sign," Maud's anxious grandmother had murmured to Maud's mother last night, when the two women were putting away dishes in the kitchen.

"Oh, I am sick of this servile waiting on the whims of rich people."

"Keep your voice down, Lily."

"I'm sick of keeping my voice down."

"The child will hear."

"So let her. She's not a child and she might as well start learning that she may have to make her own way, as I did."

"Well, if so, I hope she will make it more wisely than you did."

"That is just below the belt, Mother."

"Well, I'm sorry if I spoke out of turn. But it's not easy, you know, running this place."

"I came back to help you, to make your life easier."

"You came back because you had nowhere else to go. You had a seven-year-old child with no—"

"I will not sleep in the same room with you, Mother, if you're starting on *this* tack."

"Go sleep in Mr. Foley's room then. He won't be back until the week after next."

"I just might. You know, Mother, when you're not denouncing me, you occasionally have good ideas. Maud's Julius Caesar costume was inspired. Only you could have draped her like that."

"Then be grateful for my good ideas when I have them. I'm not going to be around much longer."

"Oh, when have I heard *that* before?"

"Then you'll have our bed all to yourself. Until you decide to fill it up with somebody else. Though, if I were you, I'd be a little more practical this time."

On Halloween, the class had voted a split second place to Tildy as David Copperfield and Chloe as little Emily. Maud would just as soon they'd gotten her own first place. Mother Malloy, handing her the prize (a volume of Robert Burns's poems), said Maud looked "completely the emperor." And she did, with her powdered short hair, her tall form draped in Granny's painstaking toga. But Maud felt she had outgrown dressing up.

Why were the lips of the prophet cleansed by a burning coal rather than burnt to a crisp? That would be an okay question to ask Mother Malloy. Neither "impertinent" nor "slangy"—two of Mother Malloy's abominations—but something Maud really desired to understand. There was a world where you got burnt if you kissed a burning coal, and another world where a burning coal, or whatever it stood for, could cleanse you. The secret was how to transform the literal burning coal into the one that could make you a clean new person. Of all the adults in Maud's smudged life, Mother Malloy seemed to Maud her best hope for learning this secret.

Maud felt hopeful every time she recalled the half-hour conference about her proposed *David Copperfield* paper. Though it had started off badly with Mother Malloy's reaction to her title: "The Pungent Ache of the Soul in *David Copperfield*."

"What made you choose the word 'pungent,' Maud?"

"Well, it seemed closest to the kind of ache I want to write about, Mother."

"Then let's talk about that first. Tell me about this ache."

"It's David's ache when he's washing bottles in that factory. He's crushed in his soul. He thinks he will never get out of this low place and become what he knows he can be. He can't understand why a smart child like himself should be thrown away. While I was reading this, the ache I felt was his ache, but there was something else happening, too, from my side. And that's what I want to write about, how you can experience more of yourself as you follow a character through his story. If the story is good enough, I mean. Most stories aren't. Or they're not good enough to help you make the *transfer*. Because you can never stop remembering that this is just something some author is making up. If you don't feel the ache yourself, you can't come to grips with what it means to your life."

"And do you plan to report these *transfers* as they occur throughout the novel?" Mother Malloy, who had been listening carefully, seemed surprised but impressed.

"That's my plan, more or less," Maud recklessly bluffed. She really had not thought much beyond her initial brainstorm about the bottle-factory scene.

"It's a very ambitious plan for a five-page paper, Maud. Maybe too ambitious. You'll have to consolidate, keep it tight. And perhaps take a less dramatic title for now. Or certainly another adjective. 'Pungent' generally applies to a taste or smell. Perhaps you meant 'poignant,' which denotes something sharply painful to the feelings, though 'poignant' has been overused by the ladies magazines. Why don't you take a simple working title that will keep you true to your intention: 'The Universal Aches of David'—something like that. The perfectly right combination of words may suggest itself to you after the paper is finished. I've often found that to be the case in my own academic work."

What was the "perfectly right combination of words" to describe Mother Malloy's beauty? Pale, cool, classic, sculpted, *ethereal:* all, alas, had the ladies-magazine taint. Maud should know. Those stacks of Granny's *Journal*s and *Companion*s and *Redbook*s and *Good Housekeeping*s. Who, after Granny, devoured those stories like chocolate bars? Only now, after David and the bottle factory, they wouldn't satisfy as completely. Things you habitually loved were always getting downgraded. Like poor Tildy, when Anabel Norton's eyebrows had shot up on Worth Avenue over Tildy's photograph.

Mother Malloy's beauty was more than just her fortunate proportions, but exactly what more? Maud puzzled over this while at the same time trying to hide her chagrin that she probably *had* meant "poignant" and not "pungent." In the nun's long face, everything was at the right distance from everything else. Eyebrows tilting outward like wings. Wide-spaced gray eyes seemed darker under the hooded lids. Her nose was a fine straight line descending from brow to tip with no indent. What you called a "Grecian nose." Habitually she tucked her firm chin into the starched and pleated white neckcloth, as if hoping to be subsumed by her religious habit. But there was reserve and also a deterring dash of—what? Contempt? Surely not in a nun. What then? You loved

to look at her when she was at the blackboard, or just now, in full profile, kneeling in the nuns' choir stall up in the chancel, but you were a
little abashed when she chose to look directly at you. Because you could
see her attention was on you; she wanted you and all the Davids under
her care to be as distinguished as you had it in you to be. It was just that
you got the feeling that she cared about something else more.

"Words are difficult," Maud had said. "I mean, finding the most . . .
apt ones is."

Mother Malloy winced at the awkwardness of the "are" against the
"is," though Maud's grammar had been perfectly correct. She saw the
nun acknowledge this also, with a slight smile.

"But you are off to a fine start, Maud. I am eager to see what you are
going to write."

☩

THANKS TO HER mother, Agnes, Chloe knew all the Latin in the
Mass, from *"Dominus vobiscum"* to *"Ite, missa est."* She knew that the
prayer of the day's offertory was labeled "secret" in your missal because
you said it to yourself and not aloud. On this, the second Mass of All
Souls' Day, the "secret" was: "Be favorable, O Lord, to our supplications
for the souls of Thy servants and handmaids, for whom we offer Thee
the sacrifice of praise, that Thou wouldst vouchsafe to grant them
companionship with Thy Saints."

Agnes was now a handmaid, carrying her immortal soul, like a new-
laid egg, through the mists and weathers of her purgatorial assignments.

In the days when Captain Merriweather Starnes was still alive but
off fighting the war, Agnes gave Chloe her catechism lessons in their
different air base homes. Their faith had sat in the place of the absent
father at their many kitchen tables, scarred and stained by previous military families on the move. After Rex Wright became part of their lives,
Agnes had her own set of brand-new maple kitchen furniture, but the
new father who now made the third at their table felt they used their
faith to shut him out. After some unhappy scenes, catechism and Latin
were banished to the booth of the downtown diner. "This is our Upper
Room," Agnes would say, leaning forward on her elbows and pulling up
the skin of her face so she looked younger. "We are like the early Chris-

tians breaking bread in secret. Only our bread is Nabs cheese crackers with peanut butter."

"So we won't be thrown to the lions," Chloe had ventured once, but Agnes, a stickler for playing fair, did not laugh. "He's trying, darling," she'd said. "Let's give him the benefit of the doubt." And then with a flash of her mischief: "Because, frankly, I don't see what choice we have."

Et resurrexit tertia die secundum Scripturas. On the third day He rose again, according to the Scriptures.

Here was the thing Chloe dearly yearned to get her mind around.

For the first disciples, Agnes had told her, the Crucifixion of their teacher was not the end, and that's why the whole thing called Christianity had started. They told stories of the empty tomb, of his appearances to friends and even to some strangers, of him showing the awful wounds to Thomas the Doubter. These stories couldn't be proved as historical fact, but they were there in your mind, Agnes said.

However, she went on, they *also* talked of how their loving teacher was now freed from the limits of human frailties so he could be present to them at all times and in all places.

"If more people," Agnes said in the diner, "could only rise to that level where they understand that resurrection is just not the same thing as *resuscitation,* we wouldn't have all this literal-minded quibbling about what 'did or didn't happen.' "

If Chloe could only get to that level in her mind, then she might have Agnes, her own loving teacher, with her again.

She didn't want to imagine her mother rising from her grave. (Even though the grave was down east in the sunbaked Memorial Gardens of Barlow, surrounded by the veterans' flags and plastic flowers on strangers' graves. Uncle Henry had wanted Agnes buried in the family plot in shady Riverside Cemetery, within walking distance from the Vick house, but Rex Wright, as husband, had prevailed.) And she certainly didn't want her mother *resuscitated,* like in those horror stories where the person came back, but with some ghastly alteration.

What Chloe did want, now that Agnes could no longer live with her, was for Agnes to live in her and through her. And there were signs of this starting to happen, if only Chloe could be faithful and silent and hold on to what she *felt* she knew.

Sometimes people bonded together and had a shared secret—or

made one up, like the Red Nun oblates she was so tired of hearing about. As far as she'd been able to figure out, the oblates' secret hadn't done anyone much good.

But sometimes a real secret slowly made itself known to you alone. This was harder and lonelier, but if you kept faith with it and let it live inside you, it made you stronger.

The first signs of how this could happen—of her secret starting to live through her—had begun during Chloe's drawing of the ninth-grade girls, destined for the updated class bulletin board. This contribution was to have enhanced them both, Chloe because she was the artist and Tildy because she was the best friend of the artist and had come up with the idea.

Well, more or less. Maud—whom Tildy chose to refer to as "our president"—had asked Chloe to contribute "something *artistic* so it won't look like everybody else's bulletin board." And Tildy, as though Maud had never spoken, had pushed Chloe forward, saying, "*You* go give it a bit of *pizzazz.*" And then Mother Malloy had invited *all* the members of the class to think of ways to make the bulletin board uniquely theirs.

But it *had* been Tildy who'd had the brainstorm of the class portrait. "You have this amazing *knack.* You make people look exactly like themselves—*beyond* exactly, sometimes. It will be a masterpiece. Everyone will just be *bowled over.*"

And Chloe had gone along without a qualm. Certainly it was something she could do. As always, she looked forward to seeing what would rise out of the paper once she started to draw. And this would be more of a challenge because fifteen people—sixteen, counting Mother Malloy—would be rising out of the paper. First-quality materials were forthcoming, along with Uncle Henry's drawing board and stool, carried reverently up the stairs to the "artist's" room. Everyone awaited the masterpiece.

First she had sketched out her composition, putting the tallest girls in the back row. Maud was one of the tallest girls in the class—Tildy said she had shot up over the summer—but Maud would not stay in the back row. She positioned herself sideways, at the right side of the group, at the very edge of the pictorial space, almost as if she were getting ready to walk out of it. She was the only one in the picture whose whole body could be seen. The standing girls (and Mother Malloy) in the back row and the standing girls in the middle row were visible from the waist up only. The five girls in the front row, including Chloe herself, were kneeling, so you couldn't see their legs. Only an occasional saddle shoe or loafer and white sock peeked out.

Well, Maud was class president, so maybe there was a kind of protocol in having her standing to the side like that. Tildy hadn't complained when she saw the composition ready to receive its details.

But then other things started appearing.

"Oh my God, that's priceless!" Tildy had screamed that Sunday night, when Gilda Gomez's cheeks suddenly puffed out below her little pig eyes and her dainty, fat hands pushed up the lamb collar of her pink coat. Without really trying, Chloe had "got" Gilda, her clownish coddling of herself in a cold country. It had just appeared on the page.

After Madeline had taken Tildy home that Sunday night, and Uncle Henry remained below to play Bach, Chloe had climbed back on the drawing stool to work some more on morose Marta Andreu in her purple shawl. Suddenly another image of the Cuban girl swam up from the paper: a young Madonna with cast-down eyes, stunned by a secret sorrow. Feeling flush with her clairvoyant powers, Chloe had gone on to "do" the two Dutch girls in their matching chesterfield coats and blunt blond hair, only Beatrix's had that twirled-up strand she constantly fiddled with, and her slightly smarmy expectancy contrasted with Hansje's face, so interestingly at war with itself.

But after she was in bed, her mother's old room lit only by the orange glow of a streetlamp through the drawn curtains, something totally new and uncomfortable *thought itself into Chloe's mind.* That was exactly the way it had felt: as though a wiser consciousness had been gently waiting for the opportunity to insert itself into hers in order to show the possible repercussions from her "masterpiece."

For a start, what would Gilda Gomez feel if she were to see herself portrayed so "pricelessly" as a swelling pig in pink, comically hugging her furs to herself in an alien climate? What would each girl feel when she confronted herself in Chloe's group portrait? Despite Tildy's snooty theory about some girls "just being background" for certain others, didn't each and every one of them privately regard herself as the centerpiece?

What a Dumbo I have been, Chloe had realized after that first bedtime infusion from the wiser mind. I must have been brainwashed by

Tildy's plan. And though Chloe continued to dabble at the picture, she no longer expected to make it public. What had she been thinking? Realistically, there was no chance their teacher would ever have let it go up on the bulletin board. *What a disaster, if I had walked into class with this thing rolled up under my arm and "modestly" presented it for Mother Malloy's approval!*

Tildy had been furious, of course. "What do you mean you're not going on with it? Are you crazy? It's already *there.* You couldn't stop now if you tried. You've even done *us.* You've colored in my beaver coat. You have Dorothy Yount wiping her eye exactly the way she does, and you've caught that furtive sideways look that Becky Meyer gets when she's trying to be remote. It's the best thing you've ever done!"

"Whatever it is, it needs to stay private."

"That is just stupid!"

"It would have been a lot stupider if we had shown this to Mother Malloy. She would have thought much less of us."

"I don't see why. You have revealed the secret sides of some of these people, what makes them *them!*"

"Has it ever occurred to you that 'these people' might not want their secret sides, as seen by somebody else, posted on the bulletin board?"

Tildy had given Chloe a long, searching look.

"Did your uncle say something?" she demanded. "Who has been influencing you?"

My mother, I think, Chloe could have answered. She might even have taken it a step further. It wouldn't be hard to convince Tildy's dramatic imagination that Agnes as spirit had been regularly "haunting" her old room at night to infuse wisdom and fair play into her daughter: this would have become Chloe and Tildy's secret; it would have made them closer.

But it would have diminished the lonelier secret, and Chloe preferred to keep faith with that.

And even this choice—to keep her secret a secret—might be one more infusion from Agnes, who herself, at Chloe's age, in refusing to join the oblates, had rejected the easier bonds of a shared secret.

"Nobody has been influencing me," Chloe had told Tildy. "I just asked myself how I would feel if I were those other girls."

"Which other girls?"

"Oh, any of the ones you call 'background.' "

Stalemated, Tildy had uttered her characteristic "hmff." But then, rallying, she had demanded, "So what *will* our great artist contribute to the communal endeavor?"

"I thought maybe a portrait of the school building, a front elevation, poking out of clouds and mist."

"Well, *that* will certainly be safe" was Tildy's scornful response.

ET VERBUM CARO *factum est,* said Father Lohan, his voice thickening with congestion. And the Word was made flesh.

Here all genuflected.

Et habitavit in nobis. And dwelt among us. *"Deo gratias,"* chimed a chorus of girls' voices.

Now they would file out of chapel, row by row, class by class, and walk around the east side of the building and down to the nuns' burial place in the cedar grove. Father Lohan would cense the grave of Mother Elizabeth Wallingford and then the graves of the other nuns. Chloe knew exactly what was coming next because Agnes had told her all about the girls' solemn yearly march to the nuns' cemetery on All Souls' Day at Mount St. Gabriel's.

She walked in silent single file down the narrow woodland path with the others, as though she had been doing it for decades.

CHAPTER 14

More Indignities

*August 11, 2001, on a rainy, windy morning, immediately following the Mass
Feast of St. Clare of Assisi*
St. Scholastica Retirement House (formerly the Sanderson estate)
Milton, Massachusetts

LORD, IS THIS another silence like my 1952–53 exile in that serpents' den on the Battery? You later said that You were with me that whole horrible year Reverend Mother sent me to care for my mother. You were there even in the outermost darkness of my mistrust, You said. I don't mistrust You now, but I have to take it on faith that You are hearing me, since You won't let me hear You.

Please, remember in me that I am worth something.

Is it that I talk too much? My retreat master, Father Krafft, kept telling me that joke about the old monk yakking all day long to himself in the garden. A new novice finally gets up the nerve to ask him, "Are you always praying, Father?" "Always! Always!" the old monk tells him. "But don't you run out of things to say, Father?" "That's what I keep hoping!" cries the old monk.

Yesterday I overheard Sister Bridget gossiping about me in the kitchen with the home helper, Lanie, who comes to see to Mother Odom's needs since her stroke.

"Every time I pass the blind nun's door," Lanie was saying, "she's in there talking a blue streak. Is she praying, or what?"

"No," said Sister Bridget, "she is talking her memoirs into a fancy machine some rich women from her old school bought for her. They are going to publish them and then she will be so swollen with pride the rest of us won't have breathing space in this house."

Well, I will keep talking into my fancy machine, but I will give You a rest.

Father Krafft gave me a prayer to say, which I never said much because I liked my conversations with You better. It's attributed to St. Ambrose, the eloquent bishop of Milan, but I have my doubts. Why would someone who prized words as highly as St. Ambrose compose such a prayer? Nevertheless, in memory of Father Krafft (how I wish I could consult him about Your silence!) I will now say it: *Let thy good spirit enter my heart and there be heard without utterance, and without the sound of words speak all truth.*

The blind nun will listen for You in the silences of her heart.

Holy Daring: A Noonday Digression

My dear girls, today at St. Scholastica's retirement house in Milton, we celebrated the Feast of St. Clare of Assisi. I stayed on in the chapel afterward, as it was too rainy and windy for my morning walk, and as I knelt there I was mulling over many things, including the provocative ideal of "holy daring" that our foundress bequeathed to us, along with her compelling concept of "a woman's freedom in God."

Clare lived only fifty-nine years (1194–1253). That seems such a short time when you think of all she accomplished. Of course, she had St. Francis as her inspiration and mentor: it was he who, accompanied by his monks, cut off her hair and gave her a rough tunic and sent her off, at age eighteen, to shelter with some Benedictine nuns until he could install her and her "poor ladies" (later known as the Poor Clares) in the monastery he was restoring for them at San Damiano. By twenty-one, she was the mother to her order; two of her sisters and even her mother joined the order. By the end of her life, Clare had founded twenty-two other houses. She was the first woman in the West to write a rule for monastics. Compared with Pope Innocent's rule, which went into great detail about what the nuns were to wear, and how many grilles and double locks it would take to shield them from womanly temptations, her rule was full of joyful good sense. Wear frugal garments, she instructed, to imitate the poverty of the Holy Child in the manger. When the serving sisters had to leave the convent on business, instead of warning them against looking at strangers and inviting evil, Clare told them "to praise God when they saw beautiful trees, flowers, and bushes, and to praise Him in all the people and creatures they met along the way." Under her rule, each community elected eight sisters "from the most discerning ones" to provide counsel to the abbess. The shared power was less demanding on the abbess, and the abbess also relinquished some of her power. Clare's life was a true embodiment of "holy daring" and "a woman's freedom in God."

Well, on this rainy day I have been mulling some more on "holy daring" ever since Mass this morning. I wish I could lay my hands on Elizabeth Wallingford's commentary on the book of Acts, "Charged by the Holy Ghost," which she wrote during her twenty-ninth year when she was drawing near to her conversion. The text, as you know, is preserved for us in the appendix of Mother Fiona Finney's chapbook, *Adventures with Our Foundress,* which I don't have, and even if I did wouldn't be able to read—someone would have to read it to me. But let me see if I can recall the apposite points for this little digression.

Luke tells us in the book of Acts that the Apostles' missionary journeys were determined by the Holy Ghost. We read how the Holy Ghost "forbids" them to preach the word in Asia, when they'd already gone throughout the regions of Phrygia and Galatia. Likewise, they get all the way up to Mysia, which was a major Jewish center in northwest Asia Minor, but when they attempt to cross the frontier into Bithynia the Holy Ghost again says no. Employing the vision of a man begging them to "help us in Macedonia," the Holy Ghost reroutes them eastward again and across the Aegean and into Macedonia.

All this is right there in the Bible for us to read, but our foundress, when she was still Elizabeth Wallingford, the Anglican spinster in Oxfordshire, was moved to apply her critical intelligence to the book of Acts because she was trying to trace that "pure line" from Peter and Paul to the present-day church. You might say the Holy Ghost was routing her on her spiritual journey. And in writing her commentary, "Charged by the Holy Ghost," she formulated the concept of "holy daring."

Now, mere "daring" by itself can lead, our foundress writes, to folly and the destruction of one's mission. What if the Apostles had "dared" to cross the frontier into Bithynia because it was, well, daring? After all, Bithynia was a challenge. It was a great source of wealth to the Roman Empire and therefore was very efficiently run by local governors. In dealing with any threats to public order or accepted institutions, the governors were allowed wide powers of discretion. We know from Pliny's letters to the emperor Trajan, which were written seventy years *after* the Apostles' missions, that Christians were still being punished in Bithynia if successfully denounced.

If the Apostles had dared to cross into Bithynia, it would have been daring, all right, but it might have been their last stop.

Which is where the "holy" part of "holy daring" comes in. Holy daring, our foundress said, lets itself be guided by divine improvisation. And divine improvisation is a matter of being in service to a work larger than yourself and being "of one heart" with the others who "belong together with you" in that work.

I think it would be a wonderful spiritual exercise, the next time you have a rainy day, to take the sixteenth book of Acts (where the Holy Ghost is rerouting them) and the life of Clare of Assisi and the life of our foundress and her "fellow adventurer," Fiona Finney, and meditate on the ways they accepted the call of service with joyful good sense and in the spirit of holy daring. I know this little meditation has certainly improved my spirits on this very gloomy day in Milton, Massachusetts.

—from *Mount St. Gabriel's Remembered: A Historical Memoir,* by Mother Suzanne Ravenel

CHAPTER 15

Tildy Struggles

Monday afternoon, December 10, 1951
Second week of Advent
Mother Malloy's office
Mount St. Gabriel's

THIS ROOM IS a far cry from Mother Ravenel's office, with its view of the western ranges and every shelf and wall crammed with trophies of school accomplishments and framed photographs of pet students and dignitaries posing with the headmistress, with and without her sunglasses.

Mother Malloy's office looks out on the gloomy cedar grove surrounding the nuns' cemetery and down on a portion of the shale driveway where young Mark, Jovan's grandson, is taking advantage of the last of the day's sunshine to simonize the school station wagon for its trips to the train station and the airport, Mark and Jovan spelling each other to get all the boarders embarked on their Christmas vacations.

Except for the textbooks on the shelves and several piles of papers arranged neatly on the office desk just now basking in the last sad burst of seasonal light from the corner window, there is no evidence, other than her accepting presence on the dreary horsehair sofa, of the room's current mistress. The pictures on the walls, old brownish photographs of Mount St. Gabriel's when the trees and shrubberies were younger and sparser, seem so settled in their places as to acquiesce in being overlooked. But Tildy would a million times rather be in this unprepossessing office than in Ravenel's dazzling and dreaded shrine to herself.

"Ah, Tildy, come," says Mother Malloy, smiling and patting a place on the sofa. There is a loved and trusted old book, with pictures carefully colored by Tildy's first-grade self, on Mother Malloy's lap, and a block of lined notepaper. Tildy, sitting down beside the nun, knows what is coming and therefore feels no apprehension and shame clumping in her chest.

"*Votre père, Tildy, est-il à la maison?*" The remembered drill sounds childish on Mother Malloy's elegant lips as she improvises from the first-grade French book, and Tildy has to suppress a giggle at the Boston nun's awful pronunciation.

"*Non, ma mère. Mon père est dans la campagne avec son chauffeur, John.*"

"*Et votre soeur, Madeline? Est-elle à la maison?*"

"*Non, ma mère, Madeline est à l'école.*"

"*Et votre mère, est-elle à la maison?*"

"*Non, ma mère, Mama est à son atelier de photographe.*"

"Tildy, you speak like a Frenchwoman. I am in awe."

"That's because in first grade Mother Hubert—she was French on her father's side—made us look at her mouth and not at the book when she was saying the words. When we said them right, she'd write them on the board, and after we'd copied them into our book, we could color that page."

"What a great plan." Mother Malloy passes the notepad to Tildy. "Now, will you write some French words as I say them?"

"Sure, which ones?"

"Oh, let's start with *dans la campagne.*"

Tildy has to repeat the words aloud slowly, correcting Mother Malloy's un-French sounds, before she can start properly forming the letters on the pad.

"Good idea, repeating them after me," the nun says, with a grimace of self-reproach. "Perhaps you'll improve my accent. I didn't have a Mother Hubert. My French was learned out of a book and taught by a nun from Ireland whose pronunciation was as bad as mine, if not worse."

They went on like this until the sun had gone from the room. Mother Malloy switched on a lamp. "How are you getting on with *David Copperfield,* Tildy?"

"I'm keeping up, Mother, with Madeline's help. We've just met Uriah Heep. At first you don't realize how creepy he is. I mean, blowing in a horse's nostril might be a good thing. But his creepiness grows on you. What Madeline and I do, we lie on her bed and read like we used to, only now it's my bed. She thought I needed a new start, so she gave me her room."

"And how is it going?"

"We're trying something different. We take turns reading and putting feeling into it, like in a play, but whenever I come to a difficult word, I tap her on the arm and she supplies it, so we won't ruin our momentum. Before, I would be dreading the bad words so much I would have to stop."

"Ah, Tildy, you were fortunate in your Mother Hubert and you are blessed indeed to have a sister like Madeline."

✠

Monday evening, December 10, 1951
Mother Ravenel's office
Mount St. Gabriel's

"AND HOW ARE *you* feeling, Mother Malloy?"

"Well, Mother. And you?"

"Oh, I'm fine. I have to be. Miss Mendoza's lost her voice and can't do Spanish conversation, and Jovan's at home for the second time with a fever of one hundred and two, though Betty tends to exaggerate when protecting her menfolk, and Mother Arbuckle has three boarders in the infirmary tonight."

"Is it—some kind of epidemic, do you think?"

"No, it's about par for this time of year. Seasonal colds combined with Christmas nerves. Please, Mother Malloy, take Mother Wallingford's wing chair. You look as if you could use a bit of propping up. You had one of your after-school tutorials with Tildy. I saw Madeline waiting outside in her little roadster."

Mother Ravenel was seated behind her English flat-top desk, flanked by her tributes and trophies. The thick velvet curtains were closed, and pools of lamplight broke up imposing shadows. Above the Victorian prie-dieu, a votive candle in blue glass flickered before a little wooden figure of Our Lady of Solitude in her brightly painted and gilded niche, a gift from a Mexican roommate on the occasion of Mother Ravenel's first vows. Mother Malloy, over the course of her visits to this room, had been apprised by the headmistress of its significant items. The desk with its three pedestal drawers on each side had belonged to Mother Ravenel's father, who had died in a quail-shooting accident two days after the Crash of 1929. The handsome silvery-blue Queen Anne wing chair propping up Mother Malloy's back had been one of the foundress's great finds. Mother Wallingford, with her sharp eye for furniture, had bought the disgraced chair for twenty-five cents from a Mountain City junk dealer and she and Mother Finney had spent weeks removing grease and layers of kitchen paint, then reupholstering it in some leftover brocade from an altar frontal.

This room had brought home for the first time to Kate Malloy, a foster child raised among indifferent furnishings, that a person could surround herself with things that reassured her of her own history.

"I gather from Tildy's second six weeks' report," began Mother Ravenel, her left hand playing with a pencil poised above the ubiquitous yellow pad on which she jotted thoughts as they arose, "that your afternoon labors with her have borne some fruit. I offer my congratulations, Mother. She is not an easy girl. They are not an easy family. That's why I had my chastening session with her first, before turning her over to your remedial care. Reading the riot act is best done by the headmistress, don't you think?"

Without waiting for an answer, Mother Ravenel plunged on: "Have you got to the root of the problem yet? The grades have come up, but they need to come up more. As I told Tildy in our little heart-to-heart, she isn't fulfilling her potential."

"The problem is the reading, Mother. Tildy has difficulty seeing words as they actually appear on the page. She transposes letters, sees 'on' for 'no,' for instance; or she partially misreads words. She'll read 'marker' as 'market,' or 'climbing' as 'clinging.' She hears her mistake as soon as she reads the sentence aloud, but it takes time. You have to wait while she sounds it out and hears it. She is a speaking-and-hearing person; her vocabulary is extremely sophisticated for her age, and she breezes along in Spanish conversation class. Her spoken French puts mine to shame. That's what we've been doing. I ask her something in French; she hears and responds orally. Then I have her write phrases we've been using, sounding them out as she goes. She seems to operate best when she can use multiple functions at the same time. French is something she learned through the ear and through watching her teacher's mouth. She told me her first-grade teacher, Mother Hubert—"

"I've often said that if we could only find a way to make carbon copies of that precious nun and scatter them up through the grades, all our girls would be bilingual without ever opening a book. Mother Hubert's teaching secrets are phonics and patient love. Not that she would think of herself as having any secrets. Mother Hubert just *is* phonics and love. But since we have only one of her, the place for her is at the start of their education. What I don't understand is why it has taken until ninth grade for us to realize that Tildy can't read properly."

While scribbling something on her yellow pad, Mother Ravenel proceeded to answer her own question: "I have concluded it's Maud Norton. Or, rather, the lack of Maud Norton. They're not friends this year, and Tildy no longer has Maud to help her with her homework. Which brings me to something else I've been mulling over, Mother Malloy. What I'm seeing in your ninth grade is *several* clusters of girls, each with its sphere of interests. I don't see a nucleus of main girls anymore. I wonder whether, if a Mrs. Prince situation arose today, this class as it is now constituted could drive her off. What I think is, the breakup of Tildy and Maud and the influx of new girls has created new patterns and diluted old forces. That's how I see it. What do you think?"

Mother Ravenel in dialogue with her doodles seemed to have provided herself with all the information she needed about the ninth-grade girls.

What insights could Mother Malloy add? There was animosity between Tildy and Maud, but also a continued attraction. They couldn't stop being aware of each other. Maud was a passionate student with a questing mind. Her home life, from what Mother Malloy could gather, was an embarrassment to her ideals. The girl who had been Kate Malloy could certainly identify with Maud's desire to transcend her origins. Herself parentless, she could also ache for the orphaned Chloe; although Chloe, to a remarkable degree, kept her own counsel—she even maintained a quiet distance from being Tildy Stratton's best friend. Chloe's artistic talent absorbed her, and she seemed to draw sustenance from the memory of her mother. It must help to have a mother to remember.

But it was Tildy who tugged at Mother Malloy's heart. During their reading sessions, she struggled along with this bright, haughty, mercurial girl who could be brought to tears by an unruly procession of black letters across a white page.

There was no doubt in Mother Malloy's mind that Tildy could have been the organizer of the sixth-grade ousting of Mrs. Prince and the three elections of Maud Norton to the office of class president. Tildy was an instigator. She could be "the main girl" all by herself. Her imagination craved drama, and she liked to form the flow of life that went on around her into distinctive scenes. She liked to make things happen.

But how much, if any, of this would it be wise to share with Mother Ravenel? Having heard Madeline's family story of the aunt left dangling by Suzanne Ravenel's precipitate entry into the postulancy, and having been privy to Mother Ravenel's animus regarding those "difficult" Stratton women, Mother Malloy was reluctant to jeopardize Tildy's progress by revealing more problematic traits. It would only add fuel to the flames. On the other hand, what sort of information might she offer to the headmistress to help Tildy escape probation while the girl struggled to improve her reading?

She said, "I think you're right, Mother, about there being several clusters of girls, each with its own interests. I'm impressed with Maud Norton's work. She's come up with a very promising idea for her Dickens paper. And I agree with you that she seems to be less concerned with friendships than with her studies."

"If she continues like this, she should have her pick of colleges," said Mother Ravenel. "And with the recent patronage of her father and his wealthy wife, things look even rosier for her. Maud will be spending Christmas with them in Palm Beach. They're flying her down."

"How nice for her. I didn't know."

"Yes, they dote on her, according to Lily Norton. Lily phoned to ask if I would let Maud miss the last day of school. They want her down there early for some Christmas cotillion dance."

Tactically, Mother Malloy proceeded. (The headmistress was a person who made you appreciate tactics.) "I don't see a nucleus of main girls, either, Mother. And lately there has been a feeling of class unity. Chloe Starnes did a wonderful drawing for our bulletin board. She stayed after school every day for a week. She asked permission to sit at my desk on the platform and drew the girls' desks, looking out on them as I do. Fifteen empty desks. With the windows behind, and the view through the windows. You must come and look at it. It is beautifully executed and the perspective is so skillful—"

"She has the blood of two gifted architects in her. It wouldn't surprise me if Henry takes her into the firm one day. It would be the natural thing. And women are getting to do more exciting jobs nowadays. But I interrupted you, Mother. You were saying—"

"Just that the girls love that drawing. Before class, there are always girls looking at it. Kay Lee Jones will point to her desk and say, 'There I am,' and Ashley Nettle will point to hers and say, 'There *I* am.' "

"Chloe does seem to be holding her own," mused the headmistress, "despite having been chosen by Tildy."

"Speaking of Tildy again, Mother, I have had some thoughts, since I've been working with her, that might be helpful."

"Oh, please, Mother Malloy, out with them. Make my Christmas a happy one. I believe I worry more over that child than I do all the rest of your brood. Of course, it's understandable, given my entangled history with the family. Poor Antonia, and then having to send Madeline away at the end of her freshman year. By the way, how did your conference with Cornelia Stratton go, when she finally found time for you? I asked her to stop in and chat afterward, but as usual she had to rush off. I've never been a favorite of Cornelia's, but she tolerates me because she knows Tildy will get more attention here than in the city schools. Madeline is boring herself to death over at the public high school; she calls it 'Mountain City *Low* School.' "

"Tildy's mother was in a hurry with me, too, Mother," Mother Malloy hastened to assure the headmistress, who seemed to measure herself competitively against the other teachers. "Mrs. Stratton is very busy with her photography studio. But she was pleased that Tildy was making progress, and I think she was happy that I had recognized Tildy's special qualities."

"Which are?"

"I believe Tildy has leadership qualities that haven't found large enough outlets yet. She likes to think up things for others to do. She was the one who talked Chloe into doing a class portrait for the bulletin board. She told me so. She even admitted that her first idea—of Chloe drawing portraits of the actual girls standing in rows—hadn't worked out. Some girls might not like how they were portrayed. Next Chloe abandoned a portrait of the school building swathed in mists, and after that asked me if she could sit by herself in the empty classroom until she came up with something. And out of that came this drawing. All from a process that Tildy set in motion."

"I will definitely step into your classroom and look at this wonderful drawing. Tell me, Mother Malloy, before we go off to Compline: How are you finding us?"

Mother Malloy was unprepared for such a question. Her soul revolted. How should she answer? *I am not supposed to have a voice. Whatever you send me, I accept.* Which, to Mother Ravenel's worldly ear, might sound sanctimonious.

Or what if she should say: I am trying to accept it as good discipline for my soul, being sent to Mount St. Gabriel's, when what I really wanted was—well, first I regretted not being a boy so I could enter the Jesuits. But, failing that, I wanted to continue earning my doctorate and teaching Greek drama and English studies to college freshmen. I like teaching young college men and women together. I like standing before a classroom and engaging with hungry minds, many of whom have never read a Shakespeare play, many of whom work night jobs to go to college. Between myself and these girls of fourteen, here at Mount St. Gabriel's, I am missing some vital link. I have been a girl, but not a girl like any of them. For the most part, give or take a struggling Tildy, they seem to be arrested by their fortunate boundaries.

What was it Madeline said to me that day in the grotto? ("It's the whole life of *school*. I feel I've been held back to repeat what I already know how to do. It's like you've learned to swim really well, and now you're ready to cross a huge body of water and see what's on the other side, and then someone tells you, No, no, dear, you have to stay in this pool and tread water until—until I don't know what. Whatever comes next. I wish I could get to it!")

I sometimes feel I am watching over fifteen young girls who are proficiently and patiently treading water in a fenced-in pool, Mother.

What Mother Malloy finally did answer came out sounding feeble and somewhat insincere: "Everyone has been very good to me here, Mother Ravenel. Sometimes I regret not having more stamina. How I envy yours! I often fall asleep before finishing my daily examen. My daily meditations are not worthy of God, but I offer up this shortcoming and hope it is a passing thing."

☩

AFTER MOTHER MALLOY excused herself to go early to chapel, Mother Ravenel reviewed the day in the company of her cherished lares and penates. Having been galvanized by Mother Malloy's confessed envy of her stamina, she felt unusually vigorous. Why did it act as a stimulant when someone admitted to having less of something than you did? Perhaps because God made us to be competitive.

Mother Ravenel had noticed that Mother Malloy was always one of the first in the choir stalls for the final office of the day. After the younger nun's disclosure about tending to fall asleep, Mother Ravenel suspected that she might use Compline to get a head start on her examen.

As was her custom, the headmistress dispensed first with the institutional loose ends.

For the third time since the opening of school, the toilet in stall number two of the dormitory bathroom was clogged. George from Lombardo's Plumbing would have to be summoned back at his hefty hourly rate to swivel his snake contraption down through the pipes until he brought up the dripping obstruction and, this time, whether he thought it seemly of her or not, she intended to stand right beside him wearing rubber gloves and examine the evidence herself. She felt certain the culprit was either Marta or Gilda. The Cuban girls had to have it drummed into them over and over again, with threat of punishment, what must not be thrown where when there was not a battery of servants to clean up the mess without a peep. Moreover, she was fairly sure she would be able to tell by the condition of the sanitary pad whether it had been Marta's or Gilda's. Gilda was the bleeder, she did everything in a big way; Marta was the withholder, and she had plenty to withhold.

Mother Ravenel knew Marta's secret, though the girls did not know she knew it, and this had its leverage. Marta's story had been tacitly conveyed by her father with his diplomat's gift for imparting things best left unspoken. Consul Andreu had flown down to Mountain City from New York last spring to look over the school and take Mother

Ravenel's measure. During their confidential stroll around the grounds, the consul and the headmistress quickly assessed each other. The daughter of his best friend, Jorge Gomez, seemed to be flourishing at Mount St. Gabriel's, Consul Andreu said, and he thought it might be just the place for his daughter, who had known Gilda since childhood. The two families knew everything worth knowing about each other. The girls might room together. Marta trusted Gilda, and Gilda could help Marta's English—which, the consul confessed to Mother Ravenel, was very poor. Marta was two years older than Gilda, but they would both be going into the ninth grade.

His daughter, the consul explained, had been held back in school in Havana for not applying herself, and during her year of shame at having to repeat a grade had formed an unsuitable attachment. Subsequently she had been sent off to Spain to spend a year with a great-aunt in Andalusia. Meanwhile, he and his wife had been surprised late in life by a baby, a little girl, whom Marta adored and had insisted on naming Angel. Perhaps if the school were agreeable to Marta, the child, who would be ready for first grade in a few years, might follow her big sister to Mount St. Gabriel's.

If it were left to Marta, he told Mother Ravenel, she would prefer to stay in Havana, living with her mother, and being "a little mother" to Angel. But there were priorities here, and Marta must finish her education first.

Mother Ravenel explained her policy about not letting foreign students from the same country room together; contrary to what the consul might think, their English would *not* improve as rapidly, because they would always be whispering in their native language as soon as the door was shut.

"Ah, now, that is too bad," the consul had countered sadly with a forewarning side glance, which the headmistress turned to meet eye to eye. By then they had reached the new athletic field, where the lower-grade girls were practicing for field day. "Because, you see, Mother Ravenel, our families are very close. Marta trusts Gilda. Trust is very important to Marta at this time. And to Señora Andreu and myself. We want Marta to—to—*empezar de nuevo*—how shall I put it, Mother? We feel it is important for our daughter to begin on a completely fresh page."

Before they reached the leafy embrace of the grotto, she had decided to risk it. He was a man with influence who would send other wellborn Cuban daughters her way. Nothing really had been said; that was the beauty, and they both knew it. Sweeping ahead of him up the steep stone steps, she lightly tossed back her concession: "Consul, you went straight to my heart. I can never resist the promise of a new beginning for a girl. I began on a fresh page myself when I came to Mount St. Gabriel's as a seventh-grade boarder. But the girls have to understand that if your daughter's English doesn't improve, I will have to separate them and put Marta in with an American boarder. Our little arrangement must be regarded as an experiment."

It had taken the out-of-shape father a few moments to reply. Having regained his breath, he stood beside the Red Nun, whose story he would shortly be told, and thanked Mother Ravenel for her generosity and great understanding. He assured her that he and his friend Jorge Gomez would impress upon both girls the importance of making this experiment a success: "Because Marta would not feel comfortable sharing intimate quarters with a strange girl. I will urge Jorge to emphasize this proviso of yours to Gilda."

Before leaving the grounds, Consul Andreu wrote a check for Marta's full first-year tuition plus the nonrefundable boarding fee.

Whoever's sanitary pad it was would be assigned to wipe down the bathroom stalls and fixtures with Pine-Sol every evening for a week. (Not the toilet bowls themselves; that would insult the dignity of a Cuban father.)

And— Elated, Mother Ravenel committed a further inspiration to her yellow pad: that girl would have to thoroughly research and make a legible diagram of the inner workings of a modern toilet.

Now for the day's larger loose ends beyond the institutional ones: those young souls in formation, the "works in progress" under her care.

It was Tildy who waited for her, Tildy's struggles that were uppermost in her mind. "She is not an easy girl," she had told Mother Malloy. "They are not an easy family." By which she had meant, of course, the women in the family: first her own classmates, the Tilden twins, Cornelia and Antonia; and then the Stratton girls, Madeline and, now, Tildy.

It galled her, the way Cornelia continued to rebuff her, after all this time. ("Won't you stop by my office for a little chat, Cornelia, after you've had your conference with Tildy's teacher?" She wished she had not chosen the word "chat." Even as it had passed her lips she'd seen Cornelia snatch at it for the centerpiece of her acid turndown. "Oh, *Mother,* how sweet. But running a business all by myself excludes such cozy treats as chats. And here I'm already tardy for the remarkable Mother Malloy.")

Cornelia's "Mother" had "Suzanne" oozing around its edges; and "cozy treats" was just flagrantly patronizing. Yes, I, too, am running a business, she might have replied, with the wry assurance of a head-mistress in charge of a first-rate school in which Cornelia's younger daughter was barely making it. But Antonia's unforgiving sister was clicking down the hallway in her pumps, already "tardy" for Tildy's "remarkable" teacher, whom Cornelia had the respect to call by her proper name.

"Tildy's mother was in a hurry with me, too," Mother Malloy had reported. But she had gone on to add that Cornelia had been pleased that Tildy was making progress, pleased that Mother Malloy had recognized Tildy's special qualities.

And what were these special qualities?

Leadership qualities, according to Mother Malloy, that hadn't found proper outlets yet. Tildy liked to think up things for others to do, "the remarkable" Mother Malloy had said.

The wall clock gave seven minutes until Compline, for which no bell was rung, because the younger boarders were supposed to be asleep.

Well, who better than I can identify with those qualities, thought Mother Ravenel, rising from her father's old desk and shaking out her skirts prior to making the rounds to shut down her sanctum. (She blew out the votive candle in front of Our Lady of Solitude and clipped the wick.) I was that way myself. I liked to think up things for others to do. When I was Tildy's age, I started writing a play during study hall for our freshman class to perform. *The Red Nun* just poured out of me. I heard the voices and already knew who was going to play all the parts. God's voice speaking the prologue was as easy as taking dictation. I knew exactly the kind of eerie music I wanted Francine Barfoot to compose on her flute for the opening ghost chorus.

The most recent production of *The Red Nun* had been in 1947, staged by last year's graduating class when they were freshmen. That class was notable for its school spirit. The girls came to me as a delegation and asked for the honor of doing it; there hadn't been a performance since 1940. It was a very respectful production. Nothing new was added. In some ways, it had the mood of a memorial service. The whole thing needed a bonfire set under it, I privately thought, but it was very well received. The newspaper covered it and there was a little sidebar on me, how my school play from 1931 had turned into a tradition at Mount St. Gabriel's. People just were so glad to be doing normal, traditional things after the war. How can five years have gone by already? Or, it will be five if I decide to let this ninth grade do it in the spring.

Now (turning off the green-shaded study lamp on Father's desk), where do I find a relatively clean script? They get so marked up over the years. Maybe I'll type out a new one, with some carbons.

First I will sound Tildy out. Ask her if she thinks she is director material. And, of course, she must realize this would be a gift and a privilege as well as a challenge.

I just hope (feeling a fresh surge of stamina as she clicked off the floor lamp behind the Queen Anne wing chair where the ninth-grade teacher had propped her weary bones)—I just hope Mother Malloy won't think I am out to compete with her or triumph over her in the shaping of Tildy, or anything like that.

PART TWO

Inside the girlhood fortress
That once ensheltered me
I dreamed a wondrous dream
Of the person I wanted to be.
But in Your almighty design
You sealed me in red rock instead.
"Take this for your cloister, daughter of mine:
Be a fortress for others," You said.

—Caroline DuPree's ghost aria
in Suzanne Ravenel's *The Red Nun*

CHAPTER 16

The Christmas Critic

First Saturday of Christmas break 1951
Downtown Mountain City

MADELINE, WEARING HER father's raccoon cap atop a silk scarf loosely draped about her shoulders, Arab kaffiyeh–style, to conceal her rag curlers for the club's Christmas dance that night, was chauffeuring her mother and her mother's cameras through a loaded afternoon of shootings. Tildy was at the Ice Capades matinee, with Chloe and that patient paragon of unclehood, Henry Vick. Daddy and John were out at the cabin, hosting Daddy's open house for those families who had trucks and liked to drive out to the Swag and cut their own free Christmas trees from Daddy's woods. John went along and pointed out the five- to ten-foot firs ready for harvesting, while back at the cabin Flavia stirred the mulled cider and set out the plates of hot sausages and fresh-baked cookies and Daddy stoked the fire and sampled his latest batch of eggnog.

Cornelia Stratton, having just uttered the closing bars of her working woman's lament ("Nobody in this town understands my schedule and nobody *wants* to understand it. . . .") was now dealing a few mortal slashes to the modern concept of "Christmas," with all its bad taste and impositions.

Madeline was enjoying herself. She liked being behind the wheel of Cornelia's stealthy, powerful automobile, with its roomy leather interior—Daddy traded in his and Mama's Packards every other year, so Mama's cars always smelled new, signed with whiffs of Ma Griffe in summer and Jicky in winter. Daddy's new cars, which Madeline seldom rode in anymore, soon reeked of gun rags and tobacco smoke and the little nips from the bottle in the bag that John kept for him in the glove compartment.

"It gets worse every year. Buy, buy, buy—guilt, guilt, guilt—please come and take a picture of me giving something to the widows and orphans. And why all these shoppers choose to dress up in Santa red to go out and buy further Santa-red articles of clothing for one another that nobody will wear after the New Year is beyond me." Cornelia glared out the passenger window at a family in Santa-red parkas heading on foot toward Sears. Her next shoot was the Christmas party for orphans at the Shriners' temple. "Who's being honored here? To my knowledge, Santa red wasn't even a color back in Our Lord's day. Their reds were more of a clayey or winey red. You're coming in with me to the Shriners, aren't you?"

"If you aren't embarrassed by this getup."

"Maddy, you could wear a washtub on your head and look exotic and smashing. Tell me again how Creighton Rivers happens to be taking you to the club dance. His parents aren't members."

"I don't think you asked me before, Mama, but I invited him."

"You wrote him at college?"

"No, I called his dorm and asked him if he would be my date."

"And this was when?"

"Back in September. I wanted to have it settled so I could turn down other invitations."

Cornelia whipped out her compact, freshened her lipstick, uttered a stern "hmff" of approval, and dropped the items back in her purse. "I take it those other invitations were forthcoming. From your"—she mirthfully snorted—"Hershey's Kisses brigade."

"Yes, and I was able to reply truthfully, 'Oh, thank you, Hershey One, Two, and Three, but I already promised someone back in September.' "

"Three! Oh, Madeline. And you don't even care. You're not in love with Creighton or anything, are you?"

"He's tall, good-looking, ambitious, and poor. He's premed at Emory and a fabulous dancer. And he's sweet and patient with children—he taught Tildy to dive beautifully. Also, I prefer older men. But no, I'm not in love with him, and he knows I'm not. That's why I could pick up the phone and ask him."

"But he must have been surprised."

"He laughed. He said he'd be honored to escort me but he didn't own a tux. I said, Is that a 'Yes, but I'll rent one' answer or an excuse for a 'No'? He said, 'Yes, but I'll rent one,' and then he asked how his best girl was, the Tantalizing Tildy, and I came close to loving him for *that*."

"I do worry about Tildy, and we haven't even gotten her to the Hershey-brigade stage yet. Will even *one* boy invite her to the dance?, that's what worries me. She's not easy and above it all, like you."

"I'm not above it all, Mama. I want things as badly as everybody else. Though lately I do seem to be going through a stage where there's just not very much on my horizon to want."

"She's just such a strange little person," Cornelia went on about Tildy, either ignoring or choosing to pass over Madeline's slender plea for some motherly wisdom. Cornelia preferred her older daughter to stay in the role of "sisterly" backup and mainstay: a sort of extension of the lost Antonia. "The child is such an enigma. First this reading thing—I refuse to believe she's been faking it all these years. If you want to know my opinion, though nobody has bothered to *ask* my opinion, she was just sitting back and letting Maud play chauffeur—like your father sits back and lets John get them where they're going, even though your father could drive himself if he wished to. But then Maud comes back from Palm Beach all hoity-toity with her new connections, and poor little Chloe is anointed Tildy's new favorite, and all of a sudden my child's grades go through the floor. What am I to make of this? I'll tell you, though it may sound unreasonable and a tad malicious: I think Maud enjoyed her power over Tildy and encouraged her to lapse—now, Madeline, hear me out—"

"I wouldn't dream of interrupting, Mama." When Cornelia warned you she was about to sound unreasonable and a tad malicious, it was admittedly titillating to give her free rein and see how far she'd go.

"Yes, I think Maud encouraged her to *let slide,* so she could have the upper hand and feel superior. That Pine Cone Lodge ménage gives Maud plenty to feel inferior about. Lily Norton, if she ever really was Norton, was recently spotted cuddling at the movies with that fancy-foods salesman who boards with them. What I think is, it gave Maud power to watch Tildy grow dependent on her and deteriorate. It would be like—not that John would ever think of such a thing—if John were to say, Now, Mr. Stratton, you don't need to bother your head about renewing your driver's license. I'm here to take you wherever you need to go. You just sit back and look out the window and enjoy your bounty. What I'm saying, Maddy, is Maud knew that this reading thing was a way to equal things out and revenge herself on our bounty. Just look at this disgusting traffic in front of the Shriners' temple. But we're supposed to pull around in back and use the potentate's parking slot. Well, a mother is entitled to her opinion, though perhaps I go too far."

Though deploring Cornelia's ascribing of such invidious motives to a fourteen-year-old girl, Madeline hastened to reassure her. "Well, Mama, whatever it was, the cloud is lifting. Tildy has a true champion in Mother Malloy. They're working on Tildy's Dickens paper in *French.* Just one simple sentence after another. *'Uriah Heep, c'est un homme de grande humilité. Il est très humble. Mais qu'est-ce que c'est que cette humilité?'* Tildy spouts out the words and Mother Malloy, God love her, 'takes dictation.' Then Tildy brings Mother Malloy's dictation home and copies it, and the next session they translate it into English, Tildy speaking the words and Mother Malloy writing it down, and then Tildy copies *that.* Isn't that an inspired way to get someone to write a paper? Next time I get stuck, I plan to try it."

"I like Mother Malloy," said Cornelia, admiring her narrow snakeskin pumps as she stepped out of the car. "She's reserved and modest and acts like a proper nun. She's quite lovely to look at behind that veil. When I was with her, I kept thinking of Antonia. Antonia would have looked beautiful in that same habit."

Madeline lugged the cameras and the canvas bag with film from the trunk. The two women walked together across the parking lot. From inside the temple rose the jovial baritones of the Shriners leading the high timid voices of the orphans: "Dashing through the snow . . ."

"And then, you know, Mama, just before school let out yesterday, Mother Ravenel told Tildy she was thinking about letting her direct the next production of *The Red Nun.* Tildy is supposed to pray over it during the holidays. Mother Ravenel told her she has leadership qualities that need to be put to use."

Cornelia stopped dead in her tracks. "No, I *didn't* know, Maddy. When I get home from the studio, nobody bothers to fill me in on anything."

"Well, it just happened yesterday, Mama. Tildy told me when we were having our little reading session last night. She wasn't even supposed to tell me. You know how the Ravenel likes to say, 'Now this is just between ourselves. . . . ' "

"I wonder what that woman has up her sleeve to inflict on our family now," Cornelia burst out savagely.

But then she switched back into her soignée social persona as the potentate, a burly, red-faced man in a red fez and a Santa-red cardigan, came tripping toward them with the light gait of an upright bear. When introduced to Madeline, he complimented her lavishly on her fetching hat.

✛

THEIR LAST AFTERNOON shoot was the Women's Preservation Society's Christmas sale at the newly restored Miles-Rutherford House, the oldest brick building in the county.

"Which means I'll have to be civil to Eloise Niles, the president," Cornelia said to Madeline as they climbed the freshly painted steps leading to the double-tiered porch. A uniformed maid took their wraps at the entrance; then they pushed slowly forward into the crowded neo-classical rotunda, through a dense cloud of cigarette smoke and conflicting perfumes and the eerie acoustics of dozens of high-pitched voices reverberating off the domed ceiling. Well-turned-out preservationists broke apart from their huddles to make a passage for the equally well-turned-out Mrs. Stratton followed by the camera-laden beauty wearing the Davy Crockett cap with seductive veil. Some called to Cornelia by name. "Oh, what a darling hat your assistant has on," cried someone else. "No, that's the daughter," said another. "And she has a twin, doesn't she?" "No, that was the—" (inaudible).

Finally they reached the Greek Revival semicircular sunroom sparkling with reflections from the river and a ceiling-high Christmas tree loaded with handmade ornaments for sale. Arranged on trestle tables covered in green felt were crocheted lap robes, sequined evening purses, knitted socks and mittens and scarves (a great many, alas, contaminated by the Santa-red color), embroidered napkins, needlepoint eyeglass cases, painted wood serving trays, silver jewelry, hand-carved soapstone angels, "and just about every other last thing on earth nobody needs," Cornelia muttered to Madeline over her shoulder as she stooped behind her flash camera to get eye-level close-ups of the laid-out goodies. "It's a wonder, though, that there's so much of it left at the end of the day."

"Oh, most of them have already been sold," confided a voice behind her that was not Madeline's. "But I explained that they had to remain on the tables until you got here, Cornelia."

"Ah," said Cornelia, straightening up to confront the eavesdropper. "Well, that makes sense." She saw that Madeline had been detained by some women stroking her hat.

"I'm Sally Goodall, vice president of the preservationists. Eloise Niles has a bad case of the flu, but she asked me to send you her warmest regards, Cornelia, and thank you for fitting us into your day."

"How very kind of her. Tell her from me to get well quickly. Listen, er—Sally, could I trouble you to stand over there by the tree, with the river view as your background?"

"Don't you want me to get some of the others, Cornelia?"

"The others can wait. Right now the light is perfect. And you look so—well, *representative* of this whole gathering." Cornelia reserved a special corner in hell for people who repeated your name over and over, as this vice president person was intent on doing.

"Well, thank you, Cornelia. That is," the woman tittered nervously, "if you meant it as a compliment."

"What else? Now turn your body a little to the left—that is really a handsome suit—and lift your chin—nice earrings, too. No, don't look at me. You're the person in command at this lovely affair, everyone is having a good time, and most of the goods have already been sold. Just look sideways at the river and think of your—um—*bounty.*"

"My bounty," echoed the vice president obediently.

"That's right. Don't move, just keep looking slightly sideways at—that's it, that's great." Cornelia snapped away, aiming the lens so the flash wouldn't reflect in the window and ruin the shot.

"Well, thank you, er, Sally. I think we got something really nice—the table with all the goodies, the river, and, of course, yourself." She expected the vice president to take this as her cue to plunge back into the surroundings, but the woman continued to stand there, beaming at her meaningfully.

"You don't remember me, do you, Cornelia? It's Sarah, Sarah Kogan, from your class at Mount St. Gabriel's, only I transferred to public high after seventh grade. And when we moved away, I decided to call myself Sally."

"Well, goodness—Sarah Kogan—now I remember you *perfectly.*" The old name had instantly plugged Cornelia into the image of an overeager girl who crept around the edges of people's private conversations. "And how is it you find yourself back in Mountain City, Sarah—er, Sally?"

"My husband was transferred here from Macon, Georgia, last year. He runs the Mountain City State Farm office."

"And here you are, practically running the preservationists. Well, great to see you, Sarah. I've got to be earning my shekels. I'm a working woman, now, you know."

But to Cornelia's amazement, Sarah-Sally was clutching at her arm. Her eyes had gone all teary and she was saying the most appalling things.

"You and she were just—everything. I used to watch to see you come into the classroom together, to see what you wore. You dressed alike, but there was always some difference. You had colored shoelaces; she wore her barrettes farther back. You were like twin goddesses; everyone looked up to you. Just before we moved away, I heard Antonia was going to become a nun, and I wondered what that would be like for you. I mean, it would be like losing a part of yourself. And then, oh, I am so very sorry—I hadn't heard until Jim and I came back to Mountain City that she had passed away. If I had known, Cornelia, I would have written you a letter. Not that my letter would mean much after all these years, but I felt so bad about not knowing—!"

Sarah-Sally Goodall née Kogan was on the verge of losing control, though she'd at least had the presence of mind to whip out a hankie and, in the process, thank God, had abandoned her *clutch* on Cornelia's person. Partly remembering, partly calculating where the downstairs restroom in the restored Miles-Rutherford House was likely to be, Cornelia shoved the vice president of the Women's Preservation Society in that direction.

"Please—Sally—go to the ladies' and pull yourself together. Thank you for your kind words and welcome back to Mountain City, but now I really must get on with my work."

☩

MADELINE, HAVING EXTRICATED herself from her hat flatterers (was that all you had to do to be thought superior and daring in this environment: drape an old silk scarf over your curlers and crown yourself with your father's old raccoon cap?), hurried to her mother, who would be wanting more film. But she was arrested by a strange scene taking place between Mama and a woman clawing at her arm. Talking urgently into Mama's *affronted* stare, the woman suddenly whipped out a handkerchief and began to cry, and Cornelia, her face gone remote, was steering her through the room and then shoving her in a specific direction. ". . . I really must get on with my work," Madeline heard her mother say.

Cornelia turned and saw her daughter. "Well, better late than never," she drily commented. "Give me the Argus and take the Kodak. And go get our coats out of hock and wait for me *outside,* on the porch."

"THANK YOU, MADDY." Madeline was driving them away from the Miles-Rutherford House. "That appalling woman. I couldn't risk still being there when she came back from the john. I couldn't have endured a second onslaught. I just wanted to shoot every face and outfit as fast as possible and get out of there with my sanity intact."

"Who was she, Mama? Why was she crying?"

"The blubbering effrontery! She was a nobody in our class at Mount St. Gabriel's. She transferred to public school after seventh grade, and then her family left town. And here she was, going on in this presumptuous way about Antonia and me."

"What? What did she say?"

"Oh, how we were twin goddesses and everybody thought we were 'everything' and how she used to lie in wait to see what wonderful outfits we wore to school each day, and how I wore colored laces and Tony pulled her hair back with barrettes. I tried to keep tuning it out—it was so inappropriate! And now she's moved back to town with her insurance-salesman hubby and she hears for the first time that no, Antonia did not become a nun and that Antonia had—oh my God—'passed away,' and, oh, wait, before that about how she had worried about me after Antonia had taken vows, would I feel I was losing a part of myself—oh, the familiarity! The emotions! I'd rather she had thrown lye in my face."

"Listen, Mama, would you like to stop at the Dairy and get a cup of tea and some ice cream?"

"I can't think of anything more comforting, darling, than sitting across the table from my beautiful daughter in her *crowd-pleasing hat* and sipping a hot cup of tea and then chasing it down with a hot fudge sundae, and then going home to my adoring husband and hearing about all the free trees and eggnog he dispensed this afternoon, and then taking a fresh perspective on my strange unique baby girl and warning her to beware of the ravenous Ravenel, who has been known to gobble up young girls, but I am a working woman and so what I am going to do is ask you to take me home so you can start primping for your lovely dance with your dashing older man. Flavia will prepare me a thermos of soup and another of hot tea, and then I'll go down to the studio and develop the afternoon's haul. I want to get it done. All the Christmas do-gooders and their tacky decorations for Our Lord's poor birthday in a stable. Also, I think I may be coming down with something." She laughed almost happily. "I think Eloise Niles has managed to infect me with her flu all the way from her sickbed."

How does she do it, wondered Madeline, turning the Packard homeward. How does she manage to shoot us down with such faultless aim—"better late than never," when I've been her faithful driver and camera bearer the whole of this Saturday afternoon, and my "crowd-pleasing hat" and "primping for your lovely dance with your dashing older man"—and make us keep loving her and longing for more of her company and her eloquent abuse? Tonight I will be leaning into the shoulder of Creighton's rented tux, knowing we are the handsomest couple on the floor, but part of my heart will be with Mama in her dark-room, venting her outrage against the presumptuous blubberer and the tackiness of the Christmas season.

CHAPTER 17

Shadows on an Outing

First Saturday of Christmas break 1951
Ice Capades matinee
Mountain City Civic Auditorium

HENRY VICK HAD taken front-row dress-circle seats so that Chloe
and Tildy could crane their young necks over the parapet to their hearts'
content and devour every move in close-up of the professional troupe of
skaters waltzing to the thump and blare of *Tales of the Vienna Woods,*
which bounced off the acoustic ceiling Malcolm Vick had designed the
year before his death, and whose installation Henry had faithfully over-
seen, along with the important ductwork and the hydraulic-plant room
below, with its water and pressure tanks that made it possible to transform a dance floor and basketball court into an ice rink overnight. The
girls were close enough to spot the plume of breath curling from the
parted mouth of a skater, to thrill to the shear and scrape of blades exe-
cuting a sudden turn, to overhear the human grunt of the leading man
as, smiling, he lifted his partner to twirl her around on the ice. "Look,"
hissed Tildy, "you can see her vaccination scar. Right there, on her
thigh. I would have made them do it on my arm." "But her arms are
bare, too," reasoned Chloe. "True, but if it was *me* with my legs up in
the air in front of crowds, I would have insisted on the arm."

There they are in their young dramas, thought Henry, bitter with
his dark news, which he had determined to keep from Chloe until after
Christmas. Mine are over. That is, if I can be said to have had any dramas. Somehow "his bride killed on their honeymoon" doesn't really belong to me. It's more like something imposed on my curriculum vitae

by others who weren't there. There was—perhaps—a drama in our marriage, but it was just beginning and could have developed to fruition; though who knows what kind of fruit it would have produced?

A woman he'd gone out with for a while, longer than he should have, told him before she broke off with him that he reminded her of a character named Marcher in a tale by Henry James. In his fifth year as a widower, friends had fixed him up with Letitia Winch, a Mountain City "girl" of good family, who'd lost a fiancé in the Battle of the Coral Sea and taught literature at the local junior college. Henry checked out the book and tried to read the story, curious to find out what Letitia Winch thought he was like. It was a lengthy, obscure narrative with paragraphs few and far between. The long sentences doubled back on themselves, frustrating your search for the main entrance. It was like trying to force your way into a perpetually revolving door. Nevertheless, he shoved his foot through the verbiage enough times to wrest the message: Marcher was a vain cold fish to whom nothing at all was destined to happen. After the death of May Bartram, who had known it all along and loved him anyway, he flings himself, an old man, on her tombstone, realizing he has missed, through her, his one chance to be human.

How can I let Chloe go back, Henry thought. Back to what? She won't want to go back. Why is he doing this? He had received Rex Wright's lawyer's letter with the copy of the startling document the day before, Friday. Forgetting his overcoat and gloves, he'd set off on foot for his own lawyer's office, the unbelievable papers clutched in his bare fist.

"Ollie, tell me I don't have to worry about this," he'd said.

"Henry, I wish I could, but she's his legally adopted daughter. There's his name on her birth certificate. You didn't know?"

"No, I didn't know. Agnes never told me. Chloe never said anything, either. And how can Merry's name—her real father's name—not be mentioned anywhere on that document?"

"Because that's the way it's done, Henry. A new beginning, legitimized by the state. For all civil intents and purposes, she is his daughter, with the rights, privileges, and duties of his child and heir."

"But her name is still Starnes."

"That's up to the individuals. Let's see, Chloe would have been ten when these papers were signed and it was midyear and they were already living in Barlow. It's hard for a kid to leave school one day and come back the next with a different surname. Perhaps that's what Agnes was taking into account."

"Well, regrettably," said Henry, "we can't ask Agnes. But why would he want to do this?"

"Maybe because, as his attorney says, he feels her loss and, now that he is going to remarry, he wants to offer her a stable home."

"But she's fine as she is. We're fine. She likes her school; she likes living in the house her mother lived in. Look, Ollie, tell me the worst. Are we going to have to go to court?"

"It's too early to say about court, Henry. And, I hate to say it, but there could be worse than court."

"You mean I could lose her?"

"Henry, first let's try to ascertain just how serious this is, or if he may be wanting something else."

"What else could he want?"

"Oh, maybe to give you a good shake-up. Or to impress his intended. We know nothing about her, but let me see what I can find out."

"But why would he want to give me a shake-up?"

"Maybe just because he knows he can. You weren't exactly a fan of his, I take it?"

"That's putting it mildly. In the last conversation I had with my sister, she told me the marriage had been a mortal mistake but she was going to try to salvage something because, well, her exact words were that she was still 'ferociously attached to her honor.' Wait, there's something else you should probably know, Ollie. Agnes was six weeks pregnant when she died. They discovered it in the autopsy. Rex didn't know and was pretty upset about it. He told me he wouldn't put it past Agnes to have told Chloe and not him. He was crying at the time—he said they were always keeping secrets from him."

"I'm taking notes, Henry. This could be very helpful. Did you ever ask Chloe about this?"

"No, I've been very scrupulous about not quizzing her."

"Well, Henry, you may have to ascertain a few things. She's what—fourteen? She's old enough to testify in court."

"But this is despicable. She's had enough sorrow without being dragged in front of a judge. She won't want to go back. We haven't discussed Rex Wright at all. As I said, she never even told me she'd been legally adopted by him."

"Let's take this a step at a time, Henry. It may all blow over. Let me first indulge in some lawyer ping-pong and see how far that takes us."

☩

Same Saturday evening
Vick house
Mountain City

For thirty-two and a half hours, Tildy had been marking time until she could be alone with Chloe and tell about the play. She'd planned out her announcement, followed by a "first reading" of the script, but, God Almighty, the intolerable string of activities she'd had to endure before reaching this hour! First she'd had to get through all of last evening, though at least she'd been able to tell Madeline about the play—and then she'd had to wake up Saturday and eat breakfast and get through the whole morning with Madeline pressing her dress and fussing with her hair for the dance and Mama in one of her swivets about too many bookings and nobody appreciating a working woman's schedule, and then waving Smoky the Conquering Hero off with John and Flavia and their carful of goodies to the Swag for Daddy to play Lord Bountiful Bear to the simple folk who liked to cut their own trees and fill up on eggnog and snacks afterward, and then—dragging it out some more!— lunch with Chloe and Uncle Henry at the downtown cafeteria (de- signed by old Grandfather Vick in the twenties) and waving to people they knew who were also going to the Ice Capades, followed by the Ice Capades itself, and then being driven across town in Uncle Henry's Jag at his favorite speed of fifteen miles an hour, his foot on and off the pedal to punctuate his sentences, enough to make you carsick, and on to the Vick house, where Uncle Henry had to sip his leisurely *drink* and the girls their accompanying Cokes (Uncle Henry could make one lit- tle jigger of scotch and a splash of soda in a tiny glass outlast two of Daddy's iced-tea glasses of bourbon and ice and water) and then they had to rehash the Ice Capades and all about the auditorium's under- ground ice-making system that old Mr. Vick had designed the year be- fore his death, and then make more civilized conversation in the echoing Vick dining room with gloomy family portraits over their supper of cold chicken, tomato aspic, potato salad, and chocolate cake, prepared the day before by Rosa. And *then* Uncle Henry, suddenly looking sad, shuffles over to the piano and begins tinkling his interminable Bach, and then his interminable Debussy, and Chloe, on cue, throws herself ecstatically into an armchair and dashes off one sketch after another (she must have a whole portfolio of them by now) of Uncle Henry tinkling at the piano.

Just when Tildy had been fantasizing that she might lose control of herself and start screaming, "I can't take any more of this torture!" and they would have to call an ambulance, since John wasn't back yet and Madeline was at the dance and Mama probably down at the studio developing the day's work, the phone mercifully rang and it was somebody wanting Uncle Henry to build them something and he excused himself and—finally!—she and Chloe headed upstairs to their room, for so Tildy thought of it, since she slept in it almost every Saturday night.

At last Tildy's announcement had been made, and Chloe had been sulky in her congratulations because she said Tildy ought to have told her sooner that it was not bad news rather than to let Chloe worry ever since Mother Ravenel had called Tildy out of study hall yesterday.

"Yeah, I know, and I'm really sorry, Chloe. You and I both were expecting the worst, but she totally surprised me. I wasn't trying to keep it from you or anything, but I wanted to wait until all the social activities were over and we could really concentrate."

"Well, Tildy, I could have enjoyed the Ice Capades and our other 'social activities' a lot more if I hadn't been worrying about you all day."

However, ruffled feathers had now been smoothed, two sets of teeth brushed, two sets of pajamas donned. The contrite Tildy, having convinced Chloe that she would be absolutely indispensable "with everything from casting to scenery—if 'we' decide to take it on," was now lying on her sofa bed, as she had been envisioning herself doing since yesterday, her bent arm shielding her eyes in order to concentrate better, and Chloe, curled up in a chair facing her, was reading aloud the fresh typescript of Suzanne Ravenel's old play, typed by Mother Ravenel herself, "with a couple of new revisions, Tildy. As long as we are on this earth—and I hope you will remember this as you go through your own life, dear—God graciously allows us to keep improving on what we have done. As I often say, we are all works in progress!"

✠

"SHOULD I JUST start at the beginning and go straight through?" asked Chloe.

"Well, of course, what else?" replied Tildy, having assumed her customary dominion. "That's the way the director of a Broadway play does it. He lies back on a couch and closes out all distractions, and the actors read through it for him, and he watches it unfold in his head. Those first impressions received in darkness often give birth to his most brilliant ideas."

Tildy, assembled on her sofa bed in her directorial pose, her arm flung dramatically across her face, looked more to Chloe like a schoolgirl in pink pajamas portraying, or perhaps parodying, her idea of "a damsel in distress on a sofa."

What a funny roller coaster this thing called friendship is, thought Chloe as she began to read aloud the prologue to *The Red Nun*. Ever since Tildy was called out of study hall yesterday, I have been sick with worry. I could see her taken from me, forced to transfer to the junior high in the middle of the year. I was already imagining the things I would miss most about her: her arrogant little pretensions, just like her pose on the fainting couch. All of today was under a cloud for me— Granddaddy's elegant cafeteria with the colored skylights and all my favorite foods on the tray, then the Ice Capades and the terrific seats Uncle Henry bought for us—because I kept reminding myself that this might be the last time, she would be making new friends at the public school and I would be left behind at Mount St. Gabriel's, a ghost walking the halls with my mother's ghost. Even Uncle Henry looked sad all day and I thought, It's because he knows. Her parents, or probably Madeline, phoned him with the bad news and they've decided, all of them, to keep it from me until after Christmas, because I'm a poor thing who can't bear any more losses. And then we come up to this room and we're hardly through the door when she springs it on me about Mother Ravenel's turnaround. Far from being kicked out, Tildy has suddenly been appointed Mother Ravenel's own artistic successor, and because

I'm not jumping up and down and slobbering with congratulations, she sticks her lower lip out and rolls her eyes when I explain how the whole day was under a cloud for me.

"Would you mind reading that prologue through again, Chloe?" mumbled Tildy from her arm-covered face. "I think I hear some creepy music but I can't decide just what."

Chloe began again:

"If you go out walking in our dark wood
When the hawk's face is tucked beneath his wing
And mist has risen in the hollows
And the owl shrieks:
Do not shrink if on your path
You meet a solitary ghost.
Ask it, 'What did you love most?
And what have you left undone?' "

"We can't use a flute, dammit, because that's what old Ravenel picked—Elaine Frew's mother composed a creepy tune on her flute."

"What about asking Elaine to compose something on the piano?"

"I'd rather go to hell and burn than ask a favor from that stuck-up prima donna."

"But wouldn't she be flattered? I mean, keeping it in the family and all."

"No, Chloe. Besides, as an instrument, the piano isn't spooky enough. It's too damned tinkly. Go on. What comes next?"

"Well, it's God speaking. Haven't you read it?"

"Of course I peeked at it, but I tried *not* to read it. I wanted to do it like the directors. Hear it in the dark of my mind. Mother Malloy said in our reading tutorials that hearing things from the lips of others is a whole other way of receiving the word. I told you, I'm dictating my Dickens paper to her in French. It gives things more body. I want this play to have more body. It can't be all streamlined ghosts marching in a straight line across a page, you know, Chloe."

"I didn't say it should be."

"No, I know you didn't. But—go on, read God's lines."

" 'I smashed continents together to make these mountains. I buckled them into sharp peaks before my doomed dinosaurs reached their fated growth. This big and no bigger, I said . . . and they became fossils. Then I sculpted my rough peaks, sent hundreds of millions of years of my wind and my rain down upon them, and then polished them with my glaciers. And eons passed like a day and a night, and on one good day, on one particular hill, in my own good time, I decided to set a school.' "

"Cut! Damn it all, who is going to do God's voice?"

"My mother said Mother Ravenel—or Suzanne—did God, as well as some of the other big parts."

"Well, I *know* that, from Mama, but that was in 1931 and we're in the 1950s. You can't have a freshman girl doing God's voice anymore. Theater has become more sophisticated. Can you go through it once more—don't try to change your voice, but read each word slowly and then leave a pause before the next. And please try not to yawn."

" 'I smashed—' "

"No, no: 'I' (pause) 'smashed' (pause)—like that. The pauses make it sound otherworldly, like He's speaking slowly in the language of His creatures so they'll be able to understand him."

" 'I . . .' " (Yawn.) "Sorry, Tildy, let me start over.

" 'I . . . smashed . . . continents . . . together . . . to . . . make . . . these . . . mountains . . .' "

"Well, the pauses make it better, but what we really need is someone like John's rumbly Paul Robeson voice that vibrates out of his nostrils."

"You mean Flavia's John? I don't think we'd be allowed to ask people who aren't in the ninth grade."

"I *know* that, Chloe. But why couldn't we *record* John's voice? I'll have to coach him, of course. What I'd do is say each word and then he'd say it after me and some technical person could string it together and God's voice would come out of a tape machine offstage. That gives me the shivers; it would be perfect!"

"Who's going to do all this technical work?"

"Oh, we can find somebody. Go on with God."

CHAPTER 18

Two Nuns on a Walk

Saturday, September 1, 2001
Feast of St. Giles, abbot; Commemoration of the Twelve Holy Brothers
Grounds of the St. Scholastica Retirement House
Warm evening, clear and bright, following Compline

"I LOVE OUR evening walks, Mother Galyon. You are very kind to let me hang on your arm. And please stop me if I rattle on too much. There's so much in my head. We recorded just twenty-eight Catholic deaths in the Boston area today. That's one of our low numbers, isn't it? I try not to dwell on it, but one day my name will be on that list, only I won't be at the other end of the phone to repeat it so you can take down the particulars. And Sister Bridget will have to call down to Mountain City and have somebody spread the word for my old girls to offer up prayers for my soul. I just hope I will have finished the memoir by then, but that's in God's hands."

"How far have you gotten, Mother?"

"This morning I finished the—well, let's call it an *overture* to the 'fifties' chapter. I've been procrastinating by offering a capsule history survey of 'the decades so far.' The French would call it *reculer pour mieux sauter:* I balk for fear of jumping in. Remember those girls on the playground who never could dart right into a moving jump rope but stood there teetering back and forth, bobbing their necks like chickens?"

"What are you balking at, Mother? Watch your step; the gravel's uneven here."

"Thank you, dear. You know, I can still see the stars out of the corners of my eyes. You know what I'm balking at? The class of fifty-five. I mean, the class of fifty-five in its ninth-grade year. Those girls and their catastrophic play and the awful aftermath, with its repercussions. You were there."

"Yes, but I wouldn't have called the play in itself catastrophic. To anyone seeing it for the first time—and most people in the audience were, you must remember—it came across as an ambitious performance with some obscure passages and some funny parts, all of which probably weren't intended to be funny: that offstage voice of God, for instance. The aftermath was tragic, but not necessarily a direct outcome of the play."

✠

FOR THE GOOD of us both, help me establish some coordinates, invokes Frances Galyon, Order of St. Scholastica, age seventy-nine, slowing her pace to accommodate this older, shorter, all-but-sightless nun on their nightly walk.

This diminished chatterbox clinging to my arm has been in my life longer than any other person. I have admired and hated her by turns. She was the tall one when I began looking up to her. When I arrived at Mount St. Gabriel's as a freshman boarder on a Knights of Columbus scholarship, she was in the romance of her novitiate. She floated about the school in her short white veil. She was taking courses at the junior college and also teaching second grade. As soon as I said where I was from, girls began linking us and comparing us. "Oh, Charleston is where *she* is from. Her name was Suzanne before she became a nun, she was president of her class all four years of high school and the first girl ever to take vows before finishing her senior year. She received her diploma in her postulant's habit. I suppose you knew her family in Charleston?"

I said I thought my father knew her father. That seemed safe enough. I was a new girl and wanted to have the right connections. "Oh, but her father is dead," I was quickly informed. "It was a hunting accident the weekend after Black Friday. He was alone in a cramped blind and his elbow slipped and he ended up shooting himself rather than the bird. At least that's the official story. She had only just come to Mount St. Gabriel's as a boarder. They wouldn't let her go home for the funeral."

Her father had been a prominent attorney who handled a number of

trusts, one girl said, and there were rumors that he may have been bor-
rowing from clients, planning to replenish the shortfall with no one the
wiser; but then Black Friday came and all his clients wanted to be assured that their investments were safe. No charges were ever brought.
That was because, said another girl, quoting her own father, the brothers promised to make good on the shortfalls, and who wouldn't gamble
on keeping your mouth shut in the chance of being reimbursed one day
rather than bring charges now and make an enemy of the family and
end up with a great big nothing?

The girls my age at Mount St. Gabriel's (these days I would call
them my "peers") seemed so knowing about worldly things like motives and money. I had expected them to be more pious and innocent, as
I am sure my father did. He was pious and innocent himself, went to
Mass every morning and prayed for my dead mother, then walked to the
roundhouse and began inspecting the flock assigned him. He was a
master mechanic on the Southern Railway. In those pocket-size memo-
randum books the insurance companies used to give away, he recorded
for over twenty years his daily ministries to the steam engines under his
charge.

Eng 4882 not getting steam to water pump and pump won't supply boiler . . .
1369 stoker elevator wasting coal bad . . .
Eng 4877. Put indicator on superheater damper . . .
Sand pipes on 4567 not putting sand on rail. Needed pulling
out . . .
4877 flue rod tied on hand rail. Get it off.

Little wonder that I had no difficulty imagining a God who knew
the exact number of hairs on my head and kept track of every sparrow
that fell to earth: didn't my father keep track of every beloved steam
engine assigned to his care?

As I count myself assigned to Mother Suzanne Ravenel, fellow sin-
ner and sister in Christ, sharing an enforced proximity in this retirement enclosure, and both of us heading toward our diamond jubilees as
members of the all but extinct Order of St. Scholastica.

So now, on this evening walk, how do I keep us firmly on the path of the truly present and steer us away from those tempting culs-de-sac of resentment and remorse?

"Do you have a deadline, Mother?" I ask.

"What?" I feel her stiffen on my arm. "Oh, the memoir. I thought for a minute you said 'death line.' Well, I promised the girls I would work diligently through the months, and if nothing untoward happens and if I keep my marbles, I hope to bring the final tapes in my suitcase when they fly me down to Mountain City next May."

"Today is the first of September"—Mother Galyon counted off the intervening months on her fingers—"so you have eight months to go and you've already done how much since you began?"

"Well, let's see, I've done all the groundwork chapters—the history of our Order and the establishment and beginnings of the school, with some homiletic digressions about holy daring and a woman's freedom in God—haven't those two concepts of our foundress's always fascinated you?—and I've completed the decade chapters all the way up to the fifties, and, as I just told you, I've been procrastinating, via my little overture to the fifties, by going back and reviewing the highlights of where we've already been."

"So in four months, aside from all the groundwork and the homiletic digressions, you have covered the first four decades. As the school closed in 1990, you have eight months to cover the remaining four decades. Just doing the math, Mother, your prospects look very good."

She jerks us both to a standstill and wails, "But what do I do about the class of fifty-five in its freshman year?"

It is as close to her as her own face.

"In the past decades, Mother, the decades you have completed, how did you go about reporting on each class? Say, the class of 1915 or 1930 or 1944?"

"Well, you can't put in everything, can you? You put in the highlights. The funny things. The inspiring occasions. The outstanding girls. And it's only just *my* memoir; it all has to come out of what *I* can remember. And even if I have been part of the school longer than anyone, there are bound to be gaps. Of course, Beatrix, who's transcribing the tapes, has been invaluable with the old yearbooks. She phones me faithfully every few weeks. We go through whatever decade I am on—

she reads aloud from the yearbooks, and that nudges my memory. For years, you know, when I had my sight, I used to pore over those old yearbooks whenever I had insomnia. I kept them all in my office, and I'd take one or two at a time to my room and leaf through the pages. Old pictures and the way girls characterize one another and what they leave to one another can tell you so much."

"Have you and Beatrix begun on the fifties yearbooks yet?"

"Funny you should ask. When she phoned last Saturday, she said, 'Well, Mother, we're up to the fifties. Shall I read from the 1950 *Scholastica*?' I had it on the tip of my tongue to say, 'No, let's wait. I am meditating on an overview of where we have been so far and what was going on in the world at the time.' But then, you know what? I felt this sudden sense of *reprieve*. Because the 1950 yearbook would only have the classes of 1950 through '53. The awful year, with its 1951-through-'52 freshmen faces, wouldn't come until the fifty-*two* yearbook. And it will be the only yearbook that contains that unforgettable cluster of freshmen girls that haunts my soul. In the very next *Scholastica* their faces would be gone. So I said, 'Onward, dear Beatrix, full steam ahead into the fifties.' And she began reading through the graduating class of 1950—that's the way we do it; the focus is on the seniors. I could call up their faces as she named them and read the little captions under their pictures—do you remember your own caption, Mother Galyon?"

"I believe it was something like 'Ever studious and thoughtful.' What was yours, Mother?"

She lightens her grip on my arm, straightens herself, and drops thirty years on the spot. "Energy incarnate," she crows, with a triumphant cackle.

And I have to fight down the bile of resentment. We are here in the present under these constellations, the Virgin and Swan and Archer and Winged Horse of this autumnal tilt, in the year 2001, Common Era, crisscrossed by the winking reds and greens of the Logan jets. Two old nuns, without a convent or a resident priest, without a school or pupils, shuffling along in the starlight on their retirement compound in a suburb of Boston. This old girl on my arm is no longer the ruddy-faced novice mistress in her prime who rebuffed the new postulant ("There are so *many* Charlestons, aren't there, Sister?") when, to ingratiate myself with her, I had referred to the city in which we had both been raised

as "our mutual hometown." Further along in my postulancy, she had
dangled before me the specter of a worse exclusion: "Whatever length
your stay with us in the Order, Sister Galyon, we must both keep in
mind that God will be using it, whether it is a mere six months or your
whole life, for His good."

And then, after I had taken final vows, had done my graduate work
summa cum laude at the university, served as principal of the grammar
school for one year, and filled in for her as headmistress of the academy
during her leave of absence in 1952–53, she returns to administer the
coup de grâce.

Reverend Mother calls me in and says I am being sent to be headmistress of the Order's academy in Boston. Though a nun isn't supposed to ask why, I couldn't hide my dismay. "But I had thought," I
protested, "that I would go back to being principal of the grammar
school here." Vague, unflappable Reverend Mother Barrington. Her
glasses shone at you, while the soft gray eyes behind swam with a pre-
occupied rapture. Some said she prayed ceaselessly and that was the secret of her equanimity. But if you insisted on her attention, the eyes
sharpened and fastened on the petitioner, who then felt like a fledgling
being swept away from ground-level dangers by a great mothering
bird. When you landed again, after advice and higher wisdom had been
dispensed, you shook out your ruffled feathers and flapped off to obey
orders. The wisdom and advice on this occasion being that when I had
been serving as headmistress in Mother Ravenel's stead while she cared
for her dying mother in Charleston, Reverend Mother and others had
seen that my gifts would be put to fuller use with older girls. And so,
when Mother Ravenel returned to resume her duties, Reverend Mother
had made a proposal. The academy's enrollment was on the increase.
And, considering the loss of Mother Malloy and the marriage of Miss
Mendoza to the new headmaster of the boys' division, might Mother
Ravenel not welcome having Mother Galyon as her assistant headmistress?

"Unfortunately," said Reverend Mother, her eyes already going remote behind the glint of her glasses, "Mother Ravenel was not too keen
on the idea, and that, my dear, is all I shall say. You are an exceptional
teacher and a fine example to the older girls. Mother Ravenel is a dy-
namic headmistress and very popular in the Mountain City community.

She has been devoted to the school since she came to us as a girl in 1929. Our own foundress, in her final days, made provisions for her to stay on at Mount St. Gabriel's. It was perhaps a little selfish of me to want to keep two stars under the same roof."

DADDY LEFT HIS sorrows at the altar rail each morning and went forth to tend to his ailing engines. Given my coordinates—time, place, age, life history—what else do I have to do on this September evening but play master mechanic to a sister in religion spinning her wheels in the roundhouse?

Steam pipe to hot-water pipe on Engine Ravenel leaking pride. Flue clogged with remorse. Take guilty twist out of brakes.

Full steam ahead into the fifties.

A Confessional Cassette

Late Saturday night
September 1, 2001
Mother Ravenel's room
St. Scholastica Retirement House

My dear Beatrix,

Please consider this tape as a personal letter from me to you. The whole tape is from me to you.

I have just returned from a very restorative evening walk with Mother Frances Galyon, whom you will remember from the school year of 1952–53, when she filled in as your headmistress while I was on leave of absence. And then in the fall of 1953, our Order transferred Mother Galyon to our academy in Boston, where she served for many years as headmistress and later as teacher of Latin and higher mathematics. Like me, she was an old Mount St. Gabriel's girl, entering the Order her senior year—as I did—and now that we are old women she is being a good sport about leading me around in the dark, keeping me "on the track," as she puts it. I didn't realize until tonight how much she had loved Mount St. Gabriel's and how unhappy she was about leaving the South. She said it would have broken her heart if she had not already given it over to God. Until recently I have always thought of her as rather unapproachable and not very socially inclined, but isn't it wonderful how God keeps loosening our biases and showing us more sides of one another?

Tonight I learned that Mother Galyon is possessed of a discerning heart along with her intellectual gifts.

Tonight I admitted to her that I was holding back from my chapter on the 1950s because I dreaded reliving that "toxic year" that you and I spoke of last June at the picnic on your mountaintop.

And she said the most perceptive thing, Beatrix. She said, "But haven't you been reliving it ever since? Could it be that it has grown to occupy so much space in your mind that it crowds out the material that truly belongs in your account of that decade in a school history?"

"But how do I account for *it*?" I persisted.

That's when Mother Galyon reminded me that I had said that our focus is on the seniors as we go through the yearbooks. "And they never became seniors at Mount St. Gabriel's," she went on. "When the class of 1955 gets the spotlight in their 1955 yearbook, those girls who haunt you aren't there anymore. Yet it's obvious that you still feel the need for some accounting. Have you gone into this with your spiritual directors over the years?"

"I have tried," I said, "but aside from Father Krafft, who could be very rigorous, they've all been in a rush to absolve me and tell me not to be so hard on myself. One of them suggested I take up yoga and learn to play the guitar. In my last conference with him, Father Krafft told me I was rendering God's grace nugatory by continuing to 'scrape the cauldron' of that year for more 'evil snacks,' and that I had already done my penance during my year of exile. My last director, who wore a Red Sox cap and flip-flops, said my refusal to forgive myself was pure pride. He told me to read some fantasy by C. S. Lewis about people on a bus and what keeps them from getting off the bus and entering the great freedom and spaciousness of heaven."

"Well, did you read it?" Mother Galyon asked, and when I said no she laughed, and then, I'm afraid, we exchanged anecdotes about some less-than-helpful spiritual directors. She said it had been years since she'd heard anyone in religious life use the word "nugatory," which had a ring of authority that "trifling" or "worthless" couldn't match. But she went on to say she did like the idea of heaven as a place of great freedom and limitless space in which we could accept the shock of being our fullest selves in God's image, whatever our circumstances.

I was very taken with this idea, too. "Yes," I said, "but how do we get there? Do you see any buses lined up outside the retirement house?"

At this point we had reached the gates at the far end of the estate, and it was time to turn around and walk back to the house. There were lights on in various rooms, and I was pleased that I could see those. As we came closer I could even make out the brightly colored wraiths in constant motion on the TV screen in the nuns' parlor.

I could feel Mother Galyon thinking very strenuously on our return walk. Finally she said, "The buses were C. S. Lewis's choice of transport, but we can get there just as well by our own means." She said trains came naturally to her because her father had been a railroad man, and she liked to think in terms of trains and their problems and how to fix them and get them back on their assigned tracks.

"All you need, Mother Ravenel," she said, "is a way to get from one place in yourself to a better place." Then she said, "Maybe your mode of transport could be your tape recorder. You're comfortable with that mode of travel, aren't you?"

"Wait a minute," I said. "C. S. Lewis gets buses, you get trains, but I am supposed to travel to heaven sitting alone in my room in front of a tape recorder?"

"Why not?" she said. "Tell your story to someone alive, someone you care about and trust. Just tell the parts that you are tired of reliving, the parts that haunt you. Get it out of the darkness and invite a fellow creature to look at it with you under some shared light. Then ask God's blessing at the end of the tape, and send it off to that person and be done with it."

I thought of you immediately, dear Beatrix.

Now that I am beginning to see, thanks to Mother Galyon's perspicacity, which things do not serve any purpose in a school memoir though they may have shaped my behavior as headmistress in the "toxic year," what I am going to try to do is to relate those parts to you, Beatrix, in order to achieve a better perspective.

This story had its beginnings back in the early 1930s, when my classmate and best friend, Antonia Tilden, and I decided that we wanted to enter the Order together. Antonia had known as early as age ten that she wanted to be a nun, and this was just fine with Antonia's parents, but Antonia had a twin sister, Cornelia, who never liked me. She kept her eye on me from the very beginning and made no secret of her misgivings about our alliance. The sisters were identical twins, but Antonia had a higher nature; she was easy, and tolerant of people's foibles, whereas Cornelia was critical of everybody and had a corrosive tongue.

CHAPTER 19

Unmerited Degradation

Sunday evening, January 6, 1952
Pine Cone Lodge
Mountain City, North Carolina

> All this time I was working at Murdstone and Grinby's in the same common way, and with the same common companions, and with the same sense of unmerited degradation as at first. But I never, happily for me no doubt, made a single acquaintance, or spoke to any of the many boys whom I saw daily in going to the warehouse, in coming from it, and in prowling about the streets at mealtimes. I led the same secretly unhappy life; but I led it in the same lonely, self-reliant manner.

MAUD NORTON'S *David Copperfield* paper was due on Tuesday, the first day of the new semester. The draft of ten handwritten pages would have to be cut back to the five Mother Malloy had specified. Getting in everything you planned to say in five pages required a whole different approach from having ten pages to roam around in. Plus, what you had planned to say kept turning into something else, and often something much less grand. "The Pungent Ache of the Soul in *David Copperfield*," a.k.a. "The Universal Aches of David," a.k.a. "Transfers," had been, in Maud's retrospective opinion, a brilliant concept. The concept being how you can experience more of yourself as you follow a character through his story if the story is told well enough to help you make the *transfer*. Maud had planned to demonstrate some of these transfers as they occurred throughout the novel, and Mother Malloy had pronounced it a very ambitious plan. Though she had advised Maud to take a less dramatic title.

During the two months she had been working on this paper, Maud had learned many things about writing and almost too much about life. The life lessons inflicted on her during the Christmas vacation in Palm Beach curled her lip and nauseated her.

She intended, however, like David, to bear the unmerited degradation in self-reliant apartness until some turn in her fortunes could rescue her or until she grew strong enough to rescue herself. There was no one she could talk to about these things. Lily, who now crept into Mr. Art Foley's room when he was in residence, was a contributor to the overall atmosphere of dishonor. Granny, downstairs, who turned her radio programs louder these nights so she would not "overhear" anything dishonorable in the Pine Cone Lodge, had not been well. Walking across a room or even speaking a long sentence made her breathless, her ankles had swollen to the size of elephant ankles, and there was a not-quite-fresh smell in her usually immaculate kitchen. The boardinghouse trade had fallen off since the recent opening of two new motels on the tunnel road behind Tildy's house. There were more traveling salesmen than ever in Mountain City, but they wanted their own bathrooms and to choose their meals from a menu. They wanted the freedom and privacy of impersonal rooms without ailing grandmothers spying on them.

Tildy would have been possible to talk to. Oh, very possible! But Tildy was no longer hers. How was Tildy managing with her *David Copperfield* paper? When they were best friends, they had discussed their papers and Maud would suggest topics for Tildy to choose from. She would make an outline and sometimes let Tildy wheedle her into sketching out a rough draft for Tildy to "take off from."

The nearest guide Maud had for her lonely self-reliance was David Copperfield; though Maud couldn't help feeling that there were certain degradations he and his creator had never experienced because they had been born boys.

Since last summer, the Palm Beach Nortons had been cast as the potential rescuers of Maud's life story: Anabel and Cyril Norton, who had made overtures to Cyril's fourteen-year-old daughter from his first marriage to Lily. There was money from this second wife to do something splendid for Mr. Norton's daughter, if she should prove worthy. On

Maud's triumphal return from her summer stay in Palm Beach, Granny and Lily had begun to elaborate upon expected Norton largesse. There was to be college, of course, with no stinting or choosing between second choices or need for servile scholarships. And the right clothes and the right travels and meeting the right people. "Mark my word, they will probably insist upon her making her debut down there in Palm Beach," Granny Roberts had predicted. "A debut is an important thing for a girl; it sets her up for life."

"Oh, really, Mother? Too bad I didn't have one, then. And too bad you didn't, either" was Lily Norton's acid reply.

"What's done is done . . . for us," declared Granny stoically, "but the child must have her chance. Mark my word, they will be wanting her to spend Christmas with them."

"If we haven't heard something by Thanksgiving, it's not a good sign," Granny had said when November had arrived with no word from the Nortons. And Lily had blown up and declared herself sick of waiting on the whims of the rich. Of course the invitation came almost immediately after, followed by long-distance phone calls about dates and planes. "You must always call us collect," Anabel Norton would instruct Lily, who smoldered each time she reversed the charges, then hurried off to mimic Anabel's self-satisfied lisp to Mr. Foley. Now, each time Art Foley departed for the Atlanta office to refurbish his stash of gourmet items, he would slip his arm around Lily's waist and croon in his oily baritone, "Remember, dear Lily, you *musth al-wathes* call us collect." To which Lily's arch retort was "I don't call men, Mr. Foley. You know where I am if you want to call me."

Then at the last minute, Anabel, all aflutter, had phoned Lily to ask if Maud could take an earlier plane. "The Dudley Weatherbys are hosting a Christmas cotillion dance on Friday for young Duddy, who's home from Groton, and when my friend Mimi Weatherby heard Maud was coming, she said Duddy would be so thrilled if Maud, whom he so admired from last summer, would be his partner for the cotillion."

So off Maud flew, on Thursday rather than Saturday, to satisfy the social ambitions of Lily and Granny and Anabel Norton. Anabel aspired to the patronage of Mimi Weatherby, Maud remembered from her stepmother's name-dropping of this personage last summer. There seemed to be staircase after staircase for social climbers in Palm Beach. Probably Mimi, whose husband was a past president of the Old Guard

Society, and who herself was on the board of directors of the Society of the Four Arts and the Palm Beach Round Table (two clubs Anabel longed to be asked to join)—probably Mimi Weatherby herself had her eye trained on some further roped-off staircase spiraling into the loftiest realms of the social stratosphere.

Maud recalled "young Duddy" merely as a boy with insolent piggy eyes in a sunburned face, always embedded in a pack of other boys who gawked rudely at girls. Having spent most of her life in the company of women, Maud hadn't appreciated until last summer how much more subtle her sex was, compared to boys of the same age.

Duddy's "so admiring her" must mean her looks, she thought; she had never had a conversation with him. It seemed strange, though, that at this late date he didn't have a partner for his own dance. Maud guessed that she and Duddy might be pawns in some social exchange between Anabel Norton and Mimi Weatherby.

This turned out to be the case, though Maud had no joy in the acuity of her foresight.

ANABEL MET MAUD at the Palm Beach airport on Wednesday afternoon, and they headed straight for Worth Avenue to outfit Maud for the Weatherbys' cotillion dance.

"Is it going to be at their house?" Maud asked.

"Heavens no, darling, at the Palm City Club. There *will* be a party at their home on Saturday, and you and I will attend that together. Your father hasn't been going out much lately."

"Is he sick?"

"I believe the medical profession is coming around to regarding it as a sickness. But the good news is, he's on the road to recovery if he can stick it out. Cyril is the sweetest man in the world, but it's all or nothing with him. One little slip off the wagon and he's . . . well, he's something else entirely. He's better staying away from the parties this season. I'm sorry to greet you with this news, Maud. Last summer he wanted to win the respect of his daughter and went without a drop for your entire stay. But as soon as you left, he rewarded himself with one little martini, and it went downhill from there."

Stunned, Maud stared out the window of the Cadillac at the palm trees that lined the road. The tropical foliage seemed a mockery of the

Christmases she had always known. This past summer she had been un-aware that her father was on any wagon. She had assumed his most self-destructive habit was snacking in the kitchen while the cook prepared the next meal. But now Anabel was all but saying that the strain of Maud's last visit with them had pushed him over the edge the minute it was over. Had Lily known about the existence of this wagon, or was it a more recent thing?

"Maybe I shouldn't have come," she said.

"Nonsense! Cyril is so proud of you. We've both looked forward to your visit." Maud wished that Lily and Mr. Foley had not made a game out of Anabel's affected speech, because her stepmother's reassurances now came to her ridiculously distorted. *Nonsensth! Thyril isth tho proud of you.* All summer, Maud had been as unconscious of her stepmother's lisp as she had been of Cyril's wagon.

"Why, you're the best thing we've got going for us—you give us something to live for," Anabel hurried on, and Maud did her best to hear the words without the debasing sibilances. "I only wanted to warn you to expect a change, because you'll see it yourself. He's lost a lot of weight, and he's being medicated."

"Is he . . . still . . . off the wagon?"

"Oh, goodness no. As I said, he's on the road to recovery—as long as he can keep it up. Since November he's been a day patient at a very exclusive—and expensive, I might add—treatment center. That's why he didn't come to meet you at the airport. He's getting his daily fix over at the center. They medicate them, you see, so they don't crave a drink, but it makes him nauseated. Then he sees his psychiatrist. Also, he gets pills for depression."

"Depression," Maud repeated. She couldn't think of what else to say.

"It's part of the syndrome. You get depressed when you with-draw. Of course, the doctors are now saying that alcohol itself is a depressant. But the alcoholic doesn't feel depressed as long as he's drink-ing, because that's his chosen form of escape. As long as he keeps drink-ing, he *thinks* he feels wonderful. Only he has to keep pouring the shots or he'll start feeling depressed."

Escape from what? Maud wished she could ask. Once again she won-dered whether the wagon had existed back in the days when her mother had been married to Mr. Norton.

"Now let's switch to a happier subject," said Anabel, turning onto Worth Avenue. "Your dress for the Weatherbys' cotillion. And you'll need a little beaded purse and the right shoes. It's such a delight to shop for you because you're tall and so young and pretty. And look, here is a parking spot right in *front* of Tat Saunders. We'll go to Tat first and then see what the other places have."

"What is Duddy Weatherby like?" Maud asked.

"Oh, he's at Groton. That is one of the top prep schools in the country. And my friend Mimi naturally hopes he will go to Princeton, like his father, and follow Dudley into the stock exchange. Let's see, what else? Well, *I* know what else!" Anabel playfully jingled her keys before dropping them into her purse. "He is smitten with you, my dear."

"But we've never had a single conversation."

"Someone with your assets, Maud, can afford the luxury of silence" was Anabel's triumphant comeback. Maud tried hard to screen out the *thomeone* and the *athets* part.

If Anabel hadn't tipped her off about the wagon ordeal, Maud might have attributed the changes in her father to a successful diet regime and simply feeling more relaxed with his daughter on her second visit. Cyril Norton had lost his potbelly and fleshy cheeks and looked, well, more as a girl would wish her father to look. His movements were slow and dignified, his speech deliberate, though on the languid side. He was far less apprehensive of her this time. He asked her questions about her school, specific questions about what she was studying and what the nuns were like, and questions about her mother, even about Granny. He ticked off, course by course, the delicious dinner Granny had cooked for him that one time he had stayed with them at the Pine Cone Lodge. His night with them, he recalled, had coincided with Granny's favorite radio program, and so they had all four adjourned to the living room and listened to *Doctor Christian* together. "I remember your grandmother turned the lights off. She said she could hear it better in the dark. Does she still do that?"

He seemed to take pride in his powers of recall. "It's one of the good side effects of these pills. I can sit and think about things for hours. The most amazing things come back. The other day I remembered how your mother would flourish those tasseled menus and set off across the dining room, her chin sky-high, when she was hostess at the resort where we met. One of the not-so-good side effects of the pills is"—here he cut an apologetic glance at Anabel—"I don't want to do much of anything else."

Maud's hours with her father and Anabel *before* the Weatherby dance on Friday were to be the brightest ones of her Christmas stay with them. Everything leading up to that event was full of hope, and Maud felt that somehow she was its emblem. They dressed up and went out to restaurants, a prosperous, handsome little family. Cyril Norton drank Sanka with his meals and sometimes looked sleepy. Maud tried on her new finery for them, and Cyril Norton fished his medically broadened memory for stories of his marriage to Lily, when he was on the road selling college jewelry for the Balfour Company. "I was their top salesman on the eastern seaboard when you were a little girl. It is dumbfounding to me now how effortlessly I got people to order those rings. I'll never rake in such gobs of money again." He uttered a weak, astonished laugh. "Luckily, Anabel has enough for us both, and"—another quick glance at his wife—"she seems to like having me around."

"As long as you are behaving yourself," said Anabel, "you are the sweetest man in the world."

DUDDY WEATHERBY, IN dinner jacket and black tie, entered the Nortons' living room holding a transparent florist's box at arm's distance, as though it might possibly explode. Inside was a white orchid with a pink center. In his own lapel he wore a white carnation. His summer tan had been replaced by a pale forehead spotted with pink pimples. He succeeded in handing the box to Maud without meeting her eyes. Everything slowed down. It was as though all of them had helped themselves to Cyril Norton's pills. Even Anabel's exclamation of how perfectly the orchid would go with Maud's dress sounded like a record played at a too slow speed. When Cyril Norton asked Duddy if he wouldn't like to take a seat while Anabel was fastening the orchid to Maud's dress, Duddy rolled his piggy eyes. "I guess not," he said to the ceiling. "We're running late because my dad, as usual, mismatched his studs and cuff links." He imparted this information with a titter of satisfaction, meaning what? That not everyone's father could rise regularly to such cavalier disregard for his effects?

At first Maud thought it was the chauffeur standing under the streetlight. But it was Mr. Weatherby in his dinner jacket. "He always wears his Rolls-Royce cap when he drives his 1929 Phantom," explained Duddy. "And I wear it when I drive it, but I have to go on the back roads with it till I get my license. Mother went on ahead to the club to greet the guests who get there too early."

Duddy's father doffed his chauffeur's cap to Maud and introduced himself. He smelled like Tildy's father after five o'clock in the afternoon, and sometimes before, and Maud was reminded why her father was better off staying away from the Christmas parties.

She and Duddy were tucked away ceremoniously in the backseat of the Rolls and Mr. Weatherby instructed Maud not to lean against her door, because it had been known to fly open. Duddy gave a sinister little snicker. Maud wondered why, if that was the case, she had not been seated on the other side. Or did that door fly open, too? There were many things Maud was thinking, but she was not about to say any of them aloud. (*Thomeone with your athets, Maud, can afford the luxury of silence.*) Maud was even feeling nostalgic for her stepmother before they were three blocks from the Norton house. Luckily, Mr. Weatherby had launched into a monologue about vintage Rolls-Royces, which lasted them most of the way to the club, but then suddenly he was asking about the Nortons. "I run into Anabel almost every day, but I haven't seen Cyril around town recently. What's your dad been up to?"

"He's been staying at home mostly," Maud answered. But then, to dispel any notion of *sickness,* she added, "He's been doing a lot of thinking about things."

This was met with a silence lengthy enough for Maud to imagine ways in which this information might be misconstrued.

"Well, good for him," Mr. Weatherby finally responded. "Hell," he cheerfully continued, "I wish *I* could find some time to do some thinking about things. Though Lord knows what I might catch myself thinking."

Beside her, Duddy gave another sinister snicker.

Maud's country club experience had been limited to the one in Mountain City. She swam in its pool ·as Tildy's guest and ate dinner with the Strattons on its outdoor terraces or in the smoky grill room. Hiding in the bushes outside its ballroom windows, she and Tildy had given themselves flirting tutorials by watching Madeline enchant partner after partner at a Christmas dance. The Mountain City Country Club was a low-lying building of golden-gray stone whose rooms you could count and most of which opened straightforwardly into one another. It was surrounded on three sides by its golf course and was approached from the fourth side so that you or the automobile in which you were riding would not be smacked by an errant golf ball.

On first approach, the Palm City Club, which Anabel spoke of with such reverence, presented itself to Maud's eye as a picturesque imitation of a Spanish mission with a lit-up bell tower. But as Mr. Weatherby's Phantom purred along between high hedges and giant palms, the mission image sprawled into a bewildering maze of extensions and facades.

Even after her ill-fated "tour of the grounds" of the Palm City Club, which would occur later in the evening, Maud would be unable to recall whether the ocean or the lake was to the left or right of the club, or where the sequestered tennis courts were in relation to the golf course, or up which spiral stairs she had fled to repair her own compromised facade. The labyrinthine club, with its overweening prolixity of styles, would serve in the future as Maud's mental image whenever she felt like reflecting upon the treacherous route of the social climber. Its standoffish byways were so much truer to the nature of the journey than her previous notion of simple stairways leading the climber up and up into the next roped-off sphere of belonging.

Mrs. Weatherby, flanked by stone urns bristling with spiky flowers, stood in a tiled-and-mirrored alcove, welcoming guests to her son's dance. Maud, who was nearsighted, glimpsed a handsome, beautifully dressed girl. Moving closer, she was sorry that the girl's nervous smile ruined the whole effect, and even sorrier when she saw that she was facing her own reflection. Mimi Weatherby, whom she scarcely knew, grabbed her by the shoulders and lavished praise on her. "I know where *you've* been, young lady! Isn't Tat Saunders just the best?"

She forced Maud and Duddy into the alcove with her to welcome the guests. They were mostly Duddy's contemporaries but there was a sprinkling of adults, who bantered back and forth, alluding to events that had taken place as recently as this afternoon, some at this very same club. They all seemed to have been to the same parties this week. Most of them had Smoky Stratton's after-five odor on their breaths. Mr. Weatherby, who had insisted on parking "his own baby," sauntered past his wife's reception line with a jovial wave and headed for the bar.

Mimi Weatherby presented Maud to the guests. To some, she was "Maud Norton, who is with us from North Carolina." To others, she was "Maud Norton, you know, Cyril and Anabel Norton's daughter—

she's spending Christmas with them." And then certain others Mimi would kiss or nuzzle, after which she would say, "Oh! And this is Duddy's friend Maud Norton, visiting from her school in North Carolina," making it sound like Maud was boarding at this school. Occasionally Mimi would murmur, "Isn't she precious?"

Maud shook hands and dropped the occasional curtsy when some older person seemed to expect it. Having deplored the handsome girl's nervous smile in the mirror, she kept her face still. A lady asked which school in North Carolina and said she knew someone whose cousin had gone to Mount St. Gabriel's. Duddy, after swapping mumbles with friends and putting in his share of "Yes sir"s and "No ma'am"s to adults, turned to Maud and said, "Oh, wait." He fumbled in his pockets and extracted a palm-sized dance card, equipped with a tiny pencil. "You know what this is for, don't you?"

"I hope I'm not *that* sheltered," Maud snapped back crossly. A nearby man gave an appreciative chortle. Duddy reddened, but saved his dignity with his trademark snicker. "And here's Timmie Veech," exclaimed Mimi, embracing a plump red-haired boy who wore his dinner jacket more like a straitjacket. "And Troy Veech. I thought you were off breaking wild horses in Montana or something. What brings you back to placid old Palm Beach?"

"Someone had to drive my little brother to the Christmas parties. Our folks are in Bermuda. You're looking very attractive this evening, Mrs. Weatherby."

"Thank you, Mr. Veech. I try."

"But unlike most, you never look as though you had to try. After the holidays, I'm off to join the Army."

"The Army! Why?"

"Why not?" Troy Veech countered languidly. He looked some ten or fifteen years older than his little brother. His hair, a silky faded red, flopped insouciantly over his brow, and he emanated a contemptuous elegance. He wore his evening clothes as if he had tugged them off their hanger at the last minute and trusted them to fall into place, and they had. Maud recognized him as the man who had laughed when she'd snapped at Duddy.

"And this is Maud Norton, Duddy's date," said Mimi. "She's visiting from her boarding school in North Carolina."

"How do you do, Maud Norton." Troy Veech raised Maud's hand to within an inch or so from his lips, then puckered his lips at the air in between. "Timmie, let's see if Miss Norton has any dances to spare for the likes of us," he said. Maud handed her card and pencil to Timmie, and the brothers stepped to one side of the receiving line. "Take this one and that one," Maud heard Troy say. "But I can't do that one—it's a tango," protested Timmie. "Just shut up, will you," said Troy Veech, "and put your name down for those two."

When Troy was returning the card to Maud, Mimi Weatherby whirled away from the lady she was speaking to in midsentence and snatched at his sleeve. "Please don't tell me, Troy, that you're going to *enlist*."

"Whatever gave you that idea, Mrs. Weatherby?"

"Well, you said you were off to join the Army."

"Off to Officer Candidates School, then, if that makes you feel easier on my behalf. But off to join the Army sounds more irrevocable."

"Since when did *you* go in for the irrevocable, Troy Veech?"

"It attracts me more and more, Mrs. Weatherby, the older I get."

Maud was puzzled by the facetious animosity between Duddy's mother and Timmie's older brother.

The dancing, she was relieved to find, was going to be the least of her worries. Duddy had done his time in ballroom classes: he was light on his feet and knew how to lead a girl without clutching at her dress or colliding with her feet. Maud relaxed during their second dance, a fox-trot. Too bad Duddy hadn't simply materialized as her dance partner on this terrace surrounded by palm trees, without any of the stiff, snickering preliminaries they had been put through.

Now she felt safe enough to look around herself and enjoy her situation. She was the official date of the host, booked by him for three more dances, which included the last, and he seemed as proud as she that they could display themselves so professionally before his parents and friends. He didn't try to make small talk, and he came off much better as the silent type. In this torch-lit evening setting his blemishes were not noticeable, and she could visualize him as the man he would become when he was as old as Troy Veech. And she looked as well as she had ever looked in her life: the dress from Miss Tat cinched her waist snugly and floated about her calves, its taffeta petticoat rustling against her sheer stockings. Her feet moved airily in the high-heeled sandals. Her envelope-sized evening bag ("I was set upon a beaded one," said

Anabel, "but the sequins will glitter on this one when you're out on the dance floor") came with its own comb and mirror, and there was just room besides for a lipstick and for the dance card—with all its spaces filled in.

The two partners after Duddy must have skipped some dance classes. The waltz boy stayed a beat ahead of her, and the shag boy seemed to forget that he had a partner. Next came Timmie Veech, who led her in wide circles around the terrace, vigorously pumping their joined, sweating hands, while his nonchalant brother leaned against a palm tree, smoking and watching them. Timmie's thatch of red hair barely crested her shoulder, recalling to Maud her dance practices over at the Stratton house, Tildy's Orphan Annie curls butting against Maud's shoulder. "Oh, Norton, what a divine dancer you are!" Tildy had crooned, and Maud found herself sweetly missing her old friend, with none of the rancor that had come after their breakup.

Then Duddy was back, manfully guiding her through the two-step until his father tapped him on the shoulder and danced off with her himself. Mr. Weatherby's level of cheer had risen since his sojourn in the bar. He praised Maud's dignity and bearing, wished he was thirty years younger, and hoped she wasn't having too bad a time with old Duddy. To which she could reply truthfully, "Oh, no, sir, he's a wonderful dancer."

Next on Maud's dance card was the tango, to be followed by "intermission with refreshments." Maud looked around for Timmie Veech, whose name was scrawled beside this number, but it was Troy Veech who was swaying before her, inviting her into his arms. "May I have the honor of this dance, Maud Norton? My little brother says he doesn't tango."

He led her to the floor and raised an eyebrow when he saw she could follow him.

"Surely you didn't learn this at your sheltered boarding school."

"Our Spanish teacher, Miss Mendoza, teaches us all the Latin dances. Next we're going to learn the fandango, with castanets."

"And can you play the castanets?"

"No, but she's going to teach us. She knows how to do a little bit of everything, Miss Mendoza. She says a modern woman has to."

"Miss Mendoza sounds like my kind of person. Is she pretty?"

"She's more the elegant type. Calling her pretty would be almost an insult."

"And how about yourself?"

"Excuse me?"

"Would you call yourself elegant or—since pretty is an insult—how about beautiful?"

"I wouldn't call myself anything. Certainly not beautiful. I would like to be elegant someday, but I don't think I am yet."

They did their dips and sways on the floor with a few other couples. Mrs. Weatherby watched them from the sidelines, her mouth pursed in a thin sarcastic smile. Troy Veech's tango was passable, but he was nowhere near as secure as Miss Mendoza when she took the man's part.

"Oh, I think you are well on your way, Maud Norton," said Troy. As he caught hold of Maud's waist and bent her backward, he looked across at Mimi Weatherby and almost fell over Maud in the process. "That's enough of this," he said peevishly. "What say we go out to the orange court and have a smoke? Though I'm sure your sheltered boarding school forbids smoking."

"I don't smoke, but most of the men I know do," said Maud, letting him lead her by the elbow down some steps, into a sunken court. "My father does. Our priest at school does. And Mr. Foley smokes a cigar."

"And who is Mr. Foley?"

"He boards at my grandmother's house. He's a salesman for a gourmet food company. And he's a friend of my mother's."

"Ah, I see. While you're away at school. The proverbial traveling salesman." Troy Veech leaned against a palm tree and lit up. The flare of the match elongated his features and gave them a cruel cast. It occurred to Maud that he was, and had been, making fun of her. How rude would it be to excuse herself and go back to the dance? Instead she decided to stand up to him. "There's something I'd like to clear up about my school, Mr. Veech."

"Oh, please, please! Just Troy. I feel worn and ancient enough as it is."

"Well, if you'll stop calling me 'Maud Norton,' like the whole thing is a joke."

"I assure you, the last thing in the world I meant— Come, let's walk, Maud. I'll give you a short guided tour of our eminent club. The architect who designed it said he was striving for 'deteriorated magnificence,' and that pretty well sums up all of us."

He sounded almost penitent. He led her along a path that zigzagged through closely planted trees. "How old *are* you, anyway?" she asked.

"Old enough to look in the mirror and wish I saw somebody else. A thousand years older than you, my dear Maud. Far from being a joke, you smite me. What was this thing you wanted to 'clear up' about your school?"

"It's not my 'boarding school.' I mean, it is for some girls, but I'm a day student. I live at home with my mother and grandmother."

"Ah, where the cigar-smoking salesman boards."

She cut through the mockery creeping back into his tone. "I don't like false pretenses. Mrs. Weatherby was making me sound like somebody I'm not."

"Mrs. Weatherby does that. It's her style. If you're her friend, you might say it's a form of idealism. If you're someone who can't stand her, you'd say she's a petty snob."

"I'm trying to figure out which you are."

"An idealist or a petty snob?" He sounded delighted.

"No, whether you're her friend or someone who can't stand her."

Troy Veech took a deep draw on his cigarette. "I guess I slink back and forth between the two camps. Listen, Maud, do you want to go back and nibble bite-size sandwiches and dazzle the adolescents and be eyeballed by their drunken fathers, or would you like to stroll down to the marina? If we're lucky, there'll be a yacht embarking into the great unknown. It's one of the few sights that arouses what idealism I've got left."

"I'm not really hungry, if you think it's okay." She was frankly curious to have a glimpse of Troy Veech's idealism. "How long is the intermission?"

"Oh, we've got plenty of time," said Troy Veech. "I'll do my best to make it an educational tour."

There was no yacht embarking that evening, but before Maud made her scandalous reappearance on the dance floor, having missed three dances on her card, she had learned a few more things, both incidental and otherwise. The first house on the barren sandbar now known as Palm Beach was built by a Confederate draft dodger. Those towering palm trees that loomed over you everywhere had washed in as Cuban coconuts off a shipwrecked Spanish vessel as recently as 1878. People planted the coconuts, and when they grew into palm trees, they named the town Palm City. Later they found out that there was already a town by that name in Florida, so they renamed it Palm Beach. Then came Henry Flagler and his railroad, and he saw the skinny little palm-covered island as a luxurious winter resort. He bought up the property on both sides of Lake Worth, directed the layout of the streets, installed waterworks, landscaped everything to his taste, and invited his rich friends down from Philadelphia.

"And at that point," Troy Veech told Maud in his never-far-from-mocking drawl (for how long had his fingers been linked with hers?), "Palm Beach shed its upstart beginnings and became the enclosure we find ourselves trapped in now."

Flagler's first big hotels were by invitation only: to be invited you had to be gentile. Automobiles were not invited. Flagler allowed only bicycle-propelled padded wicker chairs operated by Negroes to transport guests between hotels and trains. He called them Afromobiles.

Most clubs, including the Palm City Club, still excluded Jews, and Anabel Norton's father, a Jacksonville department store millionaire, had been a Jew. Everybody had known this when the Nortons moved to Palm Beach, but Mimi Weatherby had taken a shine to Mrs. Norton and chose to keep Anabel's hopes up as long as Anabel paid court to her and supported her charities liberally.

Duddy Weatherby was an epileptic, had been known to "have fits" in public, and girls and their mothers started weeding out potential disasters early around there.

"LET ME JUST indulge in a short fantasy before I take you back," said Troy Veech, as they stood pressed against each other in the shadows of the marina. "One of those yachts is mine. I help you on board, just as you are. We can always dock somewhere later and buy casual clothes. We have a captain, because I don't want to be bothered with the sailing part. And since this is a fantasy, why not a crew as well? The captain gives the order, the crew hauls anchor, and you and I make our way to the prow. The engines fire up and we're under way. We don't look back at receding lights or receding people. Will you come with me, just as I am, Maud, into the great unknown? If you say yes, you will make me a new man. Please say yes. Remembering, of course, that this is only a fantasy."

Troy Veech was saying: "I can't believe you've never kissed before. No, I can believe it. Your kisses are as fresh as you are. But my, you are a passionate little thing. You feel what you're doing to me, don't you? Better watch that. Some cad will press your passion button and you'll be overboard."

Troy Veech said: "I have a good mind to walk you right out of this citadel of pretensions and whisk you off as my own. No, I'm not talking fantasy now. I don't have a yacht, but I have a pretty good car. Would you come?"

"I couldn't—" Maud's voice came out ragged and strange. She had not known she could feel like this and was truly baffled as to whether such feelings were sinful or sublime.

"Why not?" His lips moved against her ear, setting off more of the feelings. The mockery was completely gone. "Do you realize what I'm talking about, Maud? I'm offering you my heart. You make me think I still have one. I would marry you like a shot. It sounds crazy, but so crazy it could be the making of us both. You could be a soldier's wife. I would send you to school and college."

"I'm *fourteen*," Maud moaned against the chest of this troubling man. She felt her power where their hips locked, but she wasn't really tempted. She knew he spoke out of a place too deeply at odds with itself. Nonetheless, she sorted through the people in her life. Who would miss her? Who would envy her? Who would feel betrayed? Who would pronounce her a crazy fool? She could read everyone's thoughts and hear each voice speaking them. With a pang she realized it was Granny who would miss her most, the Granny who turned the lights off to live in her radio programs and who infuriated Lily by her stoic reminders that "What's done is done for us, but the child must have her chance."

"I have to go back now," said Maud, pulling away. "Especially after what you told me about Duddy."

"Ah, vanquished by epileptic Duddy. Well, let's look at you. You can't go back looking like a ravished maiden." The mockery had returned, but also a note of relief? "I'll show you where the locker room is for the women golfers. There won't be an attendant on duty to stare while you put yourself to rights. Go through that archway, then straight across the cloister through the other archway, and up the spiral stairs."

Another dance was missed because Maud got lost after "putting herself to rights" in the women golfers' bathroom. Her cheeks were rubbed raw and her lips were swollen. Her eyes had a hectic shine. Her dress had not suffered, but Duddy's orchid was crushed. She dropped it in a wicker wastebasket and covered it with paper towels.

The dancers were in the middle of the Virginia reel when she made her entrance. She took out her dance card to see whom she had let down. Someone named Jabbo Trowbridge. Suddenly Mrs. Weatherby was beside her, consulting the card with her. "Jabbo's got a partner. I've covered for you, Maud. Now you're back and on your own. The last dance is with Duddy, and I'm counting on you not to miss that."

The drive home with Troy Veech was bizarre. Mrs. Weatherby had arranged that, too. She and Mr. Weatherby had to stay behind and settle with the band and the servers, she said. "Now, Maud, please give my best to Anabel, and tell her I hope to see her after the first of the year. Probably not before then, tell her." Maud was about to say, "But we're coming to your party tomorrow," then realized what was being conveyed. Mrs. Weatherby was uninviting them to her party because of Maud's behavior tonight. Poor Anabel! "You *will* remember to tell her that, won't you?" reiterated Mimi, looking hard at Maud. "Yes, ma'am," Maud assured Mimi Weatherby, "I won't forget."

Troy and his little brother bickered back and forth in the front seat of Troy's not-so-new Oldsmobile. ("I don't have a yacht, but I have a pretty good car. Would you come?") Maud and Duddy rode silently in the back. Maud was glad that Duddy had already asked what happened to the orchid during their last dance. "It just suddenly wilted," she had told him, adding feebly, "I'm sorry."

Troy Veech pulled up in front of the Norton house. "Well, here we are," he said in his mocking drawl. But he sounded beaten and tired. "It was a pleasure to meet you, Maud Norton. I wish you every success in life." He kept the motor running while her date walked her to the door. "Thank you for everything, and good night," said Maud. She offered her hand and Duddy, without looking at her, gave it a limp squeeze. "Good night," said Duddy Weatherby.

CHAPTER 20

Grading Papers

Late Tuesday afternoon, January 8, 1952
Octave of the Epiphany
Mother Malloy's office
Mount St. Gabriel's

MOTHER MALLOY PRAYED before beginning the papers.

Your parents found You in the temple, sitting in the midst of the teachers, listening to them and asking them questions. You were twelve years old. Help me to be mindful of my students' questions, and the needs behind those questions, and grant me the sagacity and the stamina to guide them toward wisdom and understanding. I ask this in Your name. Amen.

She graded the papers in alphabetical order. This was her system.

Elaine Frew's self-complacent, underresearched paper, "The Artist as Outsider," required some adjustment after Lora Jean Cramer's workmanlike presentation of David's two marriages and her conclusion that "sometimes in life you have to make a serious mistake before you find true love." Mother Malloy went through Elaine's ornate script, crossing out all of Elaine's capitalized nouns. Then she laid down her pencil and went to stand by the window. It was half past four. The last of the day's sun crimsoned the west wall of the garage and brushed the tops of the crosses in the nuns' cemetery below. As she found herself doing more and more lately, Mother Malloy fantasized an alternate self setting off on an outing. This other self, possessed of more stamina, flung on her cloak and headed outside into the falling light. She breathed in the mountain air and felt better for having come out. The gravel crunched beneath her brisk steps until she veered off onto the woodland path leading down to the cemetery. She remembered Mother Ravenel's offer, that first day, to give her tennis lessons so they could play together. Another alternate self branched off from the one on the woodland path, and Mother Malloy smiled at the unlikely vision of this tennis-playing self, sash and garments flying, rushing about the court to return the headmistress's volleys.

In the cemetery she walked along the rows, pausing to read the names and dates on the marble crosses, all carved to the same format, including the cross of the Englishwoman who founded the Order of St. Scholastica.

Elizabeth Mary Wallingford
O.S.S.
1863–1930
Professed February 10, 1893

One day she would lie beneath such a cross, either here or in Boston, and it gladdened her that in death her dates would be no less complete than those of her sisters. For Kate Malloy knew neither the day nor the month of her birth. Sometime in the late autumn of 1926, it was thought. In the foster home they celebrated her birthday on October 2, the Feast of the Holy Guardian Angels. But in the life she had chosen, the date of her profession was the only one that mattered: August 28, 1948, the Feast of St. Augustine.

Back at her desk from the fantasy walk, she reapplied herself to grading papers.

She stopped by the chapel to calm her stomach before facing yet another Mount St. Gabriel's dinner. If it were only possible to draw caloric sustenance from the smells of beeswax and incense, whetted by a burst of cold air from a transom window left ajar in the sacristy by Father, so he could smoke.

When You went among us as a man, were there things You hated to eat? All those meals in other peoples' houses—surely there were certain dishes put before You that made Your gorge rise. I wish I knew what they were. Then as I pick up my fork to address my portion of gluey macaroni bubbling with bacon and Velveeta cheese, I could say, "This is the equivalent of the dish that turned Our Lord's stomach, prepared by some loving Martha, and He got it down." But when I imagine Your food I see dates, nuts, flat bread, fruit, fresh fish—in Boston we had so much fresh fish!—washed down with water from a well, per-

*haps a serving of wine. All things I would welcome on our table at Mount St.
Gabriel's.*

Four boarders and two nuns sat at each of the round tables in the
dining room. Seating assignments changed every fortnight, beginning
with the Sunday evening meal. These first two weeks of the new semester, Mother Malloy and Mother Arbuckle, the infirmarian, were sharing
a table with Marta Andreu, Gilda Gomez, Elaine Frew, and a high-
strung new tenth-grade boarder, Jiggsie (Juliana) Judd. The advance
word from Mother Ravenel had been that there was "a lot of work to be
done" on Jiggsie. Her father, a golf pro, went back and forth between
Florida and the Poconos, and Jiggsie had been in the habit of attending
two schools per academic year. Now the parents were at war with each
other, and the paternal grandmother, Mrs. Judd, of Spartanburg, South
Carolina, an old Mount St. Gabriel's graduate (class of 1913) and a good
Catholic, had taken responsibility for Jiggsie's education in hopes of
preventing the girl from following in the footsteps of her "unreliable"
mother. All this from Mother Ravenel, who had added, "If Jiggsie can
profit from her surroundings here, she will be invited back for the fall.
If not, she won't. That's what I told Mrs. Judd in our telephone interview. She understood perfectly, being an old girl herself."

Jiggsie looked like a delicate cinquecento angel until she moved or
opened her mouth. Jiggsie's jitters seemed to be manifestations of a war
being played out inside herself. Her behavior at meals could have been
a parody of bad table manners. She shook out her table napkin as if she
were airing a throw rug. She plucked a roll from the bread basket,
screwed up her eyes at it, then returned it to the basket. She jumped
like a rabbit when anyone spoke to her, blinked frantically when asked
a question, then mumbled an answer in her flat, wispy voice, usually in
monosyllables or with one of several pat phrases, all of which came out
sounding rude.

All the more, then, did Mother Malloy appreciate Elaine Frew's attempts, during this third evening meal of the new semester, to take
Jiggsie Judd under her wing. It was done, of course, in Elaine's typical
condescending manner, and with her visible fastidious recoil, but after
a few "What?"s and "Huh!"s and "Oh, yeah?"s, Jiggsie was actually
heard saying, "Uh, okay" and then, wonder of wonders, "Oh, thank
you, Elaine." It was enough to make Mother Malloy feel sad about the
D Elaine didn't yet know she was getting.

While Mother Malloy was still laboring over a quivery slab of bread pudding clotted with raisins, Mother Arbuckle excused herself—two sick boarders with intestinal flu were awaiting their cup of bouillon from her hot plate back at the infirmary. In passing, she laid a small brown package on Mother Malloy's lap.

"I picked that up for you. See the note inside."

"Why, thank you, Mother."

Back in her office, Mother Malloy unwrapped the package. It was a bottle of something called Geritol. The note read:

Take a nice good swig before bedtime and another before breakfast. Supposed to give you more pep and appetite. Lots of key vitamins and iron. It's fairly new, but they're advertising it all over the place. Let's see if it helps!

Clara Arbuckle, R.N., O.S.S.

So her wan appetite had been professionally observed. She realized she must take even smaller portions if she were to continue eating everything on her plate, as the girls were expected to do.

A few ninth graders had asked permission before the holidays to change or modify the topic of their paper. This was to be expected and was generally a good sign. Chloe Starnes, whose first proposal was to examine the influence of mothers in *David Copperfield,* had changed her focus to the influence of Agnes Wickfield upon David. "I want to explore how a person's strength of character can guide someone to maturity, even when that person stays in the background. What gave me the idea was my mother's name also being Agnes, and even though she isn't with me anymore, I feel influenced by her. I feel her watching over me and guiding me in my choices."

The initial plan of Josie Galvin, the doctor's daughter, had been to compare and contrast Little Emily's fall (her elopement with her seducer, Steerforth) with that of her friend Martha the prostitute. But before Christmas she made an impassioned plea to concentrate on Martha alone. "There's so much there, Mother; Martha can take up my whole five pages all by herself. My father says that prostitution was Victorian England's biggest can of worms. They spent millions of pounds a year on their prostitutes, but the average prostitute, even if she was young, was dead in four years. I'd like to call my paper 'Martha's Redemption.'"

"So you think she is redeemed?"

"Oh, yes, Mother. I mean, she had no mother or father, so it was easy for her to fall into bad ways."

Mother Malloy considered taking a few of the papers to her room. Though sleep threatened to ambush her at untimely moments during the school day, it eluded her when she lay down on her bed at night. Why not get more of the papers done? But in a recent rereading of the Order's rule, she saw, in chapter 42, "Silence After Compline," that the foundress, who must have fought against night reading herself, warned against letting it become a "form of conversation that interferes with God's most private communing with us just before sleep."

And so, after Compline, she went empty-handed to her room, removed her veil, folded it according to custom with the two straight pins arranged in the form of a cross, exchanged the habit for the flannel gown, washed her face and brushed her teeth at the little sink, took her first exploratory swig of Mother Arbuckle's tonic (it was both "bitter and sweet," like the angel's little book in Revelations), and dropped to her knees on the prie-dieu to perform her Examen of Conscience. Twice, during her review of the day, she felt an auspicious drowsiness, but as soon as she lay flat on her pillow, she was wide awake again and vaguely apprehensive. Sometimes she managed to diminish the unease by sitting up and saying the confiteor and striking her chest three times ("through my fault, through my fault, through my most grievous fault"). But other times, like now, it exacerbated her nervousness, and she resorted to her alternate remedy: making a second pillow out of the extra blanket from the closet, then lying at the new elevation with her eyes closed and reciting Hail Marys without counting them until something floated up, then something else, and on and on until she fell asleep.

What floated up first tonight was the pang she continued to feel as an adult when someone spoke slightingly of people without parents. Josie Galvin, heaped round with the fruits of family life, took it for granted that it was easy for Martha to "fall into bad ways" because she had no mother or father. And this in turn evoked in Mother Malloy the spring of her ninth year, when a strep throat followed by a setback of bronchitis had kept her in bed for weeks, and she had watched the sun rise earlier each day and heard the other children leaving for school and, at the end of the day, heard them playing outside in the lengthening twilight. She was infinitely sad and unable to comfort herself or explain why. Everyone was attentive to her; she was a favorite with the foster parents and with the other children. Mrs. O'Neill fussed and worried over her. Mr. O'Neill, a carpenter, made her a pencil box carved with her initials, K.M. The doctor told her she was a very good patient; her fourth-grade teacher visited from school and assured her that she would catch up easily because she was disciplined and smart.

The parish priest came to see her and encouraged her to start thinking about her confirmation name. He taught her a prayer to St. Joseph, which made her want to weep, though she could not have explained why.

O blessed Joseph, happy man, to whom it was given not only to see and to hear that God Whom many kings longed to see, and saw not, to hear, and heard not; but also to carry Him in thy arms to embrace Him, to clothe Him, and to guard and defend Him.

She had chosen Joseph for her confirmation name, and the parish priest had backed up her choice when others, including the loving O'Neills, had suggested that Josephine might be more suitable.

CHAPTER 21

Realignments

Saturday evening, January 19, 1952
The Stratton household
Mountain City, North Carolina

THE STRATTON FAMILY at dinner, minus Cornelia, who had at last found time in her busy schedule to succumb to the flu, had finished Flavia's vegetable soup and was anticipating the next course: her meat loaf, mashed potatoes, and the big yellow butter beans put away from last summer.

Tildy, whose every gesture had become more theatrical since she had been appointed director of *The Red Nun,* dabbed at the sides of her mouth with her napkin, replaced it primly in her lap, and took a thoughtful quaff from her water goblet. "I was wondering, Daddy, do you and John have any urgent plans for *Monday?*"

"This coming Monday? What's up, honey?"

"Maud's grandmother's funeral's at eleven, at First Methodist Church, and I feel I ought to be there. So I was thinking that if Madeline would drop me at school that morning, then you would have John until ten-fifteen or so, and then he could come and take me and any of the other girls who want to go to the funeral and the cemetery and then drive us back to school afterward. I really think I owe Maud that."

"Poor little Maudie. Finding old Mrs. Roberts like that. It was the first shock of my young life when my granny passed on, though she had been bedridden for a long time."

"I'll be glad to take Tildy to school," said Madeline. "I would offer myself and my little roadster for the funeral, but you can fit more girls into the Packard, and Tildy would obviously prefer it."

"John driving the Packard is more seemly for the occasion," said Tildy. "If Daddy can spare him."

"Oh, I can always borrow your mother's car while she's laid up," Tildy's father said. "If I can remember how to drive an automatic shift." He winked at his girls and included Flavia, entering with the platters.

After supper, Flavia prepared Cornelia's teapot while Madeline simmered a perfect poached egg in a small skillet and slid her handiwork onto lightly buttered toast points. She tucked some slices of peeled orange at the edge of the plate, rolled the silverware into a linen napkin, and arranged it all on a bed tray. "There, Flavia, how does that look?"

"She going to want her salt," suggested Flavia, nodding toward the omitted shaker. "I can take that up to her, Miss Madeline."

"I know you can, Flavia, but it's not every day I get Mama trapped in bed."

Sunk deep into her bedcovers, Cornelia Stratton had the canny look of an invalid anticipating her treat but not wanting to appear eager.

"Now, Mama, I poached this egg for you myself and Flavia hovered like a hawk and reminded me you liked your salt. Are you feeling up to having a bite?"

Cornelia hoisted herself up and inspected the tray. "What's going on in the world, Maddy? If you can spare a moment."

"Well," said Madeline happily, pulling up a chair, "you already know about poor Mrs. Roberts."

"Yes, Daddy told me she popped off during one of her radio programs. Maud was in the room with her, but didn't know until the lights came on. Daddy said Tildy was the first one Maud told about it at school."

"Tildy's behaving very loyally. She asked Daddy for John and the Packard on Monday to take classmates to the funeral."

"Frankly, I'm glad Maud and Tildy aren't in each other's pockets anymore. A gesture of loyalty for a nice dead friendship is one thing, but I can remember when Tildy was always after us to adopt Maud. I wouldn't want that to start up again."

"Here, let me pour your tea. Why should it start up again?"

"Ouch! Too hot. Whip into the bathroom, sweetie, and splash in some cold water from the faucet."

Madeline obliged. "Try it now."

The invalid warily tested. "Exactly right. You're too good to me,

Maddy. You remind me more of Antonia every day. Wouldn't it be odd if you turned out to have a vocation."

"I don't think so, Mama. Even if I could look as beautiful as Mother Malloy."

"You'd look more beautiful; she's pale as chalk. But if it meant you'd have to knuckle under to that archfiend Ravenel, I think I'd take a leaf from Medea and slay you first."

Madeline suppressed a shudder as her mother deftly disemboweled the poached egg. She spread it over the toast points, then salted everything heavily, including the orange slices.

"What I meant was, now that Mrs. Roberts is out of the way, Lily Norton, if that was ever her name, will undoubtedly take up openly with that fancy-foods salesman."

"Do you think they'll try to run the Pine Cone Lodge, Mama?"

"What's to run? Nobody stays in boardinghouses anymore. Except salesmen with something else on their minds. No, I wouldn't put it past Lily Norton to have the house on the market the day after the funeral."

"But where would they live?"

"My guess is that they'll move somewhere else so they can start fresh and put on airs. They might even get married. Lily will have herself a dowry. Your father says she could get as much as ten thousand for that old pile. Enough to give them an uppity start in a new place. Daddy says that street is in zoning limbo and it's in walking distance from town, which will attract the entrepreneurs."

"Oh, dear," said Madeline. "Then what happens to poor Maudie?"

Cornelia snorted. "Beginning to get the picture, eh? Either she goes with them, they drag her out of Mount St. Gabriel's, or they allow her to stay on as a boarder—Lily would have to fork over some of the dowry for that. Whereas if Maud still had Tildy wrapped around her little finger, we would be badgered by Tildy to take her in. What's one more at the table? And even if she did board at Mount St. Gabriel's, where does she go in summer? The whole thing would start up again. Swimming every day at the club. Maud sleeping in Tildy's room, and those simpering, nervous manners at our table. Thank the Lord Tildy has little Chloe now. An altogether more manageable person. Though Chloe's got her problems, too. She told Tildy that her stepfather, who's unfortunately her legal father, is threatening to haul poor Henry into court for custody. What a mess. Be glad you have your original father and mother, at least till death do us part. And by then, with any luck, you girls will be old enough so if you get dragged anywhere it will be by a loving husband."

"But what about Maud's father and his new wife? Maybe they'll want her."

"Oh, I don't care if she goes or stays. I'm just saying Tildy is much better off without that friendship. Look how much she's improved on her own steam. A B plus on her Uriah Heep paper! Of course, we both got behind her on that. You read with her every night, and I made a few suggestions to make Uriah more odious. But she wrote the whole thing herself. I only went through at the end and corrected some spelling."

"Mother Malloy's tutoring sessions helped her a lot. And you know, Mama, even Mother Ravenel deserves *some* credit, for putting Tildy in charge of the *Red Nun* production. It's done a world of good for Tildy's self-esteem, and she's thrown herself into it."

"My child has never lacked for self-esteem. And don't be fooled: everything that woman does has an ulterior motive. I just wish I knew what she has up her black sleeve to inflict on our family now."

"I have a feeling the play's going to be a huge success. Tildy's got all these ideas for putting new life into it. She's even asked Daddy to record John's voice for God's lines."

Cornelia giggled. "Not such a far-fetched idea. John's voice has a spooky kind of authority. It always puts me in mind of 'The Shadow knows.' "

"Why don't I bring you another pot of tea, Mama?"

"No, thank you, dear. All this gossip has made me a little tired. That's the thing with the flu. Even after the worst is over, you've still got to recover your strength. I suppose there's a horrid pile of unanswered messages for me down at the studio."

"No, Mama, we're completely caught up. Your new secretary is very organized, and I double-check with her every afternoon that all the calls have been answered."

"You do so much for me, Maddy. I don't know when you have time for your young life."

"Oh, my young life. Mama, when you were my age, did you ever go through a phase where you wished for some bigger assignment? I don't mean the school kind, but something that would make a larger demand on you?"

Cornelia pushed her tray away. "Lord, child, don't you have enough demands on you?"

"But they're just family and school stuff. Sometimes I wish I could have been, oh, I don't know, an ambulance driver in World War One."

"That would make you about fifty now. I would be years younger than you. I sometimes feel that I *am* years younger. Right now I feel like a pampered little girl with the flu who's had a nice poached egg on toast and is ready for sleepy time."

Trying to hide her disappointment, Madeline removed the tray. "You didn't eat your orange slices, Mama."

"You eat them for me," murmured Cornelia, burrowing deep into the bedclothes, eyes already shut.

☩

Monday, January 21, 1952
First Methodist Church
Mountain City, North Carolina

Tildy seldom set foot in Protestant churches, but each time she was obliged to do so she thanked her lucky stars she was Catholic. Everything was so dour and colorless and *kept down* in Protestant churches. There were no statues or candles, no sanctuary lamp, no vestments, no Latin, no incense, no rituals—in other words, no mystery; no *theater*. But she owed this to Maud, who sat, looking stricken and inconsequential, in the front pew, between Lily Norton and the traveling salesman. There were few people here, and most of them were old and dreary. Tildy was proud of her Mount St. Gabriel's contingent; they were young and looked nice and the five of them took up a whole pew. The Packard could seat four in the back, with Tildy riding in front with John. Chloe, of course, was a given, and then since it was the class president's grandmother's funeral, Tildy had thought it would be appropriate to invite the other ninth-grade officers: Rebecca Meyer, vice president; Kay Lee Jones, secretary; and Josie Galvin, treasurer. And here they all were, in their smart hats and coats and gloves, giving the occasion a cachet it would have otherwise lacked.

The minister, in his plain black gown, met the coffin at the door, and four old men and two representatives from the funeral home wheeled it up the aisle on its trolley while the congregation sang, "Love's redeeming work is done, fought the fight, the battle won . . ." Then the minister said some prayers in English, facing the people, and an old man crept up the stairs to the lectern and read from the Bible. The minister and congregation then recited "The Lord is my shepherd," after which the old man read from the Bible again and almost fell coming down the stairs. Then the minister, who was called Dr. Clark, went up into the pulpit and talked about the importance of hospitality in a community. He said that was what Cleona Roberts had practiced for thirty years, opening her house to strangers passing through, and he read some parts from the Bible about different people who opened their homes to strangers and by doing so found themselves entertaining angels unaware. Abraham and Sarah had some angels to dinner, and because of their hospitality Sarah was rewarded by bearing a son in her ninetieth year.

Tildy was glad her mother was not here, because Cornelia's lips would have twitched with cruel mirth and Tildy might have lost control. Mama would have been thinking *loudly* one of her uncharitable thoughts about possible "rewards" to be visited on Lily Norton by that gourmet "angel," Mr. Foley. However, Tildy couldn't wait to get home and make Mama smile: "When Dr. Clark was talking about people entertaining angels, I read your mind, Mama, though you weren't even there."

A lady with a trembly chin sang a trembly solo, "O for the wings, for the wings of a dove," and then Dr. Clark stood over the coffin and said a long prayer, with lots of "thy servant Cleona"s sprinkled throughout, and everybody stood and sang a closing hymn, "Love divine, all loves excelling," which sounded too perky for a funeral, during which the coffin was wheeled out again.

Mother Ravenel had thrown a monkey wrench into Tildy's original plan for John to drive the five ninth graders to the funeral and then on to the cemetery. "Your idea that Maud's fellow officers should attend Mrs. Roberts's funeral was a good one, Tildy. It shows your natural bent for leadership. But there is no need for you girls to miss an extra class period by going out to the cemetery. Strangers have no business at a burial. The interment should be for bereaved friends and family members."

"Mrs. Roberts was not a stranger to me, Mother Ravenel. I've stayed over at Maud's hundreds of times, ever since we were little girls."

"Ye-es," drawled the headmistress, eyeing Tildy sharply from across the big desk. "Though you and Maud aren't so close anymore. But if you feel *you* must go to the cemetery, Tildy, have your mother write Mother Malloy a note saying she wishes you to go."

"That woman!" exploded Cornelia, dashing off the note. "Always meddling in our lives!"

The other girls having been chauffeured back to school, Tildy rode with John to the cemetery, mulling over her new relationship with Mother Ravenel, who was still an adversary, but suddenly an advantageous one. The Ravenel had power—she could expel you or uninvite you back. Or, as she had done after Tildy's first report card, she could threaten probation, with its threat of failure and expulsion. But she could also, as people with power were privileged to do, suddenly bestow power on chosen ones. As she had done when she'd suggested to Tildy that she might direct a 1952 production of *The Red Nun.* But why had Mother Ravenel chosen Tildy? Mama was suspicious of her motives. "Suzanne Ravenel has meddled in our family life from the very beginning. The first day she entered Mount St. Gabriel's, she started weaseling her way into my sister's affections—Antonia, who never could resist a sufferer, befriended the lonely little boarder from Charleston, even before that father did away with himself the weekend after Black Friday. And then there was talk that she would be sent home because there was no money, and she had a sort of junior nervous breakdown and was packed off to the infirmary, where she had her legendary meeting with the foundress—God only knows how much of *that* was true and how much she made up out of whole cloth, because Mother Wallingford was on round-the-clock opiates for her brain cancer. Following her death, Suzanne was free to fabricate whatever would serve her own legend best. After that, she never left the school—who paid for it is anyone's guess. Old Mother Finney once told Agnes Vick, who was her pet, that Mother Wallingford had arranged a full scholarship for her before she died."

Tildy's mother now watched her anxiously for any evidence that she might be "going over" to Mother Ravenel. The knowledge gave Tildy an exhilarating flush of power: her hard-to-pin-down, contemptuous mother fearfully examining her baby for signs of desertion to the enemy.

"She isn't trying to maneuver you into thinking you have a vocation, like she tried to do with Madeline, is she?"

"Good grief, no, Mama, I'm far too egotistical to make a good nun. She says I have leadership qualities that haven't found their proper outlets yet. She says she was the same way. One day in freshman study hall she just picked up a pencil and started writing a play for her class. She said it was like taking dictation from a higher source."

Cornelia made a sour face. "I've never understood why writers think they have to blame their scribblings on 'a higher source.' Why can't they just own up to the job and let it go at that? And, Tildy, you have always enjoyed bossing other people around. Your leadership qualities didn't just burst into bloom because she has condescended to notice them. Anyhow, I hope you can infuse something new into her tiresome girlhood theatrical. It needs a shot of new life. It needs—"

"What, Mama? It needs what? Each class is allowed to add its own material, you know. That's part of the tradition. Tell me what you're *thinking*!"

"Oh, some sort of breakout from the traditional old party line. *Her* party line. Maybe some scenes from behind the scenes."

"Like *what*, Mama? Please be specific. Look how you helped me sharpen up Uriah Heep's disgustingness. What *kind* of breakout? What scenes behind *what* scenes?"

"Don't be so importunate, Tildy. You know I can't stand to be pinned down. Let me go away and think about it."

⊹

Monday, January 21, 1952
The cemetery

Maud knew she would remember every detail of Tildy's grand arrival at the cemetery for as long as she lived.

There they had stood around the open grave, the pitiful remnants of

Granny's funeral. The old people in their shabby hats and coats looked half dead themselves in the cruel winter light. Her mother leaned in a little too close to Mr. Foley, who had overcreamed his pompadour. The raw wind pasted the minister's black gown against his skinny body and he held the prayer book at an absurd distance from his eyes. Maud had heard him jokingly apologize to her mother, as their paltry little group of mourners labored up the hill to Granny's waiting grave, for leaving his reading glasses behind in the pulpit.

Everywhere, in this sad little scene she found herself part of, Maud perceived elements that boded compromise and outright danger to her best hopes.

It now seemed sinister that she had chosen "The Downgrading of Dreams" as the final title for her *David Copperfield* paper, which had earned her an A plus and a note of high praise from Mother Malloy. This triumph had taken away some of the sting of the Palm Beach debacle and the aftermath of having to explain to Granny and Lily why she probably would not be invited to stay with the Nortons again, but it was a short-lived triumph because Granny had slipped away from them soon after the paper was returned.

Though it departs from your original and perhaps overly ambitious plan of pinpointing the universal aches throughout the novel and showing how they achieve the transfer from character to reader, thereby enlarging and authenticating the reader's experience, your paper's narrower and sharper focus has the power of felt emotion kept in service to a theme. Yes, it is a fact, as you point out, that unmerited degradations abound in our fallen world, but it is also true, as you go on to say, that they often call out the finest creative strengths of the human soul. "The Downgrading of Dreams" is a testament to reading and writing at its best. This is excellent work, Maud.

Mother K. Malloy, O.S.S.

Tildy's trilby hat with uptilted black feather appeared at the rim of the hill just as Dr. Clark was inviting the assembled mourners to come forward and cast a handful of soil on the casket. Then came the rest of her: the mop of tawny hair that had caused Anabel Norton to compare her to Orphan Annie, a too long black coat with a fox collar (probably from Madeline's closet), an old-fashioned lace fichu that looked like plunder from an old trunk, the outfit completed by black gauntlet-length kid gloves, dark stockings, and opera pumps. Oh, glorious, dramatic Tildy, moving smartly across the turf to stand by her side! Maud, who had not been able to weep at the funeral, felt welcome tears sliding down her cheeks. She had assumed that Tildy had returned to school with the other girls.

Maud's mother went first to cast her handful of soil on Granny's casket, followed by Maud. Had it not been for Tildy, who stuck to Maud close as a bodyguard, Mr. Foley would have slipped into third place and made it look like he was the appointed protector of Maud and her mother. Maud had that remembered sense of Tildy anticipating her requirements sometimes before she herself knew what they were.

"Now, here is what I'm going to suggest, Maud," Tildy said, jumping right in with her old officiousness as soon as the mourners began to disperse. "John is waiting below with the Packard. You have the rest of the day off, am I right? So do I. Mama wrote a note. Why don't you come home with me? Flavia will make us some lunch. I have a new room—it's much nicer. Madeline switched with me. We could just hang around for the rest of the day. If you want to, that is."

"I don't know. I mean, I want to, but I don't know whether I'm supposed to ride back with my mother and—them—in the limousine."

"Well, let's go ask your mother and see what she says."

Monday afternoon
The Stratton house

"How did you get Madeline to switch with you?" asked Maud, curled up in the window seat of Tildy's new room.

"It was her idea. She did it one Sunday when I was spending the day at the Vick house. She and Flavia slaved all afternoon to surprise me. The bed was too big to move, so here I am in it." Tildy luxuriously stretched out her arms and legs in four directions, like spokes in a wheel. "It was back in October, when everyone was feeling sorry for me."

"Why were they feeling sorry for you?"

"Oh, my grades took a dive and old Ravenous called me in and said I had to shape up or she'd put the black mark on my eternal record. And

I was having a pretty awful time with old David the Copperfield. Then Mother Malloy offered to tutor me twice a week to improve my reading techniques, and Madeline worked with me at night. We'd read together, like you and I used to do, Maud."

You mean I'd do the reading and you'd lie with your eyes closed and listen with a superior look on your face, and then afterward I'd explain the significance of everything we'd read, thought Maud, feeling bitterness over Tildy's family security, over her private hours twice a week with the beautiful Malloy, and fear and disgust at what was probably going on right now between her mother and Mr. Foley back at the Granny-less Pine Cone Lodge. But she also felt exultant to be alone with Tildy in this large sun-filled room.

"I can't imagine giving up a room like this to anybody," she said.

"Oh well, Madeline is like that. She's always thinking of others. Mama says our aunt Tony was just the same. This was Aunt Tony's room when she was a girl. And then when she came back to live here with Mama and Daddy when Mama was expecting Madeline, it was her room again. There's still stuff of hers in boxes under the window seats. Old clothes and things she left behind when she married Uncle Henry."

"Was that her lace fichu you wore under your coat today?"

Tildy shot up to a sitting position. "God, you are *amazing,* Maud! How did you *know*?"

"I just had a feeling," Maud played along. With Tildy, nothing could be as mundane as a simple deduction. It had to be magical, supernatural.

"You always did have a jillion dimensions, Maud. You must be psychic, too. Chloe has some psychic powers. But"—Tildy rolled her eyes in exasperation—"she uses *hers* mainly for contacts with her dead mother."

Tildy's mentioning of Chloe at all transferred them to slippery ground. The second revelation, however, especially accompanied with the eye rolling, could be read as a breach of loyalty to her present best friend and an invitation to "talk about" Chloe. If Maud were to remain above reproach, she must not rise to the bait.

"With her . . . *dead mother*?"

She nevertheless had risen.

"I really shouldn't be discussing this with anyone," said Tildy. Frowning, she carefully rearranged her legs tailor-fashion on the high bed and leaned forward, a hand on each knee. Both girls had shed their funeral clothes and wore jeans. Tildy had found a pair in Madeline's closet that fit Maud's longer body. "But it's been a bit worrisome."

"What are these contacts like?" Maud asked, throwing shame to the winds.

"Well, she constantly draws her. You know how she's always drawing. She can make anything look like the spitting image of itself. She fills page after page with drawings of her mother. Agnes when she was our age, at school. Agnes the way she looked in the days before she died. Collecting eggs from the henhouse, or sitting across from Chloe at this diner where they went to get away from Rex, the stepfather. She must have hundreds of these drawings."

"But drawing someone—that's not exactly contacting the dead—"

"Wait," said Tildy ominously. "I haven't finished. Then she *consults* the drawings. She doesn't do this much when I'm around, but she does it enough that I know she must do it a lot more when she's alone."

"How do you mean 'consults'?"

"Oh, she'll snatch up her pad and flip to a drawing, or sometimes she'll start a new Agnes, and you can see her *meditating on it,* like you would a holy icon. Sometimes she'll speak to it, ask it questions."

"What sort of questions?"

"Like, 'Is it right for us to do this?' I mean, at first you think she's asking *you,* because you're the only other person in the room, but she's not. She's asking the picture; she's asking Agnes. It's like she's praying to the Virgin or something. It gives me the heebie-jeebies."

"Is it right to do what?"

"Oh, whatever is in the plans. She was going to do a class portrait for the bulletin board. Remember? *You* asked her to contribute something artistic."

"Yes, I remember." Maud also remembered the look of hate Tildy had shot her that day, and the way Tildy had pretended not to hear Maud's request but had acted as though it was her idea for Chloe to do something.

"Well, she had the portrait all sketched out and was starting to color in the faces and do the clothes—God, Maud, it was fantastic, it was like watching each girl came alive on the paper. She'd done Hansje and Beatrix in their matching chesterfields, and Marta Andreu hugging herself in her purple shawl, and then I had to go home, and the next thing I'm hearing from Chloe is that she's not going on with the portrait—it's all off. I mean, she'd finished it by then, she'd done my beaver coat to perfection, and Dorothy Yount wiping her eye, but she told me she wasn't going to present it to Mother Malloy for the bulletin board."

"Why?"

"*Because.* She said people might not want their secret sides posted on the bulletin board. That's when I asked her who'd been influencing her. I thought maybe Uncle Henry."

"Was it?" Maud wished she knew how she herself had looked in Chloe's portrait. Would she recognize her own secret side?

"She said nobody had influenced her, but she got that look she gets when she's ganging up with Agnes against me. And then what she said after that was pure Agnes. She said, 'I just asked myself how I would feel if I were those other girls.' Agnes was so *fair-minded.* That was her big thing, Mama said. I never met Agnes, but I feel I know how she feels about everything, through Chloe. Chloe is *haunted* by her."

You are beginning to sound like you are, too, thought Maud. "You really think so?"

"If you want to know what I *really* think"—Tildy was scowling—"I think Chloe is trying to *become* Agnes."

"But why would she want to do that?"

"To keep from being herself and making up her own mind about things."

Maud's next obvious question would have been "*What* things?" and she could see that Tildy was waiting for her to ask it. The old rhythms of her exchanges with Tildy were back in play again. She knew she would get more by slowing them down and expressing scruples.

"After all," mused Maud, looking down intently at her own knees, "her mother only died last spring. That isn't even a year ago yet."

Then Maud had her awful thought: It might have worked out better for me if Granny had lived on with her tricky heart and Lily had died. Granny and I could have carried on the Pine Cone Lodge trade; I could have shopped and kept accounts and finished at Mount St. Gabriel's on the day scholarship I won at the end of eighth grade. I could have made perfect grades and earned a scholarship to college. I would have escaped, even without the Nortons' help. Now I'm not sure I will escape. I've heard them talking. Art Foley wants to move to Atlanta and take us with him. It will be like David Copperfield losing ground at the bottle factory. All the gains I have made for myself here in Mountain City will pass away and I will have to start all over at the bottom again. But I'm not a genius like Dickens, and I'm not a man, and I'm not the favored character in a novel under the loving protection of a biased creator.

I may never reclaim my lost ground.

"Maud!" cried Tildy. "I have to know what you are thinking *right this minute*!"

How much have I missed her? Her bossy commands, her infuriating dramatizing of herself, of everything that touches her life. Do I want to be part of those dramatics again? Give up the autonomy I have built for myself in ninth grade and go back to sleeping over at the Strattons' and feeling grateful to shelter under her security? Do I want to go back to those fits and stabs of jealousy that used to make me hate myself and her?

"Maudie, are you crying?" In one motion, Tildy had sprung from the bed and was nuzzling against Maud in the window seat. "You have *got* to tell me. I know that look. It's not just your granny. It's more."

She may not be able to read worth a damn, but she sure can read me.

"Everything is just awful," Maud said. Her face felt rubbery; she fought to control it, then gave herself over. "My life is going down the drain," she sobbed into Tildy's Orphan Annie curls. "They'll take me away from Mountain City. Before she died, Granny told me she suspected they were already married, but she intended to stay alive so I could live with her and keep my scholarship to Mount St. Gabriel's. But now they're going to sell the Pine Cone Lodge and the Nortons can't rescue me anymore—they've got their own problems and Anabel may leave my dad. He fell off the wagon when I was there at Christmas because I disgraced myself at a dance with this awful person named Troy Veech, who necked with me and asked me to marry him and said he'd send me to school, and then went off to join the Army. I ruined Anabel's chances for getting into Palm Beach society and she's fed up with my father and now I am going to lose everything."

"No, you are not," declared Tildy. Maud could feel her old friend shudder with the thrill of this outpouring of new melodrama. "You must tell me every single thing that has happened, and then we will decide on a plan."

Confessional Cassette, Continued

Dawn, Monday morning
September 10, 2001
Feast of St. Nicholas of Tolentino, confessor (1245–1305)
Mother Ravenel's room
St. Scholastica Retirement House

I guess you've been wondering what happened to me, Beatrix. But no, you didn't know I'd begun this personal tape to you ten days ago. That was after Mother Frances Galyon had suggested during our evening walk that I turn over the "toxic year" to someone I trusted and cared about, and that certainly describes you, dear Beatrix.

There is nothing like a week's vacation in the hospital to make a person put her priorities in order and show her where she has been fudging. Don't worry, I'm perfectly fine now. It was something I have trouble pronouncing in which the intestine knots itself up in little kinks and you have to watch your diet carefully from then on, but it took a while for them to diagnose it and make sure it wasn't something worse. I spent several days on a painkiller drip, drifting in and out of fugues. At one point I was sure I had already died, and at another, time flattened itself out like an intricate carpet and I saw the episodes of my life woven into their divinely appointed places, and not all of it belongs in a school history. What I came to call the "toxic year," after I had lived through it, was fallout from things set in motion long before. I must accept responsibility for the role I played throughout, but I must also accept that mine was only one of many roles and, furthermore, that it is insulting God's mercy to go on flagellating myself as prime blamee, if I may coin such a word.

At the start of this personal tape to you, I said my story had its beginnings in the early 1930s, when my best friend, Antonia Tilden, and I decided we wanted to enter the Order together. I think it is best to go back to that time, maybe even further back, to our first becoming friends.

Antonia and Cornelia Tilden. They were identical twins but easy to tell apart. Antonia's superiority of soul shone through her beauty like a light from within, while Cornelia's identical features seemed harder, as though chiseled from without. Cornelia was dreaded for her critical eye and scornful tongue. In contrast, Antonia was comforting and unthreatening to be with. In her there was none of the meanness and silliness of most girls her age. She had a way of treating everyone as equally worthy of her regard. Now, this is a rare and admirable quality—I think Our Lord Himself must have had it—but it can certainly exasperate someone who hopes to claim a major share of that person's attention or be chosen as that person's "most beloved." You have only to page through the Gospels to come upon Peter making a pest of himself again and again: "Whom do you love most, Lord? Who will sit next to you in Heaven?" Impulsive Peter, stepping out of the boat, into the waves, to get to Our Lord first, and having to be saved from drowning.

Antonia befriended me; I would never have approached her first.

I was a new boarder from Charleston. My mother had told my father that she would divorce him if he didn't send me away to school. She said our eighteen-room house on the East Battery was no longer large enough to contain us both. She had always called me her "pelican child," saying I'd come out of her body determined to tear her slowly to pieces, whereas my older brothers had slid out like "little greased otters." She loved telling people in my presence, "I first thought Suzanne was the beginning of early menopause." She called me her "sneaky surprise package." By the time I reached adolescence, she had compiled a whole list of "Suzanne" epithets. I was "sneaky, sanctimonious, self-advancing"; so many of her adjectives began with *s* that I came to believe she had chosen my name because it would alliterate well with those qualifiers. She also liked to call me things prefaced by "old": "Old Frump," "Old Stumpy," and "Old Stubby," the last of which seemed particularly unfair, since I was better built, with a longer torso and legs, than either of my brothers. I had my father's wandlike body and his finer features.

But this is not going to be the story of my mother's dislike of me. It has taken a good portion of my lifetime for me to comprehend that there is, and has been all through recorded history, many a mother who cannot stand her child. I was merely one of those children. That was part of my pattern, one of the episodes in the "carpet" I saw spread out before me during my painkiller fugues in the hospital. But I wanted to provide you with a little background of how I came to Mount St. Gabriel's as a boarder. "One of us must go," my mother had said, and my father, who had probably seen this coming for some time, did not want to lose his comfortable home. Furthermore, since he was from an old Catholic family, divorce was anathema to him.

I loved Mount St. Gabriel's from the moment I set eyes on it. Unlike the other new boarders, I was not the least bit homesick. From the very first, I felt that

Mount St. Gabriel's was my home. I loved the thin, clean air of the mountains, so energizing and bracing after Charleston's sultry closeness. I loved the nuns, old and young, sweet and crabby, every one of whom behaved more like a mother to me than the woman I had left behind. I was enchanted with my adorable little roommate, Soledad, who'd had her own hand-carved prie-dieu shipped to her from Mexico City. I liked going to Mass in the chapel and following in the daily missal my father had given me, with my initials in gold on the cover. I loved knowing and following the church seasons and the feasts of all the saints and martyrs. Even Mount St. Gabriel's cuisine satisfied me, though it was fashionable among the boarders to complain. The school was founded by an Englishwoman, so its normal fare was roast meats or savory pies, boiled vegetables and stewed fruits, with bread-and-butter puddings or sponge cake for dessert—and trifle on special occasions.

I had been given a chance to start over and win love for myself, and this I set about doing on the very first day of school.

The Tilden twins were in the row next to mine, Antonia at the front of the row and Cornelia just behind her. I was at the end of one row and they were at the head of the next, so I could observe them simply by looking forward. At first I studied them as a unit: What would it be like to have a twin? What if there had been another of me? Would my mother have devised epithets for us both? They dressed alike, which made their individual "touches" stand out more. Cornelia wore colored shoelaces in her oxfords, pink or yellow or light green; Antonia's were always brown. Antonia pulled her honey-gold hair back rather severely from her forehead with tortoiseshell barrettes; Cornelia let hers loop forward, and she would regard you slyly from behind its heavy side wave.

I listened more than I talked, those first weeks at Mount St. Gabriel's. I listened to what the old girls said about the other old girls and about the nuns. I heard that the English foundress, Mother Elizabeth Wallingford, then in her late sixties, had a deadly tumor growing in her brain and all anyone could do for her now was "make her comfortable" up in the infirmary. Mother Fiona Finney was pointed out to me, the Irishwoman who broke horses in her youth and had come over with Mother Wallingford. She was very busy, performing a great many jobs at once, from sacristan to baker to riding instructress, but you would see her rushing through the halls or picking up her skirts and flying up the stairs. "There she goes," someone would say. "She runs up to that infirmary every chance she gets. Poor Finney is going to be devastated when Wallingford goes!"

I learned that the Tilden twins' father was in the state legislature in Raleigh and that their mother was an accomplished homemaker who sewed all the girls' clothes. But Cornelia went into a "humor" or fainted if she had to stand still to fit dresses, so Antonia had volunteered to do it for them both. Cornelia, they said, had the cruel tongue. A new girl, wanting to make an overture of friendship, had asked "which kind of twins they were," and Antonia was gently explaining that they were the identical, not the fraternal, kind when Cornelia spoke up and completely dashed the poor girl. "Actually," Cornelia announced in a baleful voice, "we are triplets, but one of us died."

I was good at sports, as most girls are who have older brothers. I could run fast and played a good game of tennis and I liked organizing team sports. At the end of the school year I was voted one of the four field day captains for the grammar school, and our team, the Green Team, won the trophy. I had chosen Antonia Tilden as my cocaptain. Cornelia Tilden, captain of the Red Team, was very put out that I, rather than she, had gotten her sister for cocaptain because I'd drawn the straw for first pick. But I think Cornelia had begun to resent me long before this.

However, I am jumping ahead.

Back at the beginning of the school year, it was Antonia who befriended me—forgive me if I am repeating myself; I may have already said this— because I would never have approached either of the twins and risked the fate of that poor girl who had made an overture of friendship by asking what kind of twins they were. I let people approach me as they felt inclined to. I was surprised how well this worked. I just did my work, ran the races, played the games, was courteous and pleasant to everyone, and had an easy, approachable demeanor, but I never went out of my way to attract the notice of any particular person. As I think I have indicated, God had favored me with presentable looks. I was not a beauty, nor did I radiate a superior aura like the Tildens, but I was slim and well made and had curly brown hair with interesting lights in it and straight white teeth. I moved lightly and quickly but always with purpose, and I once overheard Mother Finney saying, "The Ravenel girl holds herself straight as a switch." My classmates knew little about me other than that I was from Charleston, that my family lived on the East Battery, and that my father was an attorney specializing in trusts and my mother a semi-invalid. I am afraid I was the one who set this last story going. It seemed the least my mother could do for me. I put her in a nice big bedroom with everything she could need, the curtains drawn against the heat of the day: a nice quiet back bedroom, away from the hustle and bustle of the promenade traffic. My brothers were grown, the older already a partner of my father's, the other still in law school. I had been a late child—which was true—and she just didn't have the strength to keep track of an energetic young girl on the cusp of womanhood, much less take charge of that girl's social life and properly chaperone her.

The funny thing was that after a while, I almost came to believe this version myself.

But Antonia and I, how it began.

It was after lunch on one of those dazzling September days when the mountain air was so pure it could make a person light-headed. Especially someone like myself who had grown up in the sultry lowlands. My roommate, Soledad, and I were headed to the playground for recess. She was chattering in her excited nonstop Spanish-English. I wasn't paying close attention to what she was saying; she didn't seem to require it. She always stuck to me at recess because I was the known quantity she slept beside every night, and she would twitter away, like some charming exotic pet bird who had fastened itself on your arm. I found myself laughing from sheer physical well-being—I flourished in this high altitude—and from joy at having this devoted little creature hanging on me so that I appeared desired and chosen in the eyes of the others.

Antonia Tilden was strolling slowly ahead of us on the path, head bent, appearing deep in thought. For once, her twin was nowhere in sight. Soledad blithely tugged me along, completely wrapped up in her polyglot chatter and my laughter, and that's when Antonia suddenly stepped aside to let us pass. She gave us both this respectful, rather wistful smile, the kind of smile an older person might bestow on young girls enjoying high spirits.

As soon as we got to the playground, Soledad made a beeline for the Ocean Wave, which was the preferred ride of the boldest girls. It was a circular bench attached by steel cables to a high pole in the center. Riders would climb on, spacing themselves around the circle in kneeling or crouching positions, and grab hold of the bar in front of them. The last girl on—this time it was Soledad—would give it a great push to set it rocking before she jumped aboard. It was a hazardous ride to have on a school playground; today it would not be tolerated, even if the riders were wearing helmets and had brought letters from home absolving the school of all liability. Yet I don't recall any injuries. The Ocean Wave served decades of bold girls into the sixties, when the playground was leveled to make way for the new school and convent.

I watched Soledad fling herself with a little shriek onto the rocking contraption. The girls aboard shrieked back and began working their knees and writhing their bodies to keep the thing in motion and see how many times they could make it clang against the pole. Soledad and I were both thirteen, but the Ocean Wave separated us into child and adult. Now it was my turn to smile benignly at the high-spirited girls. The smile was for the benefit of Antonia Tilden, who had come to stand beside me. I knew she was going to speak first and tried to guess what she might say. She could have begun in many ways—with something wryly conversational: "You're not a devotee of the Ocean Wave?" Or a direct personal question: "How are you finding Mount St. Gabriel's?"

I was floored when she looked up at the sky and murmured, as much to herself as to me, "What a beautiful day."

Oh Lord, I prayed, please don't let Antonia Tilden be just some vapid Pollyanna.

"When I was little," Antonia went on, "I thought that God lived in the wind. But now I think He lives in the clouds, too."

"He's always more than you can get your mind around," I said as we watched a cumulus cloud collapse from an old man's stern profile into a slouching beast.

"Yes!" said Antonia.

"Have you ever been in a hurricane?" I asked her.

"No, have you?"

"Oh, we get them every year in Charleston. I can watch them from my bedroom window. Trees snap in two and roofs go flying through the air. I think God dwells in destruction, too. I mean, for His own purposes, of course."

"For His own purposes, of course," echoed Antonia, recognizing me with a smile that went straight to my heart.

This was the exchange that launched our friendship on that September day back in 1929. Since then, I have watched generations of girls begin friendships. Wryly, cautiously, coyly, pushily; setting up rules and dividing up powers; vying for advantage or trying to fascinate. We were just two girls speculating on how God went about revealing Himself through His world.

After we became known as best friends, I'm sure others assumed that Antonia and I told each other everything about ourselves. But we always kept a respectful reserve between us. I know I held back because I didn't want to risk alienating this superior person. In fact, it took a while for me to acknowledge

202 / Gail Godwin

what everybody else took for granted: that Antonia sought out my company and seemed most content when she was with me. But why did she not pry more into my life? When Reverend Mother called me out of class on that Monday after Black Friday to tell me Father had died in a hunting accident, she said I could go to the chapel or to my room for the rest of the day. "Is there anyone you would like to have with you?" she asked. I thought of Antonia but was afraid she might feel obligated. So I told Reverend Mother something that led her to suspect I might be blessed with an early vocation. "The only one I want to have with me is always with me anyway," I said. "I would like permission to go to my room and get my rosary and then to pray for my father in the chapel."

Of course, the news spread through the school like wildfire. Coming so soon after Black Friday, which had wiped out the savings of many girls' families, my father's death was bound to cause speculation: had it been an accident? My father handled many large trusts. What had been revealed about the state of those trusts when everyone was demanding reassurance about their solvency? Why did my mother not want me to go home for the funeral? Was it because the body could not be buried in hallowed ground? (Just for the record, Beatrix, it was, following a full Catholic Mass; and no one ever brought a suit against my father for mismanaging funds. Indeed, my brothers, both now deceased, honored every one of his obligations.)

While I was saying my rosary, I was aware that the chapel was filling up with people. Our teacher, Mother O'Hara, had sent our class to pray with me until lunchtime. Little Soledad plunged into my pew and wept ardently beside me while I went, decade by decade, through my beads. The day being Monday, the meditation was on the joyful mysteries and their corresponding virtues: the Annunciation and humility; the Visitation and charity; the Nativity and poverty; the Presentation (obedience); and the Finding in the Temple (piety). When the Angelus bell rang at noon, the nuns came in for Sext and my classmates left for the cafeteria, all except Antonia, who had been somewhere behind me. Now she moved into my pew and knelt beside me. She had her rosary out. "Which mystery are you on?" she asked. I said I had reached the Finding in the Temple. "Then I'll begin there with you," she said, "and go back and do the others later."

That was Antonia.

As I said, I wondered back then, at the beginning of our friendship, why she did not pry more into my life. But later I realized she didn't have to. Her twin would have supplied her with the kinds of information and hearsay Antonia would have thought too intrusive to inquire about. With me Antonia went to places Cornelia didn't or couldn't go, and I think Cornelia resented that. On the other hand, Cornelia sought out the places Antonia kept aloof from. Cornelia loved gossip; she loved assessing people, winkling out their faults and scandals. She specialized in the shocking put-down ("Actually, we are triplets, but one of us died") and in summing up someone with a shrewd but unkind pronouncement that lingered in your mind. I heard her say once that a certain boy smelled like he had "dried with a sour towel," and I could never see that boy again without thinking of a sour towel.

We had a lay teacher, Mrs. Prince, who taught arithmetic in the grammar school. She was popular with the girls because she brought us fudge and read us Uncle Remus stories, doing all the voices, until some of us were in hysterics. And then one day Cornelia said, "The trouble with Mrs. Prince is, she wants to be liked too much. And that can be the undoing of anyone." And though we went on enjoying Mrs. Prince and eating her fudge and laughing at her Uncle Remus renditions, we now saw her as "someone who wanted to be liked too much" and were on the lookout for signs of this pitiful weakness in ourselves. Well, twenty years passed, and Mrs. Prince was still popular with the grammar school girls. Until Cornelia's daughter Tildy Stratton and her best friend in sixth grade, Maud Norton, organized the other girls and drove the poor woman out. I had just become headmistress of the academy when this occured. Mrs. Prince told Reverend Mother she could no longer go on teaching at Mount St. Gabriel's. And Reverend Mother called me in and I heard the story. I begged Mrs. Prince to at least continue her home economics classes with the academy girls, which also were very popular, but she said she now felt nauseated every time she drove through the school gates. Tildy's putsch had completely undermined her. And it was so diabolically organized! I remember wondering, after this sad interview with Mrs. Prince, whether Tildy's cruel act had been "inspired" by her mother. If a parent shows contempt for a teacher, the child is more than likely to follow suit. Perhaps Tildy did it to win favor with her mother. For it should come as no big surprise that Cornelia as a mother treated her daughters very much as she had treated her school friends. She kept them in thrall to her with her contemptuous tongue.

The last thing I could have imagined, when I offered Tildy the chance to direct her class in a new production of my old school play, was that I would be setting myself up for a treachery that would have more fallout for the school than the ousting of poor Mrs. Prince.

Looking back now, I see it is all too likely that Tildy's adulteration of the play was one more attempt to win favor with her mother. I also believe that

Cornelia not only egged Tildy on but went out of her way to contribute suggestions: such as the clothes worn in the treacherous scene and other background material Tildy could not have known about.

I have asked myself many times why I offered Tildy the opportunity that was to bring down so much censure on my head. Tildy Stratton was a difficult, headstrong girl, not as lovable or as lovely as her older sister, Madeline, but she had leadership potential that was going to waste or—as we have seen in the case of Mrs. Prince—being put to the wrong uses. Mother Malloy, who had been tutoring Tildy in the afternoons, agreed with me about this. She said Tildy hadn't found large enough outlets for her leadership qualities. I was the same way myself. I liked to think up things for others to do and direct them in the doing of it. I liked to see my effects go forth in the world around me. But I was fortunate to seek healthy outlets. When I was Tildy's age, I wrote a play for my freshman class to perform. I called it after the unfinished sculpture in the grotto. I wanted it to honor that girl who had died before she could realize her vocation.

Maybe, I remember thinking in those minutes before Compline, it was time for a new production of *The Red Nun*. The last one had been in 1947 and, though those students worked very hard and were very loyal to what they believed were my intentions and the "traditions" of the play, I felt the whole thing could use some new blood. And I thought, maybe that is the answer for Tildy: give her something to sink her teeth into. I will sound her out. But she must realize that I am offering her a gift and a privilege as well as a chance to prove herself.

You could say I offered my play as tinder and threw in the first lit match myself.

But I have jumped ahead. I was telling about how Antonia and I became friends and something of the quality of that friendship. Actually, it was my play and the working on it together that solidified our decision to join the Order of St. Scholastica together.

Lord, help me keep all these stories going and fit them into their proper places.

CHAPTER 22

An Errand for Agnes

Saturday forenoon, February 2, 1952
Downtown Mountain City

MADELINE, HAVING PURCHASED the required supplies for her mother's studio, stopped at the front of Commercial Stationers to examine the rack of Valentine's Day cards. Tucked among a preponderance of sweet and safe offerings ("I really think you're mighty nice . . ." "To the One I Love . . .") were a few spicier alternatives: "It's leap year and you've caught my eye, / You great big handsome wonderful guy," with a girl frog ogling a bullfrog. And "Where's the fire? Now don't be smart. You know you set it in my heart," with a dog driving a fire truck. Boldness in love, it seemed, required animal stand-ins. Madeline burst into giggles at the tuxedoed skunk holding a glass of champagne ("For a Man of True Di-STINK-shun"), but there was no male in her life with the kind of humor that could tolerate receiving such a valentine. Her father, perhaps, but from a daughter it might seem disrespectful. If Mama sent it to Daddy, he would guffaw and be tickled she'd thought of him; but Mama, being Mama, was not a card-sending person. ("I don't need a Hallmark hack to express my feelings.")

"Oh, Madeline, hello."

It was Henry Vick, also carrying parcels. He looked gray-faced and hollowed out. "I thought I recognized your laugh," he said.

"It was this card." She plucked it out of the rack and handed it over, watching him study the picture with a bemused smile, then break into laughter when he read the message inside.

"Were you thinking of sending it to me?"

"Oh, Uncle Henry, I would never—!" Madeline felt her face flame.

But then she was doubly embarrassed when she realized he had been making a joke.

"What have you been buying?" she asked him.

"Tracing paper, India ink, more pen nibs. Have you had lunch?"

"Oh, I was just going to grab a Coke and a grilled cheese at the Woolworth counter."

"We can do better than that," said Henry Vick.

They walked to the Park Cafeteria on the green; it had Beaux Arts trim and colored skylights and had been designed by Henry's father, Malcolm Vick, in the 1920s. The cafeteria had been Madeline's eatery of choice since she was a little girl, and today she loaded her tray with all her childhood favorites: slices of moist white turkey meat wrapped around a generous scoop of dressing, mashed potatoes puddled with gravy, lima beans swimming in milk and butter, red Jell-O with whipped cream, and sweetened iced tea. Henry had Salisbury steak with the mashed potatoes and gravy, a pineapple salad, and black coffee. It was too early for the Saturday lunch crowd, but several people greeted Henry warmly as they moved through the line. Madeline felt sophisticated to be "dining out" with a prominent man in town. She also had the pleasure of noting her own positive effects on poor Uncle Henry, who already seemed a different person from the gray-faced old bachelor who had crept up behind her in the stationery store. He was being almost debonair. He asked where she preferred to sit, upstairs or downstairs. "Wherever you want," she said, feeling suddenly shy and deferential.

"Let's take that booth, where we can have some privacy. I want to ask your advice, Madeline."

"*My* advice?"

He unloaded both their trays, hers first, arranging her dishes and silverware in front of her. Then he carried the trays to a nearby stand, to be collected by a busboy. From behind, Henry could still pass for a much younger man. As he bent deeply from the knees to stack the trays on the bottom shelf—saving the top shelf for the people who could not bend so easily?—she saw him as a desirable man through her late aunt's eyes. What had sex been like between them on that short honeymoon?

Flustered, Madeline ducked her head and gazed intently at her mashed potatoes.

"You should have started without me," said Henry, folding himself into the booth across from her. "You don't want that wonderful gravy to get cold."

"I love their gravy."

"Evaporated milk, bouillon cubes, flour, and a touch of molasses."

"How do you know that?"

"The cook is Rosa's cousin. Rosa thinks it's a pretty poor excuse for brown gravy, but health departments don't like to see jars of pan drippings and grease sitting around on restaurant stoves. Rosa adds a splash of sherry to ours."

"Isn't food *great*? The last thing I'd want is to take one of those capsules they're talking about that fulfill all your nutritional needs."

Henry sipped his black coffee and smiled at her indulgently. Was he already regretting asking a sixteen-year-old girl to lunch?

"How is Chloe?" she asked. Since Mrs. Roberts's funeral, Tildy seemed to be getting thick with Maud again. Tildy and her intense, exclusive friendships!

"That's what I wanted to talk to you about. You're a discerning person, Madeline. You know about the stepfather business, don't you?"

"Rex Wright wants Chloe to go back to—what is the town?"

"Barlow. He's her legal father, you know. He's going to marry again and wants to start them right off as a family."

Madeline thought: Both Tildy's best friends have stepmothers—or stepmothers-to-be—who want to add them like charms to their lives. Though she'd gathered from Tildy that there was some disenchantment going on vis-à-vis the Palm Beach stepmother. Maud had acted "fast" at a dance, or something, and thrown a wrench into the second Mrs. Norton's social aspirations.

"How does Chloe feel about it?" she asked Henry.

"At first she wanted no part of it. When I told her about the letters going back and forth between Ollie Coxe and Rex Wright's lawyer in Barlow, she gave me a wide-eyed stare, like Agnes used to when someone brought up something she disapproved of. She asked me couldn't I just have Mr. Coxe write back to the other lawyer and say she was happy with me. But now she's suddenly come up with this idea of taking the bus to Barlow by herself and spending the weekend with them."

"What would the point be?"

"To get to know Brenda, the fiancée. She's a widow with grown sons. Both sons work for Rex; one sprays crops and the other teaches flying lessons."

"But why should Chloe want to get to know Brenda if she's happy with you?"

"Well, now, this is the thing—" Henry, looking uncomfortable, passed his hand slowly over his receding hair. "Chloe thinks that her mother—that Agnes—wants it."

Madeline recalled Tildy's recent outburst. ("All this drawing, drawing, drawing of Agnes, Agnes, Agnes! And then she *consults* her like she's the Blessed Virgin or something. It's downright creepy. I don't have the *patience* for that now, with the play to direct and all.")

At the time Madeline had assumed Tildy was presenting excuses to the family for taking up with Maud again.

"But why would Agnes want it? What is Chloe's reasoning?"

"I'm not sure reasoning comes into it. I don't like to say this, but my niece seems haunted. She spends hours drawing pictures of her mother. And I can't help overhearing her talking in her room at night. It was my sister's room as a girl, you know."

"Yes, Tildy said."

"Chloe and Tildy aren't as close as they were, and I'm sorry about that. Tildy is such an *unhaunted* little person. But I can see why Chloe, the way she is at present, would strain a friendship. There just isn't a lot of her to relate to. I include myself. Lately I've been wondering whether I wouldn't have done better for her to let her board with the nuns, as planned. But Chloe wanted to live at the house, so I forfeited her boarding fee. I've even considered consulting Mother Ravenel, but she tends to take over in these matters. And Agnes always had reservations about Suzanne."

"Will you let her go to Barlow for the weekend?"

"Ollie Coxe says I'm crazy if I do. He says it's playing into their hands. What's to stop them from keeping her? Possession is nine tenths of the law, especially since Wright is her legal father anyway."

"But they couldn't just hold her hostage. If she had her round-trip bus ticket—"

"Yes, I considered that. The trouble is, what if she didn't want to come back?"

"But why would she want to stay? She told Tildy he used to hit them."

"Ah, she never told me that. I haven't wanted to cross-examine her, you see."

"Couldn't you send her down on the bus and then pick her up yourself?"

"I offered that. But," he laughed dolefully, "it seems Agnes has decreed that I'm not to be a part of this. Chloe is to go to Barlow of her own free will. It's something she must accomplish for her mother. You see how troublesome this is getting. I am not in Chloe's mind, so I don't know how much of this is the wishful fantasy of a girl who desperately misses her mother and wants to pretend they're in communication, or whether she really hears Agnes, or something she believes is Agnes, dictating to her from within. At any rate, what I have decided I have to do is speak to Monsignor after he hears my confession this afternoon."

"What does the church say about—hauntings?"

"Well, there is the doctrine of the soul's immortality. And Aquinas held that we can prove the fact of the soul's conscious life even after it is separated from the body. But I'm hoping Monsignor can shed some light of a more practical kind. A priest is bound to have had more experience of haunted young people than an old bachelor architect. I can't even claim the experience of a single haunted house."

"Listen, Uncle Henry, why don't I drive Chloe down to Barlow? We could make it a day trip. Leave early on a Saturday morning, and I'd drop her off and then pick her up a few hours later. Do you think *that* would pass muster with Agnes?"

Henry winced slightly, and Madeline regretted her flippancy. Why, oh, why was it so hard to strike a balance between wit and kindness? Not that she'd had the greatest teacher in her mother.

But the next thing she knew they were working out the logistics.

"What would you be doing during those hours?" asked Henry.

"Oh, I could be visiting an old school friend in Barlow. No, they might want to know my friend's name. What is the nearest good-sized town to Barlow? I'm not smart like my granddaddy Tilden; he carried the state map in his head—he could close his eyes and rattle off the counties for you, west to east, and who they were named for."

"My father used to say that Archie Tilden was one of the rare state legislators who could see things whole. But you're plenty smart, Madeline; I won't have you running yourself down. Barlow's about twelve miles below Statesville."

"In that case, my friend is going to live in Statesville."

"You have to go through Statesville to get to Barlow, so it would mean doubling back for that visit with your friend."

"What's twenty-four miles round-trip for a friend?" said Madeline merrily. "But, wait, why would I suddenly be going to see her? Maybe a bridal shower. No, my friends are still too young for those. I know: her big sister's bridal shower. I always admired her big sister. And I happened to mention it to you, Henry, and you said, 'Chloe's thinking of taking the bus down there—when would you be going, Madeline?' "

"And when *would* you be thinking of going?"

"How about next Saturday? That would give Chloe time to phone them, and it would save her the bus fare and all. Of course, we still don't know if—"

Shut *up,* she thought, stopping herself.

"If it will pass muster with Agnes," Henry finished for her, smiling sadly.

"Listen, Uncle Henry, you don't have any scruples about—well, my imaginary friend and her big sister, do you? I mean, if you told Chloe, 'Madeline has offered to drive you down and wait for you and drive you back,' it might seem as though we're in cahoots, like I was your stand-in, your spy, sort of."

"I'd much rather she be in your care than sending her off on the bus. I may have overdone my scruples regarding her. But what about you, Madeline? If you're going to be gone all day, your family will want to know where you are."

"I will tell Mama the truth. She enjoys covert operations. But I won't tell Tildy, because you never know with Tildy. She might or might not spill the beans to Chloe."

"That's wise, I think. I'll propose your offer to Chloe this evening and she'll probably want to—sleep on it. Will you be at Mass tomorrow? I may be able to let you know something then. Of course, it will depend on the weather, too."

☩

Early Saturday morning, February 9, 1952
Mountain City to Barlow

The weather was just what Madeline had wished for: crisp, bright, not cold. If it had been cold, Mama had offered, they could switch cars so Madeline could drive the better-insulated Packard. Cornelia had entered with gusto into the intrigue, which she had drolly christened "the errand for Agnes."

"But don't you think a bridal shower is a little incautious, Maddy? What if Rex Wright and his intended bride hunt through the newspapers for your friend's sister's upcoming wedding?"

"Well, we'll have left Barlow by then."

"But you might need to go back. You don't want to destroy your credibility. Have your friend's sister expecting a baby—the dates are vaguer. Make it a baby shower. And, of course, you'll need a present."

"Isn't buying a present taking it a bit far, Mama?"

"Who said anything about buying? How about your silver baby mug? You can wrap it prettily and sit it in full view on the backseat, where everyone can poke their heads in and admire it. Then you can stow it in the trunk before you go back to pick up Chloe."

"But what if Tildy sees it when I'm leaving the house?"

"Do you really think Tildy is likely to be anywhere but fast asleep in her nice big bed—the bed you so generously bequeathed her—at six on a Saturday morning? But your point is taken. Wrap it in secret and carry it to your car inside an old shopping bag. Before you get to the Vick house, pull over and display it on the backseat. But after you come back, you *should* tell Tildy you drove Chloe to Barlow. In case Chloe says something to Tildy. Goodness! It makes one pause, doesn't it? Think of all the things you'd have to plan for before setting out to commit a real crime."

"Mama, what was Agnes Vick like?"

Their dialogues took place in Cornelia's darkroom at the studio, the best setting, Madeline had learned, for successful tête-à-têtes with Mama.

"She thought very highly of herself and was something of a prig. The only person at school who loved her unreservedly was old Mother Finney. Agnes was an expert at making you feel you weren't quite as principled as she was. She was always name-dropping virtues like 'integrity' and 'honor.' Some people thought she had a wonderful sense of humor, but I never saw it. All her jokes had that treacly wholesomeness. You know, 'This is funny, it will make you laugh, but it's still within the bounds of good Catholic taste.' Her big achievement was that she could put down Suzanne Ravenel. All during high school when Suzanne was scrabbling for power, she had sense enough to keep her distance from Agnes. My, but it was fun to watch!"

"She wouldn't join the Oblates of the Red Nun."

"That was something Suzanne devised to keep her and my sister's vocations hot and bubbly. Everything Suzanne cooked up, like the play, was designed to keep Antonia close. The oblate idea was rather fervid and naive, but I kept my feelings to myself. I joined to keep an eye on Tony. If they'd formed a little club to take regular tours to hell, I would have insisted on my right as a twin to go along. Suzanne didn't dare exclude me. Whereas Agnes Vick was president of Sodality for three years in a row. When you're already a high-muckety-muck in the Society of Mary, which sponsors the most lavish reception at the end of the school year, when the Queen of the School is crowned, why should you need to take secret vows to a hulk of old marble memorializing a girl who never did anything but die? But Suzanne was very annoyed by Agnes's turn-down. I've always thought it was Suzanne who spread the rumor that Agnes couldn't take the oblate vows because she had petted too heavily with Merriweather Starnes. Suzanne had to ask Francine Barfoot because there had to be five of us to start a club. The other oblate was Suzanne's little Mexican roommate."

"I guess you wouldn't ever divulge the secret vows, would you, Mama?"

"Tildy was trying to winkle that out of me the other night when I dropped by her room to tuck her in. You know how Tildy *importunes.* But I can't stand to be pinned down like that. I told her I would think about it."

"Are you in the mood now?"

"The truth is, darling, I don't recall exactly. Nothing was written down; it was much too secret. I can recall the gist, of course. It was typical of the things fervent girls love to swear to in their cliques and sororities. The premise was that your worst fate would be not to fulfill God's plan for you, and so you had to dedicate yourself under oath to seek the self God had in mind for you, and put everything else second. Oh, now

I do seem to remember: one of the vows was to forsake any person who tempted you away from God's plan for you. I'm going to tell you something, Madeline. After Antonia's death I had a really bad time. I almost went out of my mind trying to figure out why this bizarre accident had to happen to my sister. I entertained all sorts of crazy ideas, one being that perhaps during the honeymoon Tony had told Henry about the secret vows of the oblates and then it suddenly struck her that he might be the person who was obstructing God's plan for her and that her duty was to forsake Henry. And she became so confused and distraught about what she should and shouldn't do that she stepped in front of that van. And now please help me pin up these prints. Not bad for a plain bride, are they? That's because I understand lighting. I'm seriously considering expanding into portraiture. What do you think? Making people look good is always worth some dough."

+++

THE WEATHER ON Saturday morning was so agreeable that Henry Vick and Chloe were waiting for her on the front porch. Faithful to her mother's "crime plan," Madeline had pulled over a few blocks from their house and placed the wrapped baby gift in full view on the backseat.

Chloe could have passed for nine instead of fourteen in her pleated plaid skirt, school blazer, white knee socks, and loafers. She was also carrying her book bag. Madeline knew Chloe's closet sported more sophisticated attire than this and wondered whether the *jeune fille* effect was deliberate.

Henry accompanied them to the car, carrying a basket covered with a checkered dishcloth. "Rosa packed you all a midmorning breakfast. She can't stand the thought of anybody arriving anyplace hungry. It might reflect on her. Where do you want me to put this, Madeline?"

"Oh, on the backseat will be fine. Next to the, er, baby shower gift."

DURING THE CORKSCREW descent between Black Mountain and Old Fort, Chloe grew pale and silent. Up until then, she had been doing her best to respond to Madeline's attempts at sociability.

"You okay over there, Chloe?"

"I'm feeling a little woozy."

"Is it urgent woozy or the kind that can wait till I find a place to pull off?"

"It can wait." A pitiful whisper.

"Then I won't block that sandpit for runaway trucks. There's a better spot farther down. Can you last till then?"

"Yes," came the muffled reply. The girl had put her book satchel to her face. Madeline recalled her own bouts with passenger nausea on this dizzying descent of road that dropped you eight hundred feet in less than thirty minutes. As soon as she was old enough to drive herself, it had stopped.

As soon as Madeline pulled off the road, Chloe flung herself out of the car and dashed behind a clump of underbrush. She emerged with her dignity intact. Thank you, but she had her own Kleenex, as well as a traveling toothbrush and a small tube of Ipana.

Down they went, through Marion, Morganton, Valdese, and Hickory, dropping another three hundred feet toward sea level. Madeline told Chloe about Granddaddy Tilden, the state representative, who could close his eyes and recite all the counties from west to east and the people they were named for. "This morning alone, we'll have crossed through six. We left our own Buncombe, then we went through McDowell, Burke, and Catawba. Next comes Iredell, that's when we hit Statesville, and then we'll dip on down to Barlow, which is in Rowan."

"Who were the people?"

"Well, let's see. I could rattle them off as a child because it tickled Granddaddy. Colonel Buncombe, Edward B., commanded a regiment in the Revolutionary War—on our side, meaning the side that wanted our independence from Britain. Charles McDowell and his 'Over-Mountain Men' slaughtered the Loyalists at Kings Mountain. The Loyalist troops underestimated what they called a band of ragtag mongrels, but the Over-Mountain Men called themselves that because they knew what a real mountain was, and to them Kings Mountain was just a little bitty hill. Thomas Burke and Matthew Rowan were royal governors when we were still a colony. Burke was kidnapped by the Tories, escaped from his prison, and left politics in disgrace because he had broken his oath to the Tories not to escape. James Iredell was the first North Carolina judge appointed to the U.S. Supreme Court after we became a state. He was for states' rights, but, interestingly enough, he was also a strong advocate for the abolishing of slavery. The Catawbas were a big important Indian tribe, and so were the Cherokees, so they got two counties named after them after they were defeated or driven out of the state. There, that's Madeline's state history lesson for the day, compliments of Granddaddy Archibald Tilden, who was a loving man who believed in justice and never talked down to children."

They stopped at a roadside picnic ground between Hickory and Statesville and ate Rosa's sausage biscuits, washed down with sweetened hot tea in a thermos. The sun was warm for February, at least ten degrees warmer in the lower altitude.

"I think it's important to keep the dead with us," blurted Chloe suddenly. "Don't you think it's important?"

"I don't know how we can help it," said Madeline. "They remember themselves in us every day. We carry on their work. And, oh, probably we repeat their mistakes. In a way I was carrying on Granddaddy's work back there in the car. And I'm sure you will influence the world around you in ways that would do credit to your mother."

"What do you mean, repeating their mistakes?"

"I'm not sure. It just popped out of my mouth."

"No, you meant something," Chloe persisted.

"Well, it would seem logical, wouldn't it? If we take on their good qualities, some of the less desirable parts of their natures may get swept in, too. You know, weeds with the seeds."

"But like *what,* for instance?" Going into Tildy's favorite attack mode.

Examples unsuitable to pass on to Chloe crowded eagerly to the forefront of Madeline's mind. Old Mrs. Vick, Henry's dipso mother and Chloe's own grandmother, teetering in the soused haughty footsteps of father and grandfather before her. The previous mayor's wife, who had left her prosperous marriage and had a child out of wedlock, just as her mother had done with her. The thirty-year-old father who shot himself with his hunting rifle on his son's birthday; the son—a close friend of Smoky Stratton's in high school—finally managing to extinguish himself, after two botched attempts in his twenties, on his thirtieth birthday with the same hunting rifle. Old Mountain City stories, polished up dagger-shiny and sharpened to perforation point, then handed down by Cornelia to her daughters at a tender age.

"The closest I can get to a 'for instance,' " Madeline temporized, "is . . . well, think of someone you love or admire—they don't necessarily have to be dead—and then ask what qualities of theirs you would like to take on as your qualities. And then ask yourself what things about them you would rather *not* take on."

BEFORE MADELINE HAD switched off the ignition in front of Rex Wright's farmhouse, a frowning man in a brown leather flying jacket was quick-stepping down the walk.

"That's him," murmured Chloe.

"Well, remember, I'll be back to collect you in just a few hours."

Agnes at Rest

Saturday afternoon and evening, February 9, 1952
Rex Wright's house
Barlow, North Carolina

CHLOE WOULD RATHER have come alone on the bus. He would have met her at the station and it would have been all on his terms. Rex liked things all on his terms. That's the way he stayed in the best mood. Agnes had learned that, and Chloe had learned it with her.

But Mr. Coxe, the lawyer, told Uncle Henry it would be "playing right into Rex Wright's hands." Rex Wright might cajole or use other means to make her stay. And then the legal battle would begin all over from the other end. The uncle in Mountain City trying to get back his sister's child from Barlow. But a legal father, if he was also an upstanding, solvent person, a decorated World War II pilot, a widower about to remarry, would be much more likely to triumph in court over a bachelor uncle, Mr. Coxe said.

And then Uncle Henry found out that Madeline Stratton was driving down to the Piedmont and would be glad to drop Chloe off in Barlow, even though it meant going out of her way. He told Chloe she could ride with Madeline and visit with Rex Wright and meet his fiancée, and then maybe later a weekend in Barlow could be arranged.

When the visit business had first been proposed by her stepfather, Uncle Henry had offered to take her and bring her back, but Chloe knew that wouldn't work. Rex Wright hated Uncle Henry; he said he was the last sterile remains of the snobbish Vick clan.

The only time Rex had met Uncle Henry, except for Agnes's funeral, the circumstances couldn't have been less favorable. It was the time Rex had surprised them all by flying up to Mountain City in his new Beechcraft and whisking Agnes and Chloe away before their visit had hardly begun. On the flight back, in a fit of rage, Rex had threatened to crash the plane into a mountain.

So Chloe had turned down Uncle Henry's offer to drive her to Barlow. "Agnes wouldn't like it," she'd said.

Oh, Agnes, if only they would let us do it our way. We aren't afraid. We know too much.

But maybe this would work.

At first Uncle Henry said it was to be a bridal shower of a friend's big sister, but it turned out it was a baby shower. The kind of thing an old bachelor would be expected to get wrong, Uncle Henry said, laughing at himself.

Chloe could see that Rex was not in the best mood. He advanced upon them with the demeanor of a man who had been anticipating all the ways he would be patronized by this social butterfly who would drive down the mountain and back in a single day just to go to a goddamn baby shower—and condescend to drop off his daughter as a favor to the sterile remnant of the moldering Vick clan.

But Madeline kept her greeting brief and respectful and was her charming self. Before she drove away she had coaxed from Rex Wright a begrudging smile of admiration and a gallant bow. Chloe glimpsed him through Madeline's eyes: a nice-looking war hero in immaculately pressed fatigues and a flight jacket bearing his squadron's patch. She liked him the better for this vision, and he registered his stepdaughter's approval. Thus their visit got off to a propitious start. As they headed toward the house, he did not try to kiss or hug her, merely chafed her hands briefly between his. "I'm surprised they aren't little blocks of ice," he said. "Riding all this way in that drafty vehicle of hers. I expected she'd have a better car."

"Oh, it was warm inside. And we—we had a thermos of tea." She left out the hot biscuits and sausages that Uncle Henry's cook had come early to make.

Be with me, Agnes.

They went inside. Some furniture had been changed around, but the things left as before took away her breath with the absence they proclaimed. Who would now reach out and snatch the suddenly wanted verse anthology or the golden legends of the saints from the shelves that

Rex had so proudly built and stained when he had first brought Agnes and Chloe into their new home? ("Now you girls have a place for your library.") The books appeared unconsulted since last spring, though she knew they had been regularly dusted. Rex was an obsessive house-keeper. He had taught Chloe how to make a bed military-style, so you could bounce a quarter on it, and how to polish her shoes and iron her blouses.

She sat on the edge of the sofa, book bag across her knees, waiting for the glass of water she had said yes to because he wanted to bring her something.

"I don't hear the chickens," she said.

When Rex's features started to go all putty-like, it was the signal that he was about to cry. But he pulled himself together. "I had to sell them. A stray dog tunneled under the electric fence and got Cackles; then Bomber went sullen and the others wouldn't lay."

"Poor Bomber. He liked Cackles best."

"So did your mother."

"Cackles was the dowager duchess. Mother always said, 'Thank you, Your Grace' when she took an egg from under Cackles."

"She worried over them like family. She could have brought Bomber around. Well, we've got a busy schedule today. You aren't here for very long."

His mood lifted as he ticked off their agenda. First they'd drop by the coffee shop to show her off to his buddies. ("You've been missed around here, honey.") Then out to the airfield to meet Eric and Jack. ("My grown sons-to-be. Brenda did a hell of a good job raising them.")

Then on to the cemetery to see her mother's new gravestone, after-ward meeting up with Brenda for lunch. ("Then the three of us will come back to the house. Brenda wants to do some redecorating, and she'd value your advice.")

Careful!

She hadn't given Rex's coffee shop cronies a single thought since leaving Barlow, but there they all were in their same old places, waiting for her like Little Boy Blue's toys. Ole from the filling station, with his black nails; Jimmy, the dapper little court recorder, who laughed at Ole's teasing him for his manicures; Andy from the feed store; old Bill Castle, the domestic court judge; and Miranda, the waitress, who was at least sixty.

"Well, look who's back in town!"

"Rex's been so excited about your coming."

"He says to me, But, Jimmy, she's only here on Saturday, which means you and Judge Bill will miss seeing her. I said, What's to stop us coming here on a Saturday? Is Miranda going to refuse to serve us coffee just because there's no court that day?"

"Hasn't she gotten pretty!"

"Favors her mother."

"Would you like a do-nut with your coffee, hon? Well, sure, we have tea, if a tea bag's okay."

"Up there in Shangri-la, they have fancy tea parties with their silver services every afternoon. But I guess she can make do with a bag among friends." Rex's voice seesawing between scorn and pride.

"How do you like your new school?"

"I like it. My mother went there."

"Are the nuns real strict?"

"Some are, but we have this beautiful—"

"I've never laid eyes on a nun, except Ingrid Bergman in that movie."

Chloe unbuckled her book bag and slid out a spiral drawing pad.

"What you got there?"

She folded back the pad and laid it on the table. Mother Malloy in three-quarter profile, chin tucked in, wide sleeve in motion, long fingers bunched around a short piece of chalk, writing on the blackboard. "That's our ninth-grade teacher."

"Did you do that, honey?"

"She can draw anybody." Rex boasting. "Make it just like them—sometimes more than meets the naked eye."

"How do you do it, honey?"

"I just have to want to—to get the true person. And if I want it badly enough, it comes out that way."

"Handsome lady! Even in that nun's getup."

"The girl's got talent." Judge Castle to Rex. "She ought to be seriously trained."

"I expect I could arrange that." Rex was in an excellent mood now. "Miranda, how do you stay so beautiful?"

"I never let anything touch my skin but Camay."

"Put everybody on my ticket."

Judge Castle lingered after the rest had gone and Rex went off to the men's room.

"It's been good to see you again, honey. We've worried about you, Rex especially, but you're looking well. You've got people who care about you up in Mountain City, and you've got them here in Barlow. I get cases in my court every week—I tell you, they sicken my heart. Kids who probably aren't going to make it because they've been dealt such a mean hand. There are way too many parents who don't deserve the children they've got. Whereas you've got a superabundance of good people on your side. Don't close any doors prematurely, Chloe. Give us all a chance to do right by you."

Eric and Jack looked older than their father-to-be. Eric, when he rose from Rex's former desk, revealed a sloping belly. He was now the office manager, keeping the accounts and scheduling the crop dusting. Jack, trimmer and shorter, serviced the planes and taught flying lessons with Rex; he was wearing Rex's old flying suit with the trouser cuffs turned up. Their voices, boyish and high-pitched, tumbled together, eager for her approval. Chloe was ashamed of herself for being disappointed in them. Here her day in Barlow had hardly begun and she felt like a weary dignitary who was counting the apperances she still had to make.

At the cemetery she had to struggle to hide her distress over the wording on the gravestone with which Rex was so pleased.

Agnes Wright

1916–1951

Beloved Wife of

Capt. Rex Wright, U.S. Air Force

Where was her mother's middle name, Teresa? Her maiden name, Vick? Her first married name, Starnes? It was as if Agnes had possessed no life before she belonged to Capt. Rex Wright. And couldn't he have saved the Air Force stuff for his own stone?

Look on this as a good thing, Chloe. It hardens your heart for your task.

On to the Angus Barn, where Rex's wife-to-be, her countenance set in an expectant smile, awaited them at a table. She was a petite woman, nicely though not stylishly dressed, and younger-looking than her sons, though she must have been Rex's senior by a few years. She had let her feather-cut hair go gray, but you could still see the "cute" girl she had been in high school. She was not at all what Chloe had pictured. After this, there remained only the return to Rex's house and the completion of her task.

To Chloe's relief, they did not act like an engaged couple. They behaved like people already married taking an out-of-town guest to lunch. Brenda did not question her about school or her life in Mountain City. She did not call her "honey" but addressed her by name, on a person-to-person basis, particularly as a person who had lived in the house she herself would soon be running. That Agnes had also occupied the house during those four years was not mentioned, and yet she was present to Chloe in much of Brenda's proposals for better living. "I've been thinking, Rex could move the washer and dryer out of the basement, to the porch off the kitchen. Does that sound okay to you, Chloe?"

"It would save a lot of stairs." (Hearing in memory Agnes's footsteps running down and up, down and up, between loads of laundry.)

Rex had allowed himself a Budweiser, since he wasn't flying that day.

"And I'd like to put in a fenced garden where we could grow vegetables and flowers for cutting. All the fertilizer we'll ever need is there from the chickens you used to keep."

("*Thank* you, Your Grace." Agnes bowing to Cackles as she backed away with the hen's fresh-laid egg cupped carefully in crossed palms for her daughter's breakfast. As carefully as she now carried her soul through its daily round of purgatorial assignments.)

THEY WERE BACK at Rex's house by a little past two. Madeline was due at three.

Soon now. Then it will be over.

Agnes was speeding things right along. After a tour of the rooms, upstairs and down—except for the upstairs one whose door remained closed—with Brenda respectfully submitting to Chloe her ideas for redecoration, and after they had finished their slices of Brenda's lemon chiffon pie in the kitchen (Chloe saying it was the best she'd ever eaten and Brenda offering almost shyly to teach her), Rex, as if on cue, started praising Chloe's drawing.

"Show Brenda that picture you did of your teacher, Chloe."

Chloe reached for book bag, which had been biding its time beside her feet. She kept the pad close to her chest as she leafed past other drawings. Folding back to the requested one, she placed it on the table.

"Oh, my," said Brenda. But instead of following up with gushing superlatives, she inspected the pencil rendering of the nun at the blackboard.

"There was a better one I did first," Chloe said. "But I gave it to a friend for her birthday."

"I feel I am *seeing* this person," said Brenda. "Don't you think this is good, Rex?"

"Bill Castle said she ought to have lessons."

"It looks to me like she was born with the lessons inside her. But I could speak to my neighbor, old Mrs. Ledbetter. She taught art at Converse for years and still takes an occasional private student."

They believe it is all going so well, thought Chloe sadly. They see me in their life, picking vegetables and flowers, learning to make Brenda's pie, and studying art with old Mrs. Ledbetter.

No sympathetic scruples, Chloe. Now it's time.

"I wonder," she asked Rex, "would it be all right if I went into the room upstairs for a few minutes?"

It was clear from the look they exchanged that they knew which room she meant. "Well, sure, honey. We didn't know whether you'd want to go in—"

"But naturally you would want to," Brenda quickly put in.

"There wasn't time after the funeral. Uncle Henry wanted to get back to Mountain City." Chloe was helping them along, as she had felt Agnes helping her along all day.

"You want to go up alone, or you want someone to go with you?" Rex asked. "The room is pretty much the same. I couldn't—. I sleep downstairs now."

"I'd like to be in there by myself for a few minutes. To say some prayers. And then, Rex, maybe you could come up in about five minutes."

"Just me?"

"If that's okay."

"Well, of course it is," Brenda warmly assured her. Brenda would have been a loving stepmother, quick to understand and to back her up.

But that doesn't have to happen now, does it?

Chloe heard her own light footsteps climbing the stairs as if she were the two of them listening from below. As she proceeded down the hall, carrying the book bag, she was thinking of Tildy. This would be Tildy's dream of a scene.

Rex said the room he had shared with Agnes was pretty much the same, only now it could have passed military inspection. All evidence of daily habitation was gone. The room was chilly: the radiator was turned off. Rex probably had to sponge dried blood from where Agnes hit her head on the rungs when she fell. There could have been blood on the floor. Rex would have cleaned the room after the funeral, when he could take his time, sobbing as he carried up the mop and bucket and Pine-Sol and the Old English lemon polish and his dust rags and sponges. Rex yelled at Agnes if she kept a sponge longer than a month. He went around the house smelling them and throwing them out.

As he had scoured and buffed this room toward the memorial aspect it bore now, he would have changed his mop water frequently, emptying the dirty water down the toilet, perhaps choking up as he refilled the bucket from the bathtub tap.

You could have bounced your quarter off their double bed. Her toiletries had been removed from the dressing table's glass top, but a fresh antimacassar had been placed under the gilt-and-pearl music box Malcolm Vick had given Agnes when she graduated from Mount St. Gabriel's. When you lifted its lid, it played "Toora Loora Loora."

From the book bag, she took out the drawing pad and laid it on the dresser. She unscrewed the little bottle, one of Rosa's many scalded and saved containers, that held holy water filched last Sunday from the stoup after Mass.

Do the radiator first.

She sprinkled the water along the top, rubbing it gently with her fingers into the cold rungs.

Absolve, O Lord, the soul of Your faithful departed Agnes from every bond of sin. And by the help of Thy grace may she be enabled to escape the judgment of punishment and enjoy the bliss of everlasting light.

Now the floor.

Eternal rest grant unto her, O Lord. And let perpetual light shine upon her. May she rest in peace.

When Rex knocked she was still kneeling on the floor.

"Just give me another second."

"Take your time, honey."

Get up from floor. Replace bottle in book bag.

"Okay, you can come in now."

He had no idea what he was coming into. She had never seen her stepfather look so humble and anxious.

Now is not the time for softening of the heart. Stay firm. It's almost over.

"Did you get all your prayers said?"

"There weren't many. Just the prayers we say for the dead."

"I never properly understood your mother's faith. If I had it to do over, I would make more of an effort."

"She forgives you," said Chloe.

He didn't like this. "Oh, really?" The old Rex creeping back into his tone. How easy it was to summon the old Rex back!

"Agnes is in purgatory now. It's not a bad place or a scary place. It's a place that makes perfect sense; it's where you go to get cleaned up. You want to go there before you go somewhere better. Rushing off before you're ready would make you feel soiled. Agnes used to say it would be like coming home from school all tired and sweaty and then putting on your best dress and going off to the dance without taking a bath first."

"Oh, yes, those catechism lessons of hers." The corners of his mouth twitched. His arms hung at his sides, his hands clenching and releasing. He was struggling to keep his temper.

Walk to the dresser and pick up the drawing pad. Open to the first drawing and hand him the pad.

"Back at the coffee shop, you said I could make people—you said I could show more things than the naked eye could see."

It was like watching a pantomime of a man going from indulgent curiosity to shock, and then from shock to disgust.

"What the *hell*—? What is this—thing?"

"It's her. After she fell against the radiator."

His whole body stiffened. His eyes boiled at her with their old hatred. "What kind of damn fool trick—?"

"Turn the page," she practically whispered. "There are more."

"Who wants *more*? This is just—" But he turned the page. And the next and the next.

"Just what are you trying to do here?" His lower jaw had begun to tremble, and his voice had taken on that impacted, choking sound that always came from deep in his throat as the violence rose in him. You could watch it rise up his neck and spread out into his shoulders and arms and down into his blunt, hard fingers.

"It's how she looked. After you left the house. After you hit her."

"After I—? What the *fuck*?"

She flinched and was sorry. He would think she'd flinched out of fear of his next move, when she had simply been caught off guard by a word she had not heard since leaving his house almost a year ago.

"The way you always hit us. Then you'd leave the house and forget about it and come back in a better mood. But we hadn't forgotten."

Now something was beginning to dawn. He stepped back, as though she had suddenly turned radioactive. She knew he was afraid he might hit her and fulfill her prophecy and prove his own viciousness. He flexed his fingers, then crumpled one fist inside the other. His whole body seemed to crumple. "You think—" His voice came out high, incredulous. "You think I hit her—that day—and knocked her against the radiator and then left the house? What kind of monster would do that?"

"No," said Chloe, keeping her voice low and careful, "you didn't do that. But you two had an argument and you hit her, the way you always did, and then you left for the airfield. She lay down on the bed for a while, and then she got up and felt dizzy and fainted and hit her head."

"You misguided little ninny, you weren't here! You were up in Mountain City with that fatuous uncle. You never saw how she looked when I found her. I can assure you she didn't resemble any of these— these bleeding Madonnas. Have you ever seen someone who's been dead several hours? I'll spare you the details, you sheltered little fool."

"It's just that—she forgives you," Chloe whispered, her voice shaking. "That's all these were about. So she can—get on with her cleansing in purgatory." But now her words sounded stupid and ridiculous to her.

"What do you mean she 'forgives' me? For what? For loving her? For aspiring to her? For putting up with her airs and her high-minded expectations and that goddamned religion? I still miss her. There'll never be another woman like her. Not even Brenda. I like Brenda better than I ever liked Agnes, but I could never love another woman the way I loved your mother. And she loved me. Right up to the end, she wanted me. Yes, ma'am, she wanted me. I suppose since you two have been having your Catholic afterlife conversations, you knew about the baby. Or had she told you she was pregnant when she was still alive?"

"I—didn't know about a baby." Chloe's mouth had gone dry. "It's just—I understood things while I was drawing the pictures. When I'm drawing people I can go inside them. And I saw what probably happened that day and that—that she forgives you. She would want you to know that. It's all okay now." This last sounded lame and foolish, even to her. "Fatuous," Rex might say.

"Well, you missed the mark this time, young lady. I think we have all flattered you too much about your artistic abilities and it's gone to your head."

He was getting back his self-mastery and his mastery over her. He leafed on through more drawings, lips twitching, then paused over one that made his repugnance soften. "There she is in that head scarf of hers. Collecting the eggs. Why couldn't you have stopped with that one, you sanctimonious little bitch?"

╫

AFTER MADELINE DROPPED off Chloe at Rex Wright's, she had become so involved in her lie that she drove away thinking, "Where exactly in Statesville *does* Nan's sister Dolly live, anyway?" Prepared for intensive questioning, she had provided her characters with names, histories (the fictional Nan had been a sophomore with her at Mountain City High, before Nan's father was transferred to Statesville), and lots of other ephemera that nobody asked for. (Dolly had eloped while still in high school, but the family was now reconciled because everyone was looking forward to the baby. Dolly's married name was Johnson because you could always count on plenty of Johnsons in the phone book.)

For veracity's sake, she went all the way back to Statesville, as if someone were checking up on her from a helicopter above. She lingered over a cheeseburger and fries at a drive-in, singing along with Nat King Cole on the car radio and wondering how Chloe was faring back in Barlow with that tense stepfather. Then she doubled back to the movie theater she had spotted. She had missed a few minutes of the early matinee, but she had already seen *A Place in the Sun* with her friend Cynthia, whose chief interest had been in Elizabeth Taylor's wardrobe. Madeline's favorite scene had been the one after Montgomery Clift has gone to jail for drowning Shelley Winters, when lovesick Liz is languishing at her parents' summer lodge during a storm, being fussed over by her worried mother.

This time she noticed incidentals and discrepancies: those shrubs outside the lodge in Liz's languishing scene were being blown too hard by a wind machine. The windows of Montgomery Clift's rented room were much too spacious and nicely curtained for a boardinghouse. But the worst was Montgomery Clift's sloppy preparations for the drowning. Leaving the car parked on the road by the lake, giving a false name when he rented the rowboat, stumbling into a campsite and waking everybody up, dropping clues like candy, right and left, on his trail. By contrast, Madeline's imaginary baby shower had been plotted masterfully. "It makes one pause, doesn't it?" Mama had remarked when they were creating the minutiae of this trip. "Think of all the things you'd have to plan for before setting out to commit a real crime."

She emerged, blinking, into the bright wintry sun and was mystified to see a gift package perched on the backseat of her car. I've been living in too many fantasies today to keep them straight, she laughed at herself, stuffing the ungiven baby gift back into the shopping bag and tucking it behind the spare tire in the trunk of her car.

"It's a good thing we planned better than poor Montgomery Clift," she heard herself reporting to Mama later. "Because Chloe came out of that house loaded with stuff, with Rex and Brenda following right behind her, each carrying boxes, and guess where everything had to go? Wouldn't I have had a red face if you hadn't thought of that shopping bag!"

But Mama was still out when Madeline returned home shortly after dark. Daddy was off somewhere, too. She hurried upstairs, armed with a fresh lie should Tildy erupt from her room demanding to know what was in the shopping bag. "Something for a nosy little person who'll have to wait until Valentine's Day," she would say, letting her have a peek. Which would mean buying a gift roughly the size of the package and wrapping it with this same paper and ribbon and giving it to Tildy next week. Lies went on and on, like tapeworms. But Tildy's door remained shut.

This whole Saturday felt unreal to Madeline. She had driven a fake package two hundred miles and gone to a movie she had already seen.

Neither Rex nor Brenda—nor even Chloe—had questioned her about the baby shower in Statesville. Brenda had hugged Chloe to her in what seemed a burst of genuine affection, but Rex Wright, stiff and remote, had shaken Chloe's hand and brusquely enjoined them to have a safe trip back.

As soon as they were out of sight of the house, Chloe had asked Madeline to pull over. No, she wasn't feeling sick, just terribly tired. So Madeline had driven home with the radio playing softly. She couldn't be sure whether Chloe slept or not. The girl lay without moving on the backseat, using her book bag as a pillow, and covered up to the chin with a coat that had belonged to her mother. She was taking all of Agnes's clothes home, she had told Madeline, and they had kindly packed up all of the books that had belonged to Agnes and herself. Also a music box that Malcolm Vick had given Agnes as a girl. That was all Chloe volunteered about the errand for Agnes.

Madeline closed the door of her own room and hastily unwrapped the "gift" and put away the ribbon and paper for another time. How she wished she were a fly on the wall over at Henry Vick's. After they had stowed away the boxes of Agnes's things, Henry, reticent as he was to "cross-examine" his niece, would surely have asked, and surely been entitled to, some account of Chloe's time in Barlow. All Chloe had said, when Henry asked her how the day had gone, was that it was "all finished" but she was very tired.

Feeling curiously unrelated to everybody, Madeline wandered down the hall and knocked tentatively on Tildy's door. She found herself absurdly grateful to be welcomed into her old room by her baby sister, who was full of her own day. At the last minute, Maud had canceled out on Tildy because she had to help Lily get some stuff ready for a household sale at the Pine Cone Lodge. "So I decided it would be a good day to inventory Aunt Antonia's old belongings from under the window seat. I thought we might use some of the clothes for props in the play. But you will never guess in a million years what I found in the back of this old trigonometry blue book! I can't wait for Mama to get home."

Tildy didn't ask a single question about Madeline's day.

CHAPTER 24

Trigonometry Midterm

(front cover)

Honor Examination Book
Name: Antonia Tilden
Date: October 11, 1933
Subject: Trigonometry
I certify on my honor that I have neither given nor received
assistance on this examination

ANTONIA MARIA TILDEN

(inside back cover)

Since that evening at the Swag, Suzy, I have been
wondering whether we should go on with our plans.
Something tells me it would be wrong in a way I can't
find words for. Only that there is a good reason for
things, but when you know there ought to be a better
reason, then the good can turn bad.
Has that happened to us?

Confessional Cassette, Continued—and Interrupted

Dawn, Tuesday morning, September 11, 2001
Feast of Saints Protus and Hyacinth, brothers and martyrs, burned at the
*   stake; Rome, 260*
Mother Ravenel's room
St. Scholastica Retirement House

Sentences have been forming in my head all night, Beatrix. Finally I gave up on sleep and dressed in the dark and here I am at dawn, having just pressed the Record button. We have Mass at seven-thirty on weekdays now because Father has to do three nuns' retirement homes, and then we eat a cold breakfast because that's too early for our cook. I'd like to complete this cassette today and send it off.

From what I am able to discern with my limited sight, augmented by my other senses, it is going to be a fine September day here in Boston. The sky is golden, not milky gray. The air is crisp, not humid. The bird chorus is in full voice, soon to be drowned out by the roar of jets departing from Logan. Sister Bridget's brother-in-law who is an air traffic controller at Logan says our retirement house, formerly the old Sanderson estate, lies directly beneath the first minutes of all southbound flights.

I am now on the second side of the tape. But you of course know this because you would have turned it over! I was starting to tell you about writing *The Red Nun* for my class to perform and how working on it with Antonia intensified our plan to join the Order together at the end of our senior year. We were now freshmen in the academy. I had been elected class president and Antonia vice president. In the previous year, 1929–30, much had happened. I had lost a home and a father, but I had found a new home at Mount St. Gabriel's and the chance to re-create myself. Nothing was stopping me from becoming the person I wanted to be. And I knew I was treasured by the friend closest to my heart.

Our foundress had died at the beginning of 1930 and there was the big funeral at the basilica, then a Requiem Mass at the school, and lots of write-ups in the local and state papers and Catholic periodicals about the growth of Mount St. Gabriel's and how it had become so much a part of the community in its first twenty years. Mother Finney was kept busy giving interviews, and along with all her other chores she was writing her chapbook, *Adventures with Our Foundress,* while, as she said, so much was still fresh in her mind, though overlaid with sorrow. The reason it was fresh, Beatrix, was that during Mother Wallingford's final months in the infirmary, when nothing more could be done for her, Mother Finney would sit by her bed whenever she could steal a free moment and they would try to recollect the stages of their remarkable journey together, "charged by the Holy Ghost," just like the Apostles in Acts. Of course, with the brain tumor, Mother Wallingford was not always cogent and sometimes Mother Finney would get very sad and frustrated. I had a spell in the infirmary myself for several days following the death of my father and I overheard snatches of their conversation. It was so odd: sometimes they sounded like old crones and other times like young girls congratulating themselves. Once I heard Mother Finney ask breathlessly, "Did we really do all this for God?" And Mother Wallingford answered with a chilling laugh, "No, I think God used us." Once I heard Mother Finney begging, "Please, Lizzie, please speak to me," and Mother Wallingford screeched at her: "Fie! Fie! Fie!" I thought she was cursing Mother Finney, but later I realized she could have been screeching, "Fi! Fi! Fi!," which may have been her nickname for Fiona.

(I will break here, Beatrix. Sister Bridget has just rung the gong for seven-thirty Mass.)

Back from morning Mass and cornflakes.

I had started to tell you about the play I wrote for our freshman class. Each academy class presented a play during the year and the freshmen went last, usually at the end of April, so they would learn from seeing the older girls' plays. Most of the plays chosen were by well-known playwrights. The seniors that year were in rehearsal for W. B. Yeats's great morality play in verse *The Hour Glass*, about the smart man who has taught everyone in his village that there is no soul and then an angel arrives to tell him he is going to die and go to hell unless he can find one person who still believes in the existence of the soul. He will still have to die, of course, but if he finds that one person he will only have to go to purgatory.

And I had been sitting in study hall wondering, "How will we ever top that one?" Even back then, Beatrix, I was very competitive. Some good has come out of my ambitious nature, I believe, but I have also been told that it has chipped away parts of my soul. I was class president and I wanted us to do something that would make our class be remembered for years to come.

I also wanted to impress Antonia and get her involved in a project that would bind us closer.

The academy study hall had been the ballroom, back when this building was the old Sky Top Inn. Couples danced to an orchestra in this vast room where we now studied; and then around the sides were smaller parlors and smoking rooms, which were now our classrooms.

Well, suddenly all kinds of voices started swirling around in my head, voices coming from different times in the building's history. I heard a couple exchange platitudes while they waltzed around this room, and I heard the auctioneer ask for opening bids for the hotel's furnishings (the auction had also been held in this room) after old Sky Top went out of business, and

Mother Wallingford made her offer for "every piece of furniture throughout the hotel and in all the eighty bedrooms." Her bid was snatched up; the liquidators were overjoyed. Here came this English nun with her hoity-toity accent and her banker's draft, freeing them from having to pay a single penny to drag it downstairs and truck it all away.

Later that day, Mother Wallingford bought the hotel.

And I heard the pure soaring voice of the girl, Caroline DuPree, who was carried off by malaria in the summer of 1912, so early in the school's history, before she was able to make her first vows. And then I heard God ruminating on how He had gone about creating this place.

It didn't come out, when I was writing it, in chronological order. It was more like God's kind of time; God Himself isn't chronological. I can't remember who said that. Father Krafft, perhaps.

Then I did the deck scene of Mother Wallingford and Mother Finney crossing the Atlantic on their ship back in 1898, feeling like they are in a tale they are making up as they go along.

I loved imagining these two, and so did Antonia: these two close friends, bound up in God, writing their own rule. The more we fleshed out their story, the more it seemed we were filling in our own future. We already knew that Antonia was going to play the part of the foundress.

There were certain lines I wrote for the play that could have doubled as our lines, Antonia's and mine.

WALLINGFORD: I couldn't have done this without someone to go with me.
FINNEY: Yet it all seems so easy.
WALLINGFORD: It seems easy because the Holy Ghost is blowing us onward.

At first we thought I'd play Finney, but in the end I cast Agnes Vick. Agnes was close to Mother Finney, who helped her get all the details right. And Finney had been more of a follower, whereas I was so much a leader. "It's too bad you and I can't both play the foundress," Antonia once joked. And I joked back that I'd try to console myself with just being God's voice and the narrator and the playwright. Oh, Antonia looked so beautiful in Mother Wallingford's own cloak. Everyone said so.

Which brings me to the regrettable subject of envy, my envy of Antonia.

In an unfallen world if you love and admire someone, you rejoice when they are loved and admired by others. But ever since our first parents' envy of God's knowledge caused them to eat of the tree, we have been living out variations on the envy theme and reaping the consequences. Cain's face fell when Abel's firstborn lamb found more favor with God than his own offering of fruits. Jacob covered himself with skins so he could steal his hairy brother's blessing from their blind old father.

Regarding my envy of Antonia, I hardly know where to jump in. I'm like those little girls on the playground who never could dart right into a moving rope.

I want to jump in with this more than I do not want to jump in, yet I am also tempted to divert from the plunge by inquiring into the jealousies of others. Who smote your heart with envy, Beatrix? Best friend? Archenemy? Colleague? A passing stranger who had some quality you wished for? A family member?

God's angel Lucifer was not content to be the brightest in heaven. He wanted to run his own show.

But I am "divaricating," as you girls tell me I used to point out when someone was beating around the bush.

Antonia Tilden, beautiful, secure, and good, had known as early as fifth grade that she wanted to give her all to God. And she was backed up by her family. They started a fund for her dowry. Antonia had so much and she knew it and she wanted to put it all to the service of God. It was as simple as that.

Were my desires so simple?

In our sophomore year, we founded this little society, the Oblates of the Red Nun. It was my inspiration, but Antonia liked the idea. Each member pledged to dedicate herself to fulfil God's plan for her. We wanted to put a wall around our intentions, to protect them from all harm, to keep out any second-best desires. That was all it was about. We chose the Red Nun as our mascot because she stood for the unfulfilled desire of an earlier pupil at Mount St. Gabriel's. And yet God was able to use her unfinished monument, and her legend, to be a fortress for others.

There were only five of us oblates. Cornelia insisted on joining anything Antonia did. And there was my roommate, Soledad Ostos, from Mexico. And we asked Francine Barfoot, a boarder who played the flute. She was a helpful, modest girl who didn't insist on being the icing on every cake. Her daughter, Elaine Frew, was in your class.

That's all we were, a small harmless society of girls who wanted to become the best they could be and not let God down by settling for anything less. Yes, we also pledged to forsake any person or influence who tempted us to shortchange God's major plan for us. After that debacle of Tildy Stratton's production of *The Red Nun* in the spring of 1952, her mother, Cornelia Stratton, said some unwarrantable things to me at the reception. She accused me of being the indirect cause of Antonia's death in Rome. She said I had been a pernicious influence on her sister, had "fed on Antonia's vocation like a tapeworm" and poisoned it with my own desires. She said that the "silly old pledge" I had dreamed up, the pledge to forsake all second-best influences, had stuck in Antonia's conscience and troubled her heart on her wedding trip, causing her to step in front of that van.

I do not believe that Finney was ever jealous of Wallingford. She knew Wallingford was the superior one and was content to share a grand adventure with her.

Those two, no doubt, provided a model in my young mind for Antonia and myself. But I didn't identify us as much as Antonia thought. "Suzy, we're not *them*," she said to me one day, early in our senior year, when she had started to question her vocation.

It was around that time when I realized I might have to go it alone. I was already having conferences about it with Reverend Mother.

But there was something else, too, Beatrix. And here I must come back to envy and its first cousin, competitiveness.

I knew, even back in September of our senior year, that the school would vote Antonia the Queen of the School for the May First festivities. She was the inevitable choice: beautiful and good; she was that year's embodiment of the Mount St. Gabriel's ideal. Oh, I had been class president four years in a row, I was the best leader in my class, but I was not its best embodiment of the ideal, and I knew it. Though it gave me pain and I was envious.

And so, when Antonia began to have doubts, I decided to subdue my envy by entering early. Because, you see, as a postulant I would be ineligible to be voted queen.

(Beatrix, someone downstairs is frantically ringing our gong. It makes no sense. The next gong is scheduled for the Angelus at noon. I must go see what is the matter.)

CHAPTER 25

Silent Skies

Late Tuesday night, September 11, 2001
St. Scholastica Retirement House

Two nuns setting off for a walk

"THE STARS — DO they seem closer tonight, Mother Galyon?"

"They do, Mother."

"That's what I thought. Even though I can only see them out of the corners of my eyes. The Carolina Cherokees believed the sky was a great overturned bowl that we live under. They called it the sky vault. Did you ever hear that when you were in Mountain City?"

"No, Mother. But you were in Mountain City a great deal longer than I was."

The former headmistress, who had been instrumental in curtailing Mother Galyon's teaching career in Mountain City, did not respond to this. They continued along the gravel drive, the crunch of their steps amplified by the uncanny new silence of the skies. All aircraft, except for military fighter jets and medical helicopters, had been grounded, all airports closed indefinitely. The nation was on high alert. Were these coordinated attacks only the beginning of more of the same—or worse? Would we go to war, as we did after Pearl Harbor? But against whom, and how?

Knowing that the chatterbox fastened to her arm could not endure silence for very long brought a paradoxical measure of relief to Mother Galyon. When the next unimaginable thing could strike from the sky vault at any moment, you welcomed the familiar intrusions.

"Well, you and I logged in forty-one Boston Catholic deaths tonight. I was surprised there were that many, weren't you?"

"Why, Mother?"

"I guess it would have seemed more natural if they had waited."

"Waited for what?"

"Oh, to hear the president's speech—to see what was going to happen next. To—I don't know—hold out for some singularity in their deaths. Thousands, the president said. All those bodies in flames falling through the air. Innocent people starting work at their desks—or thinking they were safely aboard flights to California. Forgive me, I know I'm rambling, but those two planes from Logan were supposed to be headed west; by the time they went over us the real pilots may already have had their throats cut. Probably the exact moment the hijackers were flying over our house, some passenger who knew the route was thinking, Why have we suddenly turned *south*? What were *you* doing, Mother, when Sister Bridget started banging away at that gong?"

"I was reading a detective novel."

"You know what I was doing? I was dictating that little confessional tape that you suggested. I had almost reached the end of the second side. But after the events of today, how could I possibly send such a cassette to Beatrix down in Mountain City? It would seem all out of proportion, and she would lose respect for me."

"Why don't you put it on hold for now, Mother. For all we know we all may be dust and ashes within a few days."

They reached the gates at the end of the estate and retraced their steps: the cautious homecoming of four old safely shod feet. Tonight the TV screen in the nuns' parlor, usually visible through the window, was blocked by heads gathered round it, watching the endless replay of falling bodies, crumpling towers, dust-covered people running, running . . .

CHAPTER 26

Henry

Thursday midmorning, February 14, 1952
Henry Vick's office
Downtown Mountain City

"MR. COXE FOR you, Mr. Vick."

"Oh, put him through, Sherry."

"No, sir, I mean he's come to see you on foot. Want me to send him in?"

"Ah, please."

This may not be good.

But Ollie Coxe's face was beaming as he entered. "Well, old buddy, here's an unexpected valentine for you. I thought I'd deliver it in person." The lawyer pulled a folded letter from the breast pocket of his overcoat and handed it over to Henry, who scanned it disbelievingly. It was from Rex Wright's lawyer, J. D. Wheeler, who quoted the full context of his client's short letter within the body of his own.

" 'Brenda and I are bailing out,' " Henry read aloud.

"Of course, if Mr. Wheeler could have bothered to pick up the phone and call long-distance, he'd have spared us half a week's worry. He had Wright's letter on his desk this past Monday. Wright wrote it a week ago Saturday."

The same day Chloe had been with them in Barlow.

Henry reread the lawyer's letter, searching Rex Wright's brief incorporated missive for a subtle snag. He found none. Rex Wright was bailing out, which was as final as an ex–squadron leader could get. After a day spent in his stepdaughter's company, Rex Wright wrote, it had been made clear to him that she would be better off remaining in the care of her Catholic uncle and the nuns' school where her mother had been so content. He withdrew all future claims as legal guardian. In turn, he asked to be absolved from any future obligations to the young lady. The remainder of Mr. Wheeler's letter addressed those concerns.

"Can it be this simple, Ollie? Does this mean it's really over?"

"Unless you want to hold out for Chloe's college expenses in an escrow fund. After all the fuss he's made about being her legal father, we'd have a damn good shot at it."

"I'll be happy if you can fix it so he won't bother us again."

"I can do that, you rascal. So, you let her go to Barlow against my advice."

"She was bent on going, Ollie. She said her mother—she said Agnes would have wanted it. I let her drive down with Madeline Stratton, who was attending a baby shower over in Statesville. I knew Chloe would be fine with her. Madeline dropped her off and picked her up a few hours later."

"Well, our little Chloe sure must have been busy during those few hours."

"Busy enough to change Rex's mind, it seems. She said he flew off the handle and packed up all of Agnes's things and sent them home with her and Madeline."

"You didn't have an inkling he might bail out?"

"I thought it was more likely he was planning a switch in tactics. When Sherry told me you had come in person to see me, I was expecting you to tell me a new bomb had dropped."

"Well, here's your bomb, old buddy. But I need it back for my files. I'll have a copy made for yours. Sure you don't want to press for that college escrow fund? I'd enjoy the back-and-forth with Mr. J. D. Wheeler of Barlow."

"Absolutely sure. May I offer you something from Malcolm's sideboard?"

"You know the answer to that, my friend. Like you, I don't touch the stuff until sundown, and then only a solitary savored ounce. But I'll settle for my usual nostalgic peek inside those handsome cabinet doors. Yep, it's still the mirror image of Daddy's bar over at my place of work: the single malt and the Cutty snubbing each other in the forefront, the

Woodford Reserve standing apart in isolated splendor, poor Tio Pepe and Cinzano languishing in their dusty corners. If you ever decide to part with this magnificent piece of Sheraton, you've got a buyer."

"I'll will it to you," Henry told this person he had once ridden tricycles beside, the man who, like himself, inoculated himself nightly against alcoholism before it could sneak up on him. Henry's mother and Ollie senior had taken their drying-out vacations at the same West Virginia retreat, often at the same time. "What do you think those two get up to in that sequestered spa?" a not-so-well-meaning colleague had once teased Malcolm Vick. Henry, drawing plans in an adjoining office, had held his breath through the appalling silence that followed. "Oh, mainly walks and cards, I would think," came Malcolm Vick's unruffled reply in its own good time. "Once a pecker is pickled, I understand it can't get up to much else."

His workday thrown off balance by the capitulation from Barlow, Henry put on an overcoat and scarf and headed down windy Patton Hill to take a fresh look at his library site. The south corner lot at the end of Church Street had been empty since First Savings had burned to the ground in 1949. Vick & Vick's brown-and-gold sign, set in the lavish winter grass planted last fall, announced the home of the future library. Groundbreaking was scheduled for the first Saturday in April.

Sheltering in the portico of the Shriners' temple across the street, Henry tried to envision four unnecessary Doric columns inflicted upon his clean, open design. What would Alvar Aalto have done? But the Finnish architect was a genius and a free spirit, and Henry knew he was neither. Aalto's first set of plans for the municipal library in Viipuri had encountered its own snags. They turned down his idea for a rooftop garden with outdoor reading rooms. Then the site itself was moved and Aalto had to start over. However, the new location, in a spacious park, gave him more freedom. His thinking changed. He pared away classicism and simplified radically, concentrating on the uses of light: keeping it off the stacks but giving the patron plenty of natural light through strategically placed barrel skylights. The Viipuri, an early masterpiece of International Modernism, opened in 1935, when Aalto was thirty-seven. Three years younger than Henry today.

En route to Rome, Henry and Antonia had stopped overnight in New York to see the Aalto exhibit at the Museum of Modern Art. Both of them were moved by the architect's simple, childlike sketch of a reader at a library table, arrows representing light zeroing in on his open book from many directions. Antonia had loved the slapdash modesty of the drawing. "He was so intent on working out his problem he couldn't be bothered to make it pretty." She liked people who kept their focus on what mattered.

After the war, the Viipuri library, no longer in Finland but in Russia, had been abandoned and left to fall into ruin. Antonia was buried beside her in-laws in the Vick family plot at Riverside, a five-minute walk from Henry's house.

Two Saturdays ago, he and Madeline had devised their plan to get Chloe safely to Barlow and back. How pleased she would be to hear how well their efforts had turned out. On the off chance that she might be buying more supplies for her mother at Commercial Stationers, he set off in that direction. But then he remembered that today was a weekday and sixteen-year-old Madeline would be in school.

He examined the offerings in the window of Winston's Men's Store, contrasting his wintry reflection in its prewar overcoat with the mannequins arrayed in spring suits with narrower ties and rakishly tilted panama hats. Henry had put off buying new clothes for years. Now, since he would have Chloe permanently in his life, he'd better smarten himself up. He would take them both shopping for Easter clothes.

In the window of Skyland Studios was a single photograph on an easel against a drape of gray velvet: a black-and-white portrait of a pensive bride looking down at her bouquet. As he stood there trying to fathom the source of its charm, Antonia's face seemed to float in the gloom above the portrait. Then he realized it was Cornelia Stratton, in her black developer's smock, wryly observing him from the other side of the glass. She motioned him into the studio.

"That's an intriguing photograph," he said. "I didn't realize you did that sort of thing."

"And what 'sort of thing' is that?" Cornelia challenged him. Would Antonia have had those dry lines at the sides of her mouth? Or would living fifteen more years have left different etchings on her face?

"There's a psychological quality in an old-fashioned pose."

"Tell me more, Henry. Yes, I've hit on something and I know it. Do you have a moment? Where were you going, anyway?"

"I've been over at the library site, aggravating myself over those damn columns they're hell-bent on sticking on."

"Well, you can do a modified Howard Roark. Stick on their columns in some sort of freestanding way that won't compromise the structure and then dynamite them some dark moonless night."

Henry wasn't always in the mood for Cornelia's aggressive wit, but today it hit the spot. "To tell the truth, I'm at loose ends. I've just had my major worry pulled out from under me like a rug. Chloe's stepfather is withdrawing all claims. He leaves her to me and the nuns and wants no further business with any of us."

"I *knew* something was up when Madeline told me about Rex packing Chloe off with all those boxes. So our errand for Agnes was a success."

"It looks that way, though I'm still not sure what went on down there."

"Madeline said Chloe slept all the way home under her mother's coat."

"Then she went straight up to bed and slept all day Sunday. Sunday evening she came downstairs and said everything was going to be all right now. As if she were the one reassuring me. Apparently she and Rex had this confrontation over purgatory. Chloe said she saw exactly the moment when he let go of her. 'I disgusted him' was how she put it."

"Disgusted how, I wonder?"

"Well, you know, I don't like to cross-examine her. I want her to feel she can tell me what she's comfortable with and stop at that."

"I'll send Tildy over. Tildy is a champion cross-examiner. She's been exhausting me, trying to winkle school memories out of me for that play. Listen, Henry, she found this note Antonia had written to Suzanne. It was inside the back cover of an old trigonometry midterm, the fall of our senior year. My sister alluded to something that happened out at the Swag and said it might be wrong to go on with their plans to take vows together."

Henry waited.

"It must have been that night Smoky and I threw our engagement party. I have no idea whether the note was just a draft that never got sent, or whether Suzanne received it. Tildy found it in a box of Tony's things under the window seat. It was very oblique. Just that something would be wrong in a way Tony didn't have words for, and then something else about good turning to bad. I don't quite know what Antonia was trying to say, and yet somehow I feel I do."

"Yes." He nodded, having been caught off guard.

"Henry, come back into my inner sanctum and let me show you my new toy."

Cornelia locked the front door and hung up the Out to Lunch sign. "I'm between secretaries. Madeline says I'm too hard on them. But I'm no harder on them than I am on myself."

Cornelia's new toy was a beautiful old view camera, a Deardorff, of glowing red wood and gold-painted metal. It was mounted on a tripod with its bellows extended, and Henry found himself seated on a low wooden stool in bright light. His sister-in-law's voice from under the photographer's hood informed him of her progress. She was composing her image of him upside down. All he was required to do was sit there, in three-quarter profile, as she had arranged him. He could keep his eyes closed so he would be less likely to blink when she was ready to shoot.

"This is interesting, Henry; I can see things in your inverted image that I hadn't seen before."

"Uh-oh. Watch out."

"Aren't you curious about what things?"

He gave a purposely bland laugh. "Are you sure I could take it?"

"Just for that, I am going to leave you in suspense."

"Probably best."

"Now open your eyes and count to ten and please don't blink."

"Was the bride's portrait done like this?" Henry asked, after they had gone through the procedure several more times.

"Oh, no. That was an inspired candid shot. It was right after the marriage—the party was back in the vestry signing the register and she was standing off to one side examining her bouquet, thinking who knows what? But the moment I saw the image forming in my developer pan I knew I had caught something. What you called psychological. So I splurged on a platinum print. With platinum prints you get the deepest range of shadows. I've been teaching myself how to do them. I've tried to learn fast because the failures are expensive. Listen, Henry— now do *not* move your head!—what did you mean when you indicated you knew what Antonia may have been saying in that note to Suzanne?"

Well, I gave her the opening, Henry thought, so no use equating myself with the deer who suddenly discovers that the friendly woodland photographer has crosshairs in her lens. I have known Cornelia and her crosshairs ever since she was a supercritical little girl. And both of us loved Antonia.

"We talked about it some before we got engaged," he said, deciding to tell her some but not all. "She said Suzanne's determination that they do this thing together was diluting her own vocation."

"That was her word—'diluting'?"

"Yes. At first I thought she might have said 'deluding.' So I asked, to be sure. Suzanne had somehow gotten between her and God, she said, and as time went on her intention felt watered down. Whereas Suzanne's fervor seemed only to increase. As if she was feeding on Antonia's former vocation, was how Antonia put it."

"Oh, God, Henry," came Cornelia's affronted protest from beneath the hood. "This is the first time I'm hearing this. Why did she never tell *me* that?"

"Maybe because she thought you had other things on your mind. You were about to become a mother for the second time. And also maybe because I came right out and asked. I was wanting to ask her to marry me by then, but I didn't want to be competing with a vocation, even a stalled one. Antonia assured me that she no longer had the least desire to be a nun. She did want to give her life to God, but she trusted that He would show her how. And then she told me how being with little Madeline so much had given her the notion that she would make a good mother herself. The funny thing was—well, she practically proposed to me that day, if you want to know the truth."

"Henry, hold that expression and don't blink. Count to ten. There, I may or may not have captured something. But that's enough for today. Suddenly I am worn out."

When Cornelia emerged from her covering she had a persecuted look.

"Am I going to get the platinum treatment?" Henry asked.

"That depends on what develops on the plates. But either way, this little interlude of ours has been an unexpected development, hasn't it?"

"Let me take you out to lunch." Thinking better of it even as he was proposing it.

"Thank you, but I never go out to lunch. Flavia makes me a thermos of soup. Since I fired my last secretary I've got a backlog of stuff to do. But what do you think she meant about the Swag? What could have happened out there?"

"I wasn't there, Cornelia. I was off at college, remember?"

"But what do you think it could have been? Did Antonia ever say anything about it after you were married?"

"Ah, we were only together such a short time," Henry answered, taking refuge in his standard equivocation. He saw no reason to offer further confidences to his sister-in-law, especially considering Cornelia's animus toward Suzanne. Lying beside Antonia in the dark and talking, after they had diligently worshipped each other's bodies, as per their wedding vows, had been the most daring and intimate thing he'd ever done with anyone. Antonia had felt the same. She had told him about the disturbing kiss in the woods, out at the Swag. ("It came out of nowhere. I'm not saying I didn't respond; it was the first time anyone outside my family had kissed me on the lips. But everything became muddied after that. I started wondering whether she wanted God in the same way I did, or did she want to have God through me.")

"I just know Antonia was heartbroken when Suzanne joined early," said Cornelia. "She completely lost her spirit. She wouldn't even be Queen of the School. Suzanne's betrayal left her stunned."

"But isn't that a normal response to a friend's betrayal? You are stunned. You thought you knew someone and then you find out you didn't. Isn't it possible that, deep down, Antonia was relieved?"

"Oh, I don't know, Henry." Cornelia looked as though she couldn't wait to be rid of him. "All these revelations are too much for an ordinary working day. All I know is I still get convulsive when I think of poor Tony's ruined senior year. And now she's dead, and I'm just learning she never got her wish to be a mother! And meanwhile that devil continues in power, still worming her way into our lives. You know what she is up to now? She wants to win Tildy away from me!"

CHAPTER 27

Auteur/Directeur

Saturday afternoon, March 15, 1952
The Ides of March
Suite of Nita Netherby Judd
Sunset Park Inn, Mountain City

TILDY WAS PLEASED with how things were going with *The Red Nun*. The play had been cast, and everybody had a part; some girls had more than one part. The scenery was being constructed and painted by Chloe, with offstage supervision from her architect uncle, and Daddy and Tildy had finally finished recording John's (carefully coached) delivery of God's lines, with creepy pauses in just the right places.

So far, not one disgruntled murmur had reached Tildy's ears. Nobody had gone complaining to Mother Ravenel, either, because Tildy would have been informed by the headmistress. The two met regularly so Tildy could update her on the progress of "their" production, as the Ravenel now indulgently called it.

Art was turning out to be easy, compared to people. People kept behaving out of character, or exposing alarming new facets. Take—well, take anyone in her *life*, for that matter.

First, take Chloe, since Chloe was still her official best friend. Chloe had now gone into the second stage of her mysticism, or whatever it was. After she and "Agnes" had done whatever they did down in Barlow to shake off the stepfather forever, she admitted to Tildy there had been "teamwork" between (dead) mother and daughter, but offered no details. However, Chloe was throwing herself into the scenery, and, thanks to Uncle Henry's help with the movable sets, it was going to be really spectacular.

Tildy had continued to spend Saturday nights with Chloé because the play needed to be blocked out in scenes, and Tildy found that her creative faculties worked best when she lay on her sofa bed with her eyes closed and Chloe read slowly through the play until Tildy envisioned a kind of *square* around a certain body of material; then she would cry "Stop!" and have Chloe make a big colored block around that scene. They had done this so often that Tildy knew the play pretty well by heart. She could *see* it, stacked up in its red, blue, yellow, green, brown, purple, and black scenes, on the insides of her eyelids when she lay in bed at night. And Chloe was patient and steadfast: she would read a scene over and over until Tildy had seen whatever it was she needed to see. Very unlike Maud, who used to sigh heavily at some point and say, "All right, Tildy, open your eyes and let's move on, okay?"

Maud posed a dual problem these days. On the one hand, she seemed grateful, almost humbly so, for their revived friendship; she sought Tildy's counsel about the smallest things. But there was at the same time in Maud a disturbing new standoffishness. Tildy could not remember this holding back in their previous friendship. Maud seemed to be keeping certain parts of herself in reserve. Tildy was at the moment in the midst of puzzling this out. She felt sure that if she could get to the reasons, it would be more like the old Tildy-and-Maud equation, though of course now Chloe had to fit somewhere into that equation.

Maud's life over at the Pine Cone Lodge was disintegrating by the day. It wasn't even the Pine Cone Lodge anymore: the sign had been taken down and an up-and-coming real estate firm had put a binder on the house. If the city planning board gave the go-ahead next week, the sale would go through and the company would start turning it into apartments for older people who wanted to be within walking distance to town. And that meant Maud and Lily Norton and Mr. Foley would have to move out immediately and leave the house "broom clean" within thirty days of the closing. That was part of the negotiated sale price, which Maud was being coy about, though Daddy had said he had heard Lily had done very well because this same real estate bunch was buying up more old houses on the same street and planned a sort of enclave for well-heeled oldies who'd had their driver's licenses revoked.

Recently Maud had overheard her mother and Mr. Foley discussing whether it would be more economical to rent temporary lodgings in

Mountain City so that Maud could finish out her school year "at home" or for them to go ahead and invest in a house in Atlanta, where Mr. Foley's home office was, and fork over a boarding fee to Mount St. Gabriel's for the remaining month or so.

"Oh, Christ, Maud, don't be silly—you can stay here with us!" Tildy had expostulated, though she knew she would have to win over Mama, who seemed to have taken against Maud.

But it had become easier to bring Mama around to her wishes since Mother Ravenel had made Tildy the director of the play. Tildy exulted in her new power over Mama: Cornelia was on jealous alert for the first sign that her baby was being stolen away by the enemy.

But Maud had rebuffed Tildy's offer. "Thank you, that's really sweet of you, Tildy, but, you know, I am going to *pressure* them to let me board. That's what will work out best for me, I've decided."

Why being cooped up as a boarder would work out best for Maud was beyond Tildy's comprehension. There was something being kept from her, but she could not figure out what. It had to be more than Maud's antipathy for Art Foley, because there was certainly nothing new about *that*.

Meanwhile, Maud was devotedly immersed in *The Red Nun*. She had learned all of her lines for both of her parts—although Tildy was still writing more lines for the second part.

Before Tildy had cast the play, Maud had respectfully asked if she might "try out" for the part of Mother Wallingford, the foundress. "We're not going to have tryouts," Tildy told her. "They take too long and people tend to imagine themselves capable of roles that are completely unsuited to them. You waste valuable time paying lip service to the democratic process. Mother Ravenel feels the same. She cast all the parts for the play's first performance in 1931."

Then Tildy had let a suspenseful pause go by before she put Maud out of her misery—and granted her double what she'd asked for. "It so happens, Maud, that I have *already* cast you as Mother Elizabeth Wallingford. You have the gravity and bearing of an aristocratic English foundress. Nobody in our class could wear Mother Wallingford's own cape as well as you."

Tildy watched Maud's countenance change from disappointment to relief. Only there was a shadow of the new aloofness, too. As if she were having a small side thought about how juvenile all this fuss about a mere school play was.

"But in my production, the person who plays the foundress has to play another role, as well," Tildy went on.

"What role is that?"

"It's a character I haven't finished creating yet. Each class is allowed to add their own material, as long as it honors the spirit of the original production. Mother Ravenel has given me permission to add new characters who come later in the history of the school. Your second character will be a girl named Domenica. She's the best friend of a girl named Rexanne. The two of them plan to emulate Elizabeth and her friend Fiona by becoming nuns together."

And then take John and Flavia, those monoliths of dignity in Tildy's home life. They had behaved totally out of character after Tildy invited them into the dining room to listen to Daddy's and her finished tape of John speaking God's lines. She had ceremoniously brought the machine to the table, laid it on a mat, and pressed the button. After a series of hisses and pops, the hollow magisterial voice caused both John and Flavia to step back in alarm from the reel. But as it rolled on ("I smashed continents together . . ."), with its pregnant word spacings indicated by the director, the couple regained their usual composure. However, by the time God got to the part about deciding to create a school "in my own good time," where God's voice swung up a notch, both John and Flavia turned away from her, and Tildy saw their shoulders were shaking. Her first thought had been "They are so moved they're *crying*," but then Flavia gasped that something was "boiling over on the stove" and ran to the kitchen, even though it was midafternoon and nothing was cooking. John held out a few moments longer before blurting a strangled "Thank you, Miss Tildy" and bolting through the kitchen's swinging door after his wife. From the other side of the door came a horrid release of stifled laughter as the couple made a hurried escape to their quarters over the garage.

And then, just yesterday, Friday, there had been the completely out-of-character behavior of Mother Malloy during their tutoring session. They had been working up Tildy's medieval history paper the way they had worked up her *David Copperfield* paper. Tildy was first encouraged to extemporize aloud, and then together they'd narrow her enthusiasms down to manageable proportions. Tildy had chosen Eleanor of Aquitaine as her topic and, having anticipated being congratulated by Mother Malloy at finding a perfect fit for herself, was dashed when the teacher said many others in the class were writing on Eleanor, too. "Well," said Tildy, rising above her setback, "but it's what you do with the topic, isn't it, Mother?" "There's certainly enough of her to go around," the nun agreed, smiling. "What do you plan to do with her, Tildy?"

And Tildy had launched confidently into her extemporization: "I would like to use a lot of *French,* Mother, maybe compose it in French, the way we did with my Uriah Heep paper. This time it seems *really* appropriate because she was a French queen before she was an English one."

Last time, when they had been working up her Uriah Heep paper, Tildy had simply tossed out highlights of things that had caught her fancy about this grotesque figure, relying on her gift for pulling excitement (or repulsion) out of the air, and liberally sprinkling it with what people called her "precocious" vocabulary, meanwhile watching Mother Malloy closely to measure the quality of her nods. Steering by the more vigorous nods, Tildy had been able to narrow down to the topic that had earned her a B plus: what made Uriah so disgusting and what parts of his disgustingness were truly evil?

But this time the nod method wasn't working so well. None of the nun's nods could be called vigorous.

Tildy had chosen Eleanor of Aquitaine because that was the person in the period they were studying who seemed most worthy of her imagination. Given the right parentage and all those lands, Tildy felt sure that she, too, would have made a superb queen at fifteen, which she would be on her next birthday.

Given more encouragement, she was about to voice this certainty aloud, but Mother Malloy was sitting very still, hands folded on her lap, head bowed, and so Tildy searched for something less egotistical and hit on the idea of *fifteen alone.* Mother Malloy loved concision and modesty—she was always counseling them about "not biting off more than you can chew" in their presentations.

"I was thinking, Mother, maybe I could just take Eleanor at fifteen, basing it on all the history that was going on around her, all the fascinating people, and why she and Louis had to consolidate their holdings, and . . . no, wait, Mother, I've got a better idea. I could just do the marriage—or even Eleanor, on horseback, a fifteen-year-old duchess, riding toward the young king she has never met, with all her vassals and trappings, and show why—"

Mother Malloy did not raise her head. She seemed scarcely to be breathing.

Then she stirred herself and apologized, explaining that she had been having trouble sleeping lately, and asked Tildy if she would mind going over her proposal again.

Three of the most dependable people in Tildy's life: the teacher who had spent hours encouraging her to express herself in new ways and the two house servants whose adoration she had taken for granted ever since they had taken turns pushing her wherever she wanted to go in her stroller; within a single week, two of them had run out of the room laughing at her, and she had put the other one to sleep sitting bolt upright.

It made you think twice before taking anybody's fealty for granted. Thank goodness there were some new people in her life to make a fresh impression on today. At the moment, Tildy sat next to Jiggsie Judd, the new boarder who had recently been demoted to ninth grade by Mother Ravenel, on the scratchy backseat of Jiggsie's Spartanburg grandmother's ancient Oldsmobile, being driven by "Bob," a cigar-smoking man in Levi's and a plaid wool jacket. They were on their way to the Sunset Park Inn to have afternoon tea with Mrs. Judd in her suite. Bob seemed to be an uncertain mixture of friend and retainer to Jiggsie's grandmother. Jiggsie said he "went everywhere with her" and "stayed in the room smoking when she had company at home," but Granny wrote him a check for fifty dollars every week; Jiggsie had seen her doing it. Since Tildy had been in the car, Bob had related several bits of information about Mrs. Judd, whom he referred to as "Nita," in his sarcastic smoker's voice: "Nita" still had her license, but she liked him to drive so she didn't have to pay attention to where they were going; "Nita" refused to part with the 1937 Oldsmobile, whose yearly upkeep cost them more than a new car, because her late husband had bought it for her the year before he died; "Nita" tended to dwell in the past, but she was right good company. His tone teetered between affection and condescension. Tildy was encouraged by the "dwelling in the past" part, however, because this afternoon she planned to ransack the memory of Mrs. Nita Netherby Judd, class of 1913, for the purposes of the play. Think of it: 1913 was only three years after Mount St. Gabriel's opened. Mrs. Judd would have known the foundress in her prime!

Jiggsie's being put back a grade—a secret dread of Tildy's for years—hadn't appeared to faze the girl. If anything, she seemed to regard it as a reward. As a ninth grader she got to spend her entire school day in the same classroom with her adored patron Elaine Frew, who had taken the girl under her wing.

And for Tildy, Jiggsie's demotion to the ninth grade had been pure gold. Jiggsie looked like a delicate, if slightly unstable, angel and sang like one in a keen, otherworldly soprano. Tildy at once conceived a new part for her in the play. Since she could hardly revoke Dorothy Yount's singing part of the doomed Caroline DuPree, Tildy made Jiggsie the ongoing "Spirit of the School." Like an angel, this spirit didn't age, and it had perfect hindsight and foresight. It could shed light on things that had happened a long time before and predict things that were going to happen in the future. It could see behind the scenes and right old wrongs. The character inspired by Jiggsie provided the new dimension Mama had said the play needed to make a "breakout" from Mother Ravenel's "old party line."

Tildy, feeling magnanimous, had invited Elaine Frew to compose the piano music for Jiggsie's songs. "I'd have to see some lyrics first," hedged haughty Elaine. "I'll have a sample of them for you by Monday," Tildy promised, swallowing her ire and spending her weekend dictating and revising "The Spirit's Theme Song" as she lay on her sofa bed over at Chloe's:

> My pitiless light routs out dark schemes;
> My brilliant flame revives old dreams;
> Yesterday and tomorrow are for me the same.
> Call me Spirit of Now if you need a name.

"Who wrote this?" Elaine asked, frowning.

"I did," said Tildy. "What's the matter with it?"

"It sings well—or will, when it has the right music. It will suit Jiggsie's queer little countertenor."

Though Mrs. Nita Judd was definitely old, she did not look or act like a grandmother. She paced compulsively about the suite, plying them with her opinions. She obviously felt it was her role this afternoon to instruct and entertain two young people and was doing her best by her lights, not expecting them to contribute much. Which was understandable, thought Tildy, if your idea of a young person was someone like Jiggsie. People on Mrs. Judd's good side were labeled "poor," and the rest had to do without her favorite adjective. Her wide-bottomed gray silk trousers swished as she paced the carpet in her Mexican huaraches, her bracelets clanked and tinkled, and when she bent forward to pour the tea in her loose V-necked sweater, you could see the whole front of her black lacy brassiere and the crispy folds of her midriff below. Her skin was the color and texture of a gingersnap, and her hair, swept back in a cruelly tight Spanish knot that made her eyebrows look permanently in shock, was what Mama would have called "suspiciously black."

Her topics tumbled out in no particular order, usually trailed by insurrectionary backlashes. First she had reminded the girls that today was the Ides of March, "the day poor Julius Caesar was murdered by his so-called friends. 'Et *tu,* Brutus?' You see, I did learn a few things at old Mount St. Gabriel's, even though I was the sort of girl who couldn't wait to see the last of school." Next came the history of Jiggsie's slapdash schooling ("deplorable, really, poor child, but what could you expect, with those parents?"); and on into Jiggsie's home life, due to Jiggsie's poor father having spent his inheritance and become a golf pro and Jiggsie's mother being "well, let's just say capricious in her affections, to put it kindly"; then detouring somehow into Mrs. Judd's firm adherence to her Catholic faith ("When everything's in turmoil around you, you have to have something constant to steer by—though the Lord knows His poor church is not without stain"); and then on to the perfections of the late Mr. Judd ("Poor Harold was perfect, the perfect husband. And I'll tell you something, girls, and you can remember this when you are widows: he was even more perfect after he died").

And then back to Jiggsie: "When Mother Ravenel phoned to say she'd had to put Jiggsie back a grade, I made poor Bob drop everything so I could rush up here and console my only grandchild. And what do I find? Jiggsie like a pig in clover, surrounded by friends like you, Tildy, and this nice Elaine Frew—I'm so sorry Elaine wasn't able to come today—"

"Oh, Elaine is *brutal* about sticking to her Saturday practice schedule," Jiggsie proudly announced without looking at anyone. Her fingers hovered over the sandwich tray. Finally she picked up a triangle with the crusts cut off, peeled back the bread and sniffed at the filling inside, then popped the whole thing into her mouth with a shrug.

It was the first Tildy had heard that Elaine had been invited.

"So I guess this old granny will check out of here tomorrow morning," Mrs. Judd cheerfully resumed, swishing and clanking. She had yet to sit down. "I'll go to Mass at the basilica and stop off and have my conference with Mother Ravenel and see if I can find Mother Finney, who was always my favorite, and then poor Bob can get back home to his tools. You know that archaic old buggy you rode here in? I don't dare sell it because poor Bob would have nothing to tinker with at my house."

Tildy decided the time had come to divert this going-nowhere monologue about all these poor people onto a more purposeful track. "I was hoping, Mrs. Judd, that you would tell us about *your* time at Mount St. Gabriel's. You know, we're doing this play about the history of the school—"

"Yes, Jiggsie was saying. You wrote in a new part just for her. That was very sweet of you, Tildy."

"*Elaine* is writing some songs especially for me," said Jiggsie, tearing a petal from the single rose in the silver vase on the room service tray and setting it afloat, like a little boat, in her teacup.

"Actually," Tildy informed Mrs. Judd, "I am the one writing the songs. Elaine is supplying the music."

"However," said Jiggsie with a shrug.

"You girls are so clever!" said Mrs. Judd. "What do you call your play, Tildy?"

"*The Red Nun,*" said Jiggsie rather scornfully, still not looking at anyone. She tore off a second petal and set it afloat in her teacup.

"It's not really *my* play," said Tildy. "I mean, as director I'm allowed to add material, but Mother Ravenel wrote it when she was a freshman back in 1931, and it's a tradition for the freshman class to revive it every few years."

"The only red nun I know is that red buoy that had better be on the starboard side when you come back from sailing," said Mrs. Judd. "But yours is undoubtedly the nun kind of nun, since your play is about the school. How come she's red?"

"Well, it's a statue in our grotto made out of red marble, in honor of a devout Mount St. Gabriel's girl, Caroline DuPree, who died before she could become a nun, and her parents gave this memorial, only it never got finished—"

Mrs. Judd stopped pacing and looked dumbfounded. "Surely this can't be the Caroline DuPree I knew."

Tildy gasped. "You *knew* Caroline DuPree?"

"Sure, she was a boarder a grade ahead of me. But I must be missing parts of the story, because she was hardly devout, and Mother Wallingford sent her home in the middle of her senior year."

"You mean, for good?"

"Well, *yes.* She tried to jump off the water tower. But the tower windows were either stuck or hard to open and Mother Finney raced up the stairs and grabbed her in time."

"You mean she wanted to *kill herself?*"

"That was the story. She was madly in love with Mother Wallingford, and wrote about it to her younger sister, and her parents came to pack her up and take her home. They were all meeting in Mother Wallingford's office and when they told Caroline what had been decided, she ran off to the tower. I knew she'd succumbed to malaria, because the next fall we held a little Requiem for her. I was a senior by then—class of 1913—and engaged to Harold Judd and finished with school in my heart. I must say, I haven't given Caroline much thought since."

Tildy was floored. "Was Mother Wallingford in love with *her?*"

"Good Lord, no, child. Mother Wallingford wasn't in love with anybody. I doubt she was in love with God. She was a monster of efficiency. She should have been a man, a governor or a prime minister or something. God was her sovereign, that was clear, but certainly not a lover. Yes, that was the way it was with Mother Wallingford. I always thought she was ashamed of being a woman, even though she did dedicate her life to the education of females. She was always berating the girls, including yours truly, for 'thinking like a woman.' It was poor Mother Finney everybody loved. She was so witty and quick and fun to be with, and she had the cutest freckles, and she sat a horse fantastically, even in that nun's garb. Mother Finney's the one I'm looking forward to seeing tomorrow, though I expect forty years has taken its toll."

The inside of Tildy's head felt like an earthquake about to erupt.

Mrs. Judd's offhand recollections, those of an old girl who had been "finished with school in her heart" since 1913, were shaking Tildy's assumptions from the ground up. They threatened the very underpinnings of the play. It was one thing to want to add some new characters, to shed light on some old vanities and avenge some old wrongs— to make a breakout from what Mama called Mother Ravenel's "old party line." But where did you put this new stuff that had so casually issued from Jiggsie's grandmother's mouth—stuff that had preceded the time of Mother Ravenel herself? If people weren't who you had thought they were—if they weren't the people Suzanne Ravenel had thought they were—where did this fit in the play?

And if it didn't fit, what was a creative director to do?

Tildy couldn't wait to report all this to Mama. In the old days, she wouldn't have been sure of an audience with Mama on any given evening, but since Mother Ravenel had made her director of the play, she could count on Mama coming to her room every night.

"So how is my baby?" Mama would say. "What's new with the play?" And, smelling of chemicals and her winter perfume, Mama would curl up on top of the covers next to her daughter and encourage Tildy to tell her, like a child telling a mother a bedtime story, everything she had been doing with the play. Tildy had discovered that she had some of her best inspirations during these storytelling reviews with Mama nodding and snuggling beside her and egging her on.

But no, dammit, she wouldn't see Mama until tomorrow night, because she was spending tonight, as was her custom, with Chloe.

CHAPTER 28

Revising the Dead

Saturday afternoon, March 15, 1952
Riverside Cemetery
Mountain City

CLUSTERS OF CROCUSES, yellow and purple and white, poked up in their appointed spots in the Vick family enclosure. Soon it would be the first anniversary of Agnes's death, but Agnes was not buried here.

From the wrought-iron bench inside the pebbled enclosure designed by Malcolm Vick, Chloe surveyed the flat markers of Vicks who had completed their lives so far. Underneath those stones lay the remains of her grandfather Malcolm and the wife who had preceded him in death from drink. And there lay Malcolm's mother, Agnes, after whom Chloe's mother had been named. And there lay Uncle Henry's wife, Tildy's aunt Antonia. One day Henry would go in the ground beside Antonia. And one day Chloe herself, lying straight and completed in a coffin of her own, would join them.

Outside the enclosure's ornamented iron fence with the graceful latched gate were other Vicks: a great-great-uncle who had been a Confederate soldier, his wife, who'd outlived him by fifty years, some dead infants, and Malcolm Vick's father, who had perished in a flu epidemic when Malcolm was nine. Some of these lichen-crusted upright graves had sunk lopsidedly into the earth, which is why Malcolm Vick, after the death of his mother, had designed this enclosure for flat markers only. A cemetery was a place for the living, he had said, and he liked arranging things attractively for future living family members, who could come and sit comfortably in the family enclosure and contemplate their dead.

Before her trip to Rex Wright's in Barlow last month, Chloe had felt it wrong that her mother was not buried here. But things had shifted since then. Since Rex had proudly shown Chloe the memorial to Agnes with so many of her names missing and too much information about himself, it seemed to Chloe that Agnes, the real Agnes, was free to be nowhere at all and to wander where she would. She could not be contained in a "plot," either in the bright, flat Barlow cemetery or here in her father's carefully designed enclosure.

The thing was, Agnes had changed since Barlow. Chloe no longer felt her beside her, instructing her what to do next, and sometimes what not to do—like that ninth-grade class portrait that could have caused hurt feelings. Ever since Chloe had carried out Agnes's instructions in Barlow, her mother's spirit seemed to have gone on vacation. Something important had been accomplished between them: Agnes's spirit had wanted it, but Chloe's living body had been needed to fulfill it.

Chloe's body had changed, too. A couple of weeks after the trip to Barlow, she had found brownish stains inside her pajamas one morning. Fourteen, going on fifteen, and it had finally come. She and Agnes had discussed that, too, at the diner. "You may be a late bloomer, like me," Agnes said. "I didn't start until sixteen." Most of Chloe's classmates in Barlow had started. They hustled off importantly to the bathroom, borrowed nickels from one another for the sanitary pad dispenser. She had kept quiet about her "late blooming" until Tildy became her best friend. Who could keep that sort of thing from Tildy? Tildy had started at twelve and, with Madeline's coaching, had already graduated to junior tampons. "You have to angle your pelvis a certain way on the toilet," Tildy told her, "and if it goes in wrong, you mustn't try to force it or it'll go all smushy; just pull it out and splurge on a fresh one. Don't worry, I'll coach you when the time comes. Madeline didn't get the curse until she was fifteen." "Well, then I'm in good company," Chloe had said.

("Right up to the end, she wanted me . . ." Rex's high, furious voice, crumpling one fist inside the other to keep it from hitting her. "Yes, ma'am, she wanted me. I suppose since you two have been in your Catholic afterlife conversation, you knew about the baby. *Or had she told you she was pregnant while she was still alive?*")

No, she didn't tell me. I wonder why not. Was she afraid I'd be displeased? Disgusted? Would I have been? I knew what they did together, I've known the facts of life since I was ten, but all the same I never thought they would start a baby. Why didn't I allow for the possibility of a baby? What if Agnes had lived and the baby had been born? Would I have been jealous? Or would I have loved it because it was my half sister or brother, and we would all still be living in Barlow?

But Agnes sent me away without telling me about the baby. Why? Was she ashamed? Did she think it would upset me, or that I would love her less? Or, oh God, did she think *she had to choose between Rex and their baby and me?*

She wanted me to be a good Catholic and she kept saying she wished I could go to Mount St. Gabriel's one day, how happy she had been there.

Did she make some kind of promise to God? Like, Give Rex and me this baby and I will give Chloe to you, the way mothers were always giving away their sons to God in the Bible?

Maybe she had decided that if I was out of the way she and Rex could live a more normal married life, without the shadow of another man's daughter always watching them critically and overhearing them at night. She knew Uncle Henry would finish raising me according to her principles. And I was already almost fourteen.

What if all those months of her cramming me with Latin and history and religion at the diner were part of a plan? A plan to transfer me to Uncle Henry and to Mount St. Gabriel's so she could live a normal life and have this baby and others with Rex Wright?

But she loved me, I know she did. She said I was her best friend. She said we could go places together that others couldn't go. When I showed her my drawings of the way I imagined she looked at my age, she said, "It's as though you were back in my girlhood, watching over me like a guardian angel."

I believe it relieved her to talk about Rex with me in our booth at the downtown diner. She could work things out for herself about this uneasy triangle we were living. But she would never let us go too far; her fairness always stopped us before we went too far. Like sometimes she would say, "This is our Upper Room. We are like the early Christians breaking bread in secret. Only our bread is Nabs cheese crackers with peanut butter."

But when I went too far and said, "So we won't be thrown to the lions," she didn't laugh. "He is trying, darling," she said. "Let's give him the benefit of the doubt." And then with a little flash of conspiracy, she added, "Because, frankly, I don't see what choice we have."

Well, maybe later she decided we did have a choice. One of us goes, one of us stays. Or was it already "two of us stay" by then?

We talked about the hitting, too. I could see it hurt her that she felt she had to *explain* it, to make excuses. "He's hotheaded, darling. He just—some people are more combustible than others. I mean, some people are about as combustible as wet wood, whereas Rex, well, he's like . . . dry paper." She laughed at her apt comparison. "And there's also the question of upbringing," she went on. "If you grow up in a family of hitters, you learn to defend yourself and hit back. People . . . families . . ." She bit her lip, searching for words that would be fair to Rex but also get her point across. "People in families have different ways of asserting themselves. My father's weapon was scorn, a very understated scorn. He never laid a hand on any of us, but he could wilt you without raising his voice. Now, Merry's father, your other grandfather, his weapon was a kind of bland passivity. He'd say, 'Well, okay, if that's what you want . . .' Then he'd sidle off quietly and do exactly what *he* wanted. But, you see, Rex's father was a hothead, too. He'd backhand Rex at the dinner table and then, Rex said, he'd look genuinely shocked to see his son lying on the kitchen floor with a bloody nose."

"But that was men," Chloe protested. "Whereas Rex hits *us*."

She would have felt triumph for winning her point if Agnes did not look so defeated. I have really hurt her, Chloe thought, loving her mother even more tenderly because she could hurt her.

But Agnes, quickly recovering, replied somewhat sternly, "People can change, Chloe. If they love someone and learn to feel unthreatened by them and if they know they are loved, I believe they can change." Leaning forward on her elbows, she rested her forehead on her fingertips and gazed down at the table of their booth. "I have got to believe that," she said.

Did she still believe it when he went on hitting her? Did he hit her that day? Whether he did or not, it sure scared him when I said he did. "You misguided little ninny, you weren't here!" he cried, and I could see two opposite things: one, that he might not have hit her that day, that it hurt him to even imagine such a thing now; and two, that I had the power to ruin his life if he didn't let me go. I could see his fear, that such a story might get around Barlow, that he'd had something to do with his wife's falling against the radiator.

Did I really accomplish all that by myself down in Barlow? I'm not sure anymore. I thought Agnes was guiding me because she would want me to live with Uncle Henry if anything happened to her. I felt she and I were working as a team, that we had this thing to accomplish, that I was operating under her guidance and it kept her closer to me. Or did I imagine it because it kept her close?

Now I'm not sure. Since she's gone on vacation and I can't think of her buried anywhere at all, it's hard to say whether she wanted to get this thing done so she could be free from worrying about me—if she thought this thing through me—or if I created the whole thing by myself.

Just as I created those drawings of her crumpled against the radiator in her own blood. ("You never saw how she looked when I found her. I can assure you she didn't remotely resemble any of these—these bleeding Madonnas.")

Later Saturday afternoon, March 15, 1952
The Vick house
Mountain City

Chloe had been so absorbed in painting parts of the movable sets, which Uncle Henry had set up for her in the downstairs sunroom, that she hadn't even realized Tildy was late until the big Packard pulled into the drive. Tildy leapt out of the car and burst through the French doors, leaving John to follow with her things.

"Did you think I wasn't coming? Oh, what *real*-looking trees! You are an absolute genius, Chloe. Christ Almighty, you'd think that a family with three cars could get their one poor little girl without a license to her destination on time. But no, Mama was just off and Madeline was just back to get dressed for going on a date, and John and Daddy were nowhere to be found. I was beside myself. I was going to call you but then—"

"But you're here now," said Chloe. Tildy's urgency about everything to do with herself had the effect of calming Chloe and making her feel protective of them both. John edged his slightly stooped form through the French doors, carrying Tildy's patent leather overnight case and a huge old suitcase with straps. "How you doing, Miss Chloe? You want me to take these upstairs to y'all's room?"

"Yes, please, John," said Tildy. "And thank you for bringing me. Only a year and six months to go and then I'll be able to drive myself."

"It's always my pleasure, Miss Tildy."

"What on earth was in that huge suitcase," asked Chloe, now beaming because she was so happy to see her friend. "Are you coming to live with us?"

"Ah, you wouldn't like that," said Tildy. "I know you: you need to have your private time to commune with your spirits. It's a very mundane present, so don't go expecting anything grand. Actually, it's a suitcase full of Kotex. Mama buys it from some wholesale place that sells to drugstores. That way we don't have to go to the drugstore and be embarrassed."

"Oh, Tildy, how thoughtful. I just *hate* having to go in there and— and I can't very well ask Uncle Henry."

"Don't I know that, Miss Chloe. And when you're ready to graduate to the next level, I'll coach you from outside the bathroom door, like Madeline did me. And now, oh boy, do we have work to do! And do I have an earful to tell *you*! Where's Uncle Henry? His Jag's not in the garage."

"He's driven into the mountains to see a man who wants to add on to his hunting lodge but keep everything looking old and rustic. You and I will be dining alone."

"God! First they stick Greek columns on his new library and now they're trying to drag him back to log cabin days."

"He says he doesn't mind about the hunting lodge. It's the false mixing of styles he hates. We're having frankfurters and beans and Rosa left a pan of brownies and there's some ice cream."

"Poor Uncle Henry! No, I've got to stop saying 'poor.' It's Jiggsie's grandmother's pet word."

"Oh, how did the tea go? Was she nice?"

"She was very *conversational*. Even though most of it was with herself. She never stopped pacing and you could see the whole front of her black bra when she poured the tea. Jiggsie was her usual sweetly appalling self. But wait until you hear! Mrs. Judd was in the class of 1913 and *she knew the Red Nun*!"

"She knew—"

"Caroline DuPree was in the grade ahead of Mrs. Judd, and there's a whole other side of the story. Caroline was in love with the foundress, with Mother Wallingford, and her parents came to take her out of school and she tried to throw herself off the tower but Mother Finney saved her. Oh, bye, John!" She waved out the window as the Packard backed out of the driveway. "And then they took her home and she died of malaria."

"But what about the whole vocation thing?"

"Mrs. Judd hadn't heard about that, because she was one of those girls who couldn't wait to be done with school. All she knew was that there was a Requiem Mass said the next year, when Mrs. Judd was a senior. She didn't keep up with the school after she graduated. She didn't even know about the statue or Ravenel's famous play! But, Chloe, I was thinking on the way over here, you are the key that is going to unlock this whole mystery."

"*I* am?"

"Look, *who* is still at Mount St. Gabriel's who knew about all that first stuff that happened in the school, who was there right from the beginning?"

"Mother Finney."

"Dick Tracy! And which student was she closest to in the class of 1934?"

"Well, that would be Agnes."

"Right!"

"I still don't see how I am—"

"Wait, let me finish! Wouldn't it be the most natural thing in the world for you to seek out Mother Finney and have a little talk with her, say you want to know anything she can remember about your mother, and then after that you can tell her we're trying to amplify the character of the foundress for this updated version of the play, and get her talking about that, and then you could say, 'Oh, and you must have known Caroline DuPree, who died before she could realize her vocation—what was *she* like when she was at the school, Mother?' "

"But she must have wanted to be a nun at some point—I mean, her parents went to all that trouble to import the marble and hire the sculptor. I mean, it's one of the legends of the school."

"And who created the legend? That's what we want to find out!"

Tildy practically sizzled with electricity. "Was it there before Suzanne Ravenel's play? Or how much of it did she invent?"

"But surely Mother Finney wouldn't have stood by all those years and not spoken up if there was something not—"

"That's what we have to find out," said Tildy imperiously, turning her attention to Chloe's scenery panel of the grotto. "Now, I would have colored the Red Nun in first, but you've done all the trees and left her white."

"Well, this is the way *I'm* doing it. I have to see if there's anything else I need to see about her after all the background is filled in."

"I wasn't criticizing, Miss Chloe. I was just saying I'm the impetuous child dying to scribble with her red crayon and you're the subtle artist."

"I think I'm going to use a high-gloss house paint on her," said Chloe. In her backing-off moments, the articulate Tildy was impossible to resist. "That way she'll stand out from the water-based paint on the trees. She'll look more three-dimensional and *solid*. I was even wondering, should I make her a size bigger. What do you think?"

"You mean bigger than she really is?"

"Just a—a sort of impulse I had."

"You know what?" Tildy marched back and forth in front of the panel. "I think that is an excellent idea. Make her larger than life. A force to be reckoned with."

"But what if—what if I find out something from Mother Finney that will make her less of a force?"

"It won't make a difference to the *statue*. She's there, sitting on all her history of—just sitting there. She'll be the same whatever loss of force Caroline's story suffers."

"But—shouldn't we wait until we hear what Mother Finney has to say? There might not be anything."

"Oh, there'll always be *something*," said Tildy, with a toss of her shaggy curls. "Everybody has their own version of everything. What I'm trying for is to expand the scope of this play, to break open Mother Ravenel's same old party line. And Monday is St. Patrick's Day, so you have a perfect excuse to seek out old Finney and wish her the luck o' the Irish and then slip in the other stuff."

Monday afternoon, March 17, 1952
Feast of St. Patrick, bishop and patron of Ireland
Mount St. Gabriel's

In the morning sow your seed and at evening do not let your hands be idle; for you do not know which will prosper, this or that, or whether both alike will be good.

Mother Finney bent over her seedlings. The sun, soon tilting toward summer, blazed through the glass of the greenhouse and penetrated the layers of her serge habit, warming her old bones and smoothing the kinks in her joints.

Yesterday the pale sprouts had struggled to lift their tiny shoulders out of the flats. Today the trays of variegated foliage promised tomorrow's harvest. Soon there would be clusters of ripening tomatoes, snap beans, peas, summer squash, cucumbers. In Ireland her family, thrifty though prosperous, had never forgotten the 1845 famine and grew their own seed potatoes; but here at Mount St. Gabriel's, with a hundred boarders and the nuns and staff to feed, plus the cafeteria lunch for the day girls, it was more economical to buy them by the truckload from a New Jersey farm. Mother Finney's garden was no longer really a necessity, not as in those first years of the school (when she had grown potatoes to bake, boil, and store) and again during the Depression years and World War II. But the sisters and students were so vociferous in their praise: a "Finney tomato" was "the way tomatoes *used* to taste," a butterhead lettuce from her garden the crispiest and sweetest of them all. Doctoring her aches nightly with Ben-Gay cream and soaking her arthritic fingers twice daily in warm water, she submitted to their enthusiasm. She anticipated serving the first homegrown salad of the season to young Mother Malloy, who had trouble digesting the starchy Mount St. Gabriel's fare.

Light is sweet, and it is pleasant for the eyes to see the sun. Even those who live many years should rejoice in them all. Yet let them remember that the days of darkness will be many.

She rejoiced in her accrued years, though as she looked back over them, it astonished her that she could have traveled so far and done so many things. And yet her life felt exactly hers: she could not imagine any other. Of course, she'd had her companion in holy daring for two-score of her fourscore and nine. It was twenty-two years and two months now, that Lizzie Wallingford had been gone.

She could also tote up days of darkness already lived through. Surely the author of Ecclesiastes knew that dark days weren't always in the future: that they were given for you to endure and remember as you journeyed along, spreading them out, as it were, over your allotted span.

Her hearing was muted, her cataracts "ripe," as reported by the eye doctor, but when you've walked the same halls and stairs and grounds for forty-two years, and heard the same Masses and prayed the same prayers, you can make do with less acute portions of sight and sound. In the night, she was either wakeful and alert, keeping God company, or visited by episodes from all over her life. They came tumbling in as they would, in dreams and in reveries, until she sometimes wished she could give them the slip and remember episodes and scenes from some other life besides her own.

Yet in daytime she was increasingly forgetful. She could not count on herself to look at a face and match it with a name, though she knew perfectly well who the person was. She could no longer pluck the precise word she needed out of the air at the precise moment she needed it. Even the names of vegetables she sometimes forgot.

Yesterday a woman had come looking for her here in the greenhouse. A sharp-faced, jet-haired girl from the very earliest years of the school, she was now the sharp-faced, jet-haired grandmother of that new little boarder who had been put back a grade. Such a lot of questions she had, this lady, whom Mother Finney remembered as being exactly the same as a girl, always plucking you for information, yet talking as she plucked. Pluck, pluck, cluck, cluck. She had asked Mother Finney if she remembered running up the tower stairs to save Caroline DuPree from throwing herself off, the day the DuPree parents came to remove her from the school. Everybody had talked about it. Mother Finney was a heroine.

Mother Finney said her memory was not what it had been, but she was sure there had been no heroics on her part.

Then the lady wanted to know when it was that Caroline DuPree had decided to become a nun. Was it before or after she was sent home?

Ah now, I really couldn't say.

And what was this story about the Red Nun? That little girl who's directing the play was all over me yesterday when Jiggsie brought her to tea at the inn. I had to tell her it was completely new to me, this devout Caroline DuPree who died before she could realize her vocation. Yet I understand there's a memorial in red marble—

That there is, yes—an unfinished memorial, in the grotto. Would you like to see it?

The lady would love to, but was in too much of a hurry today; her driver was waiting, she was in complete charge of a magazine subscription business, very profitable, left to her by her late husband. Did Mother Finney remember how all the girls in the class of 1913 adored her? And off she had scurried, without waiting for an answer, still talking as she backed out of the greenhouse, because someone named poor Bob liked to get home before dark.

And here, this afternoon, came another visitor, a fawn of a girl with a clear-cut chin who made her way cautiously yet deliberately between the trestles of flats. Mother Finney knew exactly who she was but, alas, grasped in vain for a name. She remembered only the mother's name: Agnes, Agnes Vick, then something else, then another name after that. Agnes, the special one, though you weren't supposed to have favorites. Though Our Lord certainly did.

"It's Chloe," announced the girl, bless her. "You know, Agnes Vick's daughter? I wanted—I wanted to wish you a happy St. Patrick's Day, Mother."

"Ah, Chloe. I was just now thinking of your mother." Which was true, having seen Agnes's face approaching in the girl's steady eyes and distinctive chin. "Tell me, dear, how are you getting along?"

"Oh, I—" The girl swallowed and bent her head.

"I know, it's hard," she comforted the girl. "We know she's with God, but it's those of us left behind who feel the lack of her. I pray for her every day—and you along with her. And how are you finding the schoolwork, Chloe?"

"It's going okay, I think. I mean, I have to study to make good grades, but my mother coached me in some subjects before I came to Mount St. Gabriel's. And Mother Malloy, our teacher, is wonderful— she makes you *want* to excel."

"She's a godsend, our Mother Malloy. And you've made friends?"

"Well, Tildy Stratton and I are pretty close. I'm helping her a lot with the ninth-grade play. Our class is doing *The Red Nun*—Mother Ravenel appointed Tildy director. We're adding some new scenes. The girls are allowed to do that."

"And what scenes might you be adding, dear?"

"Well, we definitely want to amplify the character of our foundress. What she was really like, you know, in her prime. You're the only one at Mount St. Gabriel's who knew her then. Mother Ravenel talks about her a lot, but she only met Mother Wallingford at the end, when she was dying, and we have to remember that Mother Ravenel was only twelve at the time."

"That is so," said Mother Finney, pressing her lips together. With crooked but firm fingers she pinched suckers from a staked tomato plant. "Mother Wallingford wasn't herself in those last days. She should be remembered for the many things she accomplished when she was well." (The overwrought and completely imagined "deathbed scene" in Suzanne Ravenel's school drama had remained an undiminished source of distress to Mother Finney, who had, since 1931, been obliged to watch several generations of girls "play" Elizabeth Wallingford and Fiona Finney.)

"Oh, what things, for instance, Mother? We're looking for new material. We want to open up the play some. Even Mother Ravenel said it needed new blood."

"You know, dear, after Mother Wallingford died, I wrote down everything I could remember. The Order kindly made it into a chapbook. You'll find copies in the school library. At my keenest, Chloe, I was no writer, but you'll find far more of Mother Wallingford in that account than I can tell you now. I've become so forgetful. *Adventures with Our Foundress,* it's called. And it was. One adventure after another. Mother Wallingford believed in practicing what she called holy daring."

"Oh, yes, Mother Ravenel's always talking about that. And there's this other thing we were wondering, too, Mother. What was the true story about Caroline DuPree? Was it like in Mother Ravenel's play?"

The jet-haired old girl from yesterday and now young Chloe, interrogating her about Caroline DuPree.

Mother Finney was realizing belatedly that Agnes's daughter had come to the greenhouse with a purpose other than to wish her a happy St. Patrick's Day. So intent they were, these adolescent girls, about their upcoming play, which was, after all, only the latest rehash of an earlier adolescent girl's play—a play that had overrun its course, in Mother Finney's unasked-for opinion, and was best retired with all its misleading fabulations.

"Ah, child. I've become so very forgetful. She was a girl who died. And her parents commissioned the sculpture, which was never finished. And then Mother Ravenel, when she was only a girl herself, wrote the play. I'm afraid that is all I can tell you, dear."

Chloe toed up a sagging white sock with the opposite loafer, trying not to show her disappointment. "Oh, well, we were just wondering."

How Mother Wallingford would have loathed *The Red Nun* and all the wishful delusions that had gathered around the girl's "legend," thanks to a later girl's play. And yet, it was Mother Wallingford herself who had given permission for that ton of marble to be unloaded right in front of Our Lady in the grotto. From the moment of delivery things had taken on a life of their own. Veronese red instead of the pale Carrara that had been ordered from Italy. Then the First War, the death of the funerary sculptor, followed by the death of both DuPree parents. "Rather an uncouth companion for our Della Robbia, isn't she?" Mother Wallingford had soberly observed. "However, Mother Finney, let us stop and count our blessings."

And as the two of them stood contemplating the unfinished memorial, the foundress ticked off the blessings on her fingers.

"Number one, God allowed her to remain unfinished, a reprieve beyond our wildest hopes. This hulk of marble is a much more bearable concession. As you know, I was prepared to endure a life-size Caroline DuPree, sculpted down to her finite particulars, complete with the Scholastica habit and rosary, *in red*—affronting Our Lady until these mountains crumbled, so that her parents could idealize a troubled daughter rather than punish the school. Number two, the parents are safely dead, and no one will commission another sculptor to complete the job. And number three, most important, no scandal from that girl's unfortunate obsession with me has jeopardized all we have built here." Here she gave a bitter, outraged laugh, and Mother Finney knew she was recalling the girl's supreme infringement, the final straw. The lovelorn Caroline DuPree had sneaked into the nun's dormitory, off-limits to students, and spent the night in Mother Wallingford's closet. Or part of the night, until she gave herself away stifling a cough. She had come equipped to camp out in the recessive angle of the foundress's L-shaped closet, which she had reconnoitered in a previous violation of the rules, when all the nuns were in chapel. In her knapsack she had stuffed a lap robe for warmth, a Mason jar and a washcloth should she need to relieve her bladder, and had even packed herself a nocturnal snack of a sandwich and juice.

"Why?" Mother Wallingford had demanded, having fastened her veil, thrown on her cape over her nightgown, and marched the girl downstairs to her own room.

"I wanted to be with you for one night, Mother," came the sobbing plea. Then, cannily, a religious note was inserted. "Our Lord, He . . . nobody would stay awake and watch with Him. I wanted to show I could."

"You are confusing things" was the icy reply. "You are a very confused girl, Caroline. Get into bed and do not leave your room until I send for you."

"Not even to come to breakfast or go to the bathroom, Mother?"

"You have the contents of your knapsack to tide you over on both accounts."

"Won't you at least kiss me good night, Mother?"

"Certainly not."

MOTHER FINNEY'S POCKET watch now said ten to three, allowing her to release Agnes's little daughter from her unproductive visit to a forgetful old nun. "I must be on my way, Chloe, to ring the bell for None. Come and visit me again, and best of luck with your play."

"I hope you'll come see it, Mother."

"Oh, I expect I'll be there. And remember, I'll be praying for your mother and for you too, dear."

She stopped off at the kitchen to wash and soap her hands under the tap, drying them on a fresh towel with the priestly care that precedes a sacred duty, and then set off, with her slight limp from a girlhood horse fall, down the trophy-lined hall to summon the nuns to midafternoon prayer.

WITH EACH STRONG peal of the bell, she sent up prayers for her dear departed Agnes and for Agnes's slyer and more timid daughter. She prayed for all the girls, past and present, who, whether they had flourished or fallen or strayed, had partaken of Mount St. Gabriel's root system.

She recognized the footfalls of her various sisters as they crossed the landing above the gated stairwell: the discreet swish of young Mother Malloy's rubber-soled brogues; the flighty high step of Juilliard-trained Mother Lacy, humming a chant under her breath; the motivated tread of the headmistress, Mother Ravenel.

Suzanne.

"Tell me about the new girls, Mother Finney." It was the beginning of the school year, 1929, and Mother Wallingford's violent morning headaches had first sent her back to bed and at last driven her to make an appointment with the doctor.

"There's a nice new boarder, from Charleston. Suzanne Ravenel. Holds herself straight as a switch. Not a whit of homesickness. Says the air agrees with her for the first time in her life and that she has never been so happy."

"She told you that?"

"She's at my table. A forthcoming girl, but quite respectful. She'll do well with us, I think."

"One wonders, though, what such a statement says about her home life."

Then all of the apprehensive September, the blighted October. The nun's doctor had sent Mother Wallingford straight to the neurosurgeon. There were tests at the hospital. The X-rays. The spinal tap. The needle biopsy. Consultation between specialists by long-distance telephone. Medicine to alleviate the pressure on the cerebellum. The bad news, wrapped in alleviative phrases: "maximal feasible removal," meaning some of it might be cut out, giving the patient some extra time until it grew back. To take all of it would leave "unacceptable damage," meaning the patient would be better off dead. The foundress was first stoic, then angry. She was only sixty-seven, there were many things to be done for the growth of the Order, for the improvement of the schools. She metamorphosed into a demon of efficiency. Lawyers were summoned, overseas calls booked, new documents drawn up, signed, and cosigned. Just in time. Her mind and personality deteriorated daily.

The end of October brought Black Friday, followed by the Monday morning telephone call from the Ravenel brother in Charleston.

Their father killed in a hunting accident. The girl not to come home for the funeral. Her nonrefundable board and tuition prepaid to mid-December. After that, more modest arrangements must be found for her back in Charleston. No money for her to continue at Mount St. Gabriel's. However, not possible for her to live at home with the mother.

"The girl who lost her father is here with us in the infirmary," Mother Finney told Mother Wallingford, who had occupied a room there since she went on the intravenous painkiller.

"Which girl, Mother Finney? Do you expect me to keep up with every girl in my present state?"

"The nice little girl from Charleston we've talked about. Suzanne Ravenel. She's taking it hard that she has to leave us when the term finishes."

"Then why must she leave?"

"There's no more money. And she can't live with her mother. There seems to be a problem about the mother."

"There always is. The mother is an opium eater; that's the problem." The foundress erupted into the unnerving high-pitched cackle of her illness.

"No, that was— I think you're confusing her with someone else, Lizzie."

"I'll thank you not to 'Lizzie' me. What is the point of a rule if we ignore it and address one another by first names? And I'm not as impaired as you'd like to think. I know whose mother you are talking about. And a very effective method of abdication, too. Send the girl to me. Who better than myself to enlighten her about a mother's abdication?"

"When Reverend Mother told the girl about her father and asked if she wanted anyone to accompany her to chapel, do you know what she said?"

"For God's sake, Fiona, be specific. 'She' who? Reverend Mother or the girl? Doesn't the girl have a name?"

"Suzanne Ravenel, Mother. The boarder whose father had the shooting accident in Charleston. Reverend Mother was very touched. When she asked the girl if there was anyone she would like to have with her, Suzanne Ravenel said there was only One whom she needed and He was always with her anyway. Reverend Mother suspects she may have an early vocation."

Again the eerie high-pitched cackle. The tumor seemed to have robbed the foundress of her rich, mellow tones. "Reverend Mother suspects everyone of having an early vocation. Send the girl to me. I'll put her straight about mothers."

"I was wondering, Mother—"

"I'm not your mother, Fiona. Your mother died a good Catholic death from having too many babies. Now who's becoming forgetful?" Another cackle, this time triumphant and mean.

"I was wondering," ventured Mother Finney, now barred from using both first names and religious ones, "if we might look to the trust for keeping Suzanne Ravenel here with us. We could do it on a year-by-year basis, if you see fit."

"I'll be in the ground before the end of this year, Fiona. Certainly, let's sign up your little protégée and shield her under Father's munificent umbrella. You can do it yourself. You have power of attorney now."

"I'd rather we signed together. You still can, you know."

To Mother Finney's chagrin, Mother Wallingford dissolved into a squall of grief. Forlorn yowling noises poured out of the foundress's mouth, interspersed, which made it all the sadder, with completely lucid sentences. "Oh, Fiona, why do you allow me to be so cruel to you? It's the pressure, the pressure . . . some iron giant is pressing my head between his iron hands and soon I will squash like an overripe fruit. Oh, Fi! Fi! Fi! What has it all been *for*?"

The morphine drip was increased that night, and during the following week Mother Finney arranged for a sum to be set aside for a full room-and-board scholarship for Suzanne Ravenel, to be renewed annually through high school and junior college for as long as the girl proved herself worthy of it.

The foundress was given credit for the idea by Mother Finney herself. That was the kind of thing that furthered the school legend. Just as the Red Nun was allowed to become part of that legend in order to protect the school. Suzanne was brought to Mother Wallingford's infirmary room for a short "audience" with the dying foundress during what Mother Finney judged to be one of the foundress's more lucid moments, of which there were fewer and fewer. Though the audience lasted less than five minutes, it twice veered toward disaster. The first time was when Mother Wallingford went into a screed over bad mothers, shouting out some lines from De Quincey about his cold and unforgiving mother, who had driven him to opium. ("The whole artillery of her displeasure unmasked!" Mother Wallingford had screeched in the unnerving, high-pitched voice.) This was diverted by Mother Finney's quick reminder that we also had a Divine Mother who can contain all our sorrows because she herself is the Mother of Sorrows, a quote that was later to find its way into Suzanne Ravenel's report of her one and only meeting with the dying foundress, attributing these lines to the foundress.

The second close call was when Mother Wallingford, incoherently muttering something in Latin, had tried to embrace the girl, who then became entangled in the intravenous drip. Mother Wallingford screamed at Mother Finney's efforts to disengage them, accusing Mother Finney of trying to steal her rightful child. Then the infirmarian came running and Mother Finney led away the frightened Suzanne. Mother Finney sat beside the girl's bed and prayed the rosary with her until Suzanne Ravenel fell asleep.

None of this became part of Suzanne Ravenel's later remembrances. True to the spirit of romantic hindsight by which one builds a personal myth, the whole thing was represented by Suzanne as having taken place in dignity and affection between the dying foundress and the chosen beneficiary. Mother Finney had no place in this myth.

CHAPTER 29

A Letter

Mrs. Creighton Rivers
984 Cherbrooke Lane
Marietta, GA 30064

Sunday, October 21, 2007

Dear Tildy,

Rebecca Meyer (now Birnbaum) from our ninth-grade class helped me trace you through Ashley Nettle. Ashley said you go by Mary now, but I hope you won't mind if I call you by the old name, at least for the purpose of this letter.

I hardly know where to begin. Let me start by saying I was sorry to hear of your husband's death. I have such pleasant memories of Creighton Rivers. He raised me from a dog paddler to a crawler and was always so sweet with us at the pool. He used to call you "Tantalizing Tildy." You predicted he would marry your sister, Madeline.

I, too, am widowed. My husband, Max, a veterinary surgeon, died two and a half years ago. I have just sold our house, along with Max's office building and surgery. We had no children, and last February I lost our beloved golden retriever, Daisy. The prospect of my independence verges on the terrifying, but I am in good health, knock on wood, and will try to meet the demands of this new freedom.

I wonder if you knew that Mother Ravenel wrote a school memoir, *Mount St. Gabriel's Remembered,* which was published in 2006 by a Mountain City printing press. Becky told me about it and then kindly sent me a copy, at my request, advising me to read it as a fascinating document of a lost "girl world." Becky is a psychiatrist in New York working with adolescents. She "rediscovered" me through a guest column I wrote for the *Palm Beach Post* about a dyslexic boy reading to an old golden retriever.

It was a mixed experience, reading through *Mount St. Gabriel's Remembered.* Some pages made me nostalgic for the "holy daring" and the excellence of the whole endeavor (I mean the founding of the school), and on other pages I felt she was making up her own version as she went along, putting in what she liked and leaving out what didn't suit her. But then I thought, Maybe that's the way all our memories work. If you haven't seen it—and if you want to see it—I'll be glad to send you my copy.

I feel I could go on and on. The problem would be organizing all I want to tell you and ask you! Remember our five-page papers for Mother Malloy? Be concise and modest, she would say; don't bite off more than you can chew. So I am going to stop here and go out and mail this before I start finding fault with it. My street address is on the back of the envelope, and I also include my cell phone number and my email address. I would dearly love to hear from you, Tildy. It was the reading of Mother Ravenel's memoir—in which neither of us is mentioned—that made me realize how much I have missed you all these years.

Maud Norton Martinez

CHAPTER 30

Dire Alternatives

Evening of April 9, 1952
Wednesday in Holy Week
Mount St. Gabriel's chapel

MAUD HAD SPECIAL permission from Mother Ravenel to stay in chapel until the nuns' Compline and seek God's will. She had been a boarder at Mount St. Gabriel's for a week. The Pine Cone Lodge was no more. Her mother and Art Foley were living in a hotel in Atlanta while they house hunted. Lily had told Mother Ravenel that she and Mr. Foley had been married back in February by a justice of the peace and asked Maud to back her up in this little story.

"You mean tell my friends you are married?"

"Of course, what else? It would reflect awkwardly on you, as well, Maud. Mr. Foley and I want to wait and do it right, come June, when we are all three together as a family. Maybe have the ceremony in our new house."

It was bad enough telling a lie; it was even worse to have to tell a lie that made Art Foley part of her family one minute sooner than he had to be. So far Maud had not told anyone. To Tildy, who insisted on boring into your secrets, she said, "They say they are married but it disgusts me to think so, if that's all right with you."

"Of course it's all right with me, Maud. Your whole life is being turned upside down. But you've got your scholarship and you've got me. All we have to do is get you through the rest of high school; then you can go to any college you want."

"But you know as well as I do that the scholarship is just for a day girl, and Lily won't pay for me to board at Mount St. Gabriel's after May. She expects me to live with them in Atlanta."

"Well, that's not going to happen," said Tildy. "You can always live with us."

"Your mother and father may have something to say about that."

"All Daddy wants is for his girls to be happy, and Mama and I have been especially close since I've been directing the play."

"But Tildy, I can't—if I could pay something to live at your house, it would be one thing—"

"Well, look, is it totally over with Anabel and you? I know she and your dad are separating, but couldn't you write and say you know it wouldn't be wise for you to go back to Palm Beach just now, but you have this opportunity to live with your old friend's family while you finish Mount St. Gabriel's on your day scholarship and if you just had a little saving-face money to pay for your room and board—? Wasn't she always hinting that she planned to pay for your college?"

"That was *before*"—Maud had to keep herself from shrieking—"that was before I went off with this man at the dance and ruined Anabel's social aspirations. I would rather die than ask her. It's bad enough that she's going to put my father on some sort of retainer, so he can stay at a decent place and not have to go to some state institution."

"Well, all right," Tildy said, backing down. "Let's just get through the play and then we still have almost the whole month of May to think of something. If worse comes to worst, I'll cash all my war bonds and we can sell off the gold pieces that Granddaddy gave me. They are mine to do what I like with. Why are you looking at me like that?"

Maud was remembering Anabel's lifted eyebrows last summer on Worth Avenue when she was shown Tildy's picture. ("Why, she looks like Orphan Annie without a neck. She's still a little girl, darling, whereas *you* . . .")

"I'm just touched by your generosity, Tiddly, that's all."

SINCE GRANNY'S DEATH and the dismantling of the Pine Cone Lodge, it had been very hard for Maud to keep track of who she still was inside and what she was up against and who she was going to have to fool. That was why Mother Ravenel had given permission for her to stay behind in chapel.

She was supposed to be praying, only to discover she wasn't sure what real prayer consisted of. For years she had rattled off her nightly orations, but surely there was something else she was meant to be doing here on her knees if she expected God to tell her what He wanted from her.

Had Maud really indicated to Mother Ravenel that she might—? She buried her face in her hands. Could this be a possibility or was she the biggest liar in the school? Not even Tildy would be allowed to pull this out of her. It was too important—or too dangerous; she hadn't decided which. In its way it was worse than if she had gone the whole way with Troy Veech. Probably there were people who thought she had: Mimi Weatherby, probably even Anabel thought so, though Maud had tried to explain to her stepmother what had and hadn't happened during the fateful intermission at the Palm City Club that had gotten herself and Anabel uninvited to Mimi's party. But this—this new possibility that so far she'd shared with Mother Ravenel alone—if it was true, and if it became known—that she might, that she just *might* have a vocation—it would be a far worse kind of going all the way. Worse in the sense that it would alter other people's perception of her. And it might change her into something different even if she did not go through with it.

If she couldn't find her way into the proper way of praying, she could at least go back over it again and try to discern her motives. (Or, as Mother Malloy had instructed her about the martyred St. Thomas Becket, "See how far you can follow the tugs of his dilemma within those boundaries.")

All this had begun back in March during Maud's conference with Mother Malloy about her medieval history paper. You were supposed to imagine yourself at some important point in the life of your historical figure and Maud had chosen Thomas Becket, favored friend and chancellor of King Henry II and then later, by the king's wish, archbishop of Canterbury.

"It's the conscience part of it that grips me, Mother. I mean, here is his king, the person he owes everything to, they are best friends, and then, through this king and friend, he is given a job where he's supposed to answer to God first, and he finds he can't be true to both of them. So what is his deepest duty? That's what I want to go for."

"You certainly do go for the deep, don't you, Maud?" Mother Malloy had a chest cold, her eyes were bleary, and her voice was spectral.

But she had a smile for Maud. "It is an ambitious topic, and I'm not going to warn you away from it, because I know your abilities. But try to limit yourself to one or two specific instances and see how far you can follow the tugs of his dilemma within those boundaries. And remember, don't bite off more than you can chew!"

And then she had honored Maud by wondering aloud, in her congested voice, where Maud's "many gifts" would be likely to lead her.

"I'd like to do some kind of scholarship," said Maud, "history or maybe English. And"—wanting to please Mother Malloy—"maybe be a teacher, too. Also I'd like to write—if that's not asking too much."

"Why? It all goes together. And you would be *giving* so much."

The nun looked at her with something so close to admiration that Maud felt bold enough to ask, though they weren't supposed to ask personal questions of nuns, "What did *you* think you wanted to do with your life, Mother, when you were my age?"

"Like you, I wanted to study and to teach. Since I was raised in the church, it was a straight path for me. I knew I wanted to go into a teaching order and keep learning as I taught. It's a mutual commitment. You make your vows to the order, and the order underwrites your education. If I had been born a man, I would have tried for the Society of Jesus." Seeing Maud's puzzlement, she added, "The Jesuits."

"Oh," sighed Maud, "if only we had something like that. A commitment—where you could set yourself on a path and not have to worry about—"

" 'We' meaning . . . ?"

"Oh, the Methodists; it's our family's church. Not that I'm much of one. I've been at Mount St. Gabriel's so long I can flip my missal ribbons through the Mass as expertly as any Catholic girl."

"But I interrupted you. You were saying 'and not have to worry about—'?"

"Your education. Becoming what you want."

"Are *you* worried about those things, Maud?"

It was both the surprise and the concern in the nun's voice that swept away Maud's composure. "I'm so afraid, Mother," she heard herself say, starting to break down.

"Afraid of what, dear?"

"That my mother and Mr. Foley won't let me come back to Mount

St. Gabriel's next fall and I'll have to—I'll have to—to *downgrade my dreams.*"

Quoting from her own A-plus Dickens paper to underwrite her distress—how much lower could you get?

Was this what life was going to be like from now on, after you "came into," as Mother Ravenel liked to put it in her "Moral Guidance" talks, "your full cognitive powers"? When nothing was a straightforward emotional exchange anymore, and there was always a hidden motive or a sly bid for advantage.

But Mother Malloy simply said, "I am sorry to hear this, Maud, but perhaps it's good that you told me. I don't know what can be done, but I am going to speak to Mother Ravenel. With your permission, that is."

THAT HAD BEEN back in March, and this morning at breakfast she had found a folded note tucked beneath her napkin ring. "Maud, please come to my office at the beginning of afternoon study hall. Mother Ravenel." Her first thought was, What have I done wrong? She didn't connect it with her talk with Mother Malloy. It occurred to her that Mother Ravenel had somehow found out that Maud's second part in the play, that of Domenica, who, with her school friend Rexanne, had decided to become a nun, was really based on Tildy's aunt Antonia, and that the character of Rexanne, played by Tildy, was based on Suzanne Ravenel. This scene, wedged into the crucial final ten minutes of the play, was being rehearsed separately by its two principals, Tildy and Maud. Only during the performance would the other players see the scene for the first time.

"It's what playwrights call a play's 'hidden message,' " Tildy had told Maud in deepest confidence. "It's something that gives the play its special *frisson,* even though nobody but the playwright knows it's there. *You* know, Maud; I need you to know so you can incorporate it into your performance of Domenica. Nobody else knows, not even Chloe. I didn't want her to go consulting the spirit of Agnes and gumming up the works with some *scruple* or other."

"But what *is* the *frisson,* Tildy?"

"A *frisson* is a little shiver," Tildy complacently translated.

"I know what 'a' *frisson* is," Maud said crossly, Tildy's possessiveness about the French language having lately become an irritation. "What I meant was, where is the hidden message in this one? Don't you think I need to know what it is, too?"

"The hidden message," said Tildy, with a pregnant pause—Maud knew she was either choosing whether or not to confide it or thinking it up on the spot—"is . . . the unraveling of Ravenel."

"The unraveling—?" Maud saw Tildy allowing time for fear of consequences to play themselves out on Maud's face.

"Look, Maud, when she was our age, Mother Ravenel wove her version of things into a play, and now we're going to *un*weave some of it and correct it with things we have learned since. But this has to be between us. The audience will feel a burst of fresh air, and we will have done a service to those who can no longer speak for themselves, and nobody will be the wiser—except for Mother Ravenel. It will be a secret message to her."

"COME IN, MAUD."

Mother Ravenel was seated at a huge dark desk with carved legs, its flat top importantly stacked with papers and baskets of letters. Behind the headmistress, almost like a stage backdrop, were the ranges of the western mountains, with Pisgah and the Rat in prominence just above the nun's right shoulder. Maud felt spotlighted by the bright sunshine pouring through those double windows. Mother Ravenel, her back to the windows, was in shadow.

Maud took in the office, with its trophies and photographs and, on one wall, a rough-carved little Madonna wearing a sombrero, sitting inside a sort of little house. This was her first summons to Mother Ravenel's office. "It's very nice in here, Mother," she said.

"Take a seat, dear." The headmistress pointed to a silvery wing chair.

"I want you to know, Maud," said the headmistress, "that you are sitting in the foundress's own Queen Anne wing chair. It was one of her great finds. Recognizing it for the treasure it was, she bought it from a junk dealer in Mountain City. Then she and Mother Finney stripped it down and refinished it and upholstered it in that lovely brocade left over from an altar frontal."

"It's very nice," said Maud, running her fingers along the arms.

"And you suit it well. Tildy Stratton tells me she has cast you in the role of our foundress. And she says you have agreed to take on another small part as well. A new character, someone called Domenica, I believe." Mother Ravenel certainly seemed to be informed up to the minute about the development of the play, yet Maud also felt a probing edge to her tone. Had Tildy told the headmistress that this was the one scene that no one else in the class knew about and that was only rehearsed in private between the two players? Maud didn't think so.

"Yes, Mother. She's a girl from later on in the school's history. It's just a sort of cameo scene. Domenica has a vocation, or believes she does."

"I see." The headmistress settled back in her swivel chair. "That's very well put, Maud. Has a vocation. Or believes she does. Sometimes the belief grows into the reality. And sometimes it doesn't. The interim period is what we in the religious life call 'discernment.' "

"Discernment," repeated Maud, not at all sure where this was going.

"But I didn't call you in to talk about the play, though Tildy is very fired up about it. She's made me promise to attend a rehearsal as soon as everyone knows their lines. She says she's put in new bits of material, here and there, which makes it more of a living thing. Even though I wrote it, I've come to regard the play as a work in progress in service to the ongoing history of the school. I called you in, Maud, because I wanted to hear how you are doing. How are you finding life as a boarder?"

"I love it more as a boarder, Mother Ravenel."

"Would you care to elaborate on that?"

"It's so peaceful here. You always know what's coming next. I get to do more of what I want here."

"Not many of our boarders would say that, I can assure you. I guess it depends on what a girl wants. What do you want, Maud?"

"To get on with my studies. To get on with being myself, without—without—"

"Without—?"

"Without worrying that it will all be taken away. That I will have to—have to—" She lowered her eyes.

"Downgrade your dreams?" the headmistress triumphantly supplied. "Yes, you see I have been talking with Mother Malloy. She did right to come to me. And I have read your paper on the ordeal of young David Copperfield—and, by extension, the early ordeal of his creator. I found it very spiritually acute for someone of your age. But let's explore this a bit further, Maud. What is it you are afraid will be taken away from you? How would it be taken away?"

"If I have to leave here and start over somewhere else. And with— my mother's—"

"With her new husband, Mr. Foley, you mean?"

"With Mr. Foley, yes."

"Do you not get along with Mr. Foley?"

"He's all right. I just don't want to make a family with him and my mother. I'll be fifteen soon, and I wish I had some other choice."

"Do you have any idea what you would choose?"

"Well, *yes,* Mother, but it doesn't count, does it, because I'm still a minor and I don't have any money of my own."

"Well, let's hear it anyway. You know what our foundress said. She had it from her great friend Father Maturin in England, who led her to her vocation. Don't be afraid to be specific with God. God likes for us to spell out what we want in detail. The more detail we give Him, the more He has to work with, and the better we understand what we are asking Him for."

"For a start, Mother, I would like to go on boarding at Mount St. Gabriel's. You know, I won the eighth-grade scholarship to the academy—"

"Yes. And you're in good standing to continue with it next year. Your grades are very good."

"But it's just a day scholarship. Oh, it would have been perfect if Granny had lived, even if Mother had gone away with Mr. Foley. I could have taken over the housekeeping and helped Granny run things. But my mother says she can't afford to pay for me to board after this term. Tildy says I could live with them, but I'm not sure Mrs. Stratton likes me all that much. And besides, I don't want to be—"

"You don't want to be beholden."

"Yes." Having caught the flicker of approval when she voiced her reservations about Tildy's mother, Maud continued on in this vein. "Mrs. Stratton can be very—she has this way of making you feel unsure."

"You and Tildy were on the outs until recently."

"Yes, Mother. We had grown away from each other when I came

back from spending last summer in Palm Beach. And then Tildy and Chloe Starnes became best friends."

"Were you hurt by this?"

"Oh, no. I felt freed from being—what you said—beholden. I could just be myself—or find out what 'myself' was like. I was tired of being part of this thing called 'TildyandMaud.' "

Mother Ravenel laughed. "But now you two are obviously close again if she's suggesting you might board with them."

"I wouldn't say we're exactly close—Chloe is still her best friend. But I'm really enjoying working with her on the play."

"I'm very glad to hear that. I got this little bee in my bonnet that she was capable of it, and I decided to take the chance. So, Maud, are you saying it would be your choice to board if means could be found?"

"Oh, yes, Mother! I'd be willing to work. I could—I don't know—coach the younger girls or work in the kitchen—"

"I think we'd better leave the kitchen to Betty. Your mother told me things weren't going well between your father and the second Mrs. Norton, or I would have suggested that you sound them out. She's an affluent woman, isn't she?"

"My father has—a drinking illness. I think they're separating. She's going to make him an allowance so he can stay at a private place, but I don't think she's in the mood to make *me* an allowance."

"You've heard from her, then?"

"No, Mother. After my Christmas visit, Anabel wrote to my mother about the trouble with my father. And she said she wouldn't be asking me down there anymore."

"But she was so fond of you, I thought. Did you do anything to displease her?"

"Well, there was a misunderstanding about— What happened was, this boy, Duddy Weatherby, he's the son of Anabel's friend—the Weatherbys invited me to be his date at his dance."

"The dance you had to leave early for. You didn't go with him after all?"

"Oh, I went. I went. But . . . there was this misunderstanding about who I was supposed to dance with—there was a dance card with all these names filled in and I got mixed up and I guess some boys' feelings were hurt. Mrs. Weatherby was really put out and disinvited Anabel and me to her Christmas party. It was a blow to Anabel, because Mrs. Weatherby was supposed to get her into Palm Beach society."

"Was your date one of the boys whose feelings got hurt?"

"Oh no, Duddy was okay. I hadn't missed any dances with him, and we had the last dance together. But I knew I hadn't come up to Mrs. Weatherby's standards. Mr. Weatherby had brought us in his vintage Rolls, but Mrs. Weatherby made two brothers drive me home in their old car."

"Just you? Without your date?"

"Oh no, he was still with me. We sat in the backseat of the— brothers' old car and Duddy walked me to the door and shook my hand. But I knew it was over for poor Anabel. Because the last thing Mrs. Weatherby said to me as we left the dance was to be sure and tell Anabel she would see her 'after the first of the year,' which was her way of saying 'Don't show up at my party tomorrow.' "

"Hmm, it sounds like a drastic overreaction on Mrs. Weatherby's part." The headmistress's indignant tone indicated to Maud that her self-protecting revision of the event had been swallowed. But now it was high time to get off the subject of the dance, before Mother Ravenel could come up with more questions.

"Yes, well, it's all over and I'm glad. I just want to be here where I am and concentrate on what I'm doing."

"Life is not all studying, though, Maud. Or perhaps you meant more than just studying."

"Yes, I meant more—I meant the whole thing. To get on with being myself—no, that's not totally it, either. I want to be all I can be. But I don't know completely what that is yet."

"Of course you don't. You're only fourteen. Have you prayed about it?"

"Oh well, I—not in so many words, not like the way I've been talking to you. I guess my prayers are on a pretty childish level."

"How so?"

"Oh, I ask for things like 'Please let Granny be at peace,' or 'Please let me do my best on the exam,' or 'Please don't let me be forced to leave Mount St. Gabriel's.' "

Mother Ravenel was regarding her closely. "Mother Malloy told me you had been asking her about vows."

"Vows?"

"That you wished your church offered the same commitments as ours. Or am I not quoting her accurately?"

"I said I wished the Methodists had something like that. Where you could set yourself on a path and not have to worry about your education. But they don't. I'm not sure I even am a Methodist. I mean, I was baptized in that church when Mother brought us back to Mountain City—but I've been more times to chapel here than I have been to the Methodist church in my whole life."

"You know our own foundress started her life as a Protestant, Maud. She discovered the Catholic faith all on her own; she sought it out and researched it thoroughly before deciding it was for her. She knew she wanted to put all her gifts to God's use, and she wanted to figure out the best way she could do this, step by step. Talk about someone wanting to be all she could be! She kept on setting herself greater and greater challenges. I was very fortunate to know her in her last days, when she was on her deathbed. I was in a desperate situation myself. I was a boarder, in the seventh grade, but my father had died suddenly and they didn't want me at home, only there was no money for me to stay on here. Until Mother Wallingford found a way."

"What was—the way?"

"There was a trust that had been set up for emergencies. And I was a beneficiary of it. Mother Wallingford arranged a full boarding scholarship for me, renewable from year to year, as long as I proved worthy of it."

"Is there—still—that trust?"

"Oh no, it has long since been liquidated."

"Oh."

"Why do you ask, dear?"

"Only that—well, I wish I could be like her. I mean, I do want to put my gifts to God's use, but I need to go step by step, like she did, until I figure things out. And I feel I could do it better if I stayed here."

"You feel Mount St. Gabriel's provides the best atmosphere for you to do that."

"Yes, Mother, I do."

Nothing direct had been said, but Maud felt she had crossed a line.

Mother Ravenel was intently studying her. "I'll tell you what, Maud. I'm going to offer a suggestion. I want you to go to the chapel now and pray about this talk we have had. Don't try to figure anything out; now is not the time for figuring. Just make an offering of it to God and leave it there with Him. Then go on with your usual activities and trust Him to start working on it. Then go back to the chapel before you go to bed and stay there until the nuns' Compline at nine. You may be excused from evening study hall."

"And—what do I do in chapel the second time?"

"Just kneel in an attitude of prayer, and listen. See what comes. Prayer is not always talk, talk, talk. I want you to get used to being alone with God. This is an ideal time, the middle of Holy Week. The whole communion of Christ is in mourning, but we're preparing for his Resurrection. I will be praying over this, too. Let's call it your intention. And we'll keep it between ourselves, shall we, Maud?"

"Yes, Mother."

"I will just say one further thing. If we both conclude that God wants you to stay at Mount St. Gabriel's, a way will be found."

CHAPTER 31

The Play

Friday, April 25, 1952
Mount St. Gabriel's auditorium

TILDY'S MOTHER AND father accepted the nicely printed programs from girls stationed on both sides of the auditorium entrance.

"Let's go to the front row," Cornelia said. "I don't want waggly heads distracting my attention."

"There's some on the left," her husband said. "Unless they have Reserved signs on the seats."

"We'll just dispose of them. Nobody is going to unseat the director's immediate family."

"And that we are," said Smoky Stratton, with a fond chuckle. He was feeling mellow after an early light supper of shrimp Creole on rice, washed down with several iced-tea glasses of bourbon and water.

The left front row was free, except for a single Reserved sign on the seat nearest the center aisle. "It might be for the prompter," Cornelia said. "We used to have two girls in the wings with scripts, and someone posted out front to mouth things as a last resort. We'll save seats for Madeline and Henry. Put Henry next to the Reserved seat, in case it's someone odious."

BACKSTAGE, HENRY VICK, flanked by Chloe and a keyed-up Mother Ravenel, had been making some final adjustments to the flexible joining flats constructed by himself and Chloe, painted by Chloe, and delivered by truck this afternoon. Uncle and niece had come out early, to set up things.

"Henry, these exceed my expectations," said the headmistress. "*Re-*

versible flats! The economy of it! I didn't even know there were such things. Why, it's like a giant reversible triptych. How tall is it?"

"Just under twelve feet. More than twelve would need heavier reinforcement."

"You have been very generous, Henry. It would take an architect to come up with this."

"Oh, no, it's simply a matter of measurements and hinges. And deciding to cover both sides of the frames. Chloe did every inch of the artwork. I had no hand in that. I tried not to be one of those parents who do their child's homework."

"The time these will save! Instead of Mark and Jovan having to drag off the grotto and drag in the classroom, they simply walk onstage, turn this one around, and walk off again. And you haven't overstepped in the parental role. Parents have always contributed to the plays. Mothers who could sew made costumes; fathers provided masculine touches like swords and antlers and old uniforms. Remember, your father lent that handsome Sheraton sideboard from his office when our class did *Charley's Aunt* our senior year."

"So he did. For Jack Chesney's college room; Agnes was Jack. Father even provided the whiskey bottles for the sideboard. And you were the hilarious fellow they dressed up as the aunt. You had people rolling in the aisles."

"Lord Fancourt Babberly. 'Babbs.' What a great role that was. I always loved doing characters in disguise. But, Chloe, I thought you told me you were painting the Red Nun on this grotto flat."

"I did, Mother, but it didn't look three-dimensional enough, so I put in trees instead. Then Uncle Henry suggested we try some poly— poly—"

"We went to the building supply place," said Henry, "and got a block of polystyrene. The Red Nun is under that tarpaulin. Chloe wanted to surprise you. She'd like it to be our gift to the school for future productions of the play. Chloe, why don't you unveil it?"

Chloe, already costumed in jodhpurs and Mother Finney's riding boots, stepped over and removed the tarpaulin. Henry was moved and slightly embarrassed by the headmistress's girlish ecstasies when she saw the life-size reproduction of the Red Nun.

"It was real easy to carve, Mother," Chloe said, "and you can sand it and make it look just like marble sculpture. But, Uncle Henry, don't you think it needs a highlight or two?" She whipped out a little spray can and touched the hulking shoulders with creamy white. "Don't worry, it dries really fast. And it's really, really *light*." She nudged it with a Finney riding boot and it inched forward as though on wheels.

Tildy suddenly loomed in her director's choir robe. "Holy J——!" She cut off her oath on a dime when she saw the headmistress. "What is that *thing*, Chloe?"

"Well, it's the Red Nun, Tildy. The painted one looked so flat— I thought you'd be so pleased. I wanted it to be a surprise. Don't you like it?"

"Well, isn't it a bit *big*? Where do you think we're going to put her?"

"Just where the painted one would have gone. In front of the trees. You can move her very easily."

"Then where do we put Marta's *bench*?" Tildy almost shrieked.

"Just where it always goes. All this does is give a three-dimensional effect. And we agreed she should be larger, at my house, remember?"

"That was when I thought you were going to *paint* her on the flat! This is just—a great big obstruction."

"Well, I, for one, am very impressed and very grateful to you girls," Mother Ravenel diplomatically intervened. "You have put your hearts into it, and I am sure this production is going to be one of the best ever in the annals of the school. And now Mr. Vick and I are going to go down into the audience, where we belong, and just enjoy the show."

She took Henry's elbow and they exited stage right. Henry's heart had been softening toward Mother Ravenel during the past weeks, when he had dropped by the school a number of times to measure stage spaces and calculate sight lines. He always phoned ahead——he knew how she disliked anyone "going around" her—and she always accompanied him to the auditorium, letting him in with her keys to the building Malcolm Vick had designed and keeping up a running commentary about the provenance of significant items backstage: the sky cyclorama, gift of the class of '36 ("This was a huge step forward because now we could do outdoor scenes . . ."), and then the great windfall of not just one but three professionally painted canvas drops left at the school in '42 by a touring company whose members were enlisting ("I was in charge of the girls' drama club then, and when the young men asked me if they might store these drops with us until after the war, I said, 'They will be here waiting for you when you get back, and in the meantime just think what the girls will be able to do with a forest, an ocean, *and* a drawing room!' That was the last I heard from those young men—I hope they survived—I still pray for them regularly—but what a godsend their drops have been in dozens of Mount St. Gabriel's performances!").

Henry's perception of her had undergone a shift. Always before, he had been used to regarding her, whether as his sister's classmate, his wife's best friend, or the headmistress of the academy, as a controlling person, jealous of her territory. This school was her life. She was, more and more as the years passed, its custodian, its legend keeper, its repository, its very chronology. (He had completely forgotten about his father's sideboard being a prop in *Charley's Aunt*.) He could hear her, years from now, proudly pointing out the polystyrene Red Nun to someone: "This was created and given to us in '52 by one of our girls, a very fine artist, and her uncle, the architect Henry Vick, whose father designed our auditorium . . ."

Now he saw—and this was what had softened his heart toward her—that this school was her fortress.

And, in the sense that all her plans and authority were invested within its borders, it was also her prison.

Twenty minutes before curtain time, the dressing room beneath the stage was a quivering hive of nerves, excited outbursts followed by shushes, and last-minute adjustments and vanities. Gilda Gomez decided Squire Wallingford needed a mustache and had drawn one on herself with an eyebrow pencil, incurring the wrath of the director, already in a snit over a monstrous prop sprung on her by her best friend without Tildy's knowledge or consent. Tildy told Gilda that her mustache lowered the play to a grammar school farce and ordered her to wash it off. Beatrix Wynkoop and Hansje Van Kleek, satisfied with their carefully prepared costumes for Father Maturin (cassock borrowed from Father Lohan, the resident priest) and Elizabeth's Thwarted Suitor (Mr. Van Kleek's dress suit and a Victorian clergyman's neckcloth fashioned from a linen napkin), were pinning a bow tie of crepe paper on Ashley Nettle's father's baseball umpire shirt to make their protégée look more like a gentleman auctioneer. Josie Galvin, in a St. Scholastica habit, was quietly going over her lines, even though she would be sitting behind a desk and could have the script in front of her when she "told the story of the Red Nun" to two 1920s students, Lora Jean Cramer and Mikell Lunsford, both of whom wore authentic dresses from that decade refurbished by their mothers. Kay Lee Jones, in her sculptor's smock, retilted her black beret to a cheekier angle; when she saw she was being observed by friends, she kissed her mirror image.

Dorothy Yount and Jiggsie Judd had stepped out to the garage where the Mount St. Gabriel's station wagon was kept to warm up their voices.

In the auditorium's basement lunch cafeteria for the day students, Madeline Stratton was doing her utmost to calm the director. Round and round the room they paced, Tildy in a full-blown snit.

"Take deep breaths, baby."

"I *can't* breathe!"

"Maybe you should sit down, then."

"I have to keep walking! If I sit down my legs will shake. *You* sit down if you're so tired."

"Of course I'm not tired. I came early with you to keep you company and be of help if I could, but tell me if you'd rather I go. It'll soon be curtain time anyway."

"I don't care whether you go or stay. No, stay! Oh jumping Jesus Christ, Maddy, you can't trust anybody!"

"This play is going to be wonderful, honey. You've just got stage nerves, which everyone says means good luck."

"How dare she! How *dare* she drag in that clumsy old piece of garbage! And act like she's Michelangelo or something, stretching to 'touch it up' with her professional little can of paint. Wearing old Finney's everlasting riding boots that Holy Agnes once wore when *she* played Fiona Finney. 'But Tildy, I thought you'd be so pleeeeased.' And old Ravenel flapping and gloating, as if she'd ordered the thing herself. What the damn hell business did *she* have backstage anyway? This is the ninth-grade play. You don't see Mother Malloy backstage, and she's our teacher. And you don't bring in props at the last minute that the actors haven't prepared for. Any moron knows that. We'd planned for it to be painted on the flat. Then she went behind my back at the last minute and purposely deceived me. I hate surprises! It's not her place to surprise me. Every time you try to share power with someone they stab you in the back!"

"But Marta is still going to be sitting on the bench as planned, you said. So nothing is changed except"—Madeline selected her words with extreme caution—"except that instead of the *painted* Red Nun on the grotto flat, there is now—uh, a *sculpted* one in front of it. And you alerted the girl who's playing the Sculptor—"

"Kay Lee Jones—oh, *she* was tickled pink. It draws more attention to her as the Sculptor to have something that actually looks like a sculpture."

"Well, then, see?"

"You don't *understand*! It throws things off! It throws *me* off! It's supposed to be my production, but now—practically at curtain time!—it's being taken away from me!"

"Nobody can take it away from you, honey. It's yours. You have put your stamp all over it, Mama says. Now let me kiss you and go upstairs. Trust me, it's going to be wonderful."

"Hmmmf!" snorted Tildy, going limp and letting herself be kissed. "I just may have a few surprises to spring, myself."

MAUD, WRAPPED IN the foundress's long cloak, whose heft and swing she had become as familiar with as those of her own coat, walked among the marble crosses in the nuns' cemetery. She felt—she was not sure what she felt. It wasn't nerves: she knew her lines. She had more lines than anyone else in the play, but she had assimilated them into herself. "The Holy Ghost will be blowing us onward . . ." and "It would be wrong in a way I can't find words for . . ." and "But, Rexy, God isn't something that can be shared, like a pet."

And though you could know your lines perfectly and still blank out due to stage fright, that wasn't a thing Maud feared, either, because she had become curiously removed from the ninth-grade play. She felt—oh, how Tildy would hate this!—that she was participating because her presence was required, but in her soul she was already somewhere else, even though she wasn't sure where that somewhere else was.

She was going into her fifth week as a boarder at Mount St. Gabriel's, with another full month to go after that. She'd had more confidential sessions with Mother Ravenel, who watched her avidly, as though waiting for some new part to sprout. She had spent much time alone with God, but, if anything, her chapel stints had rendered God less of a presence than ever. She knelt in silence and waited for Him to reveal His plan for her life, but so far He had seemed to feel Himself as remote from her drama as she felt remote from the urgencies of Tildy's play.

Well, in less than two hours it would be over. The actors would be mingling with parents and guests in the main parlor. In her weekly phone calls to her mother, Maud had kept mum about the play; she was too afraid they might decide to come, and then Art Foley would have to be introduced as her new father. She had more important things to think about right now. She had risked telling this to Mother Ravenel, who'd agreed, which Maud took as a good sign. It meant that even though the headmistress had yet to see signs of a sprouting vocation, she was already regarding her as separate from her family, which is what Maud would be if she—

Curiously, her absorption in her two roles, that of the nun who had crossed the sea with her best friend to found schools and that of the girl who chose not to take the veil because her best friend had come between her and God, had reduced Maud's scruples about latent deceitfulness in herself. They were all playing the game to win, Mother Ravenel, herself, and Tildy, and when the game was over she might or might not have committed herself in return for three more years at Mount St. Gabriel's. And even if she did announce her "intention," it wasn't set in stone: look at Antonia, whose conscience had made her abandon hers.

Maud paused before the foundress's cross.

Elizabeth Mary Wallingford

O.S.S.

1863–1930

Professed February 10, 1893

"Yes, I have been you, a little," Maud addressed the grave. "And now it's almost time to go backstage and in your name turn down Gilda Gomez's offer to set me up with a school for young ladies on the Wallingford estate. I'll have to tell the squire that I can't accept because 'the world does not need any more schools, Father, to teach girls how to stay home and do needlework and play the piano and manage the servants.' And then I'll go to Cowley with my poor spurned clergyman to hear the famous preaching of Father Maturin (Beatrix does a great job of belting out his lines in an English accent)."

On the road above, Jovan's grandson Mark, wearing a suit and tie, ran toward the auditorium, an extension cord clutched in his hand. Mark was doing the lighting and was in charge of operating the tape recorder with God's voice on it.

"Well, Mother Wallingford, I'm going in now, wearing your cloak. And under the cloak, I have on Granny's nightgown, which will do for your deathbed scene in act two—just a bit of white collar peeking above the counterpane. And under that I am wearing an actual dress belonging to Antonia Tilden—for the scene between Domenica and Rexanne, when Domenica writes something in an old exam book and hands it over to be read aloud by Suz—Rexanne.

"Help me to convey your true spirit, Mother, as it really was. And if you have a chance, put in a word for me with God. He doesn't seem interested in my dilemma. Maybe because—could it be that the whole thing is just playacting on my part?"

MOTHER RAVENEL STOOD up from her reserved front seat and rang a piercing little handbell.

"Good evening . . . good evening, everyone. On behalf of Reverend Mother Barrington and the entire faculty of Mount St. Gabriel's, I'd like to welcome parents, friends, and townspeople to the academy's final play of the school year. As many of you know, the freshman play is always the last, that is one of our traditions, and the play the girls will be presenting tonight has become a kind of tradition, too. As you will see in your program, *The Red Nun* was first presented by the freshman class of 1931. Tonight will mark its fifth revival by a freshman class. Another tradition that has grown up around this particular play is that each class may add its own material. In that way, each revival gives it new life. And now, everyone, please just sit back and enjoy—and the freshman class will do the rest."

All right, that's enough, thought Cornelia. *You've shown how modest you are—when your name is right there at the top of the program as the person who wrote the play. Sit the hell down.*

The house lights dimmed and out swept Elaine Frew in her wonderful dress. She sat down at the piano below the stage, fiddled importantly with the knobs of her bench, then, as though silently counting to ten, rested her hands loosely on her lap before launching into the overture she had just finished composing this afternoon: a fetching weave of

Bach partita, the Mount St. Gabriel's school song, and the flute overture her mother had composed for the 1931 premiere of *The Red Nun*.

A sigh of appreciation rippled through the audience: at least the music was going to be first-rate.

Music is everything, thought Elaine, serenely spotlit on her island of melody. *It shuts people up, it lifts them out of their boring selves—it is superior to all the other arts.*

A small girl with masses of flame-red hair slipped through the curtain parting and stood quietly in the apron while the piano notes dropped to a diminuendo. The spotlight shifted from Elaine to this girl in her black velvet dress with lace collar.

The music ceased, and Becky Meyer began to speak in her precise and rather impersonal voice: "We are here in the high mountains of North Carolina, but we must travel far back in time to tell you how we have come to be here."

She waited in a poised silence that went on a little too long for comfort before a sepulchral bass voice blared from behind the curtain:

"I . . . smashed . . . *con*-ti-nents . . . together . . . to . . . make . . . these *moun*-tains. . . . Sent *hun*-dreds of *mil*-lions of years of my wind and my rain . . . and *pol*-ished them with *my gla*-ciers . . ."

Someone backstage had quickly lowered the volume. *Mistake! Mistake!* thought Cornelia, wincing. *John sounds like someone doing a* parody *of "The Shadow knows." I should have listened to it myself and stopped it. But Smoky said it was all right and Tildy had worked so hard on the phrasing with John. If I had listened, I would have talked Tildy out of it, but who has time to run a business and listen to one's child's every brainstorm? Well, it's almost over, and then we have the spooky little prologue song Francine Barfoot wrote in 1931. Francine certainly looks well put together, though who wouldn't with all that Frew money—besides which, she doesn't have a career.*

> "If you go out walking in our dark wood
> When the hawk's face is tucked beneath his wing
> And the mist has risen in the hollows
> And the owl shrieks:
> Do not shrink if on your path
> You meet a solitary ghost.
> Ask it, 'What did you love most?
> And what have you left undone?' "

Until her husband elbowed her, Mrs. Yount didn't realize she had been humming along with her daughter up there on the stage. Mavis Yount had so thoroughly ingested that song that she sang it in her sleep.

"You don't know what is in you till you try."

The stately girl playing Elizabeth Wallingford, accompanied by her thwarted clergyman suitor (Hansje Van Kleek wearing her father's dark suit), was listening spellbound to Father Maturin, played by Beatrix Wynkoop, preaching in a priest's borrowed cassock against a forest backdrop.

"Dis-con-tent may be God's catapult, His way of prodding you . . . 'Go and try yourself now!' "

Beatrix's reading of the English priest's lines was masterly.

MOTHER FINNEY, UPSTAIRS in the balcony with the majority of the nuns, was, as always, dreading the "infirmary deathbed" scene in the second act of the play, but after having consulted her program had found herself pleasantly curious to see how this production was going to do without the "ocean crossing." And now that they had reached the last scene of the first act, in which "Elizabeth" and "Fiona" were walking in the woods, she understood and admired the cleverness and economy of it. Surely God was to be praised when even this wearisome adolescent play could be changed for the better by later adolescent girls.

What these girls had done was to take the gist of the dialogue of the two nuns at the ship's railing—a dialogue that had never existed except in Suzanne Ravenel's young imagination. If truth be told, which it hadn't, Lizzie had spent the entire voyage below in their cabin, sick as a dog, while she, Fiona, stood at the rail all by herself, thinking, What is this we have done? Were we mad to cross the sea? What these ninth-grade girls had done was to move the dialogue back to the time in Oxford when they were not yet professed but defining and planning their great adventure—and emboldening each other.

Even with her growing deafness she could hear that some of her St. Patrick's Day talk with young Chloe, Agnes's daughter, in the greenhouse had found its way into the script. Chloe must have taken her advice and checked out *Adventures with Our Foundress* from the school library. From what Mother Finney could hear, which was by no means everything, they had kept Suzanne's overall scheme and momentum but mixed in lines from *Adventures with Our Foundress*—things Lizzie had actually said. Though, generously, the girls had bestowed an equal amount of the dialogue's wisdom on "Fiona."

WALLINGFORD: We can do this, Fiona. The three of us can do this.

FINNEY: Indeed, the three of us can.

WALLINGFORD: The Holy Ghost will be blowing us onward, just as he did the Apostles in Acts. As long as we keep faith with holy daring.

FINNEY: Which is when you let yourself be guided by divine improvisation—

WALLINGFORD: Which is being in service to a work larger than yourself—

FINNEY: And being of one heart with others who belong together with you in that work.

The two girls paced eagerly back and forth in front of the woodland backdrop, the one wearing Lizzie's old cloak, the other Fiona's old riding boots.

And being of one heart with others who belong together with you in that work. Close to tears, Mother Finney found herself vigorously nodding, *yes, yes.*

MOTHER ARBUCKLE, THE infirmarian, had been hoping to have a word with Dr. Galvin during the intermission, but he was occupied with the Cuban fathers. She would catch up with him at the reception after the play. (*"Doctor, I've taken down a health history of Mother Kate Malloy, which I'd like to pass on to you. When she was nine she contracted streptococcal sore throat followed by acute bronchitis with high fever and was kept out of school for five weeks. The day she arrived at Mount St. Gabriel's, she fainted, but there have been no more episodes since, though she says she is sometimes lightheaded and feels a lack of stamina. She has trouble sleeping at night except in a raised position, then falls asleep at odd times during the day. Also she eats very little; the school diet doesn't agree with her. I was wondering about some tests to rule out possible early heart damage.")*

"I DON'T KNOW about you two," Cornelia said to her husband and Henry Vick in the lobby, "but I am bowled over by Tildy's streamlining of Suzanne's tired old pageant. Of course, I've been in on it with her from the start, but I must admit I didn't expect it to be this lively."

"It sure does move along," agreed Tildy's father. "Though I never saw the original. I hadn't even met Cornelia in 1931, much less imagined a Tildy in my future. But you saw it, Henry. How does it compare?"

"I missed a lot of it—I was nervous for my sister. She was playing Fiona Finney and was terrified that Mother Finney would be offended."

"Yes, Agnes did adore her dear Finney," Cornelia reflected, adding, with a touch of malice, "I know if I had been Finney, there were parts I could have done without. Especially that melodrama in the infirmary, which Tildy agreed with me needed to be toned down."

"And Father hadn't built the auditorium yet," Henry said. "The girls performed their plays on a platform stage in the old ballroom. Everything was right there in front of you, with no backdrop or curtain. The mistakes were more noticeable."

"Where has Madeline disappeared to?" Cornelia sounded as though she'd just remembered she had another daughter.

"She was going down to the dressing room to see if Tildy needed anything," said Henry, wondering why he should feel suddenly so bereft. It seemed to arise out of the evening's concatenation of events: Mother Ravenel recalling to him that his father's Sheraton sideboard had been used in *Charley's Aunt;* his little sister, Agnes, with her early crushes and later loves, buried under a Barlow gravestone with half her history missing from it. And Antonia gone, leaving behind her acerbic identical twin to remind him, year after year, how Antonia would look as she aged. There was some other element, but he could not catch hold of it. Perhaps something to do with Madeline. How she took care of people, gave herself over to what was needed—like driving Chloe to Barlow and back—and seemed to want nothing in particular for herself.

"Listen, Henry." Cornelia linked her arm through his. "Let's you and I switch seats when we go back in. I want to sit next to the Ravenel and see how she responds to the rest of the play."

CHAPTER 32

Act Two

THE HOUSE LIGHTS went down. The pianist glided to her instrument, and an elfin figure in a long-sleeved blouse and tights and a knee-length silver jerkin materialized in front of the curtain. A single F-sharp was struck, and the girl sang without further accompaniment into the semidarkness.

> "I am the spirit of this school
>   I am the one who remembers the true.
>   I am who safeguards what's really you."

Nita Judd felt her arms prickle at this wisp of a granddaughter with a voice like spun glass. Bless lovely Elaine Frew and bossy little Tildy Stratton for befriending poor Jiggsie and making her shine!

Now Elaine came in with a series of minor chords followed by some portentous tremolondos, and then Jiggsie's choirboy countertenor soared off on its own again.

> "Stories and legends have been told
>   Some more recent, others old;
>   Each had its motive, each its hour,
>   Each contributed to someone's power.
>   But I am the spirit who sifts and sorts
>   I am the one unafraid to report:
>   I am the friend who never will tire
>   Of showing you what actually transpired."

That child's voice is just uncanny, thought Mother Ravenel, in her left-front-row seat alongside the Stratton and Vick family party.

How smart of Tildy to create this part for Jiggsie: the Spirit of the School, who remembers what's gone before and safeguards the genuine person in each of us. That is what Mount St. Gabriel's is all about. And being included so prominently in the class play has done wonders for Jiggsie's morale. If she can just scrape by with a passing average, I will be able to write "Juliana is invited back" on her final report card and Nita Judd will let her board again next year, and everyone will have benefited. It is always a risk to put a girl back a grade, though in this case it seems to have worked, for which I thank You, Lord.

But, now, what was this bit about: "Each contributed to someone's power"? "Glory" would have been a more appropriate word—but then, of course, it wouldn't have rhymed with "hour."

When a smiling Cornelia had sat down next to Mother Ravenel after the intermission and offered warm compliments on the play, unadulterated by a single caustic note, the headmistress had gotten the definite feeling that she was at last being forgiven for having been loved by Cornelia's sister, Antonia. Had her act of giving Tildy the director-ship of the play finally convinced Cornelia that she was not the family's enemy?

It had been a risk, just as it had been a risk to put Nita Judd's granddaughter back a grade. But Mother Malloy's suggestion that Tildy needed larger outlets for her leadership qualities had spurred the headmistress to take that chance.

And so far things were surpassing expectations. This production, so far, *was* "both professional and lively" (Cornelia's own words). Although in Mother Ravenel's opinion, some changes hadn't needed to be made. Why, for instance, dispense with the lovely scene of the nuns crossing the ocean when at last the school had a professional ocean drop?

But now Becky Meyer, in her beautiful black velvet with the Belgian lace collar, had replaced Jiggsie in front of the curtain and was narrating how Elizabeth had become a Catholic and the two friends were professed as nuns, opened a school in Oxfordshire, were invited by the Benedictines in America to establish their teaching order there, and how, after successfully launching their academy in Boston, they heard from Father Maturin that greater challenges awaited them in the Appalachians, and, "charged by the Holy Ghost," they took the train to Mountain City, where they discovered that a hotel was up for sale.

Of course, Mother Finney's chapbook, with Elizabeth's "Charged by the

Holy Ghost" in its appendix, didn't exist when I was writing my play—she was still working on it!—but Chloe told me Mother Finney had said they might want to look at the chapbook if they needed more material. I strongly urged them to do this. And now the curtain is rising on the auction scene and Cornelia beside me has flashed me a very friendly "Here we go!" smile.

MOTHER MALLOY, NEXT to Mother Finney in the balcony, wished she could read the old nun's thoughts as she watched her younger self and a younger Elizabeth Wallingford being portrayed by Chloe Starnes and Maud Norton. At the moment, "Mother Wallingford," confident and statuesque in her cloak, was bidding for all the furniture. Ashley Nettle as Auctioneer managed to convey both rural suspiciousness and awe of this English nun.

> AUCTIONEER: But . . . madam, that's eighty furnished bedrooms alone, in addition to the public rooms. What are you going to do with all that furniture? How will you move it?
> WALLINGFORD: I'm not going to move it. It will stay where it is.
> AUCTIONEER: But . . . madam, this hotel is up for sale. The furniture will *have* to be moved.
> WALLINGFORD: Not if I buy the hotel, it doesn't.

The gangster-style riposte had Tildy's mark all over it. A gust of laughter rippled through the audience. A dry little chuckle erupted from Mother Finney herself.

Mother Malloy wondered what actually had been said by the English foundress that day in 1909. (And surely there must have been other bidders present.) Mother Finney, the only living bearer of the community's memory, most likely remembered, but tonight she was simply being an old nun in the balcony.

("Each class is an organism," Mother Ravenel had asserted categorically last autumn when, fresh off the train from Boston, Mother Malloy was being given the tour of the grounds and hearing troubling accounts about "her" upcoming ninth grade. "Yes, a class is never just a collection of individual girls, though it is certainly *that,* too, when you're considering one girl at a time. But a class as a whole develops a group consciousness. It's an organic unit, with its own special properties. . . . They are a challenging group, those girls. They will require control.")

But just before Christmas break, Mother Ravenel appeared to have reached new conclusions all by herself. ("What I'm seeing in your ninth grade are *several* clusters of girls, each with its sphere of interests. I don't see a nucleus of main girls anymore. I wonder whether, if a Mrs. Prince situation arose today, this class as it is now constituted could drive her off. What I think is, the breakup of Tildy and Maud and the influx of new girls has created new patterns and diluted old forces.")

This evening, Mother Malloy had prayed in the chapel for each performer in the play, from Andreu through Yount, calling up each face and the progress of that girl's year to date. And there had been wonderful instances of progress—witness jittery, scattered Ashley Nettle's humorous mastery of her role as Auctioneer.

And now, the curtain falling on the purchased hotel, Mother Malloy applauded with the rest of the audience and then closed her eyes and looked ahead toward her nightly examen:

Where have I, so far today, discerned God's presence?

One: in this play. I see Your presence in the joyful, sustained efforts of sixteen girls, counting our recently acquired Jiggsie. For me, their presentation embodies what the two young nuns in the last act were setting out to do: to be of service to a work larger than themselves and to be of one heart with those engaged in it. And that message, coming down from our foundress through Mother Ravenel's old script, revised and respoken by these present ninth graders, has given me new insight into my vocation.

Two: I felt Your presence this afternoon in the heedful and caring attentions of Mother Arbuckle, my sister in Christ, who summoned me for a vitamin B shot and then gave me tea while she took notes on my childhood illnesses.

"There could have been some scarring of the mitral valves during that bout of fever when you were nine, Mother. I want to send you to Dr. Galvin for tests, dear. It's just a shot in the dark on my part—I'm probably being overcautious because I worry about you—but it's best we rule it out."

"But what if your shot in the dark should prove right on the mark?"

"The doctor would probably recommend to Reverend Mother that you be transferred back to New England at the end of the school year.

The heart has to work so much harder at this altitude, which may account for your discomfort at night, your want of energy, and your meager appetite. Astonishing breakthroughs are being made every day in cardiovascular medicine, and if it turns out you do have a problem, you'll do better at sea level until you can have it fixed in Boston, with all its excellent hospitals. I would miss you, as all of us would, but you're of more use to God when you're feeling your best. Would you mind it very much?"

"When Reverend Mother ordered me to break off my graduate work and take the train to Mountain City, I must tell you, I did mind it. But I had known, from the day I put on my ring, that my 'minding' something was going to be beside the point for the rest of my life, and that I had chosen this. I think you know what I mean: our first meeting, when you told me how you decided not to turn on the car radio on your way to the hospital and how the connection with God was made in that first silence? Well, the practice closest to me now, the practice I find central to everything I do, is living every day and night as fully as I can in consultancy with God. The questions I ask and the insights that come out of the listening—I'm not saying this very well—but the more I live this way, the more I want to—to—*pray my life* rather than stumble through it."

"Ah, so you've got there, too," said the infirmarian. "Now I'm going to miss you more than ever. But let's hope I'm being overcautious. Then we can go on having these conversations."

THE CURTAIN ROSE on the classroom side of Henry Vick's twelve-foot reversible flat, framed by the blue cyclorama behind it. Chloe had painted exact copies of the Gothic Revival windows that the academy girls in their classrooms had gazed out of since the opening of the school.

Josie Galvin, in the St. Scholastica habit, hands folded nunlike on her desk, praised the two girls who had stayed after class to make up some work. She let herself be coaxed into telling the history of the school's first years. How the foundress and her teachers had to overcome local anti-Catholic sentiment:

NUN: They say a Mountain City man jumped off the streetcar when he saw two nuns from our Order getting on.

GIRLS: No! Really, Mother?

NUN: So the story goes. But we must keep in mind that stories are
often invented to point up the underlying state of things.

But that story is true, thought Maud, waiting in the wings in
Granny's white nightgown for the upcoming infirmary scene. *The man
who jumped off the streetcar was my own grandfather Roberts, who died before
I was born. He'd turn over in his grave if he knew what I have led Mother
Ravenel to think I might do to stay on at the school he wouldn't let my mother
attend. Would Lily Roberts's life have been different if she had been a Mount St.
Gabriel's girl? Would I even exist?*

Inexplicably, inconveniently, Maud suddenly missed her mother.

Now Josie Galvin was relating to the girls the history of the unfinished statue in the grotto: Caroline DuPree's death before she could
take vows, and then the death of the sculptor before he could finish her
memorial. The mothers of Mikell Lunsford and Lora Jean Cramer
earnestly mimed their daughters' responses, then merrily elbowed each
other when they realized they were doing it. The mothers were proud
of the authenticity of their girls' 1920s costumes, exhumed from family cedar chests and lovingly refitted and refurbished. Unfortunately,
neither father could be at the Friday night performance. Mr. Lunsford
had not yet returned from his week on the road for Electrolux, and Mr.
Cramer ("Why the dickens can't they hold their things on a Saturday
like the parochial school did?") was working his usual weekday evening
shift as train dispatcher.

THE CURTAIN FELL on the classroom scene and Mark and Jovan
hastened onstage to remove the desk and chairs, carried out the ghost
girl's bench, reversed the new flat so it was now the grotto, and set
in place an awkwardly shaped last-minute prop supposed to represent
the Red Nun. Some fresh white paint transferred itself to the lapel of
Mark's only suit, and he silently mouthed a ferocious stream of cuss
words.

Marta Andreu, in her mother's wedding dress, her face covered with
her own confirmation veil, entered stage right and began her ghostlike
float toward her bench. ("You want to move *como una fantasma,*" Tildy
had directed her. "Because that's what you are: the ghost of someone
who's no longer there but has to keep haunting the place that was im-

portant to her. Gilda, tell her to think of how a sleepwalker would walk: *como una sonámbula*.")

But this evening, confused by the placement of the polystyrene Red Nun she had never practiced with, Marta misjudged her footing, swayed, and dropped to her bench with very unghostly abruptness. Tildy, watching from the wings, was livid, but mercifully nobody in the audience laughed.

Dorothy Yount, the voice of Caroline DuPree's ghost, was already hidden behind the grotto flat. She nodded and counted through Elaine's opening bars, then came in right on pitch:

> "This is the ghostly hour
> When spirits float up through the fog
> If you listen you can hear my song:
> Here I have been happiest,
> Here let my spirit dwell.
>
> Inside the girlhood fortress
> That once ensheltered me
> I dreamed a wondrous dream
> Of the person I wanted to be
> But in Your almighty design
> You sealed me in red rock instead.
> 'Take this for your cloister, daughter of mine:
> Be a fortress for others,' You said."

Then she repeated the whole song again, Elaine playing diminuendo this time, because Tildy said people needed to hear a song through twice to take in all the words.

If I do say so myself, Mother Ravenel thought proudly, *that little aria has stood up to the test of time.*

Marta rose and exited offstage with fully regained ghostly grace. The blue spotlight from above continued to shine on her empty bench, which Mother Ravenel thought was an inspired idea on somebody's part. But Mark at the lighting board, spellbound by Marta in her lovely dress and veil, had simply forgotten to turn it off.

Out trotted the Funerary Sculptor, Kay Lee Jones, in smock and beret, carrying a chisel and mallet, determined to take advantage of the opportunities provided by her new prop. Tiptoeing around the figure of the Red Nun, creeping up, then backing off, tilting her head this way and that, she acted to the hilt the artist assessing his work in progress and in doing so managed to add several minutes to her part.

Then, continuing to pace about, she recited her speech without flubbing a single line:

> "You will find my statuary in parks and cemeteries all over these United States.
>
> I am the one they send for to restore the fallen hero to his horse, to mount stern angels above the graves of children.
>
> I work from photographs and descriptions given to me by the bereaved. But I also have an instinct for feeling my way to the essence of the departed one.
>
> This girl perished before she could realize her desire to take the veil. She was a slim, slight girl in her yearbook pictures. But another side of her is revealing itself through this red marble, which was sent by mistake.
>
> I am not in the prime of life anymore, nor in the pink of health, but I will trust in God to let me complete what I can and make it acceptable in His sight."

Kay Lee's mother, the court recorder, went limp with relief. The speech was much too long and concentrated and high-flown for such a short part in a school play, and she had worked for weeks on it with Kay Lee, who had wept and raged and said Tildy and Mother Ravenel ought to have it shoved down their throats. "Listen," said Ruth Jones to her daughter, "we are not quitters. If I could completely retrain my brain and fingers and thumbs to operate that infernal stenotype machine so I could make a decent living for us after your dad died, you can memorize these lines. And we've been over them enough so that you can fudge it if you have to. If you forget the lines, just tell the story in your own words."

Tildy, who trusted no one but herself with the curtain, brought it down to enthusiastic applause. Well, Kay Lee Jones had certainly milked *her* part to the fullest, thanks to that ingrate Chloe's "surprise" horror of a prop, which had almost tripped Marta. But things were going so well, she couldn't be as mad at Chloe as she felt she had a right to be. Only two more scenes to go! Next: the infirmary scene, to which she had added some very good material from old Finney's chapbook—and that, to be fair, was thanks to Chloe, who had read it aloud to her so she could listen with her eyes closed and see what flagged her inner vision. Mark and Jovan had reversed the grotto back to the Gothic Revival windows, which would now serve as a wall in the infirmary, and were carrying in the cot and chair for Mother Wallingford's deathbed scene with Mother Finney. And here was Maud in her granny's gown, her head wrapped in gauze to simulate a nun's boudoir cap, slipping beneath the blanket, and Chloe, in the St. Scholastica habit, seating herself in the bedside chair.

The curtain went up on the dying foundress turned away from the audience while Mother Finney silently prayed the rosary.

WALLINGFORD: *(Moans.)*

FINNEY: How I wish I could do something!

WALLINGFORD: You can.

FINNEY: Tell me what.

WALLINGFORD *(making an attempt at humor):* You can take half of my pain.

FINNEY: You know I would if I could.

WALLINGFORD *(shifting in bed so her face can be seen):* Do you remember some of the names we considered for our Order?

FINNEY *(laughing):* God pity us, I do.

WALLINGFORD: When there she was all along, waiting for us to get past all our Societies of Holy Ghosts and Spirits and our long-winded Communities of This-and-That-Kind of Education and—oh! *(Clasps her wrapped head in pain.)*

FINNEY *(jumping up):* Please, tell me, what can I do?

WALLINGFORD: You can sit down and help me relive our amazing adventure while I still have brains enough to give thanks for it.

FINNEY *(Sits down and pulls herself together.):* St. Scholastica. Everything we needed in a name.

WALLINGFORD: A holy woman of intelligence and feeling—the perfect name for an order dedicated to the education of women.

FINNEY: And twin sister of St. Benedict himself. She had put herself under his rule.

WALLINGFORD: For all we know she may have helped him write it. And when he went all priggish and unfeeling when she begged him to stay overnight on a visit, she prayed and God sent a wild storm so he had to stay under her roof.

FINNEY: And glad he was that he did. For she died three days later.

WALLINGFORD (*clasping her head again, but forcing herself to go on*): And do you remember some of our worst designs for our habit? That awful bonnet!

FINNEY: But, lucky for us, you said, "Not very practical for a teaching order of nuns who need all the side vision they can get."

WALLINGFORD: No, dear friend, it was you who said that.

So far, I would give this production an A, Mother Ravenel told herself. No, perhaps an A minus: that voice of God on the tape recorder caused inappropriate laughter. However, Tildy was wise to keep the sculptor's speech exactly as it was. Some things come out right the first time and can't be improved on. But how glad I am that I urged her and Chloe to consult Mother Finney's chapbook, which I didn't have the benefit of, back when I was writing the play. This infirmary scene has benefited considerably from the tone of Mother Finney's memoir.

Tildy had shed her director's choir robe before she brought the curtain down on the deathbed scene, and Maud was simultaneously stepping out of her granny's gown and ripping off her gauze boudoir cap so she would have time to reassemble her hair for the role of Domenica. They had practiced this quick change in the tower, whenever the two of them went up to rehearse the "hidden scene."

Both of them wore 1930s outfits that Tildy had discovered, along with the trigonometry exam book, stowed under the window seat in Antonia's old room. Cornelia had helped Tildy choose from the clothes. ("This was our most successful number during our senior year—girls died of envy when Tony and I came to school in those dark green knits with the scarlet trim and gold buttons. What a fool I was not to have held on to mine! Maud as Domenica should wear that one, and then we'll put you in one of the lesser numbers and make a few alterations to suit the character of Rexanne. Maybe a Peter Pan collar.")

"I HOPE YOU are enjoying this as much as I am," Cornelia said to the headmistress as they waited for the curtain to go up on the final scene.

"From what I saw in the rehearsal Tildy invited me to, I had high expectations, but I'll confess to you, Cornelia, tonight's performance has exceeded even those."

"Oh, I'm so *glad,* Mother." Cornelia's new friendly mode bordered on the gushing. She consulted her program and quoted: " 'Two later students/best friends, Rexanne and Domenica. In the grotto.' Have you any idea what *that's* about?"

"From what Maud tells me, Domenica—that's Maud's part—is trying to discern whether or not she has a vocation. It's a new cameo scene the girls have worked up together. I was dying to know more, but I don't like to pry. Each class is allowed to contribute new material, that's the tradition, so we'll just have to wait and see."

"You are perfectly right, Mother," Cornelia crooned, laying her hand briefly on the headmistress's sleeve. "We'll just have to wait and see."

I have kept Maud's secret, Mother Ravenel congratulated herself. *Wouldn't it be exciting, though, if she revealed her decision as "Domenica" in this new cameo scene? It would be a message from her to me, because no one else would know. And what Maud still doesn't know is that it's going to be all right for her whether she decides she has a vocation or not. The money will be found— I will see to it—for her to board at Mount St. Gabriel's: there is always a surplus in the discretionary fund due to the nonrefundable fees and the interest they bring. She is a fine student and will be a credit to the school, whatever she decides. And who knows? Three more years with us may still reveal a vocation. You work according to Your own timetable, Lord.*

And now the curtain was going up.

"WITH MY POOR hearing I missed much of it," old Mother Finney later confessed to Mother Malloy after the infirmary scene, "but I liked the parts I heard. It caught her personality. Your girls have done a fine job. You must be very proud of them."

"Yes, I am, Mother. I've also learned a great deal from them."

(During the evening, some treasured lines from Hopkins had roused themselves in her and had been spooling through her brain like a precious recovered melody.

> I have desired to go
> Where springs not fail,
> To fields where flies no sharp and sided hail
> And a few lilies blow.

That is what we will do on Monday, Mother Malloy thought, excited. I will write those lines on the board, saying them aloud as I write, marking where the stresses fall. And then we will go through the verse together, sounding it out, discovering for ourselves what makes it strong and rare. I won't overload them with the terminology of prosody. We will learn it closer to the method and spirit in which he composed it, walking the English landscape as a young Jesuit. And coaching Tildy has given me this inspiration.)

MAUD AS DOMENICA, in Antonia's dark green knit with the scarlet trim and gold buttons, sat alone on the bench in the grotto. She was writing slowly and with effort in the back of an exam book.

DOMENICA: "Dear Rexanne . . ." No . . . too formal. Best to dispense with any salutation and get right to what I have to say. Or will that be too cruel? Even if it's true? But I *have* to say it. It's true.

Enter Tildy as Rexanne.

REXANNE *(accusingly):* Domenica! I've been looking for you everywhere!

DOMENICA: Well, here I am.

REXANNE: What are you doing?

DOMENICA: I was trying to draft a letter.

REXANNE *(jealously):* A letter to whom?

DOMENICA: It doesn't matter since I probably won't send it.

REXANNE *(sitting down close to her friend):* I hate it when you go all distant and remote.

DOMENICA: All of us have remote places in ourselves, where we
    go to be alone with God.
REXANNE *(unhappily):* I thought God was something we shared.

Where is this going? Mother Ravenel asked herself, puzzled. *If
"Domenica" is supposed to represent a present-day girl, why is Maud wearing
that outfit? It's in the style of* my *high school days, twenty years ago. Wait,
don't I remember both twins coming to school in that exact outfit? The clothes
Mrs. Tilden sewed for Antonia and Cornelia were so beautiful they could make
your heart ache.*

DOMENICA: But, Rexy, God isn't something that can be shared,
    like a pet.
REXANNE: What are you trying to say? Aren't we going to take
    our vows together—to the same God—at the end of the
    school year?

*If "Domenica" isn't Maud, then who is she? And who is this "Rexanne"
played by Tildy, also wearing clothes from my era—I had a Peter Pan collar
like that, which I wore with many outfits. I used to soak it in bleaching powder
to keep it nice and white—I didn't have a mother who made me stylish clothes,
so I had to make do with what I had.*

DOMENICA: Oh, Rexy. That was what I was trying to write to you
    in my letter, only it wasn't coming out very well.
REXANNE: Your letter was to me? Domenica, I don't understand.
    Are you telling me something has changed about our plans to
    enter the Order together? The way our foundress and *her* best
    friend did?
DOMENICA: We are not *them,* Rexy. Look, Rexy, perhaps you had
    better read this. *(She hands the exam book to Rexanne.)*
REXANNE *(slowly reading aloud):* "Since that evening at the Swag,
    Rexy, I have been wondering whether we should go on with
    our plans. Something tells me it would be wrong in a way I
    can't find words for. Only that there is a good reason for
    things, but when you know there ought to be a better reason,
    then the good can turn bad . . ."

At the word "Swag," Mother Ravenel's mind began moving very fast, and even before she turned and confronted the gleeful side glance Cornelia had trained on her, she was calculating just what she had to do to minimize the damage and in just what order and style she had to do it.

I have been set up, she acknowledged, *but now is not the time to analyze it. With the exception of Cornelia, these are just ninth graders. Their brains have not finished developing yet. I can still outmaneuver them.*

And even as Domenica, on stage, was telling her best friend that she, Rexy, had come between her and God and "diluted her vocation," Mother Ravenel, program in hand, was mounting the stairs to the stage.

She entered the play.

"Yes, here I am," she addressed the audience in her authoritative stage voice, standing behind the seated girls transfixed in shock.

"As we all know from Charles Dickens's *A Christmas Carol,* there are ghosts from the future as well as the past."

She gestured to Chloe's polystyrene prop. "This unfinished statue that we call our Red Nun memorializes a girl who died before she could take vows. She is a ghost from these girls' past, and I am a ghost from their future. These two girls you see here, Domenica and Rexanne, whoever they were, did not take vows together. One of them had a vocation; the other discerned that she did not. Discernment is all: each of us is required to discern, to the best of our ability, God's plan for our life. That is what we strive to teach at Mount St. Gabriel's. But what we always have to remember is—" Here she paused and magnanimously stretched out her arms like an angel guarding the two stunned girls on the bench and embracing the audience as well. "We are, each of us, a work in progress. Every one of us in this auditorium tonight is a work in progress—and will be until our very last breath."

Another pause for effect. (You could have heard a pin drop!)

"And now, we will bring down the curtain on tonight's performance and"—consulting her program—"the Spirit of the School will sing her Farewell Song, after which our pianist will play the school song as a recessional. Please withhold any applause, but do sing along with us if you know the words. After that, everyone is invited to a reception in the main parlor."

Then still in the guise of "speaking her lines," she instructed ashen-faced Tildy and Maud to remain frozen in place on the bench "like a *tableau vivant,* girls," after which she marched off to close the curtain herself, sending out Jiggsie Judd to sing the farewell.

> "I burn for you with sacred fire
>   Of my faithful commission I never tire
>   My pitiless light routs out dark schemes
>   My passionate flame rekindles dreams . . ."

After Jiggsie vanished through the slit between the curtains, a disobedient flutter of enthusiastic applause was quickly drowned out by Elaine Frew's fortissimo segue into the school song: words by Mother Elizabeth Wallingford to Edward Elgar's "Pomp and Circumstance."

> "Hail to thee, bright angel, guardian of our school . . ."

CHAPTER 33

Aftermath

Friday night, April 25, 1952
Mount St. Gabriel's buildings and grounds

"THIS SURE WASN'T the way it ended in Mikell's script!" Mrs. Lunsford protested to Mrs. Cramer beside her.

"Nor in Lora Jean's, either," said Mrs. Cramer. "The Narrator was supposed to sum up how each scene represented something in the school's history and then announce each girl by the name of her part, and that girl was supposed to come out and either bow or curtsy. Lora Jean's dad worked with her on her bow. She said she didn't feel confident enough to curtsy in front of a crowd."

"Who ever did? Oh, well, it was probably another of Tildy Stratton's last-minute additions. Mikell says she's in thick with the headmistress."

"That figures. Lora Jean said Mother Ravenel and Tildy's mother were classmates."

"You think maybe it was planned, then? *Her* rushing up on stage like that at the end?"

"I really couldn't say. But still. It was supposed to be the *ninth-graders'* play."

"THAT BITCH—THAT DEVIL—" Cornelia Stratton did not bother to lower her voice. Nobody could hear her anyway, what with Elgar's grandiose march being thumped out by Francine Frew's self-important daughter and the audience in complete disarray, some standing, some singing, others talking and making their way to exits, uncertain of what was required of them.

"Mama, what *is* it? What has happened?"

"Isn't it obvious, Madeline? That controlling fiend has sabotaged my child's play."

"But how? I don't understand—"

"Of course you wouldn't. You were with Cynthia's family at Myrtle Beach over Easter break while I was working with her every night, no matter how exhausted I was from my day at the studio. I knew every line—every change in that script. All we meant to do was plant a hidden little reminder, shake her out of her complacency. All *she* had to do was sit still and let them say *all* their lines and then let Becky reiterate what everything stood for in the summation, which I helped Tildy with myself. Nothing was going to embarrass her publicly; I had seen to that. I just wanted her to know that *we* knew her dirty little secret. But her guilty heart couldn't stand it. She commandeered a school play and robbed Tildy of her rightful ending."

Madeline realized from this outburst that her mother was very much implicated in tonight's mischief. But meanwhile, what about Tildy?

"Shouldn't we go and see about Tildy?"

"Dear Maddy, always concerned for others. But you're right. Let's go."

WHILE THE ROUSING Elgar tune still exerted some binding power upon the dispersing audience, Mother Ravenel was starting damage control behind the closed curtain. She summoned the full cast to the stage.

"Girls, tonight some things did not go according to plan. My entrance into your play was a surprise to everyone, including myself. I had to think very fast. I had to make a quick decision in order to prevent worse harm. How many of you, besides the two actors involved, knew about the scene between Domenica and Rexanne? If you were aware of it, raise your hand."

Girls exchanged nervous glances. No one raised a hand. It was Becky Meyer who finally spoke: "We knew there was going to be a scene about two friends, Mother, but since the director was working on it till the last minute, it was blocked in, but not rehearsed. All we knew was that it came after the infirmary scene and would last about seven minutes, and then after that was Jiggsie's farewell song and then the

Narrator was to sum up how the scenes represented major threads in the school's history."

"I'm sorry you didn't get to make that summation, Rebecca. Do you have it with you?"

"Yes, Mother." The Narrator pulled a much-folded paper from the pocket of her dress and handed it over to the headmistress, who efficiently skimmed it, nodding as she went along, then returned it to Becky.

"Now, I'll tell you what we are going to do, girls. When the reception in the main parlor is in full swing, I am going to ring my little bell for silence and announce to our guests that we have a postlude to the play. And then, Rebecca, you will step forward and do your summation, after which you'll call each girl by the name of her role—the Auctioneer, the Sculptor, and so on; I see from your script that had been the plan—and each will come forward and take her bow. That is what we are going to do."

"We will stay in our costumes, Mother?" Squire Wallingford asked.

"Thank you for reminding me, Gilda. Yes, everyone will stay in costume." The headmistress allowed her cool glance to take in Domenica and Rexanne, still frozen in place on the bench in their 1930s outfits. "And now, girls, go downstairs to the dressing room and freshen up—staying in costume, of course—and then go right along to the reception. Tell everyone you mingle with that we have the postlude still to come, but meanwhile to enjoy the refreshments. Tildy and Maud—remain here with me."

Having checked that nobody was lingering backstage to eavesdrop, Mother Ravenel addressed her prey.

"What was it you girls were hoping to convey to the audience in your highly secret little scene?"

"We didn't—" Maud shakily began.

"The scene was interrupted," cut in Tildy, "so *nothing* got conveyed."

"You are divaricating, Tildy, and I think you know it. I'll ask another way: who are Domenica and Rexanne meant to represent?"

"They represent nobody," Tildy declared with a set jaw. "They're made-up characters. Two best friends. One will turn out to have a vocation, and one won't. It was a scene about"—triumphantly she snatched a word from the air—"*discernment*. Which is a very important thing we learn at Mount St. Gabriel's. You said so yourself when you—"

But the headmistress's attention had shifted to the exam booklet on Tildy's lap. "Let me see that."

"You can't take it!" protested Tildy. "It belongs to our family. I found it in Aunt Tony's old things."

But Mother Ravenel, having noted the name and the date on its blue cover, was leafing through the booklet. When she came to the handwritten message inside the back cover, her brows slightly lifted. She read it through, then rolled up the booklet and thrust it into the pocket of her habit.

"That is all we have time for now," she said. "You are both excused from the reception. Maud, you may go straight to the dormitory. We will talk in the morning."

"But—couldn't I—stop off at the chapel first, Mother?"

The nun cast a cold eye on the beseeching girl wearing Antonia's beautifully sewn dress with the scarlet trim and gold buttons. The stockings and the shoes were also of that era. Possibly they, too, had been Antonia's. What a devilish lot of work must have gone on in the Stratton household to perfect this aborted little treachery. But why had Maud lent herself to something so detrimental to her own interests?

"I think not, Maud. Your chapel time doesn't seem to have profited you very much." She saw from the girl's shattered expression that Maud was realizing exactly what had been lost.

Mother Ravenel suddenly felt both very tired and very young, as if she were going to have to live through everything over again in order to understand why she had made certain decisions when she was their age. And she still had to get through tonight's reception and make sure that the postlude was properly executed.

She turned on her heel and left the disgraced pair huddled on the bench.

Tildy was the first to rise. She paced back and forth a few times, then made a rush at Chloe's stage prop of the Red Nun and began kicking it savagely. Her foot striking the polystyrene made a raspy crumbling sound.

"Putrid old prop! Never, *ever* share power with anyone. They'll stab you in the back every time. That's when this whole damn evening started going wrong, when she sprang that abomination. And then acting like the *artiste,* whipping out her little can of spray paint to 'highlight' it. Ha! I wonder if—?" Tildy bolted offstage and returned waving the can of spray paint.

"What are you going to do?" cried Maud.

"Wait and see." Tildy shook the can violently and began spraying wobbly white letters across the chest of Chloe's prop:

S-A-T-I-N

R-A-V-E-N-E-L

She spun around, exultant. "Pretty damn accurate, no?"

"I don't get it. Why the 'satin'?"

"It's not *satin,* you stupid ass. It's *Satan.*"

"Oh, Tildy."

"Oh, Tildy, *what*?"

"Oh, Tildy—dear Tildy—"

Moments ago, Maud had been far from finding anything funny, but now she was released into laughter.

"Well, *what*?" demanded Tildy.

"Oh, Tiddle-dy—'Satan' is with two *a*'s."

Tildy's face was a thundercloud. "I told you never to call me that again. It's nasty and condescending. But I guess you need to get some of your own back after having to knuckle under me as your director all these weeks."

"Oh, Tildy! I didn't mean anything nasty—and I was laughing because the whole thing is just so—you."

"My awful spelling, you mean. Well, I promise you that's one word I'll never misspell again."

CORNELIA AND MADELINE went below to the dressing room, where agitated girls consulted in small groups or checked themselves in the mirror.

"Has anyone seen Tildy?" asked Madeline.

Chloe, in her nun's habit from playing Mother Finney, came over to them. "They're still up there—on the stage. Mother Ravenel wanted to see Tildy and Maud alone."

"Let's go," Cornelia snapped, not bothering to acknowledge Chloe.

She dragged Madeline back up the stairs, but as soon as they reached the top they were waylaid by parents and acquaintances leaving the auditorium.

"Cornelia! you must be so proud!"

"I thought it was extremely accomplished for their age, didn't you?"

"They must have worked awfully hard!"

"But please, Cornelia, enlighten me so I won't make a fool of myself at the reception—what was that last scene all about?"

Cornelia pushed through the cordon of chatter, her hand locked around Madeline's wrist. "Why not ask Mother Ravenel?" she called back.

ONSTAGE BEHIND THE curtain, they found only Maud in Antonia's clothes, slumped disconsolately on the bench. "Where is my daughter?" demanded Cornelia.

"Mrs. Stratton, I don't know. She sprayed that—prop, and then she ran off in a rage. She was mad at me because I told her 'Satan' was spelled with two *a*'s."

"Listen, Maud," Madeline gently coaxed; she could see the girl was trying not to cry. "What happened with Mother Ravenel? Chloe said she kept you two behind."

"She was very put out—really cold. It was scary how cold she was. She asked Tildy who the girls in the scene were meant to represent and when Tildy said nobody real, they were just representative of—you know—discernment—she accused her of divaricating."

"A pet skewering word of hers," Madeline couldn't help interjecting. "Then what?"

"Then—then she—took the booklet and looked through it and—and confiscated it. She told us we were excused from the reception. She told the rest of the cast to keep on their costumes. They're going to do a postlude at the reception to clear up any confusion about the play. And—" Here Maud's voice broke. "She forbade me even to go to the chapel. When I leave here, I am to go straight to my room in the dormitory. I think I am going to be sent away."

SMOKY STRATTON AND Henry Vick awaited Cornelia and Madeline outside in the balmy darkness, romantically lit by the former hotel's Victorian gas lamps—now electrified—along the drive.

"Well, how are our girls?" Smoky asked.

"Mother Ravenel kept Tildy and Maud onstage by themselves for an inquisition," Cornelia reported. "And now Maud is alone onstage in tears and Tildy has sprayed 'Satan Ravenel' on that prop of the Red Nun, only she spelled it 'Satin' and when Maud corrected her she ran off in a rage."

"Oh, me," said Henry. "Did you see Chloe?"

"Chloe is still in her Mother Finney nun costume downstairs. Mother Ravenel, it seems, has arranged a little 'postlude,' to be presented by the cast during the reception. To clear up any confusion anyone may have about the play. But she has excused Tildy and Maud from the reception."

"In that case, what do we want to do now?" Smoky asked his wife.

"What *I* want to do is slap that woman's face—in front of everybody—or come up with a satisfactory equivalent."

"In that case, darling, I'll wait for you outside."

"That might be best," said Cornelia. "Just don't take too many nips from the glove compartment because I am far too mad to drive us home."

"I was planning to get *the flashlight* out of the glove compartment," her husband mildly reproached her, "and start looking for Tildy."

"I'll go with you, Daddy," said Madeline.

"No," said Cornelia, "I want you to come with me to the reception. Tildy may show up there to watch this 'postlude' that's being tacked onto her play. I certainly would, in her place. What has she got to lose now?"

"What do you mean, Mama?"

"It doesn't take a sleuth, Maddy, to see the writing on the wall. Tildy's career at this place is finished. Maud's, too, from the sound of it."

"Let's just *find* Tildy first," her father suggested, digging in his pocket for car keys.

"I'll come with you, Bernard," said Henry Vick. "I'll get my flashlight, too."

It was a rare occasion, thought Madeline, as the two men set off for the parking lot, when someone called Daddy by his Christian name rather than the nickname Mama had awarded him as an engagement present. Her heart went out to her uncle, who always seemed to know the right thing to do.

BECAUSE OF HER increasing deafness, Mother Finney avoided school receptions, except for the Feast of Our Lady and graduation, preferring to help Betty replenish the serving trays in the kitchen or get a head start on the washing up, but tonight the old nun moved resolutely through the main parlor, nodding and shaking hands with parents and old students, accepting their congratulations on Chloe Starnes's fond depiction of her. Chloe was why she had offered herself to this din, where all sounds, from the clatter of a fork to a loud laugh, were rendered equal in volume by her undiscerning new hearing aid. She wanted to thank Agnes's daughter, and to give her a hug, for taking the trouble to consult *Adventures with Our Foundress,* and for restoring some of Mother Wallingford's bold spirit to the play—particularly how Lizzie would tease, or even torment, you to ward off your pity. These girls, God bless them, had banished melodrama from the mortifying deathbed scene, and how delighted she was to have stayed alive long enough to see it gone!

ACTING ON A hunch of Henry's, Smoky Stratton and Henry Vick had gone to the grotto, where their two flashlights now played on the spray-painted Red Nun.

"Kilroy was here, all right," said Tildy's father.

"And 'Satan' correctly spelled this time," Henry wryly noted.

"Good work, Henry. We're on the trail. Where to next?"

"Chloe might know something. Let's go find her at the reception."

"You go, Henry. I'll stay out here and look a few more places. I've about had it with Mount St. Gabriel's. A good local Catholic education is one thing, but there's just too much bad history between Cornelia and her old nemesis. Tildy's benefited a lot from Mother Malloy this year, but next year she'll be better off with Madeline over at Mountain City High."

HAVING SCOUTED FOR Tildy in the academy's upstairs classrooms and bathrooms, Cornelia hastened them along the trophy corridor to the reception. She was glittery-eyed and overstimulated—dangerously so, Madeline felt. You could all but see the sparks of malice shooting ahead of her.

"Let's mingle, until I decide what to do," Cornelia instructed Madeline when they reached the main parlor. "There's the archfiend herself being fawned on by Francine Frew. Keep a sharp eye out for Tildy—I think she'll show up, one way or another." She gave a malign chuckle.

"*What*, Mama?"

" '*Satin* Ravenel.' I'm afraid I was just fantasizing how Tildy might suddenly creep up behind the headmistress and spray it on her back, right in front of everybody. Spelled properly this time, thanks to our erudite Maud. There's Rebecca's mother; I might as well start with her. She might know something I don't."

The last time Madeline had been in the main parlor was on registration day, back in September, when Cornelia was too busy to accompany Tildy. That day Tildy had been shooting sparks herself, after the unhappy confrontation with Maud, who had just returned with "airs" from Palm Beach. Tildy had blazed up at Madeline in the little side room off the main parlor where the new ninth-grade teacher was holding her interviews, and Madeline, seeing that her little sister was about to lose control, had sent her off in search of Henry and Chloe. She'd stayed behind to talk with the beautiful nun from Boston and explain a few things about the bitcheries at Mount St. Gabriel's, but most of all to put in a few words about Tildy's intrepid but fragile young soul.

Now she spotted Mother Malloy speaking to the Dutch parents over by the Infant of Prague, still in his Easter robes. Madeline waited until they were finished and then stepped forward, rewarded to see the nun's weary countenance brighten.

"Oh, Madeline, how glad I am to see you."

"Oh, Mother, I was just remembering how we met in these rooms last fall, when I brought Tildy to registration."

"And you know what I enjoy remembering? That day in the grotto when you told me about that girl's poem that sent you into hysterics and got you in so much trouble—the one about Elizabeth Wallingford's 'pulchritudinous hair'—I don't think I have laughed so hard since. Madeline, what did you make of tonight's play?"

"It was going great, then something went very wrong at the end."

"I thought so, too. Have you seen Tildy?"

"Daddy and Uncle Henry are looking for her outside. She ran off in a rage, Maud said. And Mother Ravenel sent Maud to the dormitory. She has 'excused' both of them from the reception."

"That seems hard."

"Yes, well, she was really offended by that last scene with the two girls on the bench."

"I couldn't understand where that was headed. And when Mother Ravenel went up onstage, I was completely at sea."

"She thought they were mocking her in that scene. That Domenica was based on my aunt Antonia and that Rexanne was based on herself, Suzanne, back when they were going to enter the Order together."

"*Was* it based on them, Madeline?"

"From what I've been able to gather, it was, Mother. It was supposed to be just a hidden message, addressed to Mother Ravenel alone, but she ran up onstage and stopped it before it could be finished— I mean, accounted for in a symbolic way. Now she's arranged for some kind of 'postlude' during the reception so people won't go home in confusion."

"Ah, confusion," repeated Mother Malloy, the brightness having drained from her countenance. "But where do you think Tildy is?"

"EVERYONE! MAY I please have your attention? Thank you. Friends, we have a surprise for you. There is going to be a postlude, a very short one, to the play you have just seen. Some of you may have been puzzled by the ending. I see you nodding. You thought you were missing something, yes? Well, you were. After the School Spirit's farewell song, there was supposed to be a brief but important coda by the Narrator in which she explained how each scene represented a major thread in the school's history. But this coda got left out. Yes, it got left out. Tonight's production of *The Red Nun* contained some ambitious new experiments, and some of them turned out well, while others did not. But we are not going to send you home baffled. As I said earlier, we are all works in progress, and this play, first performed by the freshman class in 1931, continues to be a work in progress, too. And now I'm going to turn this over to the present ninth grade. Just stand back and make a space for them."

Rebecca Meyer stepped forward and began to read from a paper in her meticulous, rather detached voice:

"Tonight we have traveled far back in time to tell you how we came to be. We have overheard God planning our school even before its mountains were in place. We have seen the mist rising in its dark woods and heard the owl shriek while the hawk sleeps. On its paths we have met ghosts who sang to us because we knew the right questions to ask: what did you love most and what have you left undone?"

Scanning the reception crowd, Henry Vick failed to locate his niece. He thought it probable that Chloe was off somewhere with Tildy, helping her lick her wounds. That's what friends were for. The two of them had worked so passionately on this wretched play. Hours and hours at his house. He had spent hours on it himself. Suddenly he saw its ridiculous and depressing side: a school play, written by his sister's ambitious classmate back in the thirties. His late wife, Antonia, had played the foundress, wearing her cloak, the same old English cloak Maud Norton wore tonight. His late sister had played Mother Finney, wearing the same old Irish riding boots Chloe had worn tonight. Why were they all still in harness on this moribund merry-go-round?

Preferring the darkness, he went outside again and leaned against a spindle corner post on the west porch. In night-lit Mountain City below, he could pick out many of his father's buildings. Earlier this month had been the groundbreaking for his own library—the hated columns to be tacked on so people could keep living in their fantasies of what the past was like.

Chloe might be better off over at Mountain City High with the Stratton girls. He could tell that Bernard's "I've about had it," meant business. Once, earlier in the school year, Chloe had said that if Tildy ever got kicked out of Mount St. Gabriel's for bad grades, she would feel like a ghost wandering its halls.

Had the living Vicks as well as the living Strattons "about had it" with its halls and Victorian spindle posts and Gothic Revival windows and the company of its ghosts?

Mother Ravenel's insistent little handbell pierced his meditations. Not wanting to leave the darkness of the porch, he moved closer to a window and watched through the glass. She was in her element, she who had played the comic Lord Babberly in *Charley's Aunt;* now she was playing the Headmistress in Cheerful Control. She was interpreting their evening for them, tying up any loose ends so everyone could go home assured that the fortress safeguarding their daughters was as intact as ever.

She then turned the proceedings over to unflappable little Becky Meyer, who read from a script that was apparently a review of the play's scenes. Then each girl stepped forward and took her bow, and of course there was Chloe, as she had been all along. He hadn't been able to find her because he had forgotten she was still dressed up as Mother Finney.

He went in to claim her. Running to him, she stumbled over the skirts of the habit. "Where have you been, Uncle Henry? Tildy and Maud did something awful, but nobody will say what. And she wouldn't even speak to me at intermission."

"Who wouldn't?"

"Tildy. She hated my Red Nun. I thought she'd be so pleased."

Now was not the time to tell Chloe about her vandalized prop.

"Do you know where Tildy is now?"

"She's probably up with Maud in the dormitory. They'll go back to being best friends. It's so unfair. I read that play over to her at least a hundred times while she lay on her sofa bed with her eyes closed. I took dictation whenever she had an idea and typed it up. And she kept that scene with Maud a secret from me! And now she hates me because of the prop. But Mother Finney hugged me and told me I had made her happy and that Agnes would be so pleased."

Henry found himself echoing Bernard Stratton in the parking lot. "In that case, what do we want to do now?"

"I want to put on my own clothes and go home."

"Then let's go," said Henry.

AFTER THE POSTLUDE and curtain calls in the main parlor, Mrs. Nita Judd presented Elaine Frew with a little token of her appreciation (a silver grand piano to go on her charm bracelet) for being so good to Jiggsie, but now she was uncertain what to do about her present for Tildy (a gift card announcing a year's subscription to *Seventeen* magazine), who was not at the reception. Jiggsie told her grandmother that both Tildy and Maud were in big trouble having something to do with the last scene in the play, which nobody knew about. "That's Tildy's mother over there with Mother Ravenel," Jiggsie said. "Maybe you could just leave the envelope with her. These stupid boots I borrowed are pinching my feet. I'm going up to the dorm to change into my Capezios."

"Well, come right back, sweetie, so we can say our good-byes. Poor Bob's waiting out in the car to drive us back to Spartanburg."

But when Nita Judd approached the woman Jiggsie had pointed out as Tildy's mother, she saw that she was locked in some kind of grim exchange with the headmistress. She went instead to pay her respects to Jiggsie's ninth-grade teacher, poor Mother Malloy, who was speaking with a very pretty girl. Malloy looked completely done in. Nuns punched no time clocks, drew no salaries, and belonged to no unions, but were expected to work till they dropped.

Mother Malloy had hardly finished introducing Mrs. Judd to Tildy's big sister, Madeline, when Jiggsie was back again, still in the borrowed boots that pinched. In her usual fey manner, she announced to no one in particular, "I just saw Tildy on her way to the tower. She's planning to throw herself off—like that Caroline person tried to do."

MADELINE WAS ALREADY running down corridors and up stairs. It was as though she and Mother Malloy had been suddenly able to read each other's minds. Malloy would keep the others off and do whatever else was necessary while Madeline got a head start. Thank God she knew her way around this old pile! At the third-floor landing, the wood stopped and the linoleum started. At this level, there were only nuns; nobody needed the extra touches. Her running feet slapped along linoleum corridors, and up another flight, and then pinged up the circular iron staircase to the tower room. She was panting as she flung open the heavy door. She cursed like a sailor as she felt along the walls for a switch. She had never been up here at night.

A familiar titter came out of the darkness. "Naughty, naughty. You sound as bad as me."

She found the switch. "Tildy! What are you doing?"

"I was trying to write in the dark because I couldn't find the god-damned light. But your eyes get accustomed pretty fast."

Three of the blue velvet window-seat cushions had been sprayed in jerky white letters. SATAN RAVENEL; SATAN RAVENEL; SATAN RAVENEL. Tildy, still in costume as "Rexanne," was aiming the can at a fourth cushion.

"That's enough!" said Madeline, snatching the can.

"Take it—it was sputtering out anyway. How did you know where I was?"

"Jiggsie said you were going to throw yourself off the tower."

"That little imbecile. She asked where I was going and I said I had some business in the tower and she got all excited and asked me if I was going to throw myself off like Caroline tried to do and I said I just might. She is so stupid."

"Tildy, Daddy and Henry are outside combing the grounds for you with flashlights. Mama and I have been looking in all the classrooms and bathrooms. We have all been *worried.*"

"Well, I deserve some worry!" shrieked Tildy. "My night was ruined! My play was stolen from me! I damn this whole place to hell and everybody connected with it, including Chloe and Maud."

Slow footsteps were heard on the metal stairs. A haggard Mother Malloy appeared. Leaning against the door frame to catch her breath, she asked Tildy, "Do you include me, too?"

Madeline was to isolate that scene and play it back to herself throughout her life. She would try to watch it as she had witnessed it that night, before she had known what was coming next. But in all her replayings, she could never completely block out the impurities of hindsight. Because after the experience itself, you always did know what was coming next.

Tildy made a mewing sound and stumbled forward. Mother Malloy met Tildy halfway and gathered the girl into her arms. "Come," she said, "let's sit down. Oh, dear, somebody's been at work on these cushions. Let's find one Satan hasn't claimed yet."

Then there was this—forgiving calm. The tower room seemed swathed in it, as though the three of them were wrapped in clouds. Madeline stood—but it almost seemed she floated somewhere above, just watching and hearing. Mother Malloy was teaching Tildy a poem. "It's a poem I remembered while watching your play, Tildy. I love that poem. How could I have forgotten it? I'll say a line, then you say it. You'll learn it by ear, which you do so well. And then, perhaps, you'll help me teach it to the class on Monday."

The two sat side by side, Mother Malloy bowed slightly forward, hands clasped on her lap, and Tildy, now drained of her violence, leaning against the nun's shoulder.

" 'I have desired to go—' "

" 'I have desired to go—' "

" 'Where springs not fail—' "

" 'Where springs not fail—' "

" 'To fields—where flies—no sharp and sided hail—' "

" 'To fields—where flies—no sharp and—' " Tildy balked at the startling syntax.

" 'No sharp and sided hail—' " Mother Malloy led her through it.

" 'No sharp and sided hail—' "

" 'And a few lilies blow.' "

" 'And a few lilies blow.' "

"Go and find Mother Arbuckle," Mother Malloy told Madeline. "Bring her here as quickly as possible. She'll know what to do. Go quickly, dear."

She wants the infirmarian to give Tildy something to calm her, thought Madeline, hurtling down the flights of stairs.

Mother Arbuckle was just leaving the reception with Dr. Galvin.

"Oh, Mother, come quickly! Mother Malloy needs you. She's up in the tower with Tildy. She said—she said you'll know what to do."

Then the return: the brisk rustle of Mother Arbuckle's skirts mounting the stairs, the doctor's footsteps right behind; and her own gasping babble as she raced ahead, trying to fill them in about the play going wrong, Tildy running off in a rage, everybody searching—then a girl saying Tildy was going to throw herself off the tower, herself racing up flights of stairs, then Mother Malloy herself arriving in the tower room and miraculously calming Tildy—"but now I think Mother may want you to give her a sedative or something—the poor child's had a bad night."

And now the climbers—big sister, school infirmarian, nuns' doctor, all three short of breath—have reached the tower room, and what do they find?

A nun and a young girl sitting close together on the curved window seat. Behind them the arched windows full of night. The nun is hunched forward, hands clasped. She could be deep in prayer, as Madeline had first assumed of her that afternoon in October when she had come upon Mother Malloy asleep in the grotto on the Red Nun's lap.

"She's been doing this a lot lately," a shaky Tildy informs them. "She can fall asleep sitting up." She adds, with a halfhearted laugh, "Especially when I'm around."

"How long has she been asleep?" Mother Arbuckle asks, stepping forward.

Something in the infirmarian's voice puts Tildy on the defensive. "I'm not sure. I haven't—she just—I was afraid to move in case I woke her. We were going through the poem again so I can help her teach it on Monday, but then she just dropped off and wouldn't answer me. The way she does."

Now Dr. Galvin is in motion and Mother Arbuckle is removing Tildy from the window seat. Madeline sees her noticing the defaced cushions: SATAN RAVENEL; SATAN RAVENEL; SATAN RAVENEL.

"Take her down with you," the nun says to Madeline. "And ask someone to find Reverend Mother and tell her she is needed here at once."

CHAPTER 34

Sister Bridget's Heart

Thursday, October 18, 2001
Feast of St. Luke, evangelist
St. Scholastica Retirement House

MOTHER RAVENEL WAS dreaming of her mother. In the dream it was the present time and place and her mother was just a voice in the dark room, but behind its familiar rhythms of scorn it pulsed with a new acceptance of her daughter. Together they had been puzzling things out, her mother speaking for both of them.

"Yes, there are a great many who dance in ecstasy at obliterating great numbers of us, but what is one to do? Put on the surgical mask and rubber gloves and open the mail if you dare, shut down the Senate and the House until the men in yellow can vacuum up the anthrax spores. If you ask me, it may all boil down to whether we outnumber the ones who want us dead. And whether we like it or not, the most evolved don't necessarily win."

In the dream she felt so proud. She looked forward to the cornflake breakfast after Mass, when she could report to the other nuns, "My mother came to visit me last night, and she made the most exquisite sense of what's been happening in the world."

"And here's something else to think about," the voice went on. Amazingly the eighty-five-year-old daughter and the mother dead for almost fifty years were friends at last, equals pooling their thoughts in the dark. "Consider this: all this rabid imagining going on, all over the world, on our side as well as theirs, of how to destroy your enemy most newsworthily. While, meantime, you old nuns are providing an excel-

lent example for all of us by taking the less-newsworthy forms of destruction upon yourselves. There's something to be said for good old-
fashioned day-by-day, piece-by-piece dying."

She woke with a sob of protest. She had wanted the conversation to
go on: there was so much more she wanted from this voice with the new
note of friendship she had never known in life.

AFTER MASS, FATHER Gallagher asked Mother Ravenel to carry the
host for him to the quarters of Sister Bridget, who was recovering from
open-heart surgery.

"But you're coming, aren't you, Father?" She was alarmed that he
might be asking her to administer the sacrament to the superior—his
schedule was so tight.

"I am. But she sent word for me to bring you. She misses the community. She hoped you'd stay and read the appointed psalm with her
after I've gone."

Ten days ago, following breakfast, Sister Bridget had passed out in
the half bathroom adjoining her office off the kitchen. Mother Galyon,
or "Sister Frances," whose current task it was to tidy the refrigerator,
had heard the fall. Fortunately, the superior had left the bathroom door
unbolted. Mother Ravenel, just finishing with her Waterpik upstairs,
had heard the ambulance siren, which always shut off discreetly as it entered the grounds of the retirement house. "Mother Odom has suffered
another stroke," she had thought. "How many more can she survive?"
Standing in the hallway, she awaited the footsteps of the medics.
Mother Odom's room was two doors down from hers. But no footsteps
came. Voices converged in the kitchen. She was starting to feel her way
downstairs to "go see" for herself when she heard the cumbrous ascent
of Mother Odom's home helper, Lanie, the one who referred to her as
"the old blind nun."

"Is Mother Odom all right?"

"I'm on my way to her now," grumbled Lanie. " I can't be two places
at once. Sister Bridget's heart stopped in the bathroom, but they've
shocked her back to life and taken her off. Poor thing soiled herself all
over the floor, and guess who had to clean it up?"

. . . *she sent word for me to bring you.*

. . .

FATHER GALLAGHER PLACED the wafer on the superior's tongue.

"The body of Christ, Sister."

"Amen."

"Let us bless the Lord."

"Thanks be to God."

Then the two nuns were alone with each other.

"Thank you for coming, Sister Suzanne. Sit closer. I thought we might read the psalm together. Then you'll want your breakfast."

"No rush on my account, Sister. How do you feel?"

"I feel like Lazarus. I must look a fright. How much can you see of my face?"

"I can make out the heavy bruising around your eyes and neck."

"I tipped forward on the toilet and hit the floor headfirst. So they tell me. I remember very little. There were so many procedures. They ran a tube from my groin into my heart and found I was ninety percent blocked. Then they sawed me open and replaced the valves. That is all a blank. There are days I can't account for. They also installed a pacemaker, in case my heart gets lazy again. I'm feeling somewhat unsubstantial, Sister, but I'm told I might be around a while longer."

"I'm very glad for that." Realizing she meant it, Mother Ravenel found herself blinking back tears.

"How is your school memoir coming, Sister?"

"I'm still in the 1950s."

"The school closed in 1990—so, let's see, you have three more decades to go."

"They will be gravy, Sister, if I can ever get out of the fifties."

"So much happened?"

"Certain things—*culminated* in fifty-one and fifty-two. You might say they came home to roost. It was a distressing year for me as headmistress. I was sent away on a leave of absence at the end of the school term."

"Will you tell about the distressing year in the memoir?"

"It's not the kind of thing that belongs in a school history. The girls responsible were expelled immediately, and some other students didn't come back the following year. When I get to their class year in the memoir—the class of fifty-five—those girls have been long gone. But they're stuck there in my memory like a kind of roadblock. There was a mother involved, too: a classmate of mine. The intent was to embarrass me by inserting material in a class play. The tragic part that came out of it was the death of a young nun. She had an undiagnosed heart ailment from childhood, it turned out, but I hold myself responsible to a large degree. If I hadn't overreacted that night to something the mother and daughter had planted in the play—a hidden message that they still held me accountable—that young nun might have lived longer, or perhaps still be alive. I think this is what keeps me from dictating the fifties with the same ease I've managed with the other chapters."

"You've spoken to a priest?"

"Decades of priests. They either told me I was too hard on myself or that it was an insult to God's mercy to keep harping on something He'd already forgiven me for. The one I was fondest of told me I was 'scraping the cauldron' of that year for more 'evil snacks' and to get back to work and see where I fit into God's design rather than where He fit into mine—"

Sister Bridget started to laugh, then grimaced in pain.

"I confided in Mother Galyon on one of our recent walks and she suggested I make a confessional cassette—just the parts that haunt me—then ask God's blessing, send it off to someone I trust, and let it go."

"And did you?"

"I dictated a large part of it. It was to a student in that class of fifty-five. We've remained friends; she's the one who's transcribing the memoir. But after September eleventh, I felt it would be all out of proportion. Beatrix might wonder how I can keep harping on these old wounds when so much worse is happening. I know this is prideful of me, but I just couldn't face losing her admiration and respect. At this stage of my life, Sister Bridget, someone's admiration is a precious commodity."

"Well—Mother Ravenel—we haven't been the best of friends, you and I, and part of the fault has been *my* pride. But, as your sister in Christ, I offer myself as a replacement for Beatrix. I have some time on my hands, as you can see. Why don't we say the psalm together now, and you can think it over.

" 'O God, You are my God, for You I long; for You my soul is thirsting . . .' "

Not until she was eating her cornflakes with the other nuns did it register: for the first time, Sister Bridget, that stickler for the leveling nomenclature of post Vatican II, had respectfully addressed her in the old style, as "Mother Ravenel."

Confessional Cassette Rerouted

Thursday night, October 18, 2001
Mother Ravenel's room
St. Scholastica Retirement House

Dear Bridget, sister in Christ, superior of the Order of St. Scholastica,

I'm beginning a new cassette because the other might not have enough room left on it. The initial plan was to limit myself to the front and back of one cassette. But I didn't want to risk running out of space in the middle of thanking God for His wonderful patience with me—and thanking you for yours.

If you are listening to this now, you will have finished both sides of the other cassette. I was sorely tempted to listen to it all again and try to predict your reactions before taking you up on your offer to be a "replacement" for Beatrix. But I decided to risk it and just plunge in and take advantage of the momentum your offer has generated in me.

I remember all too well where I last broke off dictating this confessional tape. How can anyone forget what they were doing on that terrible day at a little past nine in the morning?

I was telling about my envy of Antonia. And how, when Antonia began to have doubts our senior year, I had the idea of entering early to subdue my envy. Because as a postulant I would be ineligible to be Queen of the School. Well, I did enter early, and she *was* voted queen, but she turned it down, and after that the school discontinued the practice, which I think was wise. Too many feelings get hurt when only one is chosen as the best. Her family's story was that I "jumped the gun" and broke her heart and spoiled her vocation, which wasn't true. I knew she was having doubts, but I believe she kept postponing telling me because she knew how disappointed I would be. But she would say oblique things, and I picked up on them. I do think she was hurt by my entering early and not confiding in her, but she certainly wasn't heartbroken. If anyone's heart was wounded, it was mine. I had hoped to spend my life serving God with Antonia. She later married a very fine man, a prominent young architect and a good Catholic. Unfortunately, she was killed in a traffic accident on their wedding trip, and this reactivated her sister Cornelia's bitterness toward me. At the reception after the wretched play, which you heard about in the last cassette, Cornelia accused me not only of being an indirect cause of Antonia's death, but of "feeding on Antonia's early vocation like a tapeworm" until I was swollen with it and she was completely emptied out. As she was saying this to me, in a low voice with a social smile on her face in the middle of a crowded room, I remember thinking, This is the lowest point of this deplorable night, and I will somehow get through it.

But there was worse to come.

Cornelia's daughter Tildy had gone off in a rage because I had intervened onstage and changed the course of the play. Things were getting very, very bad up there and I didn't know how much worse they might get, and then I saw Cornelia watching me out of the corner of her eye and I knew I had been set up. So I acted quickly, and most people agreed later that when I went up on-stage it seemed a natural part of the play. What Tildy and her friend Maud had been doing, you see, was acting out a scene supposed to represent Antonia and me, only they called themselves "Domenica" and "Rexanne." They were acting out an occasion when Antonia is telling me that it would be wrong to go on with our plans to become nuns together—an occasion that never happened, by the way. But they had an old exam booklet of Antonia's, and Maud as Antonia/Domenica was reading words addressed to me. In the fall of her senior year Antonia had apparently drafted a letter to me in the back of an old exam booklet, a letter she never sent, but the family had kept the booklet all these years, and now they were springing it on me during a school play—a play I had written at Tildy's age and had given Tildy the privilege of directing. I had also permitted Tildy to make changes to it—that was part of the play's tradition. And in all fairness, there were some good added scenes and innovations. But the Domenica and Rexanne scene, which, fortunately, came at the tail end of the play, was aimed at me, and when I heard a certain "signal word" I had to act fast in case it got worse. And even while Cornelia was saying those unconscionable things to me at the reception, I believed I had controlled the damage.

The next thing was, Jiggsie returned to the reception and told her grandmother that Tildy was on her way to throw herself off the tower. Now, Jiggsie's grandmother was at that time talking to Tildy's older sister, Madeline, and Mother Malloy, Tildy's ninth-grade teacher. Madeline started running for the tower, and Mother Malloy was to follow her.

It has always seemed strange to me that I should have been one of the last to know what was happening in the tower. I was still downstairs saying good-bye to parents, making sure every waiter had received his pay envelope; then I stopped by the kitchen to thank Betty, our cook, and Mother Finney, who was helping put things away. I was headed for the chapel to thank God for helping me survive the evening when a girl came running after me to say something terrible had happened.

When Mother Arbuckle returned with Madeline to the tower, Dr. Galvin, the nuns' doctor, was with them. Mother Arbuckle later told me that when the three of them entered the tower room, they saw Tildy and Mother Malloy sitting side by side, the nun bent forward with her hands clasped. Tildy told them Mother Malloy often fell asleep sitting up during their tutoring sessions. Mother Arbuckle saw at once that something was not right and sent Madeline off with Tildy and told her to summon Reverend Mother.

They laid Mother Malloy on the floor and worked over her for about fifteen minutes, the infirmarian's mouth on hers, the doctor pumping her chest. But to no avail.

Dr. Galvin signed the death certificate, and Reverend Mother and I stayed with her in the tower until the ambulance men took her away.

This is as far as I can get tonight, Sister Bridget.

Later, I want to tell you a little about my year of exile, which the Order called my "leave of absence" during 1952 to '53, when I was officially caring for my dying mother in Charleston.

Early this morning, I dreamed of my mother in a new way. In the dream we seemed to have begun a new relationship. For the first time, I look forward to discovering parts of her aside from those that failed my needs.

Predawn, Friday
October 19, 2001

I have not slept well, Sister Bridget. I woke from a peculiar dream in which a woman living in our retirement house—she seemed to be a nun from some other order—was explaining to me, "You have to learn to praise God when he is behaving badly."

. . .

So I decided to get up and dress and go on with this.

The year in Charleston with my dying mother (emphysema; she was also slipping into senility by the summer of 1952, though she had more than enough moments of scathing lucidity that year). She was seventy-four when she died, which seemed quite old to me then. I have now outlived her by more than a decade.

I was thirty-six that summer. I had been a nun for eighteen years, headmistress of an academy for seven years, and yet when I walked through the front door of my mother's house for the first time since I'd left it at the age of twelve, I could feel myself shrink back into the despised daughter, accompanied by all the old epithets: "sneaky, sanctimonious, self-advancing" Suzanne, "Old Frump, Old Stubby, Old Stumpy."

It was the Feast of St. Anthony of Padua, which fell on a Friday that year. It was also Friday the thirteenth.

I seem to keep backing away from entering that front door. I will try another approach.

The frugality of my brothers. Euphemism for the stinginess of my brothers. As I said on the earlier cassette, they repaid everything my father "borrowed" from the accounts he'd held in trust before Black Friday. They worked very hard at the law firm and won back people's respect. But somewhere along the way they developed an obsession with making more and more money and spending less and less. It became a game with them: try to double the amount we made last year and spend half the amount we spent last year. My older brother had married a woman with money, and what she had didn't "count" in the game. My other brother lived at home with his mother and his mistress, who, conveniently, was a practical nurse, until his forty-ninth year, when he had his fatal coronary. That was in May 1952: another fateful conjunction whose timing couldn't have been worse—for me. My older brother thought of a way he might save on three months of summer home care for his mother. His late brother's mistress refused to stay on for the measly fee he offered. His sister was in a teaching order, and everyone knows teaching nuns don't teach in the summer. So he phoned Reverend Mother and asked if I might be spared for the summer to stay with my dying mother, who had asked for me. And Reverend Mother called me in and said she would give permission for me to have a leave of absence, which might be extended to a year. She said the recent happenings had surely been an ordeal for me and this appeal from my brother could be a blessing and a healing for all. We both knew all that was being left unsaid. After the night of the play and the death of Mother Malloy, and the bishop's subsequent visit and homily on "misguided creations," followed by the reconsecration of the tower room and the Red Nun, there were unfavorable murmurings both within the school and in the community of Mountain City. I had expelled two girls, and several more in that class were not to return, though we didn't know it then. Might it not be prudent to seclude the "high-profile" headmistress, who had somehow been "implicated," until the dust had time to settle?

And so, on Friday the thirteenth of June, in the year of Our Lord 1952, I arrived after a ten-hour bus ride (my brother would not spring for the costlier train) at my mother's house. He had a case in court that day and sent his secretary to meet me and drive me to the East Battery, where she waited in the car until the door opened, then drove away.

Just go in. You've got to go in sometime.

She answered the door herself, wheeling an oxygen tank. She was recognizable as the woman I had last seen at age twelve, only not as erect and wearing a kind of housedress she would formerly have mocked. She looked me up and down, then began laughing in a mirthless *chuff-chuff* way, until she was gasping for breath and had to put on her oxygen mask. She indicated to me that she could no longer climb stairs and pointed me up to my old room. As I was ascending the staircase with my bags, she whispered hoarsely after me, "And change out of that costume, Stubby, unless you want to kill me with laughing."

This is all I can do, now. Thank God the jets are back in the skies. Such a sweet dawn roar as light begins to filter through the blind nun's eyes.

Friday, after morning prayer
October 19, 2001

No priest today; no Mass. There were only the four of us in chapel: Mother Galyon, Sister Paula and Sister Marian from our Order's now defunct Boston Academy, and myself. Mother Galyon conducted morning prayer and read from the Common of Several Martyrs, since today is the feast of the eight Jesuits tortured and killed by the Huron and Iroquois tribes in North America between 1642 and 1649. We also said the Prayer for Holy Women, and for the first time I was much struck by these words: "Father, in our weakness Your power reaches perfection."

How does that work, I wonder? I will meditate on it when I'm riding to and from my appointment with the gastroenterologist. But the van doesn't come until ten, so I'll go on with the year with my mother.

There were the two of us, rattling around in an eighteenth-century three-story house on the East Battery. All of the good furniture and carpets had been sold by my brothers, and there were lots of bare floors and echoes. I made simple meals—canned soup, sandwiches, creamed chipped beef on toast. She ate almost nothing. I wore my "costume" when I went to Mass at St. Mary's on Hasell Street and for my walks around the Battery, but inside the house I left off the veil and wore my late brother's casual clothes. As my hair was clipped very short, I was often mistaken for a man by delivery people. When it started to grow out, I cut it ruthlessly with nail scissors. The first time I did this, I cried. I missed Mother Finney's "Clip 'n' Shave Parlor," and I missed my community. Mother Finney was to write to me faithfully during my "exile," until she died of pneumonia in the late winter of 1953. Reverend Mother had told me to say the Office at the usual time whenever possible and while I was doing so to remember that all my sisters in the Order were praying with me.

But this grew increasingly hard to do.

I did find myself thinking about Antonia more than I had allowed myself to do in years. It was probably natural, given the scene in the recent play that I'd interrupted when Tildy (Rexanne/Suzanne) began to read from the exam book in which Antonia really had written a note to me, breaking off our plans to enter together—a note that Antonia must have thought better of sending.

After I had sent the rest of the cast off to the reception, I confronted Tildy and her coconspirator Maud about the meaning of their scene and I confiscated the exam book, over Tildy's protests that it belonged to her family. Well, the family had done their worst with it; I had already made up my mind about that. What would keep Cornelia from circulating it to do more damage, which could hurt the school?

Before I appeared at the reception I went up to the nuns' bathroom on the third floor and disposed of that booklet in very, very tiny pieces. The toilets up there were still of the old-fashioned chain variety with the cistern above, and I pulled the chain five times, just to be safe. Those old toilets provided a much more powerful flush than the modern ones, and I remember thinking, as I waited for the cistern to fill up again each time, that maybe we should have kept the old toilets in the boarders' bathrooms; the new ones were frequently clogged. All modern "improvements" are not necessarily improvements.

And then I went down to the reception and Cornelia lit into me about being a tapeworm and the indirect cause of Antonia's death—and then followed the tragedy in the tower—and the funeral and the rest of the fallout, which included Reverend Mother's granting my "leave of absence." With all this going on, there hadn't been time until I was in Charleston for me to absorb this new knowledge about Antonia: that she had written me a note, pinpointing the cause of our rupture—what I had done was to kiss her at her sister's engagement party out at the Swag (that was the name of Cornelia's fiancé's hunting cabin). And "Swag" was the key word in Antonia's note, and when I heard Tildy saying "Swag," up there on the stage, I realized I had to act fast. Who knew what would come next in the note?

Alone with my mother on that long year of leave, there was plenty of time to think about Antonia, and to ask myself hard questions, such as: Would I have had a vocation if I hadn't been looking for a way to stay with her? And if the answer to that was no, what kind of vocation could I claim to have now? Was a tarnished vocation still a vocation?

On the evening of my arrival in Charleston, my brother stopped by the house to greet me. He also appeared amused by my "costume." He asked if there was anything I needed. I wanted to say, "A hug from you after all these years would be a start," but didn't. He had changed; there was no play in him anymore. He had put on weight, and his cheeks puffed out in an angry, impacted way. He was not the boy who had foot-raced with me along the beach, or even the boy who lured me up into the tree house, then jumped down and took away the ladder and laughed. This person seemed impatient of anything that might divert him from his grim objectives. He was very put out when I explained that I had never learned to drive. It was as if I had accepted a job under false pretenses. This meant he would keep having to pay for things delivered to the house and have his secretary take our mother to the doctor.

During his visit, our mother stayed in her room. I asked didn't he want to see her and he said he'd had a long day in court and was in no mood to be verbally abused. He instructed me to watch her carefully and said that when the time came when I felt she'd be better off in an institution, to let him know; he'd already found a place. "I just thought you two might like to have a little time together first," he said. He made it sound like a great benevolence on his part. As he was leaving, I made up my mind to confront him: "Did she really ask for me, Buddy?" "Well, when I put it to her that you might be available, she didn't say no" was his reply.

She liked to take her meals on a tray in her bedroom and have me keep her company. I would sit in a chair facing hers and she would fork the edges of her food, as though toying with excrement, and take tiny slurps from her teacup, and in between, without raising her eyes or her voice, drop her emotional bombs. Cornelia Tilden Stratton could have learned a lot from my mother.

I am not going to dump these emotional bombs into your lap, because they belong to the class of unsavory things you wish afterward you'd never heard. Once they are in you, they're liable to take root, against your will. I suspect that many of her bombs would qualify for that carefully shrouded "sin against the Holy Ghost," which, as far as I've been able to make out from my spiritual directors, has to do with causing a person to despise his God-given human state or despising it in yourself. One of her pet themes was the disgustingness of certain basic human activities.

However, bearing on the subject of "taking root in you against your will," there is one I will tell about because it explained something. It was not one of the more unsavory ones, though it may have been the most painful to me.

Eyes cast down, my mother asked me over lunch one day, "Have you ever known a man, Stubby?"

I said I had not. "Remember, I entered the postulancy when I was only sixteen." Though why should she remember? Not one word had come from my family in response to the invitation.

"Oh, plenty of girls have tipped over by then," she said, uttering the chuff-chuffing emphysemic laugh I was to hear so often that year. "I myself had tipped over . . . years and years before I met your father."

Then a bit of messing about with her fork, after which she decided not to bring it to her lips.

"If it's any consolation," she said, "you haven't missed a thing.

"But I wanted children," she went on. "Or thought I did. He got two sons out of me, and I thought that was the end of that. The boys were in their teens and I was home free. Then, guess what?"

As she took a tiny slurp of tea, her eyes couldn't resist checking the effect this was having on me. I felt like a small animal paralyzed by the gaze of a snake.

"When I realized it wasn't early menopause, I did what I had done the first time, when I was off at boarding school. I got into a very hot bath and forced down a fifth of gin, then jumped off a table ten times. Only this time it didn't work. You hung in there like a tick. I tried it again a few days later and this time ended up spraining my ankle. My last try was to hobble to the house of a Negro woman who was well-known for giving 'deep abdominal massages' to white women who didn't want any more children. But after she started, she told me I was too far along and gave me back the money and sent me home. You had stapled yourself to my womb by then."

As I've said already, the carpets had been sold off and the house now had many bare floors. Some of these floors, especially in the public rooms downstairs, were of very beautiful oak parquetry in a chevron pattern. Well, one afternoon after I'd "kept my mother company for lunch," I wandered into the south drawing room and the afternoon light was flowing over the unsealed boards in such a way that it brought out certain stains and dents in one corner and I decided to see what else I could do down on my knees besides praying, which was not going very well. So I brought some cloths and a bucket of warm water and a pumice stone and went to work in that corner. I worked very closely on one board at a time, going with the grain, and not looking ahead at how much else there was to do.

In chapter 48 of Benedict's Rule, "De Opera Manuum Quotidiano," he prescribes so many hours a day of manual labor for his monks. He also prescribes so many hours a day for prayerful reading, lectio divina; but that summer and the winter and spring to follow was neither a reading nor a praying time for me. Those floors were the nearest I came to God that year, and they brought me into a confraternity of sorts, for which I was very grateful.

I was noticed at the Masses at St. Mary's. Of course I was noticed. The nun who had returned home to care for her dying mother. It had been our family's church. My father was buried in its cemetery. The present pastor had come after my father's death and after my mother and brothers stopped attending that church, but he knew who I was and gave me a warm welcome and introduced me to other parishioners. At first they were shy, as laypeople generally are around nuns, but as soon as I mentioned that I was working on our floors, they couldn't stop talking. Many of them had old unsealed hardwood parquetry throughout their houses, and there was the vinegar-and-well-wrung-mop faction and the damp-rag-with-fine-sand-and-tung-oil faction, and the adherents of boiled linseed oil combined with lemon, and the advocates of handheld orbital sander versus the sandpaper-only diehards. I was given generous batches of secret recipes for old family floors and lent a grandfather's old bonnet polisher from his car-buff days. A few members of my confraternity came right out and said they'd be glad to stop by sometime and look at the floors, but I explained that we weren't having visitors. I didn't wish to be surprised "out of costume" with my shorn head and bare feet.

By the end of the summer, I had completed the floor in the south drawing room and had begun on the dining room adjoining it when the season's first hurricane uprooted a mature palmetto in the courtyard. My brother, arriving unannounced with his chain saw, looked through the window and saw what he took for a workman down on his knees. He was furious, thinking we had hired someone he would be expected to pay, but when he saw it was me in our brother's clothes, and when he had inspected the shining floor in the south drawing room, he did give me the first hug since I was twelve. He said this restored parquetry would add enormously to the sale price of the house and offered to pay me. I refused, of course, telling him it had been a form of prayer and I was glad to go on doing it as long as I was staying there. "Well then," he said, "when this is all over, will you let me make a substantial donation to your school?" And I said that was very generous of him and accepted. I thought it would be nice to return to Mount St. Gabriel's bearing a large check from my family. But after Mother was buried and all the public rooms had shining floors, I reminded him of his offer and he got very defensive and said this was a particularly tight time for him but he would send a check in six months, if that was all right. I said fine, but I think I knew then that I would never see that check. Poor Buddy—I am sure he meant it the day he offered it, but his avarice had become too deeply ingrained by then, and he just couldn't bring himself to follow through. We don't choose our families, and they don't choose us. Though sometimes they can try to keep us from coming into the world at all.

. . .

Sister Paula just knocked to tell me the van is here for us. It seems I will not be riding alone. This is the morning she goes to the podiatrist's to have her toenails cut.

Friday evening after Compline
October 19, 2001

I had planned to meditate during my time in the van on those words that so struck me this morning in the Prayer for Holy Women: "In our weakness Your power reaches perfection." But Sister Paula was nervous and needed to be distracted. Going to the podiatrist makes her anxious because a year ago they told her they might have to amputate her big toe, and she's always afraid they're going to say the infection has come back. I know she likes to hear stories about Mount St. Gabriel's, so I was telling her about our plays—though not about the disastrous night!—and about the high standards the girls set for themselves in these plays. This morning she told me that the nuns at our Boston Academy used to call Mount St. Gabriel's the Order's "cash cow"—on the evidence that all through its history, whenever we needed anything down there, the Order bent over backward to supply it. That is how Mother Malloy came to us in the fall of 1951, I remember. At the last minute, the current ninth-grade teacher had to take over the secretarial courses at the junior college, so Mother Malloy was sent down to replace her. Of course, I know now that we saw the first evidence of her heart problem on the day she arrived. Unaccustomed to the thin air a mile above sea level, she fainted when I was giving her a tour of the grounds.

On our return trip in the van, Sister Paula was overjoyed by her good report— the toe has been declared officially out of danger—and because the podiatrist has installed a new Jacuzzi-type foot tub and a young nurse gave her a thorough and loving foot and ankle massage after she had cut and filed the toenails. Sister Paula said she had to struggle to hold back tears of well-being and gratitude. "I felt completely in her hands," Sister Paula said. Then I thought, Why not ask her about that sentence I was going to meditate on, when I was imagining myself riding alone in silence?

"There was a sentence this morning in that Prayer for Holy Women," I said. " 'In our weakness Your power reaches perfection.' It really struck me. What do you think it means, Sister Paula?"

And she thought a minute and then said, "I think it means you have to admit you can't save yourself before you're fully available to God."

I have learned much today. As I used to remind the girls at Mount St. Gabriel's, "We are all works in progress." Now I will turn these tapes over to you, Sister Bridget. Praise be to God for my family in Christ.

CHAPTER 35

A Midmorning Walk

Wednesday, October 24, 2001
Anthony Claret, bishop, 1807–1870 (formerly the Feast of St. Raphael
the archangel)
Grounds of the St. Scholastica Retirement House

"I LIKE IT that Father Gallagher continues to remember the old feasts," said Sister Bridget. "In an aging community like ours, October twenty-fourth has been St. Raphael's feast for most of the nuns' lives."

"You do wonder, though," Mother Ravenel lightly rejoined, "whose idea it was to bunch up the three major archangels on September twenty-ninth just to leave some spaces free on the calendar." She was doing her best not to lean on the other nun's arm, since this was Sister Bridget's first outing since her open-heart surgery.

"Well, but new saints do keep getting born," the superior reasoned in her flat Bostonese, and Mother Ravenel had to quash a fierce bubble of indignity. This was the person who had offered herself as a replacement for Beatrix, who would have picked up instantly on the jeu d'esprit of her remark. Had it been an error in judgment to hand over those intimate cassettes? However, it was too late now. After Mass today, Sister Bridget had reported that she had listened to them and was ready to offer some "comments." What if those comments should be as stodgy as her last reply? Mother Ravenel girded her loins and resolved to keep her disappointment to herself no matter what came out of this walk.

"I thought we might sit in the summerhouse," said Sister Bridget. "It's such a fine day. All the yellow leaves. How much can you see of it, Sister?"

So we were back to "Sister" now.

"As a matter of fact, yellow is one of my better colors. They look like coins drifting down. Blurred coins, of course."

"Now there are three steps up," Sister Bridget cautioned.

"Yes, I know. I often stop at the summerhouse to regather my thoughts."

"Do you have a favorite spot?"

"I like this corner. It's out of the sun." *(And out of range from where you can see me from the house.)* Mother Ravenel's rapprochement with Sister Bridget was evaporating by the minute. She felt like a student about to have her work critiqued by a teacher whose credentials might not come up to her standards.

"You certainly do tell a good story, Sister. I felt I was there. The romantic old building. The mountain air. The safety. The excellence. Girls watching other girls, planning their next moves. My school days seemed dull in comparison. I look forward to reading the memoir."

"If God graciously allows me to finish it."

"What happened to those girls, Sister? The ones you expelled after the play."

"Tildy went over to the public high school. Her sister, Madeline, was already there. I'd had to ask Madeline to leave Mount St. Gabriel's at the end of *her* freshman year. Though Madeline was by far the more simpatico of the sisters."

"And these were Cornelia's daughters, right?"

"Yes." Where was this going?

But Sister Bridget surprised her by whinnying like a donkey. "That Cornelia! What a wicked tongue! 'Actually, we are triplets, but one of us died.' I laughed aloud when I listened to that part, but I wouldn't have wanted to come under her fire. And what became of the other girl you expelled after the play?"

"I'm sorry to say we lost all contact with Maud. Her mother wrote and asked to be reimbursed for the remainder of her boarding fee, which was not refundable. She had signed off on that, and I reminded her of this and never heard from any of them again. I have sometimes wondered if I was too hard on Maud—she and I had been close for a while—but she and Tildy were so bound up, and it was that old rotten-apple-in-the-barrel dilemma. For the sake of the school, I couldn't risk keeping her on. But Maud was a very smart and attractive girl who applied herself, and I have no doubt she did well. Her father was married to a wealthy second wife in Palm Beach, and that's where I sent her the morning after the play. Her mother had just suffered a miscarriage and she and her new husband didn't even have a home yet."

"All these lives," murmured Sister Bridget. Did Mother Ravenel detect a hint of reproof? "I didn't quite understand—that scene you said was aimed at you—that made you need to go onstage before it got worse—how much worse could it have gotten?"

"I had to guard against any sapphic hints. That sort of reputation could have brought down the school."

"But surely . . . there's a tradition of girls loving other girls—or having crushes on nuns in convent schools. I mean, who else is there?"

"We're not talking about the Boston Irish, Sister. This was Appalachia. Catholics were feared."

"Ah, I see. Did you meet Cornelia again?"

"The whole family came out to the school for Mother Malloy's burial. Tildy wanted to recite a poem at the grave. I thought it best to give in on that one. It was the Hopkins poem that Mother Malloy had been teaching Tildy just before she collapsed. And then afterward Madeline stayed behind and asked on behalf of the family if I would return Antonia's old exam book with the note to me. I told her that would not be possible and she said, 'I thought not, Mother,' and walked away. Of course, we continued to live in the same city and both girls were married in the basilica—I was not invited to either wedding and didn't expect to be. When I heard that Cornelia was dying, I phoned and asked Madeline if I could visit. She made me wait for a good long while and then came back to report that though Cornelia could no longer speak, she had indicated no."

"What had you hoped to achieve?"

"I guess I was hoping for some sign that she didn't still hold me responsible for how Antonia's life turned out—or, rather, didn't. And I would have asked for her forgiveness if she thought I had been too harsh on her daughters because of old animosities between us. Not that I think I did wrong in sending them away—there was too much accumulated poison by then: they had been brought up to mistrust me."

"But are *you* still holding yourself responsible for Antonia?"

"I think if I hadn't loved her so much—or had been more skilled at hiding my love—it might have turned out differently."

"You know where I felt closest to you on the tapes? When you spoke about envy. That's an experience I know well. I've even envied you old sisters—with all your infirmities and your airs—for having been born early enough to complete your teaching years before our schools closed. I took my final vows four years before Vatican II, and by the time I finished my graduate degree and started to teach in our Boston Academy, nuns were flying out the doors and windows to become social workers and wear pantsuits and live together in apartments. When our academy closed, in 1978, I was forty-two. I asked Reverend Mother if I might be sent down to Mount St. Gabriel's in Mountain City—I knew nuns were leaving the Order there, too—and she promised to look into it. But the answer came back no. Enrollment was falling and the trustees were hiring lay teachers on a contract basis. More cost-effective. They didn't have to be housed and fed and clothed. So that was the end of my teaching career."

Mother Ravenel chose to shift the subject. "What were your specialties in graduate work, Sister Bridget?"

"I haven't finished my comments on your tapes, Sister. They weren't what I was expecting. I'm not sure what it is you still feel you need to confess—or be forgiven for—in order to go on with your memoir. Surely not a passionate kiss, given to a girl you loved—or feeling jealous and entering early so you wouldn't be eligible for Queen of the School. And, after close to seventy years of service, surely you're not still in doubt of your vocation. Maybe you were too hard on some of those girls, but then I've never been the headmistress of a prosperous academy. The only group I've ever had charge of is this community of aging nuns, and I know I've been too hard on you. The time Sister Odelie was whisking that hollandaise sauce and all of you were jabbering in your privileged French and I made her stop because of her pride. Now every time I visit her in her room, I pray for forgiveness for that outburst. If she were responsive, I would beg her for it. It was unworthy of a superior, but that day I felt so shut out, like some servant hired to see you ladies through your dotage. But I have another question, Sister. Do you still suspect that your vocation is 'tarnished'? And why? Because you first chose it as a way to stay close to your great friend?"

"That's what I have asked myself. Did I love Antonia more than God? But if I had never met Antonia, I think I would still have chosen it. I loved the school, I loved the life, and I do love God. And maybe I also chose it because it made me feel safe and gave me some authority. I just wish the whole thing had been, well . . . *purer*."

"But Sister! How many of us entered with the pure motives of—of—well—someone like Saint Thérèse of Lisieux? I know I didn't. I wanted the authority, too. And I wanted the—exemption. I didn't want to be like my mother, raising seven kids and sipping cheap sherry. I wanted to be like a certain nun I admired, standing in front of a classroom teaching, belonging to no one but an invisible spouse. And now here we both are, my Golden Jubilee fast approaching and you headed for your Diamond. You know the thing I came away with from those tapes of yours, Sister, after I got over being furious? You are eighty-five years old and still growing as a person. Or as you would say, still a work in progress. That dream about your mother. After that terrible relationship, you find common ground with her and wake up feeling closer. There's another thing, too, and I am going to confide it to you before I tell the others, since you have already dreamed it. That nun from another order you dreamed about—who was living in our house?"

"Oh, I have no idea what she meant about learning to praise God even when he is behaving badly. We'd have to ask Freud about that."

"It wasn't that; it was that she was from another order and living in our house. You see, this is what I've been wrestling with and will present to the four of you in chapter this evening: we have been offered a stipend to take in the five remaining sisters of the Order of St. Gertrude—they were founded to run orphanages, but since the seventies their main work has been resettling refugee families. The stipend will just about cover our shortfall and allow us to go on living in this comfortable house."

"But—Sister—where are they all going to sleep?"

"That's the downside. Every one of us will have to take a roommate. The upside is that, with careful management and goodwill on everybody's part, we'll be able to stay together as a community. Your dream was very timely, Sister. Though after I considered it, it seemed natural for someone who has been organizing people for most of her life to foresee what has to be done."

"When"—Mother Ravenel was determined to keep her voice as steady as she could—"is the earliest they would be moving in?"

"As soon as we say the word. Their building was sold out from under them. But I've given some thought to the privacy you'll need to dictate the rest of your memoir, Sister. Would you accept the use of my office until, say, ten each morning? We can set up a corner for you and no one will disturb you. I can reroute phone calls and take them in the little parlor."

"That is very thoughtful of you, Sister Bridget. Thank you, I accept."

"You're very welcome. As you said at the end of your last tape, praise be to God for my family in Christ."

LORD, HELP ME SEE—whatever I need to see about this unexpected exchange. Do I feel shriven? Somewhat, but mainly through the act of shaping my own confession and handing it over to another soul for "comments." Do I feel railroaded by my stodgy, stealthy superior? Yes. Though You are mercifully permitting me to see the humor of it, too.

I think the best thing for me to do now, Lord, is to say a prayer for the person who will have me as a roommate until the ambulance comes through the gates for one of us. God, help her, and grant her the forbearance she will need!

CHAPTER 36

Reunion

MAUD

Saturday afternoon, October 27, 2007
Storage unit 1516
Lake Worth, Florida

"HELLO?"

Maud Martinez, slick with perspiration, was sitting on a crate catching her breath when her cell phone rang.

"Maud?"

"Speaking."

"It's Tildy. I just this minute got your letter. I was so excited I could hardly read it."

"Oh, Tildy, I don't believe this—"

"You sound out of breath. Are you out *jogging* or something?"

"No, I've been moving boxes."

"Where are you *right this minute*?"

"I'm in my storage unit out on the highway. I sold our house. I'm sitting on a crate."

"Are you out of the house yet?"

"No, but it's almost empty."

"What's in the crate you're sitting on right now?"

Such a Tildy question!

"My mother's china. She was so proud of it. When she married Art Foley, they went out and bought everything new."

"She's gone?"

"They both are. He died first, and Lily's been gone since eighty-eight. And your parents?"

"Oh, very much gone. And—ohhh!—but listen, Maud, what are you going to do now?"

"You mean today, or for the rest of my life?"

"Both, but let's start with today. Do you have a *date* or anything tonight?"

"A date! Good Lord, no."

"Now listen, Maud, and don't interrupt until I've finished. You could get on the Florida Turnpike and be at my house in nine hours. What's stopping you?"

Glorious, dramatic Tildy. As though they were still fourteen. "About ten more trips to the recycling center tomorrow, then the floor sanders finish Max's office and surgery on Monday, and I want to be sure they leave it spotless for the new owner—the closing's a week from Tuesday—and I have a doctor's appointment this Tuesday—"

"Are you okay?"

"It's just a routine checkup. She likes to scold me about my LDL and cross-examine me about my wine intake."

"What *time* Tuesday is your doctor's?"

"Ten-thirty."

"Why don't you plan to get here for a late supper on Tuesday night? Why are you laughing?" The old Tildy: quick to sniff out insurrection.

"I can't drive after dark. I've got cataracts."

"Oh. Well, if you started out at daybreak *Wednesday* morning you could be here before dark. We could still celebrate Halloween together."

Saturday night, October 27, 2007
Maud's house, formerly part of the Palm City Animal Hospital
Sunset Avenue, Palm Beach

Maud salsa danced in her socks in the empty upstairs living room by moonlight. Even in the pit of her depression after Max's death, she had danced, telling herself, "If I am doing this, I'm not dead yet." But she danced without sound; she couldn't have stood the songs. The songs would have turned it into a weeping extravaganza. She danced alone, without sound, taking care with the precise steps, to honor the love between Max and herself.

The last incision from Daisy's toenails had been sanded away yesterday by the machines, but Maud could still summon the resolute *click-click-thump* of Daisy's final arthritic years. When the dog could no longer climb up to lie beside her on the bed, Maud had dragged the mattress to the floor, where they'd continued to sleep together until the day Daisy snacked on the fatal debris at the beach. That was March, seven months ago. Max had now been gone two and a half years.

Max had been an inspired and passionate dancer. And thanks to Miss Bianca Mendoza back at Mount St. Gabriel's, Maud had been able to astonish him by sliding right into the tango the first time they danced.

Daisy, as a puppy with a broken hip and then as an aging dog with arthritis, had watched them dance in this room, keeping time with her tail—her contribution to the family ritual. Max had found her lying on oily rags in the lid of a cardboard box on his surgery porch a week before Christmas 1989. He set her hip and carried her upstairs, still woozy from anesthetic. "I bring you an early Christmas present," he told Maud. They made a bed for her on soft old towels in a laundry basket. She was mostly four big golden feet and terrified brown eyes. "What do you think happened?" Maud asked, already in love. "She could have been kicked or thrown downstairs or hit by a car. Then left on our doorstep by a guilty son of a bitch or a Good Samaritan. Poor little *nerviosita,* we will make it up to her."

They named her Daisy. As in "I'm half crazy, all for the love of you."

Max and Maud: twenty-eight and a half years. Max and Maud and Daisy: sixteen years. Maud and Daisy: two years.

I am grateful to have had so much.

Sunday morning, October 28, 2007

The email from Tildy had been sent at 3:48 this morning, with two attachments.

> Dearest Maud, I'm so excited I can't sleep. Now, don't you dare
> back out. Here are MapQuest directions from your house to
> mine, and a recent picture of me with my oldest granddaughter,
> Jane. Just so you won't be shocked when this old ruin opens the

door on Halloween. What kind of wine do you drink? Your Tiddly.

Maud phoned Lake Worth Haircutz. She had to look up the number; her last appointment had been before Max's funeral. The stylist's
gravel voice answered on the first ring. "Lucia, it's Maud Martinez. Remember me?"

"Maud! I thought you'd moved away."

"No, I'm still here. Sorry to bother you on a Sunday."

"I work on Sundays by appointment now. I've got this guy coming
in for an emergency makeover."

"That's what I need. Have you any openings before Wednesday?"

"Tomorrow is terrible, and Tuesdays I'm off. Could you do one
o'clock today?"

"Oh, Lucia, thank you. I'll be there."

"Good to have you back, love."

Sunday afternoon

"Well, let's undo all these clips and pins, Maud, and see what we've got
here. My God—it's Rapunzel!"

"A gray-headed Rapunzel, I'm afraid."

"But human hair's amazing, no? Who was it?—some movie star's
mother, in the thirties—sent a stylist to the cemetery every month to
keep her daughter looking good. How long has it been now since Max
passed away?"

"Two years and six months."

"And hair grows an average of a half inch a month—but I think
yours must grow faster, because it's halfway down your back. Good hair,
though. Still got body and shine, even without me. So what were you
thinking of doing?"

"On Wednesday, I'm going to get together with someone I haven't
seen since I was fourteen."

"Wow! It's none of my business, but is this by any chance an old
flame?"

Maud fished the color print from her purse and handed it up to
Lucia. "My best friend, Tildy, from grade school. We haven't seen each

other in fifty-five years. When she emailed this to me this morning, I realized how much I'd neglected myself."

As Lucia scrutinized the picture, Maud, watching her in the mirror, felt pangs from that long ago day when she had proudly handed Tildy's picture to Anabel Norton on Worth Avenue and Anabel had raised her plucked eyebrows and laughed. "*This* is the superior being called Tildy? Why, Maud, she looks like—Orphan Annie without a neck. She is such a little girl compared to you. . . . What exactly do you see in her, darling?"

"Your friend takes good care of herself," said Lucia. "So does the daughter."

"That's her *granddaughter.* And in the email I had this morning, Tildy described herself as an old ruin."

"It's a *very* clever three-color process. Her stylist must do gazillions of teensy-tiny highlights and lowlights, all mixed in together. But how does she get it to stand up in a crest like that? A brush cut usually collapses past a couple of inches. What was her hair like as a girl?"

"It was tawny and curly. Like Orphan Annie's."

"When is it you're going to see her?"

"I'm driving up Wednesday; she lives just outside Atlanta. And I'd like to look my best."

"Well, love, you've still got the basics. Bones, bones, bones. And those you can't buy with any number of processes. We used to cut it in that swingy bob just below chin level. Is this going to be a fancy occasion?"

"No, we're just going to celebrate Halloween together at her house."

"Aha! I think I'm starting to feel inspired."

Halloween, Wednesday, October 31, 2007

Six hundred and twenty-six miles, from Maud's to Tildy's. But the ideal MapQuest driver must have a steel bladder and a bottomless gas tank and a body younger than hers to make it in nine hours and twenty-nine minutes. It was already close to ten hours when Maud crossed into Georgia, and after the events of her trip she was beginning to feel a little spooky. When she'd left home at dawn in a downpour, the local radio stations were already announcing indoor sites for Halloween activities. Hurricane Noel, a latecomer in the season, was expected to blow out to sea, but not before he ruined the day for costume parades and trick-or-treaters. "You're going as Morticia, aren't you?" said the girl waiting on her in a service plaza near Orlando. "And that lavender wig is a great touch." Stopping at a Burger King for a late lunch in Waycross, Maud was befriended by four seriously costumed adults in the booth across from her. At first she had taken them for two couples; but no, they were all men: proudly they ticked off their identities: a pimp, a French maid, the grim reaper, and Bette Midler. The pimp asked her if she was in costume, adding, "Or do you just normally dress, like, stylish goth?" Maud told them she was on her way to celebrate Halloween with a childhood friend in Georgia and that she'd gotten in the habit of wearing too much black "but the hair is mine, not a wig. My stylist put a lavender rinse on the gray and wove in a few dark attachments. Do you think I can pass for Morticia?" From the way they laughed, Maud knew she had been accepted as a game old girl out to have herself a cool Halloween.

The rain had stopped by the time she crossed into Georgia, and from then on the local stations were saying this was Georgia's worst drought since 1931. From too much water to too little, in a day's drive. Eleven hours on the road at age seventy, with lavender hair and attachments, having conversed with more strangers than she'd met in months. No wonder she was feeling spacey.

Left, left, left, right, left. Charlton Terrace, Westersham Place, Denmeade Walk, Bolingbrook Drive, Cherbrooke Lane. Dusk was falling on the parched lawns. Costumed children carrying bags patrolled the sidewalks: Spider-Men, Batgirls, Wonder Women—a glut of Harry Potter robes.

A Muslim woman in red stood in a driveway passing out packages of candy to a circle of children. Maud drove on by, wondering which Muslim sect wore red chadors—or maybe it was a Hindu sect, though it was most likely a mother in costume. Then she saw that she had gone past the house number at the end of her quest. She turned around and headed back. The woman in red was at the curb now, waving her on with both arms and laughing. It wasn't a chador; it was a religious habit. In red fabric, but with the white headband and the neckcloth and the silver crucifix of the Order of St. Scholastica.

Maud pulled over, shut off the ignition, and stepped out into Tildy-land.

THE FRIENDS HUGGED. Tildy felt bulkier, yet frailer. Wrinkles fanned out from her eyes and made a little fence along her upper lip, but after fifty-five years, her way of scrutinizing you hadn't changed.

"You're skinny!" she accused. "I *hate* you. Is that a wig?"

"No, it was my stylist's contribution. She got inspired when I said I was going to spend Halloween with an old friend."

"You are still beautiful, Maud, though a little sad, I think. Tell me what you want first: bathroom, drink, or food."

"All of the above. In just that order. Should I pull into your driveway?"

"You're fine just where you are."

Carrying Maud's overnight bag ("This doesn't feel heavy enough. You *are* going to stay a few days, aren't you?"), Tildy led her through a roomy kitchen with a sewing alcove and up some back stairs, hiking up her skirts like a practiced nun. "This is the shortest way. I'm putting you in my granddaughter Jane's favorite room. It has privacy and a view of the woods—or what's left of them. Our twins grew up in another house."

"You had twins?"

"God, we do have a lot to catch up on! Yes, identical twins, just like Mama and Antonia: one sour, one sweet. Now, you take your time and do what you need to do and I'll go down and start the wine. White or red? I got your choice of each."

All Hallows' Eve 2007
Tildy's screened porch, off the kitchen
Marietta, Georgia

Before the light has left the sky, they are already tipsy. Maud reclines on a chaise and Tildy, in her nun's habit, is ensconced in a wicker chair, with her feet up on an ottoman. She is also wearing red shoes. ("The Pope wears them with his outfits, so I figured, Why not?") There's a nip in the air, and Tildy has brought out a mohair lap robe and draped it around Maud like a tender straitjacket. On a table within reach of both of them is a half-empty bottle of New Zealand sauvignon blanc in its marble chiller, cheese straws and olives, and a glass dish filled with the candy corn of their childhood Halloweens.

"I can't get over your habit," Maud says. "Except for the color, it's an exact replica of the St. Scholastica ones."

"Right after our phone call I rushed over to Fabric Warehouse and found this remnant of brick-red Tencel just waiting for me. I sewed straight through the weekend. The nuns would have killed for this material: you can ball it up and throw it in the machine and it comes out looking better than ever. It didn't exist when my girls were growing up, but I made Jane some hostess pajamas out of it. Maisie, my other granddaughter, isn't into clothes. She raises Tennessee walking horses."

"I don't remember you ever sewing."

"I didn't learn till I got to Mountain City High. You could take either modern dance or home economics as your elective, and you know how I hated to take off my clothes for gym. All those damp girl-bodies with their rancid sanitary pads."

"Oh, Tildy, I never forgot you. I went on hearing exactly how you would express yourself about something. Like just now."

"I never forgot you, either, and I couldn't understand why you never wrote. I mean, you knew *my* address, but I didn't know yours. You were just ripped out of my life. You weren't at Mother Malloy's funeral; you were just gone, and nobody would say anything. I was instantly expelled, of course, but Daddy was going to take me out of there anyway. I had to finish out ninth grade with a tutor. But I went to the funeral at the basilica and the burial in the nuns' cemetery. There was no way Raving Ravenel could stop me from that. I was the last one to be with Mother Malloy, you know, up in the tower. She was teaching me a poem when she just sort of slumped over. All our family went."

"Tildy, you haven't mentioned Madeline."

"Ah, shit. I almost told you on the phone and then I just couldn't. I guess I figured that if I let you drive here without knowing, we could keep her alive between us a little longer. And all today I kept thinking: Maddy's still alive in Maud's car! She's still among the living in Maud's mind! I miss her more than anybody, *anybody*! Are you getting cold? Would you like to go in? I'm quite toasty in my habit, but—"

"I'm fine. I like it out here in the dark. I don't want to move. I want you to tell me about Madeline."

"In that case, I'll go get another bottle. Same? Or would you rather switch to red?"

"Let's not change anything."

"I'm really glad you're here, Maud."

"So am I."

IF A STRANGER *were observing us from that clump of trees,* thinks Maud, *he or she would see—what? A veiled woman returning to the dark porch with a lit candle in a glass holder. She sets it down on the table, followed by a bottle, and then arranges some kind of wrap around the reclining person's shoulders.*

"We're advised against lighting candles outdoors in this horrid drought," says Tildy, "but those guidelines are for the stupid and the careless. Now, are you *sure* you're warm enough out here?"

"With all these things draped around me, how could I be anything but?"

"Here, let me freshen your glass. Thank you, Jesus, for twist-top wine bottles. Are you sure you're not hungry yet? Supper only has to be heated."

"I am perfect. Please tell me about Madeline."

"It was just this past December. The cleaning service found her the morning she died. She was fully dressed and lying across her bed. They said they'd seen her do that once or twice before—lie down to wait for dizziness to pass. I'd given her one of those Life Alert watches, but she wasn't wearing it, because she was going out. It was Tuesday, the day she volunteered at the hospice office. She was living by herself in Henry Vick's house. You remember him, don't you?"

"Sure, but what was she doing in his house?"

"She married him."

"Madeline married *Henry Vick*?"

"Yes, well, when Mama got her cancer, Madeline came back from the Peace Corps in Africa to be with her, and things evolved from there. Though I think in their way they were very happy. Both of them were good people who liked to take care of others. My twins thought Madeline walked on water. Whenever Liza got really pissed with me as a teenager, she'd say, 'Why couldn't Aunt Maddy have been my mother?' Finally one day I said, 'Well, go and live with her. I'll call her right now.' And then Ruthie burst into tears and said why couldn't she go, too, she was tired of being punished for being the sweet twin. So they both went and spent the summer in Mountain City with their heroine and Uncle Henry, and Creighton and I had some peace."

"How did Chloe take the marriage?"

"Oh, Chloe has gotten weirder and weirder over the years. She was almost thirty when she got engaged, living by herself way out in the country in a farmhouse she had renovated. Madeline almost killed herself preparing for the wedding and reception, and then Chloe backed out at the last minute. The groom had already flown in—he and Chloe had studied architecture together at Swarthmore—and poor Maddy had to console him and get him out of town, in addition to making all the phone calls to say the wedding was off. And she and Henry spent weeks boxing up all Chloe's presents and mailing them back."

"Mother Ravenel mentioned Chloe Starnes *Vick* in the memoir. I was trying to figure that out."

"After the canceled wedding she took her mother's maiden name so the firm could stay Vick & Vick. The latest thing she's done is turn the Vick house, which reverted to her after Madeline's death, into a haven for battered wives. And she still lives out in the country all by herself, like an old hermit witch. You know, she never forgave me for defacing her stupid prop of the Red Nun, which almost spoiled the play even before old Ravenel did the job. We were never close after that. Uncle Henry took her off to look at buildings in Europe the summer after the great debacle, and she did one more year at Mount St. Gabriel's, while old Ravenel was away; then she transferred over to Mountain City High. We weren't in any of the same classes because—well, that's another story we'll get to later."

"Did your mother live to see Madeline and Henry marry?"

"No, all that started up after she died. Who knows what her take would have been? She was glad to have Maddy at her beck and call again—Daddy died in his early fifties; he just keeled over chopping wood. Mama's cancer was in the larynx, and after they removed her vocal cords, she refused to learn to speak with that little microphone. She told Madeline it was her punishment for saying so many wicked things about people, but that had been her nature, and now she was going to be silent and listen for a change. When she had anything to communicate she would just gesture or write notes. When the priest came, she wrote out her confession and made him take it away and destroy it after he had absolved her. Toward the end, old Ravenel phoned

Madeline—she wanted to pay a visit—and Mama wrote, 'I didn't want to see her while I was at war; why should I want to see her when I'm at peace?' "

"And Henry?"

"Henry's in the Vick enclosure with Madeline and Aunt Antonia. Little strokes kept erasing parts of him till there wasn't much left. For a while there, poor Maddy really had an assignment that challenged her fervor for caring for others. And then at the beginning of last year, I challenged her again. I had a double mastectomy and then that horrid chemo, which was the worst part. At this point in my life I couldn't care less about a couple of missing boobs. And now I am going to get us something warm to drink."

Maud was left to make room in her mind for all Tildy's dead—and Tildy's cancer. She lapsed into a partial doze until she found herself being covered with yet a third wrap and handed a mug of steaming bouillon.

"This is laced with the last of Creighton's cognac."

"When did Creighton die? How long have you been alone?"

"You're up to your old tricks, Maud."

"What old tricks?"

"You let me go on and on and you hold yourself back. There's always been this aloof part you keep in reserve. You did it at our first lunch in the third grade, and you've been doing it ever since. The only time you ever came close to opening up was after your grandmother's funeral when I made you come back to our house and you said you were afraid of losing everything. You started telling me about that horrible man who came on to you in Palm Beach, but at a certain point you clammed up, and I could never find out any more. Did you ever see him again? I mean, you've lived in Palm Beach."

"What man?"

"You know. The older brother of somebody at that dance where you disgraced yourself—or thought you had. I warn you, Maud, you are not leaving this house until you fill in your blanks as generously as I have filled in mine."

"His name was Troy Veech. And, yes, I saw him again. But for now please go on about Creighton. I remember him well, so manly and good-looking and going to be a doctor. He was so patient about teaching me the crawl when I wasn't even a member."

"Yes, you were, in a sense. Daddy got you those summer passes to the pool."

"It wasn't the same as being a member. I always felt beholden. That aloof part you talk about in me? Maybe it was my pride. It's uncomfortable always to be on the receiving end. Now tell me about Creighton. It's so fitting while we're drinking the last of his cognac."

"Okay, but tomorrow it is your turn. And don't you dare say you're leaving tomorrow."

"I can stay until Saturday—if you'll have me."

"Why not Sunday? If your closing's not till Tuesday."

"Because I'm old and I need a couple of days to recover from all that driving."

"You poor decrepit thing. Creighton died in 1998. He was sixty-five and didn't need to die, but he was careless about his health. You've heard the old saw about the lawyer who dies without a will? Well, Creighton was the diabetic doctor—on the medical school faculty, for God's sake!—who neglected to drink his fruit juice. He lost consciousness and drove into a ravine coming home, and by the time they located him he was dead. I've been mad at him ever since. Leaving me a widow at sixty-one. The twins were in their forties, Ruthie's girls were old enough so I didn't have to babysit them anymore, and I'd finally got Liza out of the house—Liza had what you might call an extended adolescence—and Creighton had promised me some travel. He and I never went anywhere. Neither of us had ever been to Europe; he was always working too hard. I wanted us to go there while we could both still walk."

"You always said he and Madeline would marry eventually."

"That's what we all thought. But 'eventually' came and went, and they kept dating until Madeline joined the Peace Corps. 'Ask not what your country can do for you' was just custom-made for her. And Creighton kept on coming to see me whenever he was back in town. Remember how he used to call me Tantalizing Tildy? He told me later that he'd always had a corner of his heart reserved for me, and then one day he woke up and realized I had taken over the whole thing. You remember Mama's dry-ice remarks—when I told her Creighton wanted to marry me, she said, 'How strange. When he could have asked Madeline.' And Creighton went the whole mile. He took instruction, he became a Catholic, we had a huge wedding at the basilica, and he got to go beyond the rail. At the reception at the club afterward, Mama told me I looked 'almost beautiful.' Listen, Maud, are you sure you're not getting hungry?"

"Are you hungry?"

"No, but I'm the hostess and have to ask that."

"The bouillon is enough for me. Soon you may have to help me upstairs."

"We'll help each other. Nobody needs a broken hip at our stage of the game."

Thursday, November 1, 2007
All Saints' Day
Tildy's house
Marietta, Georgia

Maud woke uneasily in granddaughter Jane's room. Getting up during the night to go to the bathroom, she had felt the lingering presence of girls. They hadn't been friendly, but their lack of warmth had nothing to do with her. She didn't exist for them; they had conflicts of their own and she just happened to be sharing a room with them.

Morning light came through the drawn blinds, but she couldn't tell whether the day was going to be nice or not. The digital clock by her bed said eight-forty. The house was quiet. Tildy must still be asleep in her room down the hall. Maud could not bring herself to get up yet. She had drunk too much wine, but it wasn't the first time and it wouldn't be the last. She postponed another trip to the bathroom because she didn't want to risk waking Tildy and having to begin the day in the company of someone else. Curling herself into a ball under the bedclothes, she squinched her eyes shut and tried to locate the source of her unease. It wasn't like the depression after Max died. It was a dislocation accompanied by vexation of spirit and mild panic. *If I got in my car right now and drove without stopping, I could be most of the way home by dark—* But where was "home"? The empty surgery and upstairs living quarters on Sunset Avenue, where Daisy's marks had been sanded over and only a mattress and a few cooking utensils were left? It seemed so. Or was it simply that she identified "home" as a place where she could be alone to preside over her history without any intrusions from anybody?

But this was not the time or place to turn into an old hermit witch, as Tildy had called Chloe. Uncurling, Maud resolved to get herself gracefully through two more days in Marietta, and that was when she saw the folded slip of notepaper that had been pushed under her door.

> *8:15 a.m.*
>   *Dear Maud. Gone to 9:00 Mass. Coffee's made and there's cereal or last night's quiche that we didn't eat. It's best warmed up in the toaster oven. Microwaving turns it soggy. I'm so happy you're here. Love, Tildy*

TILDY RETURNED, LADEN with bags, to find Maud dressed in black jeans and Max's old black cardigan, sipping a Diet Coke at the kitchen counter.

"No coffee? Oh God, you probably drink herbal tea or something. When you and I were last together nobody had started drinking *anything* yet."

"This is exactly what I like. Max used to drink it all through the day. With a slice of lemon. His 'virgin Cuba libre,' he called it. How was church?"

"Oh, you know, church is church." Today, in a tweed pantsuit and turtleneck, Tildy was the carefully groomed lady of the email photo. Her tawny hair with its highlights and lowlights stood up as stiffly as a parrot's crest, making Maud wonder how she had managed to tame it under the veil of last night's costume. "I'm a Eucharistic minister now; I can give people Communion but I can't bless it. Today is the Feast of All Saints: for the good dead. I prayed for Madeline and Mother Malloy. And then tomorrow is All Souls'. For the rest of us."

"Mother Ravenel wrote about the origin of All Souls' Day in her 'Traditions' chapter," said Maud. "A Benedictine abbot, Saint Odilo, instituted it during the Middle Ages for all dead monks, but then later his generosity increased and he extended the feast to include all the dead, regardless of how they had behaved, from the beginning of creation until the end of time. She's at her best in the memoir when she's being informative about the past or meditating on interesting subjects, like Elizabeth Wallingford's concept of holy daring."

"Good old useful holy daring! I'll bet old Ravenous twisted *that one* around like a pretzel to suit her own agendas."

"Still, it's an exciting idea. As I was reading those passages I kept imagining what I'd be like now if I'd lived a life of holy daring."

"How do you know you haven't?" challenged Tildy, unpacking groceries and more wine. "I wonder if she thinks *she* has, up there in freezing old nun-retirement land? You know, Maud, I still dream about her, and she's still the enemy. In the most recent dream, she was at some passport control desk, telling Creighton and me that we couldn't go on together. 'You will have to choose,' she said to us, and it was exactly her laying-down-the-law voice. 'The two of you will not be allowed to proceed together.' What amazes me is, I didn't know the damn memoir even existed till you wrote me. By the way, did you bring it?"

"I did. I'll leave it with you."

"Oh, I think it would be more fun to read parts of it together. And then you can take it away. Or we can make a bonfire. I don't want any part of her living under this roof. You'd think someone at Maddy's funeral would have said something, but maybe they were being tactful, those of them who remembered that our family didn't exactly love her. I wonder if Chloe has read it. Hard to know with old Hermit Witch. She brushed me off when I asked her to have lunch with me after Maddy's funeral. Said she had a load of stone being delivered for something she was building. I felt like saying, 'What awful prop are you going to surprise us with now?' You didn't want any breakfast, Maud?"

"I'm a little hungover. Also, my shoulders ache from all that driving."

"Well, outside is not very inviting. Cold and gloomy but no rain in sight. If it weren't for this drought, I'd take you for a walk to the lake, but who wants to see a dried-up lake? So what I thought was, we'd make a big pot of Flavia's soup—remember how you used to walk in the front door and say, 'Cause for celebration! I smell Flavia's soup!' "

"It was only the best soup in the world," said Maud, recalling how the smell always roused longing and resentment in her at Tildy's taken-for-granted bounty.

"Flavia's still alive, gardening and canning at ninety-five—her vegetables that will go into the soup. Every fall, her great-grandson brings me more jars than I can use. Daddy left them the Swag, and they and their sons turned it into a truck garden business."

"I didn't think they had children." Watching Tildy attack a can of beef broth with a twist opener, Maud was touched by how knobbly with arthritis her finger joints were. She was also moved that at age seventy Tildy was still being thwarted in dreams by the family's old enemy.

"None of us did. We didn't find out till after Daddy died. Back in the forties when he advertised for a live-in couple with no children, they applied as a couple with no children. John's mother lived in town, and John told Daddy about his two little nephews she was raising after John's sister had died in Chicago. John invented the sister. Now I wonder if Daddy and Mama didn't know it all along, and that's why Daddy left them the Swag. You know, to sort of make amends for splitting up a family. You haven't become a vegan or anything, I hope, because Flavia's soup calls for steak bones and chuck meat to simmer with the vegetables. So here's the plan. I'll put together this soup, then we'll warm up the quiche and have a glass or so of the dog that bit us, and retire to our respective boudoirs for a good old lazy afternoon nap. And the soup will simmer and we'll doze and sniff it and feel like we're thirteen again. How does that sound?"

"You always had a knack for knowing what I needed, Tildy. Sometimes before I knew it myself."

"And then when you come down, I'll turn on the gas fireplace in the den and we'll snuggle up in front of it and eat Flavia's soup and sip our wine and you will fill in *your* blanks for the last fifty-five years."

Evening of All Saints' Day
Tildy's den

"Where should I begin?" asked Maud.

"Begin Friday night after the play." As if there could be no possible other starting place in Maud's story.

"I thought my life was over when she sent me up to my dorm room. I walked up and down in that tiny little enclosure and thought of wild things."

"Like what?"

"Oh, just—vanishing. Running away. Dyeing my hair and taking a new name. But I didn't even have the money for bus fare. And where would I take the bus *to*? I thought of Lily missing me and then gradually accepting that I was dead, and that made me cry. And then I just conked out. Mother Ravenel had said we would talk in the morning, and when I woke up it was early Saturday morning and the birds were chirping and it seemed like a bad dream. After all, she hadn't said anything about my leaving school. And then my door cracked open and there stood Jiggsie Judd, looking at me strangely. She said, 'You don't know what happened, do you?' And she told me about Mother Malloy. At first I didn't believe her, and then I'm afraid I thought, If something this bad has happened, Mother Ravenel will forget about her anger at me. But she didn't. Now the whole thing gets a little surreal, but bear with me. I'm going to try to tell it from my point of view."

"Well, who else's *could* you tell it from?"

"Oh, you'll see. This is where I entered the stream of other people's needs and desires, and I didn't find my way back to my own stream until twenty-five years later."

"God, Maud, this is beginning to sound ominous."

"At the time it just seemed like fate to me—the way the cookie crumbles. A woman I know in Palm Beach has this wooden plaque on her kitchen wall that says 'Life is what happens while you're busy making other plans—' "

"Oh, I *hate* that plaque! I've seen it in gift shops. I would never put something like that up on my wall."

"Neither would I," Maud countered coldly. "But nevertheless, that's what happened to me."

"I'm sorry. Go on."

"The next thing was, Mother Ravenel brought me a breakfast tray and told Jiggsie to go away. She said, 'I suppose she has told you about Mother Malloy.' Then she set the breakfast out on my desk—a bowl of oatmeal, a glass of milk, two pieces of buttered toast, and some grape jelly. I can see the measured, almost respectful, way she placed them on the desk—like she was setting up an altar or something. There was even my napkin in its napkin ring from my place in the dining room. And she told me to please sit down and eat because it was going to be a very busy, very sad day for her and she had to get me on my way. I would be leaving with Jovan for the airport in less than an hour. There was a connection I had to make in Charlotte—"

"A connection to *where*?" screamed Tildy.

"I didn't *know* yet. I told you, I'm trying to tell it the way it happened to me at the time."

"Sorry."

"While I ate—and I did eat—I was hungry—she said she had been on the phone late last night and very early this morning to Mr. Foley and Mr. and Mrs. Norton."

"What about *Lily*?"

"That's exactly what I asked: 'What about my *mother*? Why didn't you talk to *her*?' And she said, 'Your mother is in the hospital in Atlanta. She had a miscarriage yesterday. You're almost a grown girl, Maud. These things happen in married life. Mr. Foley says she's going to be just fine, though it was a disappointment to them both.' Then she said, 'Now, Maud, we are going to pack your things, and I will help you, and while we are doing it, I want you to listen very carefully to what I told Mr. Foley and Mr. and Mrs. Norton on your behalf.' She was folding my things while she talked; she seemed to know where everything was in my room and where it would best fit into the suitcase. She said she had told them I was one of the most promising girls in the school, but I had been influenced by a friend to partake in a prank of a very serious nature, which could have damaged the reputation of the school. The other girl had been instantly expelled, and because of my involvement she had no choice but to expel me, too. But she had told them that I might still fulfill my potential somewhere else, under the right guidance. She said it was a crucial period in my development, and it could go either way, and she was turning me over to their care. And then she gathered up my dishes and said, 'Maud, I am going to ask you to remain up here until I return with Jovan to take your things down to the station wagon.' And I said, 'But won't you tell me where I am going, Mother?' And she told me it had been decided that I would first go to Palm Beach, until my mother and Mr. Foley had found a house of their own. She said, 'I have been doing a little fence-mending on your behalf in Palm Beach, Maud. You know, you had told me in our discussions that you weren't welcome down there anymore, but I now believe you thought things were worse than they were. Also, there have been changes. Your father is improving and you could be the means to help them keep that marriage together. Wouldn't that be a great thing?' And then she left with the tray and I sat on my bed and tried to register what was happening and what I felt about it. But I couldn't *think*. My brain felt like it had been wrapped up for shipping with the rest of me. I was being sent off like a package and would just have to wait until they opened me at the other end to find out who or what I was."

"Oh, Maud. If only I had known!"

"What could you have done?" Maud asked with something close to a sneer.

"You could have stayed with us and shared my tutor. Hell, with you there, I wouldn't have needed that damn tutor. We could have kept up with the lessons we missed and entered tenth grade together at Mountain City High. Instead, that brownnose stool pigeon raked in my father's money all summer and pretended I was a paragon and then reported back to the principal at Mountain City that my reading skills weren't up to tenth grade! I had to repeat ninth grade over at the junior high. And have a remedial reading coach."

"Oh, Tildy!" Maud ached for the demoted fourteen-year-old girl. What a blow to her pride!

"What I suffered from, of course," Tildy went on, rather airily, "was given a fancy Greek name in the sixties, and now the schools are stocked with special ed teachers trained to guide us out of our benightedness. My daughter Ruthie is a dyslexia specialist. And you even wrote a column about it in that Palm Beach paper."

"But you always compensated with your spoken vocabulary, Tildy. I don't know when I last heard the word 'benightedness.' Do you find reading easier now?"

"Oh, much," Tildy laughed. "I get unabridged audiobooks. I even belong to a book club, and my presentations are always riveting. But words flat on a page are still like those horrible hedgerows in *Silas Marner*. I have to clamber over each one as I come to it and scratch myself bloody. And if I'm scheduled to be one of the lectors at church, I have to work up my lesson a week in advance. But everyone thinks I'm a beautiful reader. Look, Maud, tell me one thing, honestly. When you were sitting on that bed, about to be sent off like a package, did you hate me?"

"No. I wasn't thinking about you at all. I told you, I couldn't think. I was just there on the bed, and that was the way it was, and then I was being driven to the airport, and then I was on the ground in Charlotte, where an airline person met me and walked me to my connection— I was fourteen, remember? And then I was on the ground in Palm Beach, and my father and Anabel were waiting on the tarmac. Anabel was crying and my father put an arm around each of us and said, 'Come on now, girls, this may turn out to be a good thing.' And for a while, he seemed to be right."

"How long did that last?"

"It lasted me through high school. I mean, he had relapses, but they stayed together and my father got a job selling Cadillacs, which he did very well, and it kept him on the wagon—most of the time. Anabel continued to maneuver her way into society, and she liked taking me places and giving me 'advantages.' It reflected well on her to be seen behaving generously with her husband's daughter."

"What about that society woman who uninvited her to the Christmas party because you left the dance with that man who came on to you?"

"Duddy's mother, Mimi Weatherby. She had a comeuppance of her own to deal with. Her husband was suing her for divorce because she'd been having an affair with a younger man. Actually, it was with Troy Veech, the man I left the dance with."

"Good God, Maud, this is like a soap opera!"

"Well, it gets worse, and I swallowed most of the soap myself. Next comes my enrollment at the Cortt Academy, known to its inmates as the Court of the Weird Sisters. But right now we'll take a commercial break because I need to go to the bathroom."

CHAPTER 37

Reunion, Continued

TILDY

All Saints' Day, evening
Tildy's kitchen

TILDY LIKED TO be in charge of her settings, and when Maud took her bathroom break she decided it was time to move them to a new one. She had been sinking into a dangerous loss of self as she gave herself over to Maud's narrative in front of the gas fire. Maud's story drew you in like the little blue flame. You let yourself forget that it was activated by a remote control that released the propane and produced the illusion of real logs burning. You forgot you were safely who you were, having lived your life and raised your children and fascinated your husband and survived cancer and nine years of widowhood—and kept your pride more or less intact throughout. You were sinking into Maud's powerlessness as she sat on that bed like a package about to be sent somewhere else.

Maud was still beautiful. When you reached seventy, the worst that could happen to your looks had pretty much happened, give or take a few more unsightly spots and growths, a few more pieces of yourself destined to be sliced off or suctioned out. But Maud needed to get out of that dreary black. Black dress, black jeans, a dead husband's old black cardigan. Maud also needed to replace the silver fillings in her molars; they dated her every time she opened her mouth. Tildy had a brilliant idea for scuttling the black—a project that would take them through tomorrow, Maud's last full day. They would go to Fabric Warehouse and select material and she would sew Maud a svelte swishy skirt, cut on the bias. They needed a project. Tildy had picked up on Maud's old edginess, like that of an animal that lets itself be domesticated up to a certain point, then darts for the exit. When Tildy had come back from church, she could read from Maud's face and body language that she had been considering darting for the exit. Maud had always been elusive, *other.* Whether it was pride, not wanting always to be on the receiving end, or just her nature, she never let you get all the way around her. But now that they had found each other again—and, after all, Maud had come looking for *her*—Tildy was determined to keep Maud in her life. There were so many things they could enjoy together, thought Tildy, setting out napkins, bowls, and wineglasses on the kitchen counter, but she must go slowly and keep on the alert against that darting for the exit look.

"A change of scene," said Maud, entering the kitchen. "Was I putting you to sleep in there by the fire?"

"Far from it. I'm dying to hear about the Court of the Weird Sisters. But you need fuel and, besides, the Storytellers' Union of America specifies so many breaks per hour in its playbook. Ta-*ra*! Flavia's soup and, of course, more wine, and I'm warming a baguette."

"You cover all the angles, Tildy."

"I try to. Especially when I'm in the company of someone with a jillion facets."

"Oh, my facets," said Maud, actually blushing. But she did not look like an animal about to bolt when Tildy ladled the thick gumbo and brought the hot bread and poured the wine.

"Here's to friendship," said Tildy.

"To friendship," said Maud. Then she sputtered and choked on her wine.

"What's funny?"

"You—at our first lunch—in third grade. You bought us two bags of potato chips and then put yours down on the bench and sat on it. You said, 'I like to do that. It makes more of them. Why don't you try it?' And I did. And after that it became the thing to do. Every day in the cafeteria, all our class sat their little butts down on their potato chips."

"Not everyone—I'm sure Becky Meyer never did. But it's a wonder nobody stopped us, no nun came over and said, 'Girls, this is indecent.' God, we had so much power. Or thought we did. We thought we could do anything."

Later
Back in Tildy's den

"The Cortt Academy was a strange school," Maud resumed. "I mean, to me it was strange, after Mount St. Gabriel's. There was something missing, or slightly off-kilter, but I couldn't figure out what it was. The good part about that was, its unreal aspect made me less anxious about fitting in. The bad part was that because it seemed unreal—everything sort of provisional—I felt free to be whatever I wanted."

"That sounds like a plus to me."

"Well, but these provisional selves weren't me. I was trying on roles and seeing how far each one would please someone else. All the other students knew about me was that I was a new girl, something of a goody-goody and a grind, who had transferred from a convent boarding school. Nobody except the Cortt sisters knew that I'd been expelled from Mount St. Gabriel's. Miss Cortt had spoken to Mother Ravenel on the phone, and, lucky for me, took an instant dislike to her. She told me I was well out of that nun factory and she saw no reason to blot my matriculation at a new school with the onus of an expulsion."

"Why did she call it a nun factory?"

"When I saw which way the wind was blowing in the interview— I mean, Miss Cortt's aversion to Mother Ravenel—I decided to tell her about Mother Ravenel's attempt to convert me."

"*What?* Is this true, Maud?"

"We were having these talks. I was supposed to pray and ask God to show me if I had a vocation. The deal was that Mother Ravenel would come up with the money to cover my boarding fees through high school if I needed the time for discernment—"

"Good old discernment! She could play a million tunes on that convenient theme. And you never told me this was going on."

"I didn't tell anyone. I knew I might do it, if it meant securing my education—they send you to college, you know—and I felt I'd lose everything if I had to start all over from scratch with Art Foley as the head of our family."

"To think of you as 'Mother Norton' boggles the mind."

"I might have been a very good Mother Norton. I would have tried to model myself on Mother Malloy."

"So if you hadn't been 'involved in my prank,' you would have stayed on at Mount St. Gabriel's, and one day over at Mountain City High I would have heard through the grapevine that my old friend Maud had entered the postulancy. Would you have invited me to the ceremony?"

"Tildy, I hate this sort of—retrospective speculation. The whole thing makes me squeamish now. I think what probably would have happened was I would have become a Catholic and then maybe a postulant—and found I couldn't go on with it. And then I would have felt like a cheat."

"But you would have finished Mount St. Gabriel's by then, and could have taken your pick of colleges."

"Well, I finished at the Weird Sisters instead. In only two years, because they skipped me a grade. I became their pet, especially Dr. Cortt's, the one with the doctorate in classics. She was dying to inaugurate a junior honors seminar where we started reading Herodotus's *Histories* on the first day and learned our Greek that way. I also went into advanced Spanish. It was Miss Cortt's prediction that South Florida would soon be bilingual, and how right she was. They were dedicated women of purpose; I used to try to compare them with Mother Wallingford and Mother Finney. I'd think, Well, I have transferred from one academy to another, both started by two women with high educational ideals, but there was always something missing in the equation. Of course, the Cortt Academy was a day school and coed, though there were far more girls—the boys in that crowd mostly went away to boarding school. But there was an absence of something we had at Mount St. Gabriel's."

"Hmm. Maybe it was the Holy Ghost."

"Funny, I never thought of that," said Maud, looking at Tildy with respect.

We have all these memories in common, Tildy thought, gratified, and I can contribute another point of view. But I must go very, very carefully.

"Anyway, I graduated from Cortt with honors and had my pick of scholarships, from Auburn to University of Miami to Agnes Scott. Both my families were proud of me, and a few of my classmates were openly jealous. But they need not have been, because immediately after graduation I chose to fling myself into the dark stream of someone else's ruin."

"This is beginning to sound *truly* ominous, Maud. Do we need to open another bottle?"

"I THOUGHT WE should have at least a *lightweight* quilt, for psychological reasons," said Tildy, returning with more wine and a platter of cheese and crackers—and the quilt. "We need to be *under* something, so we'll feel safe, like when we used to snuggle up when you slept over at my house. Oh, Maud. I am enjoying you so much. I hope you're not wishing you could leave, or anything."

"How could I, when you're satisfying so many of my facets? Okay, here goes with the darkest chapter of my life. After it was over, I wrapped myself in all the humdrum duty I could find. I looked for things that were expected of me, regardless of who was expecting them, so I could get up every morning and fill someone's needs without having to think about what I had lost. Then one day I woke up feeling furious and realized I was going on forty—and that night I went out dancing with a Cuban-American veterinarian named Max Martinez.

"The dark chapter started at the end of my first summer with the Nortons, but it developed very slowly and insidiously. I had been accepted at the Cortt Academy, and Dr. Cortt had assigned me some books so I could skip into the junior class in the fall. I told you my father had got a job selling Cadillacs, and it kept him sober—well, except for relapses. He was a born salesman—he liked making money selling something he believed in; he said it was like getting paid for being his better self. He had been the top East Coast salesman of Balfour college jewelry when he met Lily, and now he was on his way to becoming the top salesman at the Cadillac dealership in West Palm Beach. Anabel changed her Cadillac there every other year and passed her 'old' models on to him, so he knew his product. But most important, he knew the kinds of clients he was dealing with."

"The Palm Beach supersnobs?"

"No, the supersnobs drove imported cars: Jags, Porsches, Rolls-Royces—especially vintage Rolls-Royces—or they bopped around town in these perky Hillman Minx convertibles. Mr. Weatherby drove a 1929 Rolls-Royce Phantom and had a chauffeur's cap from the same year—"

"Now wait—that's the cuckolded husband whose wife was having an affair with that reptile who came on to you at the dance."

"Yes." Maud briefly closed her eyes. "In 1952, when my father started working for the dealership, the Cadillac was beginning to carry a bit of a stigma. At the Palm City Club, members would sometimes refer to it as 'the Chosen People's car of choice.' "

"Did your father tell you that?"

"No, they weren't members. Anabel was one of the Chosen People herself. I heard it from—a cynical member who happened to be buying a Cadillac from my father. As I was starting to tell you, my father knew the people he was dealing with. They were medium-tier social climbers who wanted the most luxurious automobile made in Detroit. And part of his sales routine for the more serious ones was to invite them to his home for afternoon tea; it was always tea or lemonade and little sandwiches, served by the cook on the oceanfront terrace."

Maud briefly shut her eyes again and then appeared to have come to a decision. "This is not an oral-storytelling competition; I'm simply telling my oldest friend how I threw away my young life—threw it away with the compliance of just about every adult involved, except one. So I'm going to toss the element of suspense and plunge in. One afternoon in the summer of 1952, I came back from the beach carrying a dual-language edition of Herodotus and my new Greek dictionary. I was Maud Norton, just turned fifteen, headed into the eleventh grade of a top private school, having narrowly escaped my direst scenarios for myself. My mother wrote regularly. I knew she missed me, and I usually cried after I read her letters, but she also sounded excited by her new life, and I was sure they would be starting another baby soon and I didn't want to be around for that. So I was feeling pretty wonderful as I approached our house, and there on the terrace, drinking lemonade, were my father and a customer. Against the backdrop of Anabel's Mediterranean-style villa, the two of them looked like an advertisement for the good things of life. Both were in white, my father in white trousers and polo shirt, the younger man in tennis clothes. I watched him watching me approach, and then I got close enough to see who it was. My father introduced us and I said, 'I thought you went into the Army.' And he said, 'The Army wouldn't have me. So now I'm buying a used Coupe de Ville from your father and sitting for my real estate license. Maybe I can make myself into a new man yet.' "

"Oh, holy jumping *Jesus,* Maud, please don't tell me it was the reptile."

"It was Troy Veech."

"Maud, I can't stand it. How far did it go?"

"As far as it could. With all the trimmings. The father gave the bride away on Anabel's terrace, and the Veeches held the reception for the couple at the Palm City Club. My mother couldn't attend because she was finally about to give birth to a little Foley after two miscarriages. I was seventeen and, by the way, still a virgin, though a very pawed-over one by my fiancé. But he wouldn't let us go all the way. It was part of his myth: his redemption by a maiden."

"Yeah, I remember you said he asked you to run away with him at that Christmas dance and promised to send you to school. The whole thing sounded so implausible. But then you clammed up and wouldn't confide any more details, except that your leaving the dance with him had ruined Anabel's social hopes. I imagined him as a creepy older man who liked to prey on young girls."

"Troy was thirteen years older. He was thirty when we married. He had a sort of sinister contempt about him, and he probably spotted a budding cynic in me. He had overheard me snarl at my date for asking me if I knew what a dance card was. I think that's what drew him to me: he recognized someone like himself who saw through the fakery but chose to participate in the game. But when we went out for our walk, he surprised me by revealing another side of himself, a wistful idealism—no, more like a nostalgia for idealism he'd already lost. And we ended up necking heavily. Until then, I had never even been kissed by a boy."

"Well, who had? This was the early fifties, besides which we were more or less under convent quarantine. But I don't understand how you came to *marry* him. And he was having an affair with Mimi Weatherby at the same time?"

"That was over by then. But her husband found out afterward and she admitted it and he served divorce papers on her. Then she became the social pariah and left town and Troy resurfaced in Palm Beach and the gossip mill sided completely with him. He'd had the reputation of a black sheep for a while, but the Veeches were an older Palm Beach family than the Weatherbys and Troy was still in his twenties and might still redeem himself. It was all very romantic and idealistic and got more so when he fell in love with a young girl raised in a convent.

Everyone loves the story of a pure young girl saving a black sheep, and everybody but one adult jumped on board, even the weird sisters. I could say I got shanghaied into being the star of a fairy tale being constructed by other people, but the fact was, I was under the spell of the fairy tale myself."

"But were you physically attracted to him, Maud?"

"God help me, yes. Except when I was studying, I existed in a trance of unrequited lust for almost two years. There were times—there were times during our year-long engagement when I crawled all over him and begged him to take me. But he wouldn't—he wouldn't. He would smile and do everything else—but never that."

"Maud, I have raised two daughters and helped to raise Ruthie's daughters. And I can't conceive of myself or Creighton or even the most laid-back parent I have ever met allowing things to come to such a pass. But you said there was one adult who didn't get caught up in the fairy tale."

"Art Foley, of all people. He and my mother drove down for the engagement party, and he took me off by myself and said, 'Maud, you aren't going to like me for this, but I have to put in my two cents because you're Lily's daughter. I think this whole thing is premature. You are sixteen and you're committing yourself to matrimony in a year's time. Why not just remain free and finish college and see how you feel then? You could go to Agnes Scott and be nearer your mother. We're not fancy people and we can't offer you a mansion, but we care about your future.' And I said, 'You don't think my future is safe here, then?' And he said, 'No, I don't.' And I said, 'Why not? I'm still planning to go to college. It's just that I'll be married and can devote myself fully to my classes without all the social distractions. I'm already accepted at Florida Southern, and we're going to have a little apartment in Lakeland. Troy will be selling Palm Beach real estate during the week, so I'll have all that time alone in the apartment to study. I'll be a sort of weekday nun.' But when I said Troy's name I caught the look on Art's face. I said, 'You don't like Troy, do you?' and he said Troy didn't seem 'wholesome' to him. 'Wholesome'! I thought. 'Mr. Foley, you didn't seem very wholesome to me when you were pawing my mother on the porch of the Pine Cone Lodge and with all that glop in your hair.' "

"Why wouldn't the Army take Troy?"

"He gave sarcastic answers to some of the psychological questions. They told him he had an insolent attitude and wouldn't submit well to military discipline."

"Why did he have the reputation of a black sheep?"

"He kept getting kicked out of schools for one thing and another. Breaking rules. Attitude. Failure to apply himself—" Maud tilted her head back and raked her fingers through her lavender-tinted gray bob. She plucked at the black extensions the stylist had attached in honor of Halloween. "And then there were the drugs."

"Oh, no," said Tildy.

Some shift of angle or trick of lamplight had transformed Maud's countenance into that of a weary old sibyl reviewing her sins.

"But that was all over when you two married—I mean, wasn't it?"

"I thought so. Or maybe I didn't let myself think about it. At first it was just the occasional hash, as a sort of—enhancement to our love-making. Then we looked forward to it. And, as time went on, we got into the hard stuff."

"Ah, God!" cried Tildy. "I've been there."

"You? I don't believe it."

"No, my daughter, Liza. I'd rather it *had* been me, if I could have spared her. I went through her withdrawal in this house. In those first seventy-two hours, she called me names I didn't know existed to insult human beings."

"Is she—recovered now?"

"Well, you know how you're only permitted the gerund form. She's *recovering*. She's a licensed massage therapist now and makes a very good living just going back and forth between rehab spas. When she was in the worst of her withdrawal, I rubbed her body for hours. It seemed the one form of contact she wouldn't fight off. She says she doesn't remember it, and maybe it's better left that way so her career choice is all her idea. She still doesn't like me a hundred percent, but there's a tenderness that wasn't there before. It's now been eighteen years. It almost destroyed Creighton at the time. He couldn't forgive himself for being the physician who couldn't protect his own child. Although he gave her the Valium injections and sat by her bedside at night so I could get some sleep. Valium eases the extreme anxiety of withdrawal. You can stand your baby going to pieces a little better if you can spare her the worst of the heebie-jeebies."

"Oh, Tildy. I wish I had known. If we had kept in touch, I might have been of some use to you. I could have served as a . . . a recovering counselor or something."

"How *did* you get back? And what about Troy?"

"Troy died from mixing substances. Our marriage was pretty much finished, but we still had our 'warrior weekends' in Lakeland, though I had dropped out of college by then. After his death, Anabel paid for me to go to a rehab facility in Boca Raton. She was reaching the end of her rope by that time—this was three years later, and my father had fallen off the wagon yet again. She threatened to kick him out and start divorce proceedings. But while they were still trying to patch things up, he tripped on the stairs to the stone terrace and fell on his head and never regained consciousness. Ironically, he wasn't drinking at the time; he was carrying out a tray with a pitcher of lemonade and simply missed his footing."

"How sad!"

"Well, but it did give Anabel a chance to mourn him like a proper widow and go about reconstructing him into a more perfect Cyril Norton. I needed to do some reconstruction, too. For me, he'd been more of a vague outline of a father than a substantial person with his reasons for having become what he was. Anabel made it possible for me to recover a bit of lost ground. I lived with her long enough to finish Palm Beach Junior College and then she married again, a retired bank president and teetotaler, and they moved to Colorado and became hiking and skiing addicts and she was asked to be on all the boards—the Aspen Music Festival and so on. So that ended happily, at least as long as we stayed in touch."

"But what about *you* in the meantime, Maud?"

"Oh, I eventually got a degree in social work by teaching night courses of English as a second language. There was great need in the early sixties when the Cuban exiles started pouring into South Florida, and I was in particular demand because I was practically bilingual with all my Spanish. But after my narcotic interlude, I lost my ambition. I still loved learning things for themselves, but the desire to excel seemed ephemeral and somehow—antisocial. Thus my choice of social work, which I wasn't at all suited for. The people you thought you were 'helping to improve' kept backsliding in the most unimaginative ways. There was a disheartening rate of recidivism. You remember Mother

Ravenel's pet sign-off: 'Remember, girls, you are all works in progress!' Well, more and more mornings as I headed off to my caseload, I would catch myself muttering bitterly, 'Remember, girls, you are all works in deterioration.' To cheer myself up, I took on more night jobs teaching English as a second language. Those Cubans were ambitious—they desired to excel. One man who signed up for my class already spoke fluent English, but he told me he wanted to get good enough to understand the jokes and the nuances. That was Max. And one night after class—I had been telling them stories in English about Miss Mendoza's famous Spanish conversation class with all the dating tips and dancing lessons—he invited me to go dancing with him at a tango club. And that, old friend, brings me to the end of my tale of woe. We had almost thirty years of happiness, though he had a volatile temper and was definitely toward the macho end of the scale, but every day that passes since he didn't come through his heart surgery brings him nearer to perfection in my memory."

"It's like the time you and I went to the Sunset Park Inn to have tea with Jiggsie Judd's crazy grandmother, and she was going on about the perfections of the late Mr. Judd and then she says, 'And I'll tell you something, girls, and you can remember this when you are widows: *He was even more perfect after he died.*' "

"I never had tea with Jiggsie's grandmother, Tildy. I never even met her. You must be confusing me with Chloe."

"No, it was you and me and Jiggsie. Remember how Jiggsie kept setting things afloat in her teacup? She had the most appalling manners. It couldn't have been Chloe because she was waiting for me over at her house. We were going to work on the scenery for the play."

"No, Tildy, I wasn't there."

"Oh, well, you *seemed* to be. But you always were, that year, you know, when you and I weren't best friends anymore. Even when I was furious with you, I carried you around with me and saw things through your eyes as well as my own. You were a sort of companion consciousness. Listen, Maud, where will you live now?"

"I've rented one of those time-share places on the beach while I look around."

"Are you sure you really want to go on living in South Florida? People say it's getting awfully overcrowded down there."

"People have been saying that for the entire fifty-five years I've lived in South Florida. Besides, I have my little network there. I've become very close with the members of my writing group. We perform a sort of alchemy on one another. And also I've promised the vet who's buying Max's surgery that I'll come in several days a week. I'm a familiar face at that reception desk."

"Oh, if you're going to continue *working*—"

"I look on it as a transition. Maybe even a transformation. Maybe I'm turning into something else, only I don't know what it's going to be yet."

This way of putting it struck both awe and alarm in Tildy. What if, once again, Maud was going where she couldn't follow? "Is it anything like when you were being sent off, the morning after the play, and you felt you wouldn't know what was in the package until someone opened it at the other end?"

Maud laughed. "I guess you could say that. Only now I'm a seventy-year-old package. And who's still around to open me? It could be worth exploring in a piece of writing: the transformations at different junctures of one's life."

"With your group, you mean." Tildy tried hard not to show jealousy.

"Oh, I don't know. Perhaps just for myself. Perhaps I'll turn into a scribbling crone."

"But aren't you interested in traveling?"

"If you mean going on tours and cruises with other seniors—no. Max and I had wanted to visit Cuba, if it had been possible, but it wasn't. The only travel that still interests me is the mental kind. But what about you, Tildy? Your grandchildren are grown and you're finished with the cancer, right?"

"So far, so good. My hair has even come back, but I've gotten so enamored of this costly wig that I find it simpler just to plop it on—"

"Well, it fooled me—and it totally fooled my stylist. I showed her the photo that you emailed."

"Why were you showing her my photo?"

"Because I looked like such a hag next to you that I panicked. I hadn't been to her since Max's funeral. She cut off about eight inches of scraggly gray and put on this rinse and these silly extensions."

"You ought to consider maybe going an ash-blond, Maud."

"I think I'll wait and see what I turn into next before choosing a hair color for it," Maud replied rather frostily.

"I went through a transformation once," said Tildy, taking cover in the safer past. "It was that year I had to repeat ninth grade, over at the junior high. Also I was seeing a psychiatrist twice a week because old Ravenel had told the principal I had threatened suicide."

"How mean! Why would she do that?"

"Oh, it was stupid Jiggsie's fault. She went back to the reception and told people I was on my way to throw myself off the tower. That's why everyone ran up there—to stop me. That time we were having tea at the Sunset Park Inn with Jiggsie's grandmother—only you say you weren't there—Mrs. Judd told us that Caroline DuPree had threatened to throw *herself* off the tower—"

"Caroline DuPree? But why?"

"Because Mother Wallingford was sending her home. That's what Mrs. Judd said. She was in the class just behind Caroline. Mrs. Judd had never heard about the vocation part that made the parents want the memorial for their daughter."

"You never told me this, Tildy."

"I'm sure I must have."

"This is the first time I'm hearing it."

"Well, maybe it was just Chloe I told. We were all so *separately* busy that spring! You and I had our secret scene to rehearse, and Chloe was preparing to surprise me with that prop. I wonder what ever happened to that nasty old prop?"

"So what was your transformation?"

"Well, I went from being Tildy Stratton to being nothing. I had gained twenty pounds over the summer and nobody even looked at me in the halls. Daddy and Madeline were worried—I guess Mama must have been, too, but her way of showing it was to turn away at the sight of me—"

"Oh, Tildy!" Maud's frostiness had melted right down.

"No, it was interesting; that's why I'm telling you. First it was devastating, but later I saw it as interesting. For the first time in my life, I had no influence. It was like being invisible—or dead—and watching the world go on without me. Actually, I didn't want to be noticed, because I hated myself. I went to my classes and had my remedial reading sessions, and that was about it. The school was close enough to walk to, but John or Madeline still had to drive me across town to the psychiatrist's. He and I talked a lot about Mother Malloy. I think he wanted me to admit that I felt I had caused her death so he could talk me out of it, but I saw right through him. For that entire year I became what I used to call 'part of the background.' Madeline was my comfort that whole year, but maybe she gave me too much unconditional love. It was Creighton who pulled me out of it, the following summer at the pool. He would tease me about starting over at the senior high school and how I would be the tantalizing stranger everyone would be wondering about. He made a game out of it: What would the stranger wear? How would she look? In what *style* would she tantalize her victims? By the end of the summer, I had lost weight and was beginning to feel the old powers stirring again. It was like I was recovering from a long illness. But it changed me, you know, Maud. I could never take my powers for granted again."

CHAPTER 38

A Correspondence

Chloe Vick
Vick & Associates
5 Zebulon Square
Mountain City, N.C.

Easter Monday, March 24, 2008

Dear Chloe,

These early Easters always feel strange to me. St. Patrick's
Day was only last Monday! Our early church people should have
gotten their act together better.

I've been to your website. What exciting work your firm
does. All that green and solar stuff. I looked at everyone's photos
(two of your associates look younger than my grandchildren) and
admired their projects. And I really like your sacred spaces. Our
church could use a labyrinth like the one you designed for the
Episcopalians.

The reason I am writing (I don't know your home address) is
that I plan to drive up to Mountain City the second weekend in
April, to see Flavia (who is celebrating her ninety-sixth birth-
day) and spend some quiet time at Madeline's grave. I miss
Madeline more than I can say. She was the one person in my life
I felt was always on my side, and we all need one of those.

Look, Chloe, is there any chance we could get together? Last
time you had to rush off to meet a truckload of stone. Did you
finish whatever it was you were making with it? I do hope you
can find time, if not for a lunch or dinner, then at least for a

springtime walk. Maybe we could meet at the old campus and pay a call on the Red Nun. I never saw her again after that awful night when I went around spraying everything.

Yours,
Tildy

PS. I was unsuccessful in coaxing Maud Norton (now Martinez) away from her busy life in Palm Beach to make the trip with me. She works part-time for the vet who bought her late husband's animal hospital and now she's writing a one-act play for some competition. Says it's about two girlhood friends who meet again in their seventies and exchange life stories. I have begged her to be kind! Last October she visited me in Marietta after reading Mother Ravenel's memoir. Said it made her miss me, even though neither of us—or anybody in my family—was mentioned in it. Maybe that's why nobody brought it up at Madeline's funeral. Have you read it? Maud made an appalling marriage choice when she was seventeen and went through some rough times but married a Cuban-American in her forties and had many good years with him. No children. Maud and I spent three days drinking wine and filling in each other's blanks for the past fifty-five years.

Here is my email address, if you prefer. You are still a working woman and I know you must be very busy.

To: *Riversm200@yahoo.com*
From: <cvick Vick&Associates.com>
Subject: Your April visit
Monday, March 31, 2008

Dear Tildy: A Sunday afternoon would be best for me. Let me know when and where you want to meet. The old campus sounds fine—it's a technical college now, you know; one of our associates is designing its new EMT training center—but I'd better warn you that the Red Nun is completely covered with graffiti, both carved and spray-painted. See what you started? Yes, I finally read the memoir, but hadn't when we gathered for Madeline's funeral. The parts I treasured most were those scattered glimpses of my family: my grandfather Vick remodeling the water tower into a prayer space with Mother Wallingford, the mention of some of Uncle Henry's buildings, and most of all that image of my mother, even though not named, dressed up as Fiona Finney on Halloween and riding into the grotto on a rented horse.

I miss Madeline, too. She was always kind to me and let me have the privacy I needed, and nobody could have taken better care of Uncle Henry in his last years. And I know she and Uncle Henry had many good years, as you say of your friend Maud's second marriage. How nice that you two have found each other again.

My project with the stones is coming along—it's outdoors, so I can't work on it in winter—but I will probably be working on it for the rest of my life. At least I hope so. Yours, Chloe

CHAPTER 39

The Chapel of Secrets

Monday evening, March 31, 2008
Wooded hill above Chloe's farmhouse

THAT WAS ITS name, known only to her: a derelict corncrib refashioned by her own hands into a magically small and narrow chapel of logs and native stone. It was her homage to a few unadorned places of prayer she had been lucky enough to visit over the course of a lifetime: a Saxon chapel in the north of England, built of stones from a ruined Roman fort; an anchoress's shrine in the middle of busy Norwich; a tiny Huguenot church in an upstate New York village. Here, wearing her back brace as she mixed her cement in a wheelbarrow and set her stones, she could keep company with the people she loved, who continued to live in her and through her. Here also, in the silence of her country thoughts, she could continue work on whatever in her was hers alone to complete.

Its slanted walls were bare of any symbol or icon. No markers or plaques memorialized her personal saints, who lived and spoke only within the rhythms of her mind.

Henry: guardian and companion. ("What do we want to do now, Chloe? Go home after the reception? Go to Europe and look at some buildings? Take another year at Mount St. Gabriel's? Transfer to Mountain City High?") And eventual dispenser of selected confidences when he thought the time was right. ("We didn't have a whole lot of time together, you know, but Antonia gave me to understand that what happened out at the Swag changed the path of her life. It was hard enough, she said, to face up to their mutual attraction; but sickening to contemplate that the two of them might cheat on God after they had taken vows.")

Agnes: mother and best friend. ("It's as though you are watching over my girlhood in these drawings and preserving me for myself.") Spiritual tutor. ("Would you come straight home from a sweaty day at school and drag your best dress off the hanger and rush off to a fabulous dance without showering and fixing your hair first?")

Fiona Finney: favorite nun of mother and daughter. ("But, you know, dear, even Our Lord had His favorites.") Purveyor of requested information in her last days. ("They were just being girls, those oblates. But Agnes wanted no part of it. I told her she was wise, for someone so young, to understand there are enough necessary secrets to be kept— and God knows I have kept my share of those!—without dreaming up unnecessary ones.")

And the man she had loved—in necessary secrecy—for twenty-six years, a Catholic doctor everyone knew, dead these last fourteen, whom she named only in her prayers and when they were together in dreams. As in life, he was taciturn, but, as in life, he strengthened her, whether present or absent, by her absolute faith in his love.

She shrank from imagining her last fifty-five years packed into a Tildy summary, should she have been willing to fill in even some of her "blanks" for her former best friend.

Nevertheless, as with those few she had loved and trusted, she still could hear perfectly well the voices of the ones she no longer or never did.

("*After the play Chloe and I were never close. Uncle Henry took her off to show her the sights of Europe that summer—not Italy, he couldn't bring himself to go there again—and then she did one more year at Mount St. Gabriel's and was very close to Mother Finney in her final days. Of course, when she transferred over to Mountain City High, I was a grade behind and we moved in different circles. She was always a loner, but it was starting to show more. And then everyone got married, even Madeline and Uncle Henry, to everyone's astonishment, and Chloe insisted on moving out of the Vick house and restoring a dilapidated old farmhouse miles from anywhere that didn't even have running water or an indoor bathroom. Then when she was almost thirty she sent out invitations to a big wedding, only to cancel at the last minute. Nobody ever knew why until years later, when we got together for some wine and filled in each other's blanks. Well, I filled in mine, but she left a great deal out! She had been having a long, long affair with a married man, even before her engagement. They kept it very secret; they had to. He was a local person everybody knew, the father of many children—she wouldn't even give me the number. It started after his son was killed at eighteen. Chloe was in Uncle Henry's firm by then and she designed the son's memorial, but she wouldn't tell me where it is or what it looks like. They were never together in public, and sometimes months went by when they couldn't see each other. And for the last few years of his life he was bedridden and gaga and she was unable to see him at all. But that would have been tolerable to someone of Chloe's solitary nature. When she couldn't be with the ones she loved, she drew their pictures and talked to them and listened for their answers.")*

Acknowledgments

My deepest thanks to:

Jennifer Hershey and Dana Edwin Isaacson at Random House, for their extraordinary editing.

John W. Hawkins, for being my literary agent and friend since 1968.

Mother Tessa Bielecki, O.C.D., for the wonderful phrase "holy daring" in her book *Holy Daring: An Outrageous Gift to Modern Spirituality from Saint Teresa, the Grand Wild Woman of Avila* (Element, 1994). However, the concept of holy daring set out in this novel was formulated by the character of Mother Elizabeth Wallingford.

The late Mother Kathleen Winters, R.C.E., for fifty years of friendship and spiritual guidance.

The late Mother Margaret Potts, R.C.E., for her 1991 memoir, *St. Genevieve's Remembered.*

Father David Bronson, for his help with religious orders and English church history.

Corinne Uzzell Spencer, for her rich memories of St. Genevieve's.

John Pfaff, director of institutional advancement at Carolina Day School, which in 1987 combined St. Genevieve's, Gibbons Hall, and Asheville Country Day, for his extensive archival research into St. Genevieve's yearbooks and memorabilia for the purpose of this book.

The old Victorian building of St. Genevieve's, at various times an orphanage, a hotel, and a tuberculosis sanatorium in Asheville, North

Carolina, before it became St. Genevieve's in 1908, for providing the setting for my tale. The (now demolished) building, its rooms and grounds—with the exception of the unfinished sculpture of the Red Nun—remain vivid in my memory and dreams. The fictional characters, as well as the Order of St. Scholastica founded by Mothers Wallingford and Finney, are products of my imagination.

UNFINISHED
DESIRES

Gail Godwin

A Reader's Guide

Some Questions and Comments
for the Author from Four Characters
in *Unfinished Desires*

Mother Suzanne Ravenel: Now, Gail, there were some things I liked about your novel and there were other things I definitely did not like.

Gail Godwin: Oh. What were the things you didn't like?

MR: Well, you know, I always prefer to dwell on the positive when it's too late to change the situation, so let's dwell on the positive. I like that so many of your characters have an active spiritual life. They talk to God and listen for answers. A grown man, a distinguished architect, kneels on the floor beside his bed and asks for direction every night. A girl who has lost her mother draws pictures of that mother and opens herself to guidance from that mother in the afterlife. Oh, and here's one I especially like. On page 305, Mother Malloy is telling Mother Arbuckle, the infirmarian: "The practice I find central to everything I do is living every day and night as fully as I can in consultancy with God. . . . The more I live this way, the more I want to—to—*pray my life* rather than stumble through it." "In consultancy with God" is a very felicitous phrase and I congratulate you.

GG: Thank you, Mother.

MR: And also I thought you conveyed our foundress's "holy daring" idea quite well. That concept of hers has certainly stood the test of time, hasn't it? Even as a soon-to-be nonagenarian, you know, I am still trying to practice it in my daily life—and to recognize when others are trying to practice it. And I hope *you* are still trying to practice it.

GG: Well, yes, I . . .

MR: But I do wish you had seen your way clear to including more of the school's history. You could have quoted right from my memoir. I would have given you carte blanche to quote as much as you needed.

GG: Actually, Mother, there was a lot more of your memoir in an earlier draft of the novel, when I was still calling it *The Red Nun*. But my editors felt it was getting to be too top-heavy for the reader and—

MR: Oh, dear me, let's stop right there. Is *The Brothers Karamazov* too top-heavy for the reader? Is *Middlemarch*? Is the Bible? And whatever made you change the *title*? That unfinished sculpture of the red nun was the controlling image of the book; it figured in all the stories; it was the title of my play and the title of Tildy's wretched revision that almost brought down the school.

GG: The original whole title was *The Red Nun: A Tale of Unfinished Desires.* But the people at my publishing house had serious qualms about the nun part. Said it evoked the wrong images: nuns hitting students with rulers, that sort of thing. I put up a good fight, and I still feel ambivalent about it. My dental hygienist said: "That was the perfect title! How could you let it go?" My sister-in-law, who had gone to Estonia to find me a certain icon of a red nun, was almost in tears. My brother shouted over the phone, "You caved!"

MR: Well, dear, let's not dwell on what is too late to change. But you weren't practicing holy daring, were you, Gail?

GG: I like to think it was more a case of holy cunning.

MR: Be that as it may, I sincerely wish you success with this novel. You know, when my memoir came out in 2006, my old girls flew me down to Mountain City for a signing and the bookstore sold out! I signed one hundred copies of *Mount St. Gabriel's Remembered* in a single afternoon, and the store made me sign a hundred bookplates to paste into the reorders!

GG: That's amazing. I'm overjoyed when I sign as many as fifty books.

MR: You know how I always told my girls that "each of us is a work in progress"? Well, I'm going to go further and say I believe each book is too. Even after it's published, it goes on spooling itself out in the author's mind. And in the minds of all the readers who will be influenced by it over time. You think of the things you wish you had put in. (Or, perhaps, left out.) Well, I could say a lot more about this, but I know others have questions for you. However, I hope you will ponder this.

✠

Tildy: I absolutely *love* the time in which your novel is set—I'm mainly referring to the 1951–1952 parts—though, of course, you had to give the backstory in order to understand how everything boiled over the way it did. I downloaded the book to my iPod and listened to it going back and forth in my car. You know me and my abomination for print! But the reason I just *wallow* in that particular time is because I was at the apex of my power. God, I was the queen bee, short-lived though my reign was! Do you mind if I ask you: Did you ever know someone like me?

GG: There *was* a girl—she didn't look at all like you, and she didn't have your way with words and vocabulary. But I drew on the strong memory of my awe and envy of her to evoke your presence. She was so sure of herself and could make just about anything seem worth doing. She sat on her bag of potato chips at lunch and soon we were all following suit. Her grades were bad, but she knew how to delegate power. At the beginning of our freshman year, she told everyone, "I think Gail would make the best class president," and guess who was voted in as class president?

T: Were you two friends?

GG: We went from being best friends from third to fifth grade to being wary enemies in adolescence. But when we were in our fifties, we reconnected and found we really basked in each other's company. She'd had many setbacks but was still just as sure of herself. We made plans for her to visit me in Woodstock, but then she got a fast cancer and died within months. I can still see her opening the door to me on my last visit to her house. She was her proud, queenly self—without a hair on her head. The chemo had made her voice high, like a little girl's. We cried, and I asked her to try to visit me in my dreams. And she has, and continues to do so. As soon as I began this novel, I knew I was going to have Tildy and Maud meet again in their seventies because it was something I didn't get with her. It was going to be my treat.

✠

Maud: I want to ask you a question about writing. I'm sure you get this sort of thing all the time and it's old hat for you, but, as you know, I got a late start. I finished my play about the two best friends meeting after fifty-five years, and I submitted it to a contest. It won third place, which entitled me to a reading with established actors. This gave me such a rush, and I learned so much! People really liked it, and several suggested that in my rewrite I might consider adding the ghost of Mother Malloy. I am so tempted to do this. It would be a way to explore what the afterlife is like for a particular person. And it's been done successfully by others. I've written a scene where she is reciting the Hopkins poem she is teaching Tildy in their final scene together, and I use the poem to segue into the landscape of her afterlife, which is the landscape of the poem. It felt so absolutely right until I began second-guessing myself. What right had I to do this? Who knows what anybody's afterlife is like? Yet, other artists have dared it. Look at *Our Town,* look at *The Divine Comedy.* What is holding me back? Do you think I should stick with my two still-living characters and be solidly grounded, or should I risk the supernatural element?

GG: At our time of life, Maud, I'd say go for the risk. Let the practice of artful imagination lure you beyond that last barrier. After all, someone you knew used art to make contact with the other side.

M: Someone *I* knew? When?

GG: Chloe? Are you there? What do you think?

Chloe: I'm here. I think, Maud, you should definitely go ahead. Also, more and more I am convinced there's no such thing as a "late start." When I was young, I had the drawings. They kept the link with my mother, a link I might have died without. They kept me going; they helped me grow up. Now I am finishing my Chapel of Secrets, which honors and contains my most trusted voices over a lifetime. After that, who knows? If it turns out that we are already living in eternity, which is timeless, all our efforts are already tumbling round and round and sending strength and hope to others not yet born.

Questions and Topics for Discussion

1. In Mother Ravenel's 2001 reflections on Mount St. Gabriel's, how does she foreshadow the events that transpire in the "toxic" year of 1951? By the end of *Unfinished Desires,* do you think she's reconciled herself to this "year better forgotten"? Does she prevail? Does she leave anything undone?

2. Who is the Red Nun? How does the myth and tragedy of her origin shape, sustain, and protect the Mount St. Gabriel's community?

3. What is "holy daring" as Mother Elizabeth Wallingford, foundress of Mount St. Gabriel's, conceived it? Discuss how Mother Ravenel interprets and relates holy daring and "a woman's freedom in God."

4. How and why does Mother Malloy, at Madeline's urging, encourage Tildy to keep her "intrepid little soul"? Does her diligent tutoring change Tildy?

5. Why does Mother Ravenel place Tildy in charge of the freshman class revival of the Red Nun play? Does she ultimately regret this decision?

6. What is Agnes's "mortal mistake"? Do you think she anticipated her own untimely death? Why or why not? Is Chloe really haunted by her mother?

7. Tildy understands that "best friends have been known to do hurtful things to each other" (page 57). Does this explain why Suzanne Ravenel

decides to enter as a postulant without her best friend, Antonia? If not, why did she "jump the gun on [her] vocation"?

8. Do you agree with Tildy that "some girls are just always *background*" and "some girls just stand out" (page 96)? How does Chloe counter Tildy's argument? Why doesn't Chloe unveil her "masterpiece" to the class?

9. Discuss the impact of Cornelia Stratton's "dry ice" comments on those she loves. How does her caustic tongue influence her daughters? Her sister, Antonia? Mother Ravenel?

10. Consider Tildy and Maud's friendship from its beginning and from each girl's perspective. How does their friendship evolve? Is it, like each of them, a work in progress? How do their perceptions of each other change? How would you define their relationship at the end of the novel?

11. Reading *David Copperfield* for Mother Malloy's class, Maud is introduced to the idea that "someone else's story, if told a certain way, could make you ache as though it were your own" (page 60). Do you identify strongly with any particular character's story in *Unfinished Desires*? Which one(s)?

12. Discuss the importance and power of secrets in *Unfinished Desires*. How do they serve to either unite or isolate those who tell them and those whom they are about?

PHOTO: © JERRY BAUER

GAIL GODWIN is a three-time National Book Award
finalist and the bestselling author of twelve critically
acclaimed novels, including *A Mother and Two Daughters, Violet Clay, Father Melancholy's Daughter, Evensong,
The Good Husband,* and *Evenings at Five.* She is also the
author of *The Making of a Writer: Journals, 1961–1963,*
the first two volumes, edited by Rob Neufeld. She has
received a Guggenheim Fellowship, National Endow-
ment for the Arts grants for both fiction and libretto
writing, and the Award in Literature from the American Academy of Arts and Letters. She has written li-
bretti for ten musical works with the composer Robert
Starer. She lives in Woodstock, New York. Visit the
author's website at www.gailgodwin.com.